FEELS LIKE COMING HOME

REBECCA WRIGHTS

ISBN-13: 979-8-218-33584-7 (Paperback edition)

Feels Like Coming Home

Book Cover by Sam Palencia of Ink and Laurel.

Edits by Caroline Palmier of Love and Edits.

Proofreading by Caroline Palmier of Love and Edits.

CONTENTS

Dear reader,

Before you read this story, please note that there are potentially sensitive themes of mental health, anxiety, and sudden spousal loss within these pages. While the spousal loss is nondescript, you do see the impact of it on the main character. As someone who is an advocate for taking care of your mental health, I hope that you feel seen and supported as you read this story.

You are not alone in your struggle and it is always okay to ask for help when you need it.

Sending you love,
Rebecca Wrights

*For all the Foolish Ones who want to believe he will come around,
this one is for you.*

Stay foolish babes.

1

HALEY | THEN

I was sitting at my desk writing my last paper due before Spring Break started on Friday when my phone buzzed. I almost ignored it completely because I was in the flow and when I was in the flow, and the flow was interrupted, it took me a long time to get back into it. And I needed to be in the flow because my paper was literally due tomorrow and I had only gotten to the end of my introduction. But when I turned my phone over to look and see who texted me, my breath caught in my throat.

"Why the hell is he texting me?" I muttered to myself before clicking the 'Read' button. I knew he and his girlfriend—a girl I *personally* thought needed to be given a good scrub before you got too close—broke up a few days ago but I was only half expecting to hear from him. We had been friends since we were six years old, me and Cam Johnson—everyone else called him Camden, but I always called him Cam.

We had been friends since the first day of kindergarten when our teacher lined us up alphabetically and we went one right after the other. I remember he stood in front of me, turned around, and made a joke about how short I was. In response, I scrunched up my face in displeasure at being called small and stomped on his foot. We were friends from that day on.

Throughout school, we would always be in the same classes, join similar clubs, and see each other at the high school football games until Cam was old enough to play himself. And yeah, maybe there was something more between us at some points, but when you're in eighth grade and your hormones are raging you would fall in love with a stick if it smelled good enough.

We had this relationship that was so...easy. We could share ourselves—our real selves—with each other without feeling the need to hide the bad stuff or the stuff we kept from our other friends. When shit hit the fan, we were there for one another. When my dad left, Cam was there for me, just like I was for him when his sister got sick.

For so long, it felt like this unspoken thing between us. I liked him, he liked me, we both knew it. Shit, even our mothers knew it and would openly discuss it when they ran into one another at the grocery store. But something, *something* prevented either of us from actually acting on it and making us an 'us'.

And then our junior year, almost out of nowhere, he had a girlfriend. A real, blonde-haired, large-chested girlfriend who was a year older than us, and had a car. Cam was the baby of our class and wasn't going to be able to drive until the end of our junior year which is why half the football team gave him shit for 'sleeping with an older woman.'

Me, though, I gave him shit because I just didn't like her. Sure, my reasons for not liking her were deeply rooted in jealousy and hurt feelings because he hadn't picked me, but that's not the point here.

Actually, that is the point, because this text from him now is the first one I have gotten in over four months.

And for us, four months was pretty much a lifetime.

2

CAM | NOW

I couldn't believe how beautiful she was, standing there at the end of the bed looking at me like she was ready to devour me. Her eyes were locked on mine, begging for me to come closer and touch her.

And holy shit did I want to.

Her long, cinnamon-colored hair was falling behind her shoulders and her legs looked like they could go on for miles. She didn't have the model-type body most men drooled over, but to me she was perfect. She was also wearing nothing but a lace bra and matching panties, which any man with respect and dignity would notice. As she moved closer to me, I could feel my lower half grow and my heart started to pound in my chest.

I couldn't believe I had Haley Jones standing in her underwear at the foot of my bed, looking at me the way she was. It was as if she was ready to do things to me that would blow my mind while also hoping I would do the same to her. I continued to watch her in utter disbelief, drinking in every inch of her body that I could see from where I was lying on the bed. I had wanted this for more than seventeen years, ever since I saw her in that denim skirt all those years ago.

I had been her friend—truly just her friend—since we were in kindergarten. But when Haley came to school one day in ninth grade wearing a cutoff denim skirt and white Henley with the top few buttons undone to where you could see her bra strap, I no longer wanted to only be her friend.

No, I wanted to be way more than friends, just like I wanted her as more than a friend right now. And I was *ready* to have her as way more than a friend, I can promise you that.

My heart started to race as she started to make her way towards me. I watched as she leaned over, her breasts starting to spill out of her black lace bra, dying to touch them with my own two hands, and felt her breath on my ear. She started to open her mouth as my whole body prepared to feel her lips on mine for the first time, and when she spoke, her voice came out as a loud, blaring alarm.

What the fuck? I thought as I jerked my head back and bolted upright in bed. I looked around, and when my brain —and cock—finally caught up to my surroundings, I realized I was alone in my loft and the blaring alarm wasn't the voice of my childhood friend I'd been pining for over the last two decades. Unfortunately for me, it was the sound of my alarm clock kindly letting me know that I needed to get my ass out of bed.

4:43 A.M. was flashing on the small plastic alarm clock face as it continued to blare its obnoxious alarm.

I slapped the buttons across the back to get it to stop and took a few deep breaths. It had been a minute since I last had a dream about Haley, but holy shit did I like it. I closed my eyes for a second and tried to commit the dream to memory. Her long legs and soft hair, the lacy bra and panties that I wanted to rip off with my teeth, the way her perfect breasts billowed out over the top of her bra as she leaned over me. Suddenly, I was hard and wanted to take care of myself but knew I couldn't or I'd be late for training.

"You'll have to wait until tonight," I said to my cock in the hopes that by saying it out loud, my hard-on would go away and not distract me during morning training.

It didn't work.

I stepped out of bed and walked towards the bathroom to take a quick shower before leaving. My friends always tell me I'm crazy for taking a morning shower just to turn around and train, but I hated leaving the house feeling dirty. I quickly showered, brushed my teeth, and changed into my gym clothes before walking downstairs to the kitchen.

I had moved into my place after signing a multi-million-dollar contract to play for the major football team here in North Carolina at the end of last season. My sister always liked to remind me that I had "major mansion money now" and that I should buy something with a pool and ten bedrooms, but I liked my loft. Plus, there was a community pool if I ever wanted to use it.

Once in the kitchen, I flipped on the light and opened up the fridge to grab an apple, an overnight oats jar, and a protein shake. Once I had everything I needed, I grabbed my bag from the floor and slung it over my shoulder before walking out into the garage. I pulled open the driver's side door, slid inside, and tossed my bag into the backseat. This was my daily routine as we got closer to the season starting, and by now, I could go through my entire morning in my sleep if I needed to.

Not if you're having dreams like the one you had last night, I thought to myself.

I pulled out of my garage and started towards the

training center. Where the team trained was only fifteen minutes from my loft which was nice for early morning training days. This morning though, it didn't feel like enough time. I wanted hours to sit and remember the dream I'd had about Haley and unpack every single part of it I still remember.

Her smile, the shape of her waist, how looking at her standing there turned me on. I shouldn't be thinking about her this way—she's married, for Christ's sake. At least, she was the last time I stalked her on social media. It was almost eight years ago that I last did a deep dive into her life from the safety of my side of the internet. I could only see so much because, after our last night together, she'd unfriended me and went private with her account. But from what I could tell, she'd gotten married to the guy she started dating when we were in college. In the photos she was tagged in, she looked happy.

Actually, she looked breathtaking in the photo her mom posted of her wearing a long white dress and holding a big bouquet of flowers. But looking at her standing next to another man, married to him instead of me, made me feel like I wanted to throw up and put my fist through a wall all at the same time. She had decided to move on and be happy while I was still stuck in the past. How could I have been so stupid and treated her so poorly? Now she was married to another man.

It should've been me.

I was still thinking about how much I longed to be the one standing next to her at the altar saying "I do, forever and always," when I pulled into my parking space. Without really paying attention, I made it to the training center by 5:30 even though training didn't start until 6:00. I always preferred to be early so that I had time to myself in the quiet before things got crazy when the rest of the team showed up.

I grabbed my stuff from the backseat and headed inside to eat, change, and get to work. Today was the first day of training for the season and as the new guy, I knew I had a lot to prove. I wanted to be seen as a team player and someone who was focused on the game and nothing else.

If only Haley hadn't decided to threaten that focus by visiting me in my dreams last night.

———

"Hey Camden, you looked great out there today!"

"Thanks, Coach. I'm excited to be here and be part of this team. I can't wait for the season to start in a few weeks," I replied, drying my hair since I'd just stepped out of the shower.

Coach Mike was a good guy and a huge reason why I was excited to play for this team now. He was known for being tough and demanding, but also fair and supportive. He expected a lot from all his players, but I would too if I was the head coach of a major NFL team where the players make millions of dollars a year. The other reason I liked him so much was because he reminded me a lot of my high school football coach, who was the first person to tell me that if I worked hard, I had the potential to go pro.

"How are you liking Charlotte so far? Have you explored the city at all?" Coach asked.

"Yeah, a little bit when I've had time. I spend most of my time here or training at the gym back at my place," I explained.

"That's all fine and dandy, but be sure to have a life too. Being married to the game isn't all it's cracked up to be.

Forty years in and three failed marriages later, I can tell you that much," Coach chuckled and waved a hand at me before walking toward his office.

"Are you going to remind him he's on wife number four because he can't keep it in his pants, or am I?" I heard a voice say behind me. I turned round to see my closest friend, Harvey, opening his locker and grabbing his things from inside.

"Look, I'm the new one here, YOU can be the one to say something. I need to stay on his good side," I pointed a finger at Harvey and laughed.

Harvey and I had been friends since we played ball together in college. We met the first week of classes and became close when we realized we both had the same goal in mind.

Make it to the NFL.

We were both drafted after our senior year and have played for different teams over the years. He came to play in Charlotte two years ago and I was stoked when I got traded to the team because I knew it meant playing with Harvey again.

Still laughing, Harvey looked at me and spoke, "For real though, man, how do you like Charlotte so far? How's the humidity treating you?"

"You forget I grew up in Pennsylvania, where the humidity rolls in by May and doesn't leave until after Thanksgiving," I replied as I threw my bag over my shoulder, fully dressed now.

"Ahh, that's right. Little farmer boy from the middle of nowhere who made it big playing football," Harvey teased as we walked out of the locker room.

"Harvey, please. I grew up in the furthest thing from a farm town. The kids at my school drove cars that cost more than the down payment on a house and wore shoes that cost three hundred dollars apiece. It definitely wasn't a farm town, and I *definitely* wasn't a farmer," I reminded him for the hundredth time.

This has been something Harvey and I had discussed at least every week in college. As someone who originated from SoCal, he couldn't believe that the entire state of Pennsylvania wasn't just a giant cornfield.

Only about 80% of it was, really.

Harvey put his hands up. "I know, I know, I'm just giving you a hard time man. I'm happy you're here," he said, clapping a hand on my shoulder.

"I'm happy I'm here too. It's a fresh start in a new place. I'm ready to get through training and the preseason so we can get to playing actual games."

"Yeah, I'm excited about that too," he replied as we reached our cars. "But right now, I'm more excited to get through afternoon conditioning so I can go home for the day. Monica is cooking dinner tonight and she's making her homemade meatloaf. Damn, do I love that woman's meatloaf. I would eat the entire thing if she'd let me. Or if the kids would let me." He shook his head and smiled to himself.

Harvey met the love of his life in college and married her immediately after signing his first major contract. Within the first year of their marriage, they had a daughter, and then a son after that. I always admired Harvey for his commitment to Monica and his kids, even when his travel schedule and football career kept him away from home a lot. He would pay to have them travel where he played as much as they wanted and was always home when he wasn't on the field. I secretly dreamed of having that for myself if I ever found the right girl.

You already found the right girl. You were just dumb as hell and never did anything about it.

"Awww, wittle Harvey wants his wittle meatwoaf?" I jabbed at him, even though I was only being a dick to cover up my jealousy.

"Actually, I want to go home to my wife whom I love and can have incredible sex with whenever I want, and to kiss my two kids who drive me crazy but I love so much it hurts. You'll understand one day once you find the right girl," he tossed back, flipping me the bird as he stepped up into his truck.

"Yeah..." I said under my breath, "Once I find the right girl."

3

HALEY | NOW

"Oh my fucking god. WHERE ARE MY KEYS?!" I yelled, running around the house looking for my goddamn car keys, again. I had gotten up early enough today to go to the gym, get home, and get ready with enough time to spare before my meeting with Piper. But since my brain came up with yet another idea for work, I spent an extra thirty minutes on the treadmill, sending voice notes to myself talking through it. When my brain caught an idea, it couldn't let it go no matter how late it would make me.

As a serial entrepreneur, I have started and stopped—and sold, thank you very much—several businesses over the years. Some were more legitimate than others but all had started as a hair-brained idea that I needed to flesh out just to see if it would work. I've always been an ideas girl and always had the ambition to go after anything that got me excited. I blame my dad for this trait because he's also an entrepreneur who has a propensity to chase new and shiny things.

Unfortunately for my mom and me, sometimes new and

shiny things come in the form of a twenty-four-year-old blonde named Sarah. Once Sarah came walking by, Dad went with her and walked right out of our lives and never looked back. That was back in fourth grade, and I remember how much it crushed us both. Now at thirty-two, I couldn't care less about where my dad is or who he's with.

Right now, I really only care about where the fuck my car keys went.

"I'm so late right now, where are my keys?!" I semi-shouted again, picking up all the papers and random crap off the counters as I searched.

"Honey...honey..." I heard my husband gently say from the dining room where he was sitting behind his laptop. I peeked my head around the corner to find him holding my keys up by the little metal ring. He was looking at me just over his metal-framed glasses and his mouth was curved up on one side, showing me the smirk that made my heart flutter every time I saw it.

I gasped.

"My hero!" I gushed as I walked over grabbing my keys with one hand and putting the other around his neck. I smashed my face into his with a hard kiss—just how I liked —and when I pulled away, his glasses were sitting on a diagonal. I giggled just a little and set them straight for him before he adjusted them on his own so they were right back where they had originally been.

"You truly are the love of my life, how would I ever find my keys if it weren't for you?" I asked him with my arm still around his neck. I was bending over so I was at eye-level with him, staring into his soft blue eyes. The same soft blue eyes I had loved staring at since we got married eight years ago.

"I certainly don't know how you would find them. You'd

probably be stuck at home all the time or forced to take public transportation whenever you wanted to leave the house," he teased as he looked back at me.

"Well, we certainly couldn't have that. I can't turn the radio all the way up on the bus," I joked, making light of the habit I knew drove him crazy.

"God forbid you don't listen to music at an ear-splitting level every time you get in the car, honey." He chuckled softly, and I felt his breath on my lips because I refused to let go or move away from him.

"It truly wouldn't be a good day if I didn't," I said with a smile and stuck my tongue out at him.

"It also wouldn't be a good day if you didn't kiss me one more time before you go," he hummed as he leaned in closer. Our lips touched and I felt him press a little deeper into me. I loved the way he felt and smelled and looked. I had loved him for almost twelve years now and I couldn't get enough of him.

Connor was the first man I'd fallen in love with after high school. The first man who looked at me and instantly made me feel beautiful. The first man to hold me like he never wanted to let me go. The first man I had given myself to fully. When we shared a moment like this, I knew in my heart that I would be okay if we simply melted together and became one.

"It truly wouldn't be a good day if I didn't," I agreed as I pulled away, still smiling.

I looked at him for a few more seconds before standing upright again and moving to make my way to the front door. At this point, I was way past late for my meeting with Piper and really needed to get a move on.

"Are you heading into the office today?" I asked him as I slipped on my sneakers.

I was wearing my favorite high-rise jeans and a comfy tee shirt with a blazer thrown on top. As I'm my own boss, I liked to keep things professional, yet casual whenever I had a meeting outside of the house. Usually, I worked from home, but getting out was nice every once in a while.

"Yeah, I am in a bit. I have some emails I want to get through here first and then I was planning on heading in. We have a meeting at 10:30 with the international team. I want to get in by 9:30 so I have enough time to prepare for it."

Connor explained his morning schedule with such dedication that it made my heart swell. That was one thing I could always rely on with Connor, his dedication to the things and people he loved. Connor worked at a big corporate company doing I don't know what, but I know he loved it and I know it made him happy. To me, that's all that matters.

"Okay cool, and then are you going to stay at the office till the end of the day or head home after your meeting?"

Connor and I had been lucky that we both could work from anywhere. I had finally gotten to the point where my business was paying me a full-time salary and gave me the flexibility to work from wherever. His job was also semi-remote where he could work from home 95% of the time and was only required to be in the office whenever a big team meeting was happening, like today.

I loved this because it meant I got to see him more often and we could spend more time together. Other married women talk about how they wish their husbands would stay at work longer or not rush home from a business trip. Not me though—not with Connor. I always wanted him around because when he was, I felt safe and full.

"I'm going to just spend the day at the office and then

come home around 5:30. I can pick us up some food if you want. It is Wednesday, ya know," he reminded me with a smile.

Wednesdays had always been our days for takeout, even when we were two very broke postgrads scraping by to make ends meet. I had commented about wanting to make new traditions now that we were living together, so he suggested we pick a day of the week to get takeout.

We've done it every week since.

"Ooh, can we get Thai?!" I asked, knowing he would tell me yes even though he didn't like Thai as much as I did.

"Sure, you want your usual?" he asked, looking back to his computer screen.

"Yes please!" I exclaimed as I walked over to him again, carrying my bag, shoes finally on, and keys in hand.

I leaned over one more time and dropped a kiss on his head which prompted him to look at me. He smiled up at me, his eyes flashing between mine and my lips, his silent indicator that he wanted another kiss. I gave him what he silently asked for and leaned into it. We kissed like this for a few moments, getting caught up in one another again. Suddenly, my internal alarm went off reminding me that I was VERY late for my meeting. I pushed him away and took a breath. Is it even possible to love someone more than I love Connor? I seriously doubted it.

"I love you," I whispered to him.

"I love you more," he answered, just like he always did.

I said goodbye to him with a wave and headed out the front door, locking it behind me. Once in the car, I sent off a quick text to Piper letting her know I would be late and that I would buy her a large coffee and a pastry as an apology.

Then, I plugged in my phone, hit the start button for the

car, and turned the music all the way up as I pulled out of the driveway.

———

PIPER and I had been sitting at a local coffee shop for two hours and my phone had already rung twice from a number I didn't recognize. Maybe it was because of how I was raised, but I never answered my phone if I didn't recognize the number. I figured if it was important enough, they would leave a voicemail.

"Okay, so we need to start to organize for our annual conference which is going to be held downtown next spring. Where do you want to start?" Piper asked as she pulled out a fresh notepad and pen.

I loved Piper, but her requirement to write everything down on paper before typing it up after the fact never made sense to me.

She and I had been friends since we connected on Facebook through the "Freshman Roommate Finder" page for our college. We knew we didn't want to live with some random stranger and immediately bonded over our obsession for rewatching the same shows four hundred times and Taylor Swift. She grew up in Indiana and I grew up in Pennsylvania, so we also connected on being born and raised in states where the yearly county fairs were the major events people got excited about.

We were the perfect pair: she was level-headed, a great listener, and super organized. I, on the other hand, jumped at any new idea I had and moved a million miles a minute. It drove both her and Connor crazy sometimes, but they loved me for it. After graduating, Piper told everyone she was going to go to law school to become a public defender but by the end of the first semester, she quit and came to work for me.

For the last several years, we have worked to build She Who Thrives into a full-scale business known around the world. I started She Who Thrives as a college blog, just sharing what being in college was like. Now, it included public speaking events, courses, a podcast, and my personal favorite, our annual conference. There is nothing I loved more than what I do at She Who Thrives, which supports women in living a life they love.

I was the figurehead and CEO of She Who Thrives and Piper was my second in command. She did things like organize calls, map out new podcast episodes, and made sure that I didn't go too far off course chasing some new exciting thing. We worked well together and have made She Who Thrives something amazing, and for that, I was grateful.

"Yes! Can you remind me what attendance was last year? I think we need to start by picking a venue based on projections for attendance and then go from there," I replied after thinking about everything Piper and I had achieved over the years.

She shuffled through some papers and I laughed as I watched her.

"You know...it would be a lot faster to find these things if you just put everything on your computer. That is why I bought it for you."

"Oh hush, I have everything I need right here just give me a second to find it," she threw back at me, finally finding what she was looking for.

"Here we go! So last year we had...345 women attend live which was amazing for only our second year. The year before that we had about 275, so a clear increase in ticket sales. I think it would be a safe bet to book a venue that could seat at least 400 people if you wanted!"

"Yeah, I totally agree, I think we should—" I paused because my phone started ringing, again.

"Oh my god, this is the third time this number has called me since we've been here," I sighed before showing Piper the number on my screen.

"Why don't you just answer it?" she asked like any reasonable adult would.

"Because I don't know this person! What if it's a scam or a creep looking to get off by the sound of my voice? I have a very sexy voice, you know." I smirked.

"Oh my god, I don't wanna know what Connor has said to make you believe that, but you're full of it," Piper quipped.

"I'll just let it go to voicemail. If they need me, they will leave something for me to hear," I said, putting my phone back down.

"Oh my god, you're ridiculous, just answer it. Or better yet, let me answer it so we can move on and I can avoid hearing your sexy voice," Piper huffed as she snatched the phone from my hand to answer it.

"Hello, this is Piper speaking. Sorry, you don't get to hear Haley's sexy voice but..." She stopped talking as if she was interrupted and I watched as the color drained from her face,

"Yes...say that again...oh my god...okay, please hang on a second." She pulled the phone away from her mouth and looked at me like she was about to be sick. "It's about Connor, there's been an accident."

———

Do you remember when you were little at the local pool and you and your friend were underwater trying to talk to one another? They would look at you under the water and scream as loud as they could but what you heard was almost completely indistinguishable and muddled?

That's how I felt when I listened to the man on the phone tell me that Connor had been in an accident on his way to the office. That almost indistinguishable gurgle is all I heard as Piper drove me to the emergency room where they said he'd been taken. And it's all I heard when the surgeon finally came out seven hours later, to tell me that she had done everything she could to save him, but it wasn't enough.

"His car flipped four times."

"We did everything we could."

"He didn't feel a thing."

"I'm so sorry, but he's gone."

I continued to feel like I was underwater, unable to hear or feel anything real for the next few days. People came to see me. My mother came and stayed with me. Piper asked if there was anything she could do for me. But she couldn't. None of them could. Because nothing could bring Connor back to me.

My husband.

My best friend.

My biggest supporter and number one fan.

The first real man to love me exactly as I was and not leave me for something else.

Gone.

4

CAM | THEN

I was standing at my locker, swapping out my books when I took a quick look at my phone. We weren't allowed to be on our phones as ninth graders, so everyone just kept theirs in their lockers and checked them between classes. As long as Ms. Daniels didn't see you, you were normally okay.

I flipped my phone over and saw a new notification:

I felt a smile creep onto my face as I unlocked my phone to read it. Haley and I had been friends since kindergarten and I always called her Jones when we were with other people, like a pet name, because I knew it annoyed her. In retaliation, she started calling me Johnson. When we were alone, we were Haley and Cam—only she was allowed to call me Cam—but with other people, we were Jones and Johnson.

I read the text message from her and laughed. Haley always made me laugh.

> Oh my god someone needs to tell Hunter Ryans he needs to shower in the morning. I can smell him from my desk.

> Maybe you should tell him that tomorrow when he sits in front of you again.

> Maybe you should tell him that at football practice after school. He's your teammate after all. I'm just the poor sucker who has to sit behind him in History.

I laughed again, imagining her sitting behind Hunter trying to breathe through her mouth and cover her nose the entire forty-five minutes of class.

As I read her text, I realized that I hadn't seen her today which was weird. We always met at my locker before first period but she never showed up.

> Hey, why haven't I seen you yet today?

> Doctor's appointment. My mom just dropped me off before last period.

> Is everything okay? Why did you need to go to the doctor?

I typed back quickly.

Ever since my sister had gotten sick a few years ago, any mention of the doctor put me on edge. Haley had been an amazing friend to me during that time and was the only reason I got through my sister's treatment without completely losing my mind. My sister was the single most important person in my life and watching her battle cancer at such a young age was hard on me.

"I just needed to get my yearly physical and this was the soonest my mom could get me in," I heard from behind me, looking up from my phone and following the sound of her voice.

I almost choked on my own tongue when I saw her.

Walking towards me, smiling, her cinnamon-colored hair fell just past her shoulders. She had on a short denim skirt and was wearing a white long-sleeved shirt, with the top few buttons undone. I could see her bra strap slipping out on her shoulder because her backpack had pushed the sleeve of her shirt down. I tried not to stare at it too long.

Had she always looked like a glowing light was shining from behind her? No, right? That's just happening right now?

I blinked a few times and tried to ignore the tingling feeling in my gut and remembered that she had said something and was probably waiting for me to reply.

"Got it. Everything is good though?" was all I could string together, trying to play it cool.

"Yes, Cam, everything is fine. You don't need to worry," she said with a sweet, understanding smile because she knew that I would worry. She always knew what I was thinking or how I was feeling.

"Yo! Camden!" I heard someone say from down the hall and I turned to see it was one of the guys from the team waving at me. I turned back to look at Haley, trying to prevent her from noticing how I was *really* looking at her.

"I should probably go make sure everything's okay," I said with a shrug.

"That's alright, I'll see ya later, Johnson," Haley said, a sly smirk spreading across her face and a wink that almost made me choke on my tongue again.

"Yeah, I'll see you later, Jones," I replied before walking toward the guys who just shouted my name. As I went, I tried to shake the tingling feeling that was still lingering in my gut after seeing Haley in this new way for the first time.

———

"Yo, did you see Haley today? She looked...different," one of my teammates said at lunch that same day. Our coach always told us that we played like a team and lived like a team and that meant eating lunch together as a team too.

"Different, how?" I asked, trying to play it cool and not think about how I swore I saw a glowing light following behind her as she walked towards me earlier that morning.

"Different *hot*," another guy at the table said without even skipping a beat.

I looked at him with a mix of disbelief, disgust, and protection. Clearly, he got the message.

"Sorry, dude. I know she's your friend and all, but that skirt." He brought his hands to his chest as if he was praying and kissed his fingertips.

I took a breath before saying anything and shrugged. "She looked the same to me," I lied.

"Well, she looked different enough for Sean to notice. He was talking about her in Chem. Something about how he would like to see what she looked like without the skirt."

I had to put my fork down and take a deep breath for fear that I would take my fork and shove it into Sean's hand. Sean Hampton was the oldest guy in our class and also the biggest douche. The way he talked about girls would lead you to believe he was sleeping with the entire cheer squad, which he wasn't. Normally, I would let the comments slide, but the thought of him talking about Haley like that made me want to do something that would get me in trouble.

"Sean is a dick and should really stop talking like he's getting something he isn't," I sneered through gritted teeth. It came out a little angrier than I intended.

"Woah there, Camden, no need to get all mad about it. I know you guys are tight, but Sean's an idiot, everyone knows that. He was just talking about how he'd seen her in the hallway talking to you and then commented on her skirt. I don't think he meant anything more than that."

He better fucking not have.

I continued to eat my food and let the conversation move on to something else. Obviously, I hadn't been the only one who noticed Haley and her skirt, but I couldn't believe what Sean said about her. If he was talking, I'm sure other people were talking too and I hated to think that they were.

After Haley's dad left, I always felt the need to protect her. Not that she needed my help—the girl could handle things all on her own and she would tell you as such.

I smiled thinking about how in fourth grade Carson Pax called her small and grabbed her headband off her head and held it above his, just out of her reach. I started to try and take it from him, but before I could do anything she kicked him in the shin, which made him double over in pain, and snatched it from his hand. She then promptly affixed it to its rightful place on her head, grabbed my hand, and led us away, leaving poor Carson on the floor.

Lunch was just about over and my tray was almost clean when I felt my phone buzz in my backpack. I leaned down to grab it and once I read the screen, the tingling feeling from earlier was back in my gut.

I swiped to unlock my phone and read the message.

Hey there Johnson, how's lunch?

It's good Jones, how's your lunch?

I replied, looking around the cafeteria to see if I could find her.

It was fine until I looked over at your table and you looked like you wanted to hit something. Somethin' happen?

No, we were just talking and someone said something stupid.

I finally placed her across the room at a table with her friends, staring down at her phone, and texting me back.

What did they say?

Nothing, it doesn't matter.

Clearly it did if it made you make that face you do when you're pissed. It's a cross between 'I'm constipated' and 'Watch out, I'm about to kill you.'

I looked up at her after reading her text and saw she was looking back at me, smiling but also looking concerned. I didn't want to tell her what had been said, but I didn't want to worry her either.

I hesitated before texting her back.

Apparently people noticed your outfit today.

> What the hell does that mean? What people?

I looked at her again and watched as she adjusted her skirt and tucked her bra strap back under her sleeve.

> Just some of the guys is all. I guess Sean liked it enough to talk about you in Chem.

I hit send and held my breath. Both because I didn't want her feelings to be hurt but also because I didn't want her to be happy that Sean had noticed her.

> Gag, Sean's gross and such a dick. I overheard him talking about what he and Jill did under the bleachers over the summer and I was crushed for her. No guy should ever talk about a girl like he does, it's degrading.

I exhaled deeply. *Thank god she wasn't excited he was talking about her. Wait, why did I care? I shouldn't care, she's my friend.*

> You don't talk about girls like that, do you Cam?

She sent before I could reply.

> No, I would never. My mom would kill me and I have a sister. If I ever heard a guy talking about her in the same way Sean talks about girls, I would kill him.

> Is that why you looked like you wanted to kill someone earlier? Because Sean was talking about me that way…

I read her message three times, contemplating the right

answer, feeling like this was a test. What was she trying to get me to say? Again, I looked up toward her table and again, she was looking back at me from her table, waiting to see what I would send next.

> Yeah, I guess so. You're one of my best friends, pretty much like a sister, you know?

I looked up at her again and watched her face fall for half a second as she typed back.

> Lol yeah…like a sister.

What the heck did that mean? I thought to myself.

Before I could reply, the bell rang and lunch was over. I looked at her text one more time and then up to see where she was but I couldn't find her in the crowd of moving bodies.

Why did she ask me how I talked about girls? Or if I had looked pissed because of what Sean said? Did I really look constipated when I got angry? I would have to practice looking more intimidating in the mirror.

Something else I was going to work on was getting the tingling feeling that I felt in my gut every time I thought about her to go away.

It never really did though.

5

HALEY | NOW

Over the course of a week, I went from being married to the love of my life, running a successful business, and ready to take the world by storm, to being a widow who was wearing the same leggings for the third day in a row and couldn't seem to move from the fetal position in bed.

It had been a full seven days since the accident and I still felt like I was living underwater. Whenever someone talked to me, it was like I couldn't fully hear them. As they spoke, I would move my head in a way that made them think I was listening. In reality, I was too wrapped up in my own grief to be able to hear what they said at all.

My mom had come as soon as she could and was determined to stay with me until she saw me eat, shower, and go outside for longer than five minutes all in the same day. At this rate, she would be living with me forever.

She was waiting for me at my house the following day once I got back from meeting with the police who had taken the call for Connor's accident. She came with me to the hospital when I had to fill out paperwork on what we were doing with his body after they had taken his organs for donations—he always said he wanted his body to be used for something good once he was gone. And she slept on the couch every night without complaining because I was sleeping in the guest room.

Our bed had sat empty since the day I lost Connor. I didn't have the strength to crawl under the covers that once kept us both warm and safe night after night. I didn't have the strength to do much of anything anymore it seemed. Anytime I tried to move throughout my day like normal, I was hit with the realization that Connor was gone and never coming back, which always left me in a heap of sobs on the floor.

Grief is a funny thing. It's silent until it's not. It's something you know exists, but you never truly know what it looks like until it's staring you in the face. Like a dark creature sitting in the back of your brain, it waits for the day it's called out and when it comes, it crushes you under its massive, unbearable weight.

And I couldn't bear the weight.

I couldn't hold it, and I couldn't get it to let go of me.

So instead, I let it sit on me—day in and day out—because the thought of trying to fight it was just as painful as letting it consume me.

I was curled up in the queen-size bed that we bought for the guest room when we purchased this house five years ago when I heard a faint knock on the door.

"Hey, Hays..." my mother called to me, using the nickname she gave me when I was little. "I'm heading to the store, do you need anything?"

I was facing away from her with the covers pulled up, so if you weren't looking at me you would think I was asleep.

My mother knew better though and continued, "Piper is

coming over to see you, she mentioned bringing you your favorite from the local Thai place, would that be okay?"

Thai. We were supposed to have Thai that night.

The sheer thought of its smell brought me back to that day. The day I lost him. Thinking about not having Thai with him again made tears well up in my eyes. My stomach flipped at the idea.

"I'm not hungry," I whispered, blinking back the tears so she wouldn't come any closer.

"Are you sure? You haven't eaten yet today..." my mom pressed, leaning a little closer into the room.

"I said, I'm not hungry and I don't want any fucking Thai food in the house." My words came out more pointed than I intended, and I heard my mother take a deep breath.

"Alright, Hays, whatever you want. I'll tell Piper to just come over. She should be here in the next half hour. If you change your mind and want anything from the store, just text me."

I heard her close the door and I was alone again. I tried to sleep, or better yet, I tried to get myself to wake up from what I could only believe was a never-ending nightmare. Connor wasn't gone, I was just asleep and needed to wake up. If I did, he would be lying there next to me, just like he had for the last ten years.

Connor and I met our sophomore year at college and it was love at first sight. For so long, I had told myself that the only men in my life were the ones who left or chose other people, no matter how much I showed them I loved them. I was walking into my public speaking class and sat down at one of the tables when I looked up to see this guy with metal-framed glasses walk in. I watched him as he strolled through the class, walked up the stairs, and then pulled out the seat right next to mine and sat down. Never in my life had I ever seen a man as beautiful as he was, with his tousled ashy hair and soft blue eyes.

And the glasses—don't even get me started about the glasses.

I must have forgotten to close my mouth or move or look anything like a normal human because when he noticed me staring at him, he started laughing.

"You know, there's a lot of bugs in this room. If you don't close your mouth, one might fly into it," he leaned over and whispered in my ear.

We were dating by the following weekend and married the summer after we graduated.

Everything with Connor was so easy. He made me laugh, challenged what I said but in a way that was interesting and sparked conversation, and he told me I was beautiful every morning when we woke up next to one another. Even on the days when we didn't wake up next to one another, because one of us was traveling or before we lived together, I had a 'Good morning, beautiful' text waiting for me to read.

Every day I felt safe with him, happy with him, and loved by him. Never once in our ten-year relationship did I get the sense that he was going to bolt like my dad did or suddenly decide there was someone better. He looked me in the eyes when he listened to me, supported my crazy ideas while keeping his apprehension to himself, and never told me there was something I couldn't do. He was the first man to love me like he did.

And now he was gone.

As I was failing miserably to wake up from this life that had to be a nightmare, I heard the front door open and knew Piper had finally made it to the house. I heard her open up the fridge and close it again, then the sounds of her unloading and loading the dishwasher. After she was done, she ascended the stairs toward the place where she knew she would find me.

She opened the door, moved to the side of the bed I was facing, and put her face directly into mine.

"Hi. I spoke to Martha and she told me you were in here. When was the last time you left this room?" my best friend questioned. She was so close I could smell the coffee on her breath.

"I don't know. She made me shower this morning but I managed to put the same clothes back on and then crawled back into bed before she could stop me," I mumbled, pulling the covers even closer to my eyes.

"She texted me to not bring Thai, what's that about? You love Thai, especially from the place around the corner. I could have brought you your usual." Her voice was soft as she spoke. As I listened, I had a flashback to the last morning I spent with Connor, sitting in the dining room downstairs.

"You want your usual?" he had said as I put on my shoes and grabbed my bag to leave. I remember kissing him good-bye, fully expecting to have my usual with him that night as we sat together at the table, sharing about our days like we always did with dinner.

Before I could stop them, the tears were back in my eyes and I tried to remember to breathe. Within seconds, I was sobbing again for what felt like the hundredth time that week, unable to put words to my thoughts and explain why I was so upset.

"Oh, oh sweetie, I'm sorry! I didn't mean to make you cry, what did I say? I'm sorry!" I heard my friend say, panic in her voice knowing that she had said something to set me off. Piper was my best friend, but the way she cared for me was more like a sister. I started to cry even harder because I knew I had upset her.

Through my sobs, I watched as she took off her shoes and coat and then I felt the bed give way as she crawled into bed next to me. She wrapped her arms around my torso and held me, repeating a ritual we started in college. Whenever the other was upset, we would crawl into bed and lay with each other.

I managed to collect myself and slow my tears down enough to get out, "We were supposed to get Thai that night. The night of the accident. Connor was going to bring it home with him from the office and..." But I couldn't say anything else before another crushing wave of grief and sobs overtook me.

Piper sucked in a breath, finally understanding why Thai food was an open wound for me.

Everything felt like an open wound to me.

Instead of saying anything, Piper just held me and let me cry, which hurt just as much as the thought of eating Thai again because I knew Connor would never again be able to hold me like this. For a brief moment, I closed my eyes and pretended that she was Connor in the hopes that I would finally, *finally* wake up from this terrible nightmare.

But I knew no matter how much I hoped I would wake up, I wouldn't.

Connor wasn't coming back and I wasn't dreaming.

———

WHEN I WOKE UP, I realized I was alone and Piper was gone. At first, I thought I had made our entire interaction up as if it were a dream, but then I saw her shoes in the corner of the room and heard her voice downstairs. I listened for a second from the bed and heard a second voice, my mother's.

"I feel horrible. When she mentioned how they were supposed to get Thai food that night I wanted to crawl into a hole. She was so upset just at the mention of it," I heard Piper explain, her voice was hushed as if she was trying to prevent me from overhearing.

"Oh Piper, you are so kind to care so much about her, she's lucky to have you as a friend," my mom replied. I could just picture the face she was giving Piper, one that told you that you were okay and you hadn't done anything wrong.

"Martha, I'm really worried about her. She's not eating and she spends most of her days holed up in that room. Has she even gone into her room at all since the accident?" Piper questioned, her voice steeped with concern.

My mother sighed. "No, she hasn't. She's on this cycle of sleep, eating two bites and calling it a meal, and sleeping some more. She only takes a shower after I nearly drag her out of bed to do it. Then she goes right back into that room and goes back to sleep."

"That's not Haley, that's not our girl," Piper sounded as helpless as I felt.

"No, that's not our Haley, but this Haley is hurting and we need to let her hurt. The only way for her to come out of this is to feel and feel it all. But eventually, when she's ready, she will come out of this hurt. She's strong, our Haley girl. I raised her to be strong." Hearing my mother's words brought more tears to my eyes which surprised me because I hadn't had a full glass of water in days, and surely my tear ducts had to be empty at this point.

I thought about going downstairs to talk to them, but the thought of seeing the empty chair Connor once sat in at the dining room table made me feel like I had been permanently strapped to the bed. It hit me then that this whole house was a constant reminder of Connor, our marriage, and what we used to have.

The dining room table where he sat drinking coffee before heading into the office. The stove where he stood every night to cook me a proper meal because to him, 'Anything cooked in the microwave for three minutes isn't a real meal.' The couch where we sat next to each other, watching my favorite TV show for the fourth time because he knew it made me happy.

And our bedroom where we would sleep, laugh together in the dark, and make love like we were still in our twenties.

This whole house was a reminder of what I lost.

A home that no longer felt like home because the thing that made it a home was no longer in it.

6

CAM | NOW

The first week of training hadn't been that bad, but the second week was brutal. Coach Mike had us training three times a day to prepare for the first preseason game and wasn't letting anyone give less than their best. We trained three hours in the morning, three hours in the evening, and had an hour of conditioning in between.

Honestly, I was grateful for the demanding schedule because it didn't leave me a lot of extra time to think about the dream I'd had of Haley last week.

But holy shit was I tired.

After our final training on Friday, I asked Harvey if he wanted to grab a beer with me.

"I wish man, but Monica and the kids are waiting for me to go see a movie."

"Oh, you gonna go see that new animated whatever the hell crap they call a movie nowadays?" I replied, trying to cover up the small amount of jealousy I had toward my friend.

Part of me had always wanted to have someone waiting

for me at home at the end of the day. The same part of me wanted one of those someone's to be a child of my own. Kids were always something I knew I wanted. Growing up with my sister and taking care of her while my parents were at work taught me that.

But at thirty-one, I was still going home to an empty loft that didn't even look like anyone lived there. I didn't even have a dog for Christ's sake.

Maybe I should get one.

"Hey, don't knock them until you see them. I know they're made for kids, but a lot of animated movies these days have just as many adult jokes in them as they do kids' jokes. Sometimes I find myself laughing more than my kids," Harvey explained, pulling me out of the pity party I was throwing for myself.

"Well, if you want to do anything this weekend, let me know. I'm free as a bird, ready to do whatever I please." I swiped my hand across the air to show just how free I was. I didn't care *that* much that I had no plans, no friends other than Harvey, and no one to sleep next to this weekend.

Not really...

"I might be able to meet up on Sunday. Wanna get in an extra lift before the preseason starts?" Harvey asked, slinging his bag over his shoulder and closing his locker.

"Yeah, let's meet in the morning. I'll text you when I'm leaving and we can meet here," I replied, mimicking his actions and closing my locker right along with him.

We walked out of the locker room together and got into our cars, waving goodbye as we did. Before I closed my door, I heard Harvey answer his phone. "Hey babe, yeah I'm on my way home. I'm so excited to hang out with you and the kids tonight."

As I turned the key in the ignition, I found myself

thinking about how I had ended up where I was. No wife, no kids, not even a fucking dog to call my own. After freshman year in college, football and training became my whole life. Everything I did was for the game and to make it to the big leagues.

During those years, I didn't even think about finding "the one" let alone anything more than a casual fuck after some random house party. I've been with girls before, sure. But none of them were ever a contender for anything more than a weekend of fun. There was one girl I met my junior year, Gillian, who I thought I could fall in love with. She was nice and didn't get mad when I canceled plans to train and even came to my home games to cheer me on. Everything was great between us, or at least I thought it was until I went to her apartment one day to find her screwing the captain of the soccer team on her kitchen counter.

Ever since then, I swore off all relationships until I had signed my first major league contract to play football professionally.

But even when I had accomplished that, I never truly made an effort to try to date. It was hard with my travel and training schedule and I always used that as an excuse to avoid it all together. Now though, watching Harvey be a husband and a dad, I wish I had made an effort sooner. Shit, I wasn't getting any younger and in the next few years, I'd even be too old to play football.

And then what? I spend the rest of my days alone, getting myself off to some random girl in a porno? The thought of that made me groan and wish I could just run into the perfect girl on the street like you see in the movies.

But this wasn't a movie, this was real life. And that was never going to happen.

——————

MY ALARM WENT off Saturday morning at exactly 6:00 AM sharp. During the week, I had to get up ridiculously early to train, but on the weekends I liked to let myself sleep in. Sure, six is not sleeping in for a normal person, but I'm not a normal person. I'm a professional athlete who was committed to the game.

On the weekends, I liked to sleep in an extra hour, throw on some shorts and a shirt, and then head to the park down the road and get in a long run. Having strong stamina was important for my position and I liked to train my lungs to be able to go forever.

A skill that would also be helpful while in bed with a beautiful woman, I thought to myself as I pulled on my tee shirt. *If I had one of those.*

Last night I did exactly what I feared would become my life forever.

Pulled into the garage, made myself something to eat, and sat down on the couch while I ate my meal alone. After consuming several hours of shitty television, I decided I needed to go to bed, knowing I had an early start today. I was restless though, thinking about my lack of a family and lack of a real sex life. I felt my lower half begging to be taken care of, and after an hour of trying to fall asleep, I gave in and did what it wanted me to do.

I started by watching porn, but after a few minutes, I decided to turn it off and instead, think about the dream I had of Haley last week.

How good she looked in that lace bra, the shape of her body as it moved closer to me, the feeling I got when she touched my chest.

I pictured what she would feel like in real life, not just in a dream. How soft her skin would feel against mine, what it would be like to watch her cinnamon-colored hair fall around my face as she kissed me. How good it would feel to slip inside her, feeling her center tense up while I did. It didn't take long for me to think about her like this before I had finished all over my hand and needed to clean up. After I was done, I fell asleep without issue.

I thought about her again as I grabbed my standard morning breakfast and walked out onto my balcony to eat. While I lived alone and my loft held practically no personal items, it was still nicely furnished and decorated. I had paid someone to decorate it for me before moving in and I'm glad I did or else it would only have a lawn chair, PS5, and a mattress on the floor. Now, it had everything I needed to live comfortably and pretend like I was a real adult who knew how to do things like decorate.

As I sat on the balcony, I thought about Haley again. I wondered if she was happy and how her marriage was. I wasn't sure what she did for a living, but whatever it was I'm sure she was great at it. She was always great at everything she did because she took it seriously and never did anything halfway. That was something I always admired about her when we were friends.

After finishing my breakfast, I put my shoes on and grabbed the keys to my car. Before leaving, I checked myself in the mirror and studied my reflection.

I'm an attractive guy, I thought to myself.

My eyes were a dark shade of emerald—I got them from my mother—and my dark brown hair was a little longer than I normally kept it, but still, it wasn't unruly. I was also in peak shape because of my training schedule and commitment to staying in the best shape possible so I didn't wear out on the field.

Women find me attractive, right? I won't be alone forever...would I?

I took a breath and walked away from the mirror. I don't think my looks have anything to do with my lack of a relationship. I think it was purely because of my lack of trying, and more importantly, my lack of being able to commit when it counted most.

———

I WAS BREATHING HEAVILY as I passed the tree that I used as my stopping point on the opposite side of the park.

My route was always the same. I parked near a coffee shop on one side of the park and ran on the path that took me to the entrance on the opposite side. Then, I would turn around and run back. By the end of it, my run was an easy five miles.

The weather was warm and balmy and the park was packed with people. Whenever I ran, I liked to people-watch and take it all in. As I started back toward the other side of the park, I passed a woman pushing a stroller, cooing to the baby that sat inside, a guy who looked like he was probably ten years younger than me playing fetch with a Golden Retriever and a young couple who were definitely in high school holding hands and sitting at the base of a tall oak tree. The sight of them brought me a sudden stab of pain in my gut, thinking about a particular moment in my life that matched them almost identically. I hadn't thought about that day in a long time, but seeing the young couple brought the memory back immediately.

Finally finishing my run, I stood at the entrance of the park catching my breath and listening to the cars driving by. The park I ran through sat in the center of downtown Charlotte, and I liked coming here because of all the energy I could feel from the city. Charlotte wasn't huge, but it was just big enough to give you the sense that it was.

I was about to head back to my car when the sight of the coffee shop across the street caught my attention. I hadn't had a cup of coffee, or much of any kind of takeout, for weeks now as I prepared for the season. The thought of my favorite pastry, a bear claw, made my mouth water.

Deciding that I had worked out enough to earn the reward, I headed toward the shop. As I stood at the corner waiting for the sign to signal WALK, the images of Haley from my dreams crept into my brain again. Suddenly I felt my shorts move in a way they shouldn't move in a public setting, and I attempted to adjust myself as I crossed across the street.

There were probably fifty people in the small coffee shop when I stepped inside. A small bell above the door chimed as I pushed it open and I waved at the barista behind the counter. The menu wasn't big and I smiled triumphantly when I saw that they did, in fact, have fresh bear claws behind the counter. My mouth started to water and my stomach growled as I eyed them.

The barista took my order—a black coffee and a bear claw—and I stuck a few extra dollars in the tip jar before heading to the end of the counter to wait. Since it was Saturday morning, the shop was packed, and I had to move toward the end of the bar to wait for my drink so I wasn't in the way.

I looked up and watched as a guy grabbed his coffee from the bar. When he walked away, that's when I saw her.

Haley Jones, standing just a few feet away from the counter.

My whole body froze and my eyes slowly blinked a few

times, not fully able to believe that the girl I had grown up with was now standing in front of me, a fully grown woman. Her hair is what gave her away as it was the same cinnamon color it was when we were younger, except now it was a little shorter and she had a few pieces that framed her round face.

As I looked at her, I could see that she was slightly thinner than I remembered her being. She was wearing a black dress and carried a black bag across her shoulder that cut across her chest and made her breasts a little more noticeable than if she wasn't wearing it. I glanced at them without meaning to and quickly brought my eyes back to her face. Her beautiful, soft, round face that I couldn't forget even if I wanted to. The face from my childhood, my past, and my recent dreams. The face of the girl I had convinced myself I couldn't have and shouldn't want.

The unforgettable face of the girl who got away.

I took a few steps closer to her, stopping at a comfortable distance.

"Jones?"

7

HALEY | NOW

I almost thought my brain had made it up when I heard him call out my name. But when he repeated it for a second time, I knew I wasn't hallucinating.

No one had called me Jones since my freshman year in college, and only one person had ever called me that in my lifetime. It couldn't be him, could it? I turned my head to follow the voice and the air got caught in my throat when I saw him. Immediately, my heart started to pound so loud in my chest that I thought the people around us could hear it too.

Standing a few feet away from me was Camden Johnson.

Professional NFL player, recent trade to the local team, and the boy I grew up with.

Not just the boy I grew up with, but the boy who I had loved since I was in seventh grade.

I looked at him without saying anything, taking in everything that he was now. Tall, built, undeniably hot. His face was the same as the last time I had seen him, except older and more mature. He had stubble along his strongly formed jaw and his hair was longer than he normally kept it when we were growing up. He was wearing running shorts and a skin-tight, long-sleeved shirt that complimented his large, muscular arms.

But it was his eyes that pierced straight through every logical thought I was trying to form. Deep emerald and perfectly fit for his face. Exactly as I remembered them. The eyes I looked for every day on the playground, in the cafeteria, in the hallway, and that night in my dorm room during our first year away at school.

When my brain finally managed to reconnect itself to my body, I tried to calm my breathing as he walked toward me, but the way his hips swayed made it difficult. Once he was close enough to me, I could smell the familiar scent of pine, earth, and AstroTurf on him. Cam always smelled like this growing up, and the familiarity brought me a sense of comfort I hadn't felt in weeks.

I was staring at his arms when he finally spoke again.

"Haley Jones, I'll be damned. What the hell are you doing here?" he said with a smirk and a tinge of disbelief in his voice.

"Getting coffee," was all I could manage.

He chuckled, "I assumed that much, Jones. I mean what are you doing here *in Charlotte?*" His emphasis on the last two words brought me back to reality.

I had forgotten that Cam lived in Charlotte now that he played for the local NFL team. I had unfriended him on every social platform years ago and only knew about his trade because of my mom. She still followed the local newspaper back home on Facebook, and when they reported on his trade, she called to tell me all about it. I tried to tell her that I didn't care (even though I was happy for Cam) but she went ahead and read the entire article to me anyway. I refused the part of me that desperately wanted to look him up and send him a message to congratulate him. I knew if I let him in, I would be opening up a can of worms I wasn't ready to open yet. I had Connor and I was happy. And I wasn't going to let anything jeopardize that.

"Oh, I uh..." I lingered on my answer for fear that sharing my true purpose for being in town would cause me to break down in tears. I was never a crier growing up, but recent events have changed that. Now it felt like I could cry at any moment. I took a few deep breaths and locked my eyes on the ceiling, trying to force the tears that threatened to spill down my cheeks back. Having to explain my situation was still so fresh and caused me agony every time I had to do it.

"I'm...uh, I'm here for a funeral." I swallowed hard, looking down at my feet and pulling my bag closer to me as if it were a shield that would protect me from the pain.

I looked up to see Cam's face fall and fill with concern. I felt guilty for concerning him. I never wanted to make Cam feel anything other than happy, just like when we were younger.

"Oh my god. I'm so sorry, Haley." His brows came together in the center of his face, "I didn't realize you had family in Charlotte, I thought everyone lived in Pennsylvania?"

He was clearly confused about why I was going to a funeral in Charlotte when we both knew our families were born and raised in Pennsylvania. I was going to have to explain it to him and try to hold it together while I did.

"I don't have family here, but my husband did. It's his funeral I'm here for—my husband's."

Cam didn't say anything for a long moment, his face filled with a mix of shock, sadness, and concern. I shifted where I stood as I waited for him to respond. The people in the coffee shop moved around us like we were statues.

"Haley..." His voice was low and he swallowed hard. "I'm so sorry. I can't even imagine what you're going through."

"I wish people would stop fucking saying that. It's not that you can't imagine what I'm going through, it's that you won't," I snapped at him while looking him straight in the eye.

I didn't miss the pained look in his deep emerald eyes as my words hit him like a slap across the face. Embarrassed by my outburst, I quickly went back to studying my shoes. Cam was only trying to be kind, and I had just gone full psycho bitch on him.

"You're right, I could imagine it," Cam lamented as he sucked on his bottom lip and gently nodded in agreement. "but it still doesn't explain why you're here in Charlotte, don't you live in Wilmington?" I wanted to know how he knew that, but I moved past it and answered his question.

"We do—I do, but Connor's family lives here and his mother is insisting we do a full service for him even though it's not what he wanted. He wanted to be cremated and then have his ashes spread around places that were special to him. Not to be put on display and gawked at by people who didn't even really know him. So now I'm here, playing the grieving wife, when I haven't been able to get out of bed or eat a proper meal or even have the energy to bathe myself since his accident last week. She's being so fucking selfish and only cares about herself when I'm the one who lost the love of my fucking life...we were supposed to have Thai that night!" I threw my arms up in the air and was almost shouting.

The tears were no longer threatening to fall; they were streaming down my face at this point. I felt like the cork of a champagne bottle had just burst open out of my chest and a wash of relief and embarrassment ran through me. It felt nice to get this off my chest but I was also mortified that I had just dumped all of this on Cam not even three minutes after seeing him again for the first time in over ten years.

"Hey, hey...it's okay, you're okay..." Cam hushed as he moved closer to put an arm around me and move me toward two chairs sitting next to a big window that faced the busy street.

The touch of his arm sent something that felt like electricity down my spine, and I was instantly ashamed of how it made me feel. My husband of eight years just died in a tragic accident, for crying out loud; how dare my body react this way to the touch of another man? But the feeling of his arm wrapped around me made me feel safe and like everything was going to be okay.

I sat down in one of the big chairs, rested my elbows on my knees, and dropped my face into my hands. While I tried to collect myself, I heard Cam's footsteps walk away and then return after a moment, and I looked up to notice he was handing me a napkin to use as a tissue. I took it from him, grateful for his kind gesture. I dried my eyes using the scratchy brown paper napkin and took a few breaths.

"I'm sorry for dumping all of this on you. I'm sure you weren't expecting to have a blubbering widow crying in front of you when you came in here."

"You know, I actually woke up and had the sense that I was destined to come here and run into a blubbering widow," he joked, making me smile just a smidge. "For real though, Haley, I'm sorry for your loss. Do you want to talk about it? You don't have to, I'm more than happy to just sit with you if you want."

This was something we always offered to do for one

another growing up. When life got hard, we never forced each other to talk about things until we were ready, but always offered to sit and be there while the other hurt.

When my dad left, when his sister was going through treatment, we would just sit and wait for the other to start talking, and if we didn't, we left the words unsaid. Just being there for one another was enough.

I continued to dab my eyes because the tears wouldn't stop when I heard the barista behind the counter call my name and then Cam's. I started to get up to go grab my drink when Cam put his hand up to stop me and lifted his body from the chair again to retrieve our orders. When he returned, he handed me my drink, set his down on the table, and pulled a pastry out of the bag.

"A bear claw..." I noted, laughing at the familiarity of it. "You used to eat those things by the dozen when we were younger."

"I wish I could still eat them by the dozen now, but I'm pretty sure that would slow me down on the field or at least clog my arteries making it much harder to breathe while I ran after a football. I haven't had one of these in years but when I saw them in the display, I couldn't say no. You want a bite?" He was holding the pastry close to his face, practically drooling on it, then shoved it toward me so fast he almost smashed it into my face.

"No, I'm okay. Plus, I feel like you might bite my hand off if I tried to take it from you anyway. You look like you're ready to make love to that thing."

"Trust me, Jones, this is not the face I make when I want to make love to something."

His comment caught me off guard and my eyes flickered to meet his deep emerald eyes once more.

Was there a hint of something in that comment? I didn't

want to read too much into it, but the comment mixed with the fact that he called me by my last name made me feel like there was something more to it.

"Anyway..." Cam retracted his arm pulling the pastry back to his side of the chair and fidgeted in his seat, picking up on the awkwardness that came with his last remark. "You mentioned your husband's name is Connor?"

"Was Connor," I corrected sharply, not to be rude but because I found that speaking in the past tense about him made it more real that he was gone and never coming back. No matter how much I wish he was. "He died last week in a car accident on his way to work. It was sudden and they couldn't save him."

Cam paused and looked at me before reaching over and placing his hand on my knee, looking me straight in the eyes as he did. It wasn't sensual in any way but that same shot of lighting went down my spine again. A feeling of shame followed closely behind it.

"I'm not sure what the right thing is to say in this situation, but I want you to know that I'm truly sorry for your loss, Haley. I know how happy you were with Connor, and I'm very sorry you lost him. Is there anything I can do for you?"

I could see in his face that he meant it, but I still wished he would move his hand from where it rested on my knee.

"You're really kind to offer, but no. I'm only here for the weekend and am heading home on Monday. Plus, Piper is here to help me get through the weekend. My mom wanted to come but I told her it wasn't necessary," I explained, dreading the almost four-hour drive home. Getting here was hard enough, but going back knowing I would be going home to an empty house almost crippled me with grief all over again.

The mention of my mom made him smile, they had always gotten along and she was almost like a second mother to him when his sister was sick and his mom was preoccupied with taking care of her.

"I'm not surprised...Martha is always close when you need her. How is she doing?" Genuine interest and care for my mother was obvious in his question.

Growing up, my mom was always more of a friend than a mom, so everyone always called her by her first name. She always insisted on going by Martha instead of Mrs. Jones after my dad left, so it wasn't weird that Cam addressed her as such.

"She's good. She runs a local flower shop in Wilmington now that she's retired. She moved there maybe five years ago to be closer to me and opened the shop the same year. She says she's retired but is still working at the store every day." I rolled my eyes because this was a constant argument she and I had. Me, telling her she needs to slow down and her, telling me I need to shut up and mind my own goddamn business.

There was no doubt that I got my tenacious spirit and willingness to try new things from her.

"That's good to hear. I'm honestly not surprised, your mom talked about doing that all the time growing up. I'm glad she finally did." I took a drink as Cam talked and tried not to notice how strong his jaw looked as he took another bite of his bear claw.

When he raised his coffee to his mouth, I definitely didn't mean to stare at his muscles growing and stretching under his shirt. But I did, and another wave of grief and shame slammed into me because of how unfaithful I felt I was being towards Connor.

"Yeah, she likes it a lot and it's made her new friends. I

was in there the other day and—wait a second, what time is it?" I froze mid-sentence and set my coffee down on the table, digging into my bag to look for my phone.

Cam checked the sports watch he had on his wrist, "It's just about 11."

"Shit, I have to go or I'm going to be late. Where the fuck are my keys?" I hissed as I rifled through my bag wondering how so much crap could fit into such a small thing. When my fingers finally found them, I stood up to leave. Cam mirrored my movements and looked at me like a puppy who just had its toy taken away.

"I'm really sorry, but I have to go or my mother-in-law will have a conniption. It was so nice seeing you again, thanks for listening!" I waved my crumpled up napkin tissue at him as I sped toward the door.

As I pushed the door open, I felt the warm afternoon air on my face and watched as the cars whizzed by on the street. There was an energy to this city that I hadn't felt in a while. It was alive when I had felt like I had only been surrounded by death for the last week.

It was almost the same as the energy I felt in my core after seeing Cam at my door my freshman year in college and the same I felt now as I walked toward my car after seeing him again, so many years later.

8

HALEY | THEN

I swung the door open after hearing a knock and was surprised but happy to see him standing there, a backpack slung over his shoulder and his face a little flush. It was getting cold outside, as winter was just starting to creep in. All of the leaves on the trees had fallen, and the girls on my floor were starting to pull out their wool sweaters and heavier coats.

I grew up in Pennsylvania, but going to school in the Northeast was a whole new level of cold for me. Thankfully, fall and winter clothing were my favorite kind, so I didn't mind the required shift in wardrobe.

What I did mind, though, was the thought of Cam skipping a game to come and knock on my door. I knew he was in the middle of his football season and he had a shot of becoming the real deal if he did things the right way.

"What the hell are you doing here on a Saturday morning? Don't you have a game?"

Cam played football at a larger school a few hours away and had a full ride because of how good he was. Growing up, football was everything to Cam, and I loved his dedication to something he loved so much.

If only, I thought, *I could be one of those things.*

"What, Jones, you aren't happy to see me?" His teeth started to peek out behind his smile and part of me wanted to know what they tasted like. I pulled my eyes away from his lips and returned them to his deep emerald eyes that haunted me in my dreams.

I sighed, "No. I'm—I just don't know how you're here right now. It's the middle of your first season at school and I don't understand how the hot shot, full ride, football star is standing in my doorway. Explain yourself, Johnson." I shot his name back at him, my voice full of tease.

This is something we always did back in high school and since he called me Jones, I had to call him Johnson.

"Can I come in?" He ducked his head and pushed past me, entering my room without waiting for permission.

He looked around, taking in the room which wasn't big. My roommate Piper and I had meticulously planned out our twelve-by-twenty dorm room so it now included matching bedding, matching towels, and both our monograms on the wall.

Piper had decorated her desk with string lights and a wax melter—candles were strictly prohibited, our RA told us forty times when we moved in—and I decorated mine with inspirational quotes and pictures of home.

One of the photos on my desk was of Cam and me from back home and every time a girl from our floor came to our room they asked if he was my boyfriend. *"No, he's not..."* I would always say, silently wishing that my answer was the opposite.

"This is nice," Cam commented, doing a full circle and

looking at the desk that was clearly mine based on the photos. "It definitely smells better than mine."

"Imagine that, two girls sharing a room produces a nicer smelling environment than two football-playing boys."

"Hey, Harvey and I keep our room clean compared to the other guys on the team. It's not our fault the entire building smells like Axe and three-day-old chicken nuggets." Harvey was Cam's friend and fellow teammate that he met at school, he had told me in a text one day.

"Cam...what are you doing here?" I asked again, not allowing him to avoid the question any longer.

"It's an off week for us, and Coach gave us the weekend off. I decided I wanted to come and see what your school was like. So I got up this morning, trained, and then came here."

"You came to see what my school was like?" I asked incredulously.

"Yeah...and to see you." His eyes went from studying the photo of us on my desk to looking straight at me. Silence hung in the air as we looked at one another and I swore the pounding in my chest could be heard from down the hall.

Cam and I had had our ups and downs, but ever since we graduated in the spring and went our separate ways, we kept in touch by texting each other every few days. When we started texting each other, we didn't stop until the other person got too busy, had class, or fell asleep.

Sure, I had gotten a little drunk at a house party during welcome week and *maybe* texted him things I shouldn't have, but I laughed it off as a big joke the next morning when I woke up and read my texts. I also had a conversation about Piper that same morning, telling her if I ever got drunk again she needed to take my phone away from me immediately.

Since then, we've been friendly and talked like friends do. He asked me for advice on how to get the phone number of a girl in his general studies class and I told him how the party I went to was the next morning. Just friend things, nothing more.

So why was he here now, in my dorm room, telling me he came here to see me?

Just as I opened my mouth to say something, Piper came busting into the room, shuffling through at least a hundred papers while also trying to take a drink of the iced coffee she was carrying. Her bag was half-zipped with four very large books spilling out and she looked like she was coming back from the library. Something I loved about Piper was that she knew what she wanted and what she wanted was to become a public defender. The girl studied as if she already was one.

"Hey, Hays! Sorry I wasn't here when you got up, I decided I wanted to go to the library and get some extra studying in before we—" She stopped when she realized there was a third body in the room that took the form of a guy our age who was built like a machine and smelled of pine, earth, and AstroTurf.

"Oh...hello there," she said as a smile crept over her face, making eye contact with me as it grew. I could already hear the questions I would be peppered with once Cam was gone because not only did Piper study as if she was already working in law, she asked questions like she was too.

"Piper, this is my friend, Camden. Cam, this is—"

"Piper McClellan," she said, shoving her hand toward Cam, not even letting me finish my introduction. "It's SO nice to meet you, our Hays here has told me a lot about you." She finished by giving Cam a smile that said, *I know exactly who you are, the things you've done, and if you hurt my friend, I will bury your body and burn the clothes I wore as I did it.'*

After the drunken texting incident, Piper forced me to spill my guts to her and explain everything between Cam and me. She knew that it meant something that he was here now, standing in our dorm room.

"Hi...I'm Camden Johnson. I'm a friend of Haley's from back home. It's nice to meet you too." He shook her hand slowly, a sense of unsteadiness in his voice.

"The pleasure is all mine, Camden Johnson," Piper cooed in her most professional, lawyer voice. If this is what she sounded like now, I could only imagine what false sense of safety she would lure some poor sucker on the stand into later in life.

"Cam just got here and we were going to go get coffee, did you want to come?" I added, trying to dispel the weird energy in the room.

"No, Hays, I have a coffee already." She shook the drink in her hand at me as if to say, *'Duh, earth to Haley, pay attention and act normal and you better fucking explain everything to me later or I won't let you sleep!'* "Plus, I have some reading I want to do before we go out tonight. You guys go and we can catch up later."

"Okay, if you're sure. Text me if you need anything," I said quickly before grabbing Cam's arm and pulling him toward the door. I needed to get him out of there before Piper started asking inappropriate questions.

"Oh, sweetie, we'll be doing more than texting..." I heard her say under her breath as the door closed softly behind me.

I groaned, knowing I was in for a full-scale prosecution when she and I were alone again.

———

CAM and I spent the morning grabbing coffee from the on-campus coffee shop and walking around the small campus I now called home. He was in awe that I could walk from one end of campus to the other in less than thirty minutes because where he went, the same kind of trip required a bus ride. I showed him where all my classes were, pointed out the different dorms, and also showed him the sorority and fraternity houses.

"People only join those because they're so desperate for friends that they're willing to pay for them," he joked.

"Some could say the same about people who join their college sports teams," I snipped back. I hadn't told him this, but I was planning on rushing after the first semester and was really looking forward to being part of Greek life.

After a while, morning turned to afternoon and we headed to the dining hall where I used a guest pass to get him in so he didn't have to pay for lunch. I watched as Cam came and went from our table three times, each trip coming back with a full tray of food. Then, partially in disgust and partially in awe, I watched as he sat there and ate all of it in one sitting. I knew he needed to eat a lot to stay in shape for football, but holy shit. If I ate that much food, I would be four-hundred pounds.

Cam, though? No, he got jacked and had abs you could wash your clothes on.

Why do men always have it so easy?

Eventually, we ran out of things to do so we headed back to my room and found Piper exactly where we had left her several hours earlier. When she heard me unlock the door, she turned around and moved her large framed reading glasses from her face to the top of her head like an old librarian would do. I always like to tease her about wearing reading classes when she doesn't need to, but she said it helped her retain the information better.

Honestly, she was full of shit and she just liked the way they looked.

"Hey guys, enjoy your outing?" she said, wiggling her eyebrows at us.

I shot her a look as Cam took off his coat and shoes as if to say, *'Knock it off! You're embarrassing me!'* And she returned one that said *'Your super hot, wanna-be boyfriend is here out of nowhere, you are so not off the hook!'*

"Yeah, we did," I finally replied. "We took the grand tour and I showed him where my classes were and where all the people who pay for their friends live," I added at the end, taking a stab at Cam's comment from earlier.

"Huh?" Piper remarked.

"Nothing, we had a good time. Cam ate half the food in the dining hall and I almost threw up watching him do it."

"Hey, I'm an athlete who needs to eat a very specific way to stay in shape!" Cam shot at me from my bed, where he was now lying.

Oh my god, Cam is lying in my bed. Okay, just play it cool, I told myself but when I looked at Piper, her face said the very same thing. I shot her another look and she motioned her hand toward Cam just small enough so he wouldn't notice.

Okay, breathe, I told myself, walking toward my bed to sit next to him. There was hardly any space to sit down in our room, the only real options were a desk chair, the floor, and the beds. It wouldn't be weird if I just sat next to him, would it? Lying down would probably be too much...yeah, definitely too much.

"Sooo, Haley..." Piper started, dragging out the first word as her eyes moved from Cam who was lying next to me, to me. I was sitting straight up on the bed as if someone just affixed a metal rod to my spine. "Are we still on for tonight?"

"What's tonight?" Cam asked, looking up from his phone that had held his attention during mine and Piper's silent exchanges. He looked up at me, his head resting on my pillow, and I made a silent pact to myself to never wash it again.

"Oh, it's nothing!" I brushed off quickly.

"Uhm, excuse me? It's not *nothing*," Piper mocked me. "There's this huge party tonight at one of the frat houses, everyone is going."

I looked at my friend as if she had just thrown me under a bus. Cam was here, visiting me for the first time, and she wanted me to go to a party with her?

Absolutely not. No way. Not happening.

"Sounds fun. We should go," Cam interrupted my thoughts.

"You wanna go?" My head whipped around to look at him in disbelief. I didn't have any plans for the rest of the day, but spending it in a hot and sweaty frat house was not something I was interested in doing with Cam here.

"Yeah, it sounds like fun. I'm sure it's not like any of the parties where I go, but I'm sure a small school party would still make for a good time. I think I'd like to see what you're like at a party, Jones." He was sitting up now and looking at me, a cocky grin on his face. My insides started to melt.

Piper squealed from her seat, happy that Cam was down to go because now it meant I couldn't back out. "Oh my gosh, this is going to be SO FUN! Okay, I just need to finish this chapter, and then..."

She continued talking but my focus was on the fact that Cam—my Cam, the Cam I had hoped for so long would end up spending a weekend with me—was here and doing just that.

And we were going to spend the night at a house party.

Maybe I had gotten the wrong vibe from his comment earlier about wanting to see me and he was just here for a good time. Whether I had or not, my heart squeezed in my chest because once again, I felt like I wasn't the one Cam wanted to spend his time with.

———

WE WERE WALKING up the front steps of the house when the guy at the door asked for our student ID's. This was the not-at-all-foolproof way frat houses made sure that only students came inside the party and undercover cops did not. I was hoping that Cam's lack of ID would mean they wouldn't let him in and we would have to leave. Unfortunately for me, when Cam told the student doorman his name, the guy's face lit up because he had seen the replay of Cam's touchdown catch that ESPN had been playing as their highlight of the week and let him in without an issue.

Once inside, Piper whispered something in my ear about finding the guy from her ethics class and walked down a long hallway on her own. I smiled awkwardly at Cam and led him further into the house, waving at people I knew as we navigated the dark hallways, our shoes sticking to the floor every so often. Eventually, we made it to a room that didn't have music blaring from giant speakers mounted to the walls and found an unoccupied corner to stand in.

"So this is a small-town college party, huh?" Cam asked with a cocky grin.

"Yep, this is it." Normally I liked coming to parties on the weekend, but with Cam, it felt weird.

"Do they serve anything at these parties or is everyone here drinking lemonade out of those red plastic cups?" He leaned close to my ear so I could hear. I could hardly focus on his question because when he leaned in, his lips brushed my ear and my brain went fuzzy.

"I'm sure they have the bar somewhere!" I had to practically yell because someone had turned the music up in the once quiet room.

I walked through the house again, Cam keeping close behind me until we found the bar, which was a makeshift stand with two giant orange coolers filled with god knows what. I took a sip from my cup and felt a burn as whatever it was slid down my throat. I looked at Cam as he took a drink and felt like I was in a dream.

Here Cam and I were, drinking at a frat party as if it were a normal thing to occur. I knew why it had felt like a dream because I had had this dream before. Except, my dream ended with us in bed together doing things we had never done before, and I knew that wouldn't be happening tonight. We would have fun, maybe dance, maybe get a little tipsy, and then we would head back to my dorm and I would let him sleep in my bed while I slept next to Piper.

My dream would stay a dream, and I would do my best to enjoy the night.

———

An hour or so into the party, Piper came and found me after seeing Mr. Ethics hooking up with a different girl from their class and she asked me if I wanted another drink. I was already on my second cup and it was still more than half full, so she asked me if I wanted to do a shot with her instead. Cam was a few feet away, standing in the corner and talking with the guy who was at the door when we got to the party. Every so often I would look in his direction to find him already looking back at me.

I agreed to the shot and let Piper drag me over to the bar where a guy stood behind it, pouring multiple shots for the people around us. He tipped an empty shot glass toward the two of us and we nodded to let him know we wanted one too. We pulled the shots back and finished them in one go, smiling at one another after we finished them. My head was starting to spin as Piper pulled me toward the dance floor.

We were dancing together when a guy came up behind Piper and started dancing with her. Within a few seconds, a second guy came up behind me. When he tried to dance with me, I took a step away from him and grabbed Piper's hand. He then followed my movements by taking another step forward and placing his hands on my hips. Again, in an attempt to move away from him, I moved my body to where I was now standing next to Piper, looking at her and still holding her hands as we danced. I didn't want to dance with some random guy while Cam stood in the same room as me.

I wanted the guy I danced with to be him.

"Hey, why are you so squirmy?" the stranger said as he started to put his hands on my hips again, "I just wanna dance with you."

"I'm okay, thanks though. I just want to dance with my friend." I gave him a half smile, hoping he would take a hint and get lost.

He then put both his hands fully on my hips and pulled me into him, rubbing his crotch against my back. "Come here, baby. You know you wanna dance with me. Stop being such a fucking tease and just dance. I won't hurt you."

As he pressed his body against mine, I realized just how tightly he was holding me where I stood. My heart started to race, and my head started spinning even more. The music was so loud and I was starting to panic, looking at Piper like a deer in the headlights. Before I could panic any longer, I suddenly stumbled backward as the guy holding me in place stumbled backward too. His hands released their grip from my hips as he tried to catch himself before hitting the floor with an audible thud. Some people around us had stumbled as he went down.

"I'm pretty sure she told you she wasn't interested."

My eyes went wide as I looked toward the booming voice and saw Cam towering over the stranger who had been behind me not five seconds earlier. Cam looked like he was ready to go to battle and the fierce look on his face made my heart beat faster than I even thought possible. His jaw was clenched and the muscles in his arms were pulsating.

"What the fuck?!" the giant ogre of a guy said from the floor, still trying to figure out how to get his feet under him.

"I said, I'm pretty sure she told you she wasn't interested. And since you're clearly too fucking stupid to take a hint, let me spell it out nice and clear for you. You touch her again, and I will kick your ass," Cam said slowly.

I looked around the room to see everyone watching us.

"Come on, Haley, we're leaving." He grabbed my arm and there was nothing I could do but follow him out of the party.

———

CAM HELD onto my arm all the way back to my dorm room, not letting go even when I had to pull my keys out of my small purse to unlock the door or when I sent Piper a text making sure she was okay to get home with a friend. When she said she would be fine, I crossed that off my list of things to worry about.

Now I just had to think about Cam and how he had acted at the party in front of all those people.

We hadn't said a word to each other since he pulled me from the frat house, but now that we were back in the quiet of my room, I knew the words would have to come out.

I stood there in the middle of my room, watching Cam as he kicked his shoes off and threw his jacket over my desk chair. I didn't do anything besides look at him, a swirl of emotions wracking around in my stomach like a tsunami.

Why had he acted like that? Why was he *here*, in my dorm room, on a Saturday night alone with me? He could have spent his weekend at his school with all the pretty girls I'm sure were throwing themselves at him since he was the star football player. I looked at him until he noticed that I was still standing in the middle of my room with my shoes on.

"What?" His voice came out strong and sharp.

"I just...I was just thinking that I'm a little confused." My arms were folded across my chest defensively.

"Confused about what?"

"Confused about why you did that at the party and why you drove all the way here and why you showed up at my door completely unannounced and why you're lying in my bed and why you're looking at me like I'm being crazy right now!" It all spilled out so fast and in one breath.

"That guy was a jerk and it was clear you weren't interested, so I did something about it."

"But *why*?" I asked, hoping for a very specific response.

"Because Haley, you're my friend and friends protect one another." He sat up in my bed and ran his fingers through his dark brown hair, his eyes cast toward the cold tile floor.

"Is that why you came here this weekend…to see a friend?" My words came out just above a whisper. *Say it, Cam. Please for the love of God, tell me what I have been hoping to hear you say for all these years now.*

"No…not really," he grumbled, still not looking me in the eye.

I took two steps closer to him and unfolded my arms. I was close enough to him now that he could see my feet in his line of view. It was as if he was attempting to burn a hole into the floor with his eyes, refusing to look up at me.

"Then why did you come here this weekend?" I asked him again.

A moment passed and I was starting to think what my gut was telling me about this entire situation had been wrong. I started to move away from him when suddenly, he reached for my arm, stood from the bed, and pulled me in for a kiss, right there in the darkness. He cupped my face and I could feel his fingers in my hair as he pulled me closer. My insides began to melt because the dream I'd had for so long was finally coming true. I went to pull away but he held me where we stood, kissing me deeper, running his tongue along the inside of my mouth.

Fine, I thought. *If we're doing this, we are doing it how I always wished it would happen.*

I wrapped my arms under his and around his waist, pulling him into me. We stumbled backward because the alcohol I'd had at the party was making me dizzy. We stumbled together until Cam caught his hand against the wall, pressing me into it with his body. As he pressed against me, I could feel every muscle in his body contracting as he pushed his lips into mine even more. I answered the call of his body by forcing mine back against his and when I did, I could feel how hard he was through his jeans.

I pushed him gently, only for a moment to catch my breath. When I looked at him, Cam was looking at my lips with a coy smile across his face, breathing heavily.

"What are you smiling about?" I chuckled. Our alcohol-laced breath commingled between us.

"Nothing. This is way better than I dreamed it would be and I'm really glad I decided to get in the car this morning and come here."

"You dreamed about this?" My voice came out small as I looked into his deep emerald eyes. I was surprised that he thought of me in this way at all.

"Haley, I've dreamed about a lot of things involving you. This is just one of the many." He started kissing me again only this time more slowly than before. It felt as if the entire world had stopped moving as he held me against the wall and kissed me. I had kissed boys before but this, this was a whole other level of kissing. It was soft, yet deep and the taste of him was something I knew would ruin me forever. No kiss would ever make me feel the way Cam's did.

Tired of being pressed against the wall, I placed both hands on his chest and guided him toward my bed, kicking off my shoes in the process. When we hit the edge of the bed, Cam sat down and moved back as I followed him. Crawling onto the bed, I found his lap and straddled it, both of my legs on either side of him. I looked at him for a moment, just long enough to take in his beautiful emerald eyes one more time, and then framed his strong face with my hands and kissed him again.

We went on like this for a while, kissing and devouring each other as much as the other would allow. He would bury his tongue in my mouth and then come up for air and press his lips to my neck. When he slipped his hands under my shirt, my breath caught in my throat and my skin started to tingle. His hands traveled up and down my back, exploring every inch of skin they could find.

A few times Cam tried to bring his hands to my chest but I stayed put, pressing myself firmly against him. It's not that I didn't want him to touch me there, I was just nervous and a little scared. I had never let a boy get under my shirt before...or my skirt for that matter.

"Haley..." He breathed heavily after a long stretch of kissing. I had denied him access to my chest again by keeping my body flushed with his, blocking his hands from going anywhere they hadn't already been.

"Yeah...?"

"Are you okay?"

I continued to kiss him as I thought about my answer.

I was okay, right? I was with Cam, the boy I had been in love with since seventh grade and we were doing something I had *literally* dreamed of. Why was I being like this? He's going to think I don't like him or I don't want him when I really, really do.

But something in my brain was sounding the alarms, telling me to stop now before I get hurt.

"Haley?" he pressed again after I didn't answer him. He pulled away from me and looked me in the eyes. God, his eyes. They called to me and spoke in a language I couldn't understand but so desperately wanted to learn. They were beautiful and deep, and I wanted to jump into them two feet first.

"Yeah, I'm okay," I said, still looking into his eyes. I could feel his hands resting on my butt and his chest rise and fall, still catching his breath after our marathon make-out session.

"Do you wanna stop?" I could hear the slight hint of

disappointment in his voice. Maybe he wanted me as bad as I wanted him.

There were two voices in my head screaming at me at the same time. One saying, '*Holy shit, we are making out with Camden, in our bed, ALONE and in the dark! This is the best thing to ever happen to me!*' And the other saying, '*You know how this ends. He doesn't want you, he's told you that a million times. He's just going to leave and choose someone else. Stop now while you can, or else you're just going to get hurt.*'

"No, I don't wanna stop," I said, silencing the second voice.

Cam pushed me off his lap, laid me down, and then lowered himself onto me. He felt so strong on top of me, yet soft at the same time. The thing I noticed most was how perfect his body felt against mine. Cam paused and looked at me, a look of admiration on his face.

"Do you know how beautiful I think you are?" he hummed, leaning down and kissing my neck. "And how much I have been thinking about kissing you? How *long* I have been dying to kiss you?"

My body reacted to his lips on my neck in ways it never reacted before.

"That's why I came here this weekend. Because texting you and dreaming about you wasn't enough anymore. I needed to be with you, like this, here, now."

I moved my face to the side so he could continue to kiss my neck as he talked, his voice low and husky. I ate up every word as if they were candy.

"Why didn't you just tell me this on the phone? You didn't have to come all the way here on your weekend off to tell me. I would've been just as happy if you had called and told me, or even just texted it to me."

"Texted it to you? You would have been happy if I *just*

texted it to you, Jones?" He nipped at my ear and I giggled underneath him.

"Well...maybe not." I smiled shyly, and he started to kiss me again. I could feel his hands starting to wander toward the hem of my shirt and slowly start to pull it up above my belly button.

I shivered at his touch as his hands went from my flat stomach up toward the edge of my bra. My breath became nervously shallow as his hands continued up past my bra and to my shoulders. Slowly, he moved the straps off my shoulders and then pulled my bra down just enough to where I was fully exposed under my shirt. Cam had stopped kissing me and was instead fully focused on feeling my breasts with his hands for the first time. I was trying to slow my breath and my body was quiet as it started to feel what it felt like to be touched in this way for the first time.

"Haley..." My name escaped his lips in a whisper.

"Cam..."

"Are you still okay?"

"Yes." I spoke so quietly I was surprised he could hear me.

"I want to be with you, like this, and like more than this. I promise I won't hurt you. I'm sorry I did in the past. I know I did, but I was an idiot and I feel terrible for how I treated you. But if you let me, I will show you that you can trust me, that I won't leave you. I want you, Haley, forever and always."

Tears pricked my eyelids because he was saying the words I wanted to hear for so long. I've wanted to be with Cam this way since our sophomore year in high school. Now that it was happening, I could hardly even believe it. He was finally saying what I needed to hear and while it felt like a dream, I knew it wasn't because of how my body was reacting to his touch.

"I want to be with you too, like this and like more than this. Forever and always," I whispered back as we started kissing again.

This was the moment I had waited so long to have; the words I had longed to hear for the last three years.

It was the kind of closeness with Cam I had been starving for.

And I was going to eat up every single minute of it.

———

WE DIDN'T SLEEP TOGETHER. Instead, we kissed and made out while he played with my breasts under my shirt. He asked if I wanted to go further but I told him I wasn't ready, and he was nice enough to not make me feel bad for wanting to go slow. There was a lot of history between us, and I didn't want to ruin the progress we made by giving him my V-card.

After a while, with our red faces and chapped lips, we rolled over to face one another and just talked. Talked about how long we had been friends and about how long I had had a crush on him. He even admitted to having feelings for me our freshman year in high school and reminded me of the conversation we had over text during lunch about the denim skirt I had worn that got half the football team talking. He told me how pissed he was about what Sean had said about me because he was jealous.

We talked about being together as a couple and what that would look like with him going to another school and being on the football team. I knew Cam was dedicated to the game and I was okay with that. I wasn't going to let football be the reason Cam and I didn't end up together. While he hadn't asked me to be his girlfriend, we made plans to spend winter break and New Year's Eve together at home. We worked to figure out how I could go see him during the season and how, once football season was over, he could come to spend the weekends with me here.

I put the blanket over him and tucked myself into his side, resting my head in the crook of his arm and holding him across his waist. I couldn't believe that I was falling asleep next to Cam. I played back the last two hours with him in my head and started to get excited about the plans we had made. My head was spinning from all of the events of the evening. My face was still a little raw but my heart was so happy I thought it would burst. I fell asleep under the covers with Cam lying next to me on his back.

I couldn't wait to wake up the next day, kiss Cam good morning, and spend as much time together as possible before he had to head back to school. My heart ached knowing he had to leave so soon. I reminded myself that he wasn't leaving me, he was just going back to school and we would talk every day and see one another as much as we could.

He promised me we would.

The next morning, I woke up and reached across my bed searching for him only to find a large empty space next to me. I opened my eyes quickly and scanned the room looking for his stuff, only to find his shoes and bag were missing. I started to panic as I realized my fears from last night were coming true.

He had left me, again.

Cam was gone.

9

CAM | NOW

Before I knew it, she was walking away from me, waving with the napkin I had given her to wipe her eyes as she cried still in her hand. I couldn't believe I'd run into her today just as much as I couldn't believe what she had told me.

I'm here for a funeral. It's for my husband. There was an accident.

And then the tears, so many tears that I wasn't expecting to see. Haley had never been super emotional growing up. If she were hurt—whether it be physically or emotionally—she always held it in until she knew she was completely alone. Seeing her so upset in a public place told me just how deeply she was hurting. It hurt me to see her that way.

As I watched the door of the coffee shop close, I had the sudden urge to run after her. To tell her how much I missed her and how I had never stopped thinking about her. But instead, I cleaned up where we had been sitting and decided I needed to go home. Now wasn't the time to drop that kind of thing on her and I had something I needed to figure out first. I practically ran to my car and threw it into reverse, almost backing into the car that was waiting for my spot. Thankfully, downtown traffic was next to nothing and I didn't need to pay much attention to get myself home, which was good because my head was spinning with everything that had just happened. Once I pulled into my garage and hit the button to lower the garage door, I ran inside and threw my shit down. I passed through the kitchen, snatched my laptop from its resting place next to the couch, and opened it quickly.

'Haley Jones' I typed into Facebook. There wasn't much I could see because after that night in her dorm room, she'd unfriended me and made her page private. I could only see what she made public or what other people tagged her in. After she unfriended me, there were so many times I wanted to friend request her back, but I never did. I knew she was happy and she deserved to be. Especially with how I treated her after our night together.

This was the first time I entered her name into the search bar since I saw her wedding photos all those years ago. After that stalking session, I told myself I wouldn't look her up again because seeing her happy with someone else hurt too much. But now I was scrolling her Facebook page, trying to find anything that would tell me the full story of what happened. After a few swipes of my trackpad, I saw it —his obituary. Someone had tagged Haley in it so it was on her page.

I clicked on the link that took me to the local Wilmington newspaper obituary section and read:

> *Connor Mason died on August 2nd after being in*
> *a fatal car accident at the age of thirty-two.*
> *During his time on Earth, he was loved by all*
> *who knew him including his family, friends,*

*and coworkers. He worked as a financial
advisor for over five years and was known for
being kind to anyone he met. When he wasn't
at work, he spent his time working at the children's center and giving back to the local
Wilmington community. He is survived by
his wife of eight years, Haley Mason. Connor
will be dearly missed and remembered
always. Services for Connor will be held in
Charlotte, North Carolina.*

Under the blurb was a photo of Connor and Haley, and the information for his funeral. It was tomorrow, at a funeral home not even half an hour from my house. I sat back on the couch as so many questions swirled around in my head.

There was no mention of kids. Did they not have any kids? Was that because they didn't want any or couldn't have any? Haley always talked about wanting to have kids growing up, but now we were both well into our thirties and she didn't have any. I wondered if that was because she'd changed her mind or because her husband didn't want any. He was a financial advisor? It sounded like a boring as fuck job. Part of me wondered how Haley had ended up with someone who worked a desk job. She was always so full of fire; how could she have ended up with someone who sits at a desk all day? Should I go to the funeral tomorrow to support her?

I stopped on that last one.

Was I wanting to go to *support* her, or for my selfish reason of wanting to *see* her? I hadn't seen Haley in over ten years and hadn't thought about her—okay, maybe I had every so often—until I had that dream last week. Since then, I hadn't been able to get her out of my head. I'd been telling myself for the last two weeks that I just needed to focus on training and she would eventually slip my mind.

But she hadn't.

Then I saw her this morning in the coffee shop and all of the feelings from years ago came back like a tidal wave. It was almost as if they had just been hibernating away in my brain and the sight of her sounded the alarms and woke them up. When I wrapped my arm around her as she started to cry, the feel of her leaning into me made the crotch of my pants get tight. I hoped she hadn't noticed.

"You cannot go to her dead husband's funeral, you sick bastard," I mumbled to myself, closing my laptop and lying back on the couch. "Today was a fluke, a freak chance, a once-in-a-million weird event that will never happen again. She probably doesn't even want you there and you *definitely* should not go."

While my voice was saying one thing, my brain was thinking another. *What if it wasn't a fluke, but an opportunity? What if seeing her today, here in Charlotte, is a second chance? I would be the dumbest fucking person on the planet if I didn't go and try to see her again, right? I will just go tomorrow, be a friend, and let her know that I'm here if she needs anything. That's an okay thing to do, we're childhood friends, for Christ's sake! It would be rude of me NOT to go and support her through this trying time.*

Chewing on my bottom lip, I weighed all my options before opening my laptop once more to write down the address of the services. My mind was made up as I walked down the hallway to pull my best suit out from the back of my closet.

I was going to need it tomorrow.

———

THE NEXT MORNING, I woke up early, went for a run before the sun came up, and stopped at the same coffee shop as yesterday hoping I would run into her again, just in case. When I didn't see her inside, I tried to hide my disappointment before telling the barista my order. Once my coffee was ready and in hand, I gave up hope that I would be lucky enough to see her here twice and headed home. Once there, I showered, scrubbed my entire body, and stood in front of the mirror as I shaved close and tight to my face. I rarely shaved so close, but it felt appropriate for the event I'd be attending.

I walked out of the bathroom, towel wrapped around my waist, and started to get dressed. I picked out a solid black suit, white dress shirt, and a long black tie to go with my jacket and pants. My shoes were also black and formal, but not too formal to where they felt out of place. I paused as I glanced at the expensive bottle of cologne sitting on my dresser, toying with the idea of whether it was appropriate to wear to a funeral or not. For fear of getting nervous and sweating, I put two dabs of it on my wrists followed by the watch my mother gifted to me after I was drafted for the first time.

The only thing I could focus on as I drove to the funeral home was Haley. Her face from when we were kids. Her face staring back at me that night in her dorm room. And her face from yesterday in the coffee shop when we saw each other for the first time, so many years later. I wondered what she would look like today when she saw me. Would she be surprised? Excited? Pissed? All of the above? I settled on all three but pushed my foot down on the pedal anyway.

I did the thirty-minute drive in just under twenty and thanked the gods above that I didn't get pulled over for speeding. Once I parked, I sat in my car for a moment and watched as people dressed in black filed into the small, tan brick building. The funeral home was nice but looked like a funeral home and it gave off an energy that nothing good would come from going inside. Maybe that was just my head screaming at me to turn the car back on and go home before I made an ass of myself. I knew I shouldn't be here, I had no right. But the pained look on Haley's face from yesterday pushed those thoughts out of my head. Pulling my key from the ignition, I got out of the car, straightened my tie, and headed for the door.

As I walked through the crowded lobby, the looks on people's faces told me that I was either unknown or uninvited. I smiled politely as I walked through the hallway, following the stream of people heading toward an open set of double doors. Once inside, I noticed a large wreath of white and yellow flowers surrounding an oversized photo of a man I recognized as Connor from the obituary I read last night. I moved off to the side, letting the people behind me in, and looked around the room.

There were a lot of people here but they didn't all look like family. Would I have this many people at my funeral when I died? I found it hard to believe seeing as how I lived alone and my family was a total of ten people. Harvey and his family would come, but other than them, I wasn't sure who else would. I guess the obituary was right; Connor was loved by a lot of people.

I continued to take in the scene, noticing an older woman crying quietly at the front of the room and an older man standing next to the TV that was filtering through family photos of Connor. As my eyes made it toward the casket—which was closed, thank god—I felt a prickle on the back of my neck and goosebumps spring up on my arms.

That's when I saw her, standing alone toward the front

of the room wearing a modest black dress that hit just below her knees and a white sweater over her shoulders that was buttoned once across her chest. She was wearing black tights, which struck me as odd seeing how it was August in North Carolina and still hot as fuck outside. On her feet were a pair of black, shiny heels that made her legs look like they went on for miles. The thing that struck me the most though was her cinnamon-colored hair and how it fell softly at her shoulders. I always loved her hair and was happy to see she never colored it. Her nose was red, indicating she had been crying and her cheeks were flushed.

When I finally made my way to her eyes, I saw that they were looking straight back at me, piercing me through the busy room of people. As her eyes met mine, her expression was one I had unfortunately seen too many times before.

An expression that told me she couldn't believe what I was doing.

Pissed was the right answer then, I guess.

10

HALEY | NOW

I felt him before I saw him, a warm tingling feeling crept up my neck. When I turned and saw him standing in the doorway, I had to bite my inner lip to stop myself from crying out. Just like the day before at the coffee shop, I couldn't believe my eyes.

What the fuck is Camden Johnson doing at my husband's funeral?

I noticed him first and watched as he scanned the room, taking in all the mourners and crying people. Eventually, though, his eyes found me, and we stood across the room exchanging silent messages.

He started to smile at me when someone approached him, someone who recognized him I assumed, and started talking to him. I watched as he made friendly gestures and signed something for the man. It took me almost a whole minute of watching Cam to realize that someone was talking to me at the very same time.

"Hello? Haley? Hays? Did you hear what I said?"

I dragged my eyes away from Cam to fully register that Piper was standing next to me in a long black dress and modest heels. She was holding my arm and looking at me, concern written all over her face.

"Wh—what? What did you say?" I asked as my eyes went between her and Cam, who was now walking toward a chair in the back of the room.

"I said are you ready to get started? What are you looking at?" She turned her head and traced my line of vision. "Oh my god...is that—"

"Camden Johnson," I finished under my breath.

"What the *fuck* is he doing here?! I thought you hadn't seen or heard from him since—"

"That night in our dorm room freshman year," I finished again, more firmly than before, feeling my lungs deflate. A wave of anger, frustration, and shame built up inside me making my fingers tingle and my insides feel hot. Remembering that night while also trying to mourn Connor was almost too much to handle.

"What is he doing here?" she asked again. I didn't have an answer for her because I didn't know why he was here. I hadn't told him where Connor's funeral was, had I? I quickly scanned my memory of our conversation yesterday and couldn't recall sharing this detail with him.

"I don't know, but we should get started. People are seated." I grabbed a program from the chair behind me and started toward the woman in the corner of the room who worked at the funeral home to let her know we were ready to start the service. Before I went, Piper grabbed my arm.

"Hays, what is going on?" Her voice came out urgent and concerned. "Don't you think you should go figure out what he wants?"

I yanked my arm out of hers and bit back, "Yes, Piper, I do. But right now really isn't the best time. I'm about to lay my husband of eight years to rest in a ceremony I didn't want to have because it's not what he would've wanted. I don't care why Cam is here, I have bigger things to deal with at the moment than him." Her face fell and I knew immediately that I had hurt her feelings.

"You're right. I'm sorry, sweetie. I just didn't expect to see him and wanted to make sure you were okay. I know how badly he hurt you after that night and I'm sure seeing him now doesn't feel great either."

"It doesn't, but if I focus too much on him, I will literally break down right here on this ugly ass carpet and no one wants to see that." My words came out hotly again and I took a breath, trying to compose myself. The weight of the weekend was starting to pull me down and I was unfairly taking it out on Piper. She was only trying to look out for me. I looked at her again. "Hey, I'm sorry for snapping, it's just—"

She cut me off, "You don't need to apologize. You're hurting and I get that. I'm sorry for pushing you." She grabbed my right ring finger and gave it a squeeze, something we always did to let the other one know everything was okay. I grabbed hers and squeezed it back. What did I ever do to deserve a friend like this?

She then put both her hands on my shoulders, "You, Haley Mason, are the strongest woman I know. You are here, standing tall, and showing people that you loved Connor more than anything else. Your strength and bravery inspire me daily and I'm so lucky to call you my best friend." Her eyes were starting to mist, as were mine. "You ready to do this?"

I nodded my head and fought back tears as we both walked together toward the funeral director. It was time to lay Connor to rest and all I could do was try to hold myself together as we did.

THE SERVICE WAS short but nice. Both of Connor's parents spoke, then one of his best friends, and it ended with me.

My eulogy included the story of how Connor and I met, how his favorite thing to do on the weekend was explain the stock market to me, and how he was my best friend. As I said the last part, I used every fiber of my being to not look at Cam who was still sitting in the back of the room, staring at me without breaking eye contact. As I spoke of Connor, I could feel my heart breaking into what felt like a million pieces but I managed to stay standing and get through my speech.

Once I had finished and sat back down, I laid my head on Piper's shoulder and quietly cried into a tissue. Getting through the week after his accident was hard, but standing up in front of a room of people who knew him and talking about how much I loved him was torture.

Once I finished my eulogy, the funeral director came to the podium and let everyone know that there would be a reception and food in the room down the hall and that people were welcome to make their way there.

I knew that giving Connor's eulogy would be hard, but what I had been dreading the most was the reception. I didn't want to stand in a crowded room filled mostly with people from Connor's family that I didn't know because we lived three hours away and rarely got to travel to visit. I didn't want to hear "I'm so sorry for your loss" or "Connor was a great man." I wanted to go back to the hotel room, crawl under the covers of my bed, and never come out.

Unfortunately, I was the widow and it was my husband's funeral, so I needed to go and pretend like I was okay with all of it when I wasn't.

People were mostly nice and only one woman, a great aunt of Connor's, asked the insanely rude question of "why don't you have children?"

"Didn't you love him?" she asked. *"No, actually, I hated his guts and didn't want his sperm commingling with my eggs because he was the worst person ever and that's why I was with him for ten years,"* is what I wanted to say, but instead, I just said that we hadn't thought it was the right time, which was partially true.

After walking around and talking with Connor's family for about an hour, I found an empty table and took a seat. Piper had headed back to our hotel after the first forty-five minutes to answer some urgent emails for She Who Thrives, so I was alone for the first time all weekend. I had only started to relax when a tall, familiar figure with strong arms and an expensive suit came and sat down next to me. I didn't even need to look at him to know who he was. His scent gave him away instantly.

"Hey, Haley," he tried after a moment of sitting next to me. I hadn't said anything to him, hell, I hadn't even addressed the fact that he sat down. I just continued to stare at the water spot on the white tablecloth where someone had spilled their drink.

"What the hell are you doing here?" I finally said, my voice coming out with a tinge of anger. My eyes stayed locked on the water stain because the thought of looking at him made me even angrier.

Angry that I was sitting at a funeral my husband didn't want. Angry that my husband and the love of my life is gone. And angry that, for some god-forsaken reason, Cam thought it would be okay to just show up unannounced. He had a propensity to do that though, so I shouldn't be surprised.

"I...I thought you could use a friend," he started,

chewing on the side of his lip. I could see him out of the corner of my eye and knew he was trying to pick his words carefully.

"I have a friend here. Piper is with me."

"I don't see her anywhere..." He looked around the room which was quickly dwindling in numbers. People were saying their goodbyes to Connor's parents and exiting, their time to mourn Connor coming to an end.

"It doesn't matter if she is or not, what the hell are YOU doing here, Cam? I don't remember telling you about when this was or *where* for that matter."

That was the thing that stuck with me the most, *how did he find out where Connor's funeral was?* I was sure I hadn't told him any details about the service, just that I was in town for it and that I would be leaving on Monday as soon as everything was over. How the hell did he figure out where to go?

"I looked it up." He shrugged his shoulders as he spoke as if it were no big deal.

"You looked it up?" My head snapped to look at him finally, not believing what I had heard.

"Yeah, I looked it up yesterday after you left the coffee shop and decided I should come and be a friend, see if you needed any kind of support during the service." Hearing the concern in his voice brought me back to high school for a fraction of a second and how much he acted like my protector back then.

Now it just felt uncomfortable and sour.

"You mentioned yesterday how you weren't super stoked to have to come to this, so I wanted to come and be an extra layer of support if you needed it."

I tried to avoid the warm feeling growing in my belly as he gave me a gentle smile. As I listened to him talk, I could feel his concern and worry for me. Cam had hurt me in the past. But now, something about the way he looked at me told me he was truly here to make sure I was okay.

He'd always been like that before that night our freshman year—a protector. Growing up, I always knew that Cam was there if I needed him. Even when I didn't, because I could take care of myself, he was always there, just in case. He would stand up for me even if I wasn't around and would kick someone's ass if I asked him to. It was one of the biggest reasons why I fell in love with him all those years ago.

Seeing him now, sitting in front of me, looking at me with those deep emerald eyes that I could pick out in a lineup, made me remember just how much he meant to me. The feelings of grief for Connor and nostalgia for what Cam and I used to have started to mix, making my stomach churn and for a moment I thought I might be sick.

Cam must have sensed this because he reached across the space between us and put his hand on my knee. More concern grew on his face as his eyebrows met in the middle of his forehead, "Haley...are you okay?"

"Yeah, I'm fine," I said quickly. "Today has just been a lot. Listen, thank you so much for coming and being willing to be here for me, but I'm okay..." I put a hand on top of his which was a mistake because as soon as I did, I thought my hand might catch fire from the energy that surged between our hands.

"I need to talk to Connor's parents and ask if they need anything from me before I head back to my hotel. Piper and I are leaving first thing in the morning and I still need to go to their house and grab some stuff I left there before the service." I stood from my chair, pulling my hand from his, and watched as he matched my movements.

"Haley—" he started to say something but I cut him off.

"Camden, don't." I didn't want to hear what he had to

say. Fear of what he might bring up nearly brought me to my knees and I didn't have it in me to hash out our issues now.

"I can't do this right now. Please, just let me go."

He chewed on his bottom lip and gave me a small nod. When he didn't respond, I turned away from him again.

As I walked toward the door, I looked over my shoulder to find Cam watching me from the table we were just at, his brown hair was messed up as if he had just run his fingers through it. I paused for just a second, taking in all his features and judging myself for feeling the slightest bit of attraction toward him.

But I wasn't taking in his image because I was going to go back to my hotel and get myself off on a fantasy with him in it. No, I was taking in his image because I didn't want to forget what he looked like now, as a grown man. I was taking in a man who was once a boy I had grown up with and spent so many of my early years with. A boy who meant so much to me before one stupid night together changed everything, and he broke my heart.

I was taking in every part of him now because I promised myself in that moment that I would never see Camden Johnson again. I couldn't.

Not if I wanted to protect my heart, which was something I desperately needed to do.

[PART TWO]
• Six months later •

11

HALEY | THEN

I paused, holding my phone in my hand, debating whether or not I should even read his message. We hadn't spoken to one another in almost four months after Cam cut me off for what I said about his girlfriend. It's not my fault she's the kind of girl who looks like someone needs to get her down and scrub her. It's just my fault that I texted him that as a joke not knowing they were together, and she would read it.

From that point on, Cam and I were no longer speaking.

For a while, I thought it was because of what I said. Turns out it was because she had forbade him from talking to me if he still wanted to date her. And I only found this out because one of his teammates, who also sat next to me in Chem, told me he had overheard Cam talking about it in the locker room. Sure it hurt that Cam wasn't speaking to me, but it hurt even more that he had chosen her over me.

I tried for weeks to get him to talk to me. I sent him texts, called him at least every other day, and even tried calling him at his house. When his mom told me he wasn't there even when I knew he was, I decided it was a lost cause and gave up. If he wanted to choose his girlfriend over me, so be it. I would carry on without him and our friendship just fine. But here he was now, sending me a message, reaching out for the first time in months.

Something I'd been secretly longing for.

I took a breath, knowing good and well I wouldn't be able to get back to writing my paper without knowing what he had to say, and swiped my thumb across the screen. I tapped on the message to open it.

Hey.

Hey?

Literally just 'Hey'? Are you freakin' kidding me? He drops me like I'm a carrier for the black plague for four months after being one of my best friends since kindergarten, and all I get is a, '*Hey.*'?!

My fingers hovered over the keyboard as I struggled to come up with the right reply.

Hey.

I typed it in, deleted it, then retyped it and hit send before I could overthink it any longer. If he was going to break the ice after four months with a 'Hey.' then so was I. My phone buzzed again and I nearly dropped it, surprised by how quickly he sent a message back.

What are you doing right now?

What do I say? Do I lie to him and say I'm doing something with people? Should I make it sound like I'm super busy instead of cramming to get this freakin' paper done?

Maybe I should make up a story about some hot guy I met and how I'm getting ready for a date with him...

> I'm trying to finish a paper and you're interrupting me.

Okay, I could have come up with something a little juicier, but I was always taught that honesty is the best policy.

> That's cool...are you busy?

Is he for real? I just told him I'm writing a paper. I swear to God boys don't listen.

Or read, clearly.

> I just told you I'm writing a paper, and it's due on Friday.

> Let me guess, you're just starting?

His response instantly annoyed me. Damn this boy and him knowing everything about me. I could just see his face sending it too, smug and arrogant, knowing that I had waited until the very last minute to do my work.

Why did the thought of his face make my cheeks flush?

> No, I didn't just start it. I'm actually trying to finish it, so I'll just text you later, okay?

He responded immediately.

> I want to see you.

He'd sent it back so quickly even after I had tried to shake him off.

He wanted to *see me?* What the hell for?

I thought about it for a minute before replying, chewing on the inside of my cheek. My heart was suddenly pounding very loudly from inside my chest.

Why did Cam want to see me? He and I haven't spoken a word to one another in four months and now he wants to see me?

Part of me wanted to say, "Yes! Let's meet up, I will come right now and see you!" but another part of me—the logical part—told me I should tell him to shove off and leave me alone.

Sure, I had been in the wrong for what I said, but he was way more in the wrong for choosing his girlfriend of two point two seconds over his friend of more than ten years.

> I don't know Cam, I really need to write this paper.

> Please, we can meet when it's good for you if you're too busy now. I just really want to see you.

> I miss you.

He sent the second text right after the first and I was hit immediately with the feeling I have been avoiding for so long.

The feeling of how much I missed him too.

I chewed on my cheek harder now, surely about to draw blood, when I decided on what I should do.

> Do you have practice or training tomorrow?

It was the off-season so I didn't think he did, but Cam sometimes put in extra practice even when he didn't have to.

Not tomorrow no, what are ya thinkin'?

Meet me tomorrow after school at Haywards Park at 4PM. We'll go for a walk.

It's a date Jones.

It's definitely not Johnson. Now leave me alone so I can finish this paper.

He didn't answer, respecting my wishes to be left alone. I went back and reread all our messages. He called me Jones. He hadn't called me Jones in a long time and even just reading it again made me smile.

He also called tomorrow a *date*. While I knew he had called it that to be funny, I knew that my heart wished it was one.

———

I PULLED into the parking lot a few minutes early and checked myself in the mirror. I had my hair pulled back into a ponytail and was wearing a long-sleeved striped top with plain black leggings and white sneakers.

I ran home after school to change into something better for a walk and let my mom know where I was going. She was ecstatic to hear Cam and I were speaking again and told me to have fun and make good choices. Her voice turned up as she finished the sentence as if to indicate something might happen on our walk.

My mom knew that I was in love with Cam even though

I had never come out and said it. That's why she was so surprised when I told her we weren't speaking anymore a few months back. But true to form, she didn't push it. That's one thing I loved about my mother, she knew when to push and when to leave things alone. Cam was always a topic she left alone and I was grateful for it.

As I was pulling the strands of my ponytail apart to make it rise on my head, I saw a car pull up next to me in my periphery and looked into its driver's side window.

A small gasp escaped my mouth when I saw him. It's not that I hadn't seen him at school the last few months, but every time I looked at him I was bogged down by sadness and disappointment, knowing I couldn't walk up to him, call him Johnson, and say something smart.

Something about today felt like we were turning over a new leaf and things would be different. I was excited to see him and couldn't wait to be with him. My cheeks flushed as I thought about it. I shook my head and rubbed my cheeks, hoping that doing so would dissipate the blood that had just rushed there, and stepped out of the car.

"Jones."

"Johnson." It was like no time had passed as we made our introductions just like we had for years. I looked at Cam from top to bottom and started laughing when I saw that he was wearing jeans.

"What are you laughing at?" He looked down at his clothes, checking to make sure his fly wasn't down or he didn't have toothpaste on his shirt.

"I'm laughing at the big idiot who wore *jeans* to go for a walk in the middle of a warm spring afternoon! Aren't you going to be uncomfortable in those?" I pointed to his pants and rolled my eyes.

"What's wrong with jeans? They look good on me, don't

you think?" He gave me his signature smirk and I felt butter-flies take flight in my belly and the urge to punch him all at once. He was being very cocky for a guy who had just iced me out the last four months.

Yes, they do look good on you and your ass looks amazing in them but I'm not going to tell you that.

"You look like you, Cam, just like you always have."

He rolled his eyes and stuck his fingers in his front pockets.

"So, where we goin'? This was your idea, so you're in charge." *I like the sound of that,* I thought to myself as I walked toward the entrance of the park.

"We're going for a walk. Come along now." I walked away not even checking to see if he was going to follow me. When I heard the leaves crunching under his feet, I knew he was and smiled to myself. We walked in silence for almost twenty minutes before I heard him take a big inhale and then sigh loudly.

"Something wrong?" I kept moving, hardly glancing over my shoulder to look at him while also trying to watch where I was going so I didn't trip and fall. I was trying to be cool and the last thing I wanted to do was bust my ass on an exposed root.

I heard him grunt and turned just in time to see him cupping his right butt-cheek in his hand, a look of pain on his face. I tried not to laugh watching him, but it slipped out.

"Hey, don't you laugh at me, this was your idea!" He pointed a finger at me which made me laugh even harder.

"Aren't you supposed to be some hotshot athlete? Why do you look like you're in pain? We're just walking!"

"It's not the walk that's bringing me pain, it's my jeans. They're starting to rub where no man wants rubbing to happen." He grimaced and continued to cup his butt-cheek.

"Then why the hell did you wear jeans?!" I said, throwing my arms up and turning to face him, "I told you we were going for a walk!"

"I thought 'a walk' really meant finding a nice bench and *a talk*." Cam looked at me, pausing where he stood, his hand still cupped under himself.

I was starting to feel bad for him, even though he was an idiot because I told him we were going for a walk. Looking around, I noticed a bench not too far up ahead on the trail we were on and motioned Cam to follow me. Once we reached it, we both sat down and Cam let out a loud exhale.

"So..." Chewing on the inside of my cheek and playing with my hands, I looked at Cam, "You wanted to talk?"

Cam looked down at his shoes and played with the zipper of his coat for a minute before speaking. "Yeah... Haley, I just wanted to say I'm sorry. I shouldn't have let London come between us like that, it wasn't right how I treated you." He was looking directly at me and I was starting to get lost in his deep, emerald eyes as he talked. My eyes were going back and forth between looking at his eyes and his full lips as he spoke to me. I must have been staring a little too long because he spoke again.

"Haley...did you hear me?"

His words pulled me from my trance and I tried to recover quickly, "Oh! Sure, yeah, it's fine. I'm sorry too, ya know, for what I said about her...even though it's true," I mumbled the last part under my breath which made Cam laugh.

"Yeah, it is true..." He scrunched up his nose, lost in a thought he was having. "And truthfully, when you sent that text, I laughed because I thought it was true then too. That's why London had gotten so upset. First, she was mad at me for laughing, then she was mad because you had made me laugh so easily. That was part of the reason she told me I wasn't allowed to talk to you anymore."

"What, you never laughed when you were with her?" I scoffed, thinking that it would be completely ridiculous to be with someone who didn't make you laugh. Cam made me laugh every time I was with him.

"Laughing wasn't really what we were into..." His cheeks turned pink as he looked at me shyly. I wanted to get away from this topic as soon as possible because I didn't want to know what they were into. I knew whatever it was would make me jealous.

"So then..." I trailed off before proceeding. I wanted to ask the question but I didn't know how much was still off limits, "Are you two done?"

"Oh yeah, we're done," he said matter-of-factly. "We were done as soon as I saw her making out with Sean at that party last weekend."

"Sean Hampton?!" I had heard about the party but didn't go—mostly because I knew Cam would be there and I didn't want to see him. I hadn't heard about this little piece of news though. I suddenly felt bad for Cam. I can't imagine what that would have been like seeing your girlfriend making out with someone else in such a public setting.

"The very same. I tried to talk to her about it, asking why she did it, and she just told me we were done and walked away. That was that." He shrugged and looked down at his shoes.

"Well then...how do you feel?"

He took a deep breath. "I feel free."

I smiled, seeing the Cam I knew coming back to me. Over the last four months, it wasn't that he had changed, but something about him seemed different. Almost like he was trying to be someone or something he wasn't. Seeing him now sitting next to me, I was starting to see the old him coming back.

"I really missed you, Haley..." he dragged out his words in a low, deep tone.

Hearing him say my name made my heart skip a beat. We were sitting next to one another on the bench, his hand on the seat, his fingers stretched out. I put my hand down next to his, letting our fingers touch ever so slightly, feeling the energy running through them as soon as they connected. I looked at them quickly to make sure my hand wasn't on fire, because that's exactly what it felt like. When I looked back toward Cam, his eyes were bouncing between mine and my mouth. My heart started beating faster and I could feel my brain starting to unplug.

Oh my god, oh my god, oh my god, he's going to kiss me! Camden Johnson is going to kiss me! I've wanted this for years. I can't believe this is happening. I can't believe he broke up with his stupid girlfriend last weekend and now he's here, with me, sitting on this bench looking like he wants to kiss me. Wait a second, he just broke up with London last weekend. He can't kiss me now. I can't be the rebound!

The voices in my head were speaking at once, but the one that came out the loudest screamed, *"Mayday! Mayday! You're about to make a horrible mistake, MOVE! DO SOMETHING!"*

Without thinking, I stood up and took a few steps away from the bench, putting some space between us. I set my eyes on the open field that was just on the other side of the path. Pennsylvania wasn't much, but when you found the right spots, it could be kind of beautiful. I continued to stare out into the field, trying to calm my heart rate and process what had almost just happened between Cam and me.

Cam cleared his throat after a moment and I turned

around to see him getting up from his seat. We looked at each other, both feeling a little awkward.

I gave him a tight smile. "We should probably go. It's getting late and we still need to walk twenty minutes back to our cars."

"Yeah, sure..." he paused and then grabbed my arm as I started to walk away, making me turn and look at him again. "Haley...are we okay?

"Of course we are!" I piped back, a little too perky and eager.

"Haley..." His voice was low, and he cocked his head to the side.

Now it was my turn to sigh. "Yes, Cam, we're okay. But you know how I feel about you, and I don't want to be your rebound. I want to be the one you choose, the one you want. Not just the one you pick because you're lonely or it's convenient."

"Haley, that's not fair, and that's not what this is."

"Isn't it?" My eyebrows furrowed as I looked at the boy who could never seem to choose me no matter how obvious I was about my feelings for him.

"Isn't that what has always happened the last few years? Ever since we were fifteen and I told you how I felt about you, you always seemed to never be available or willing to choose me. And that's fine if that's truly how you feel about me, but I don't think it is. I think there's more between us, you just won't admit to it."

Cam shifted where he stood as I continued, "But I can't continue to be your second choice, Cam. I think it would be better if we were friends. *Just* friends. Okay?"

He looked at me, a mixture of disappointment and understanding on his face. "Okay," he said, nodding his head, "Okay, I get it. I'm with you. You promise we're okay, though? And that we're friends again?"

I wanted to ask him why he couldn't just pick me.

Why he'd avoided the feelings I *knew* he had for me because they were the same I had for him. At the end of our freshman year of high school, under the bleachers, I had gotten brave and told him how I felt about him, and he brushed it off like it was a joke. Embarrassed and hurt, I went along with it for fear that our friendship would be ruined if I didn't.

But there were times when he led me to think that he felt the same way about me. Certain texts he would send me between classes and the way I would find him looking at me from across the cafeteria. How, after he caught the winning pass at last year's championship game, he ran to *me* in the stands and pulled me into a hug in front of the entire school. Cam's actions told me he felt one way about me, but his words told me something else.

And it always left me feeling like I was never enough.

"Yes, Cam, we can still be friends. Forever and always."

I spoke the words even though I didn't mean them. I didn't want to only be his friend, I wanted to be something more. I wanted to be the one he picked. The one he wanted. The one he loved.

Forever and always.

12

CAM | NOW

While my first season in Charlotte wasn't horrible, it wasn't great either.

We had a winning season but lost in the first round of the playoffs. Now that the season was over, we'd be done with games and official training for the next few months. Coach Mike told us to go and enjoy our time off and to not do anything so dumb that our names would end up in any papers or tabloids.

A lot of the guys who were married or had families were going to take big trips and travel, Harvey and his family included. Since we played over the holidays, the post-season was when a lot of the guys celebrated with their families.

"Got big plans for the off-season?" I asked Harvey as we packed up our lockers for the last time before we had to return for pre-season training.

"Yeah, Monica and the kids have been begging to go to visit their grandparents in California for a few months now. With the season being over, that's where we're headed." The thought of seeing family sounded nice. I hadn't seen my own family much over the last few years because of training and our game schedule.

There was only one person I wanted to see though.

"That sounds nice, I hope you guys enjoy your time out there. I'm sure it's beautiful this time of year." We walked through the hallway of the training center together, heading toward the parking lot.

It was mid-January now, and thankfully I'd been drafted to a team that plays in a warm weather state. The temperature had dropped considerably compared to the summer months and if you didn't dress properly, the wind would cut right through you. My morning runs through the park were bearable, but only slightly.

"Monica is just excited to see me in person more than she sees me on the field," Harvey replied. He threw his bag into the backseat of his truck and looked at me inquisitively. "What about you, what are you doing in the off-season? Going anywhere fun?"

I knew exactly why he was looking at me the way he was.

I had let him in on what had happened with Haley back before the first game of the season and all the history between us. I told him how we hadn't seen or spoken to one another since we were eighteen but before then, we spoke almost daily. When I told him about how I went to Connor's funeral after seeing her in the coffee shop the day before, he called me an asshole. He then told me I needed to mind my own goddamn business and keep my hands to myself.

"I'm only trying to be her friend!" I'd said defensively when he lectured me. I hated it when Harvey used his dad voice on me. It made me feel like a child.

"Yeah, no you fucking aren't. I know you, Camden. Don't be fucking stupid and leave her alone. She just lost her *husband.* She doesn't need some dickwad like you rolling up and trying to get into her pants."

"I wasn't trying to get into her pants..." I told him, intentionally leaving out the wet dream I'd had about her not even two weeks before running into her.

It had been six months since I'd seen Haley and after talking to Harvey about it, I decided he was probably right. Plus, I couldn't get her words out of my head.

"Please, just let me go."

If she wanted me to let her go, I would. Because I would do anything for her. So I decided to keep my distance and respect her need for space and time to grieve. I sent flowers the week after the services though, just to be a friend. *'Thinking of you – Cam'* was all I put on the card, and that could be interpreted in a multitude of ways. It could mean, *I'm thinking about you during your time of grief.* or *I'm thinking about you naked and on top of me while you suck me off.*

I decided to let Haley choose how she wanted to perceive it.

There were so many times I wanted to reach out to her, call her, and reconnect with her. Several times I stared at the cursor on my laptop, watching it blink over the 'Add Friend' button on Facebook. But I never did. I only found her address through the obituary listing that I dug out of my search history. With how busy the season kept me, I never had the chance to reach out any further. But that didn't mean I stopped thinking about her.

Or dreaming about her.

"Nah, I don't have many plans right now. I'm just going to go where the wind takes me," I tried to be coy. Almost as if Mother Nature could hear me being so full of shit, a strong gust of wind whipped through the parking lot and flung my bag right off my shoulder and onto the ground where it landed in a giant puddle.

Okay, maybe I'm not going where the wind takes me, I thought to myself as I picked up my bag and threw it in my trunk. *Maybe I'm going after the girl who can't seem to escape my dreams.*

13

HALEY | NOW

"I think it would be good if you started to go out every now and then, leave the house, be part of society again. Even if it's just once a week for a few hours." Crossing her legs and holding a notepad on her knee, Deborah looked at me, trying to gauge how I felt about her suggestion.

I chewed on the inside of my cheek and considered what she'd said. It had been six months since Connor passed away and about five and a half since I started seeing her for grief counseling. I liked Deborah a lot. She reminded me of what a quintessential Southern grandmother would be like. Sweet and kind, but will also drop an F-bomb out of nowhere and tell you when you're being over dramatic. Two things that she'd done in our sessions before.

I knew why she was suggesting I get out more often. Ever since getting back from Charlotte for Connor's funeral, I had become a sort of recluse. I rarely left my house, even though I felt like it was suffocating me at times with its reminders of Connor, and even after I started working again,

I always asked Piper to come to my house for our meetings. Not only was it hard for me to leave my house, but it was also impossible for me to go to places that reminded me of Connor. I hadn't been back to the coffee shop I was at when I got the call about his accident and ordering Thai food was out of the question.

But my time of being a hermit was running out. The She Who Thrives Live! conference is in another four months and there was no way I was going to be able to shove 400 women into my living room to attend. *Thankfully, we are hosting it at the convention center downtown so I won't need to leave Wilmington,* I thought to myself. I wasn't going to tell Deborah I felt this way though to further avoid proving her point.

"Haley," she continued, shifting in her big, plush leather chair again. "I know that the world seems scary right now, and it's been hard losing someone so suddenly. But you can't live the rest of your life like this." Her head tilted to the side as she spoke with genuine concern. "Have you slept in your bedroom yet?"

I looked down at my hands, embarrassed by the fact that I hadn't. I couldn't even open the door to our bedroom for six weeks after the funeral because the thought of opening the door and Connor not being on the other side broke my heart all over again. As a result, I wore the same three outfits repeatedly for weeks. It wasn't until one day that my mom came over and wouldn't let me escape her until I opened the door and walked inside. Once I stepped inside, I was crushed with memories of Connor that felt so heavy, that I collapsed to the floor sobbing. My mom dropped down on the floor next to me and apologized for pushing me too soon. While it stung at first, I was grateful she had pushed me to go inside because I was able to move throughout the room without the weight of my grief completely crushing me.

But I still couldn't bring myself to sleep in our bed alone.

Realizing I still hadn't answered Deborah, I took a deep breath and answered her question.

"No, I'm still not sleeping in our bedroom. My bedroom," I corrected myself quickly and shifted where I sat, uncomfortable and embarrassed. Why couldn't I just get over this?

Deborah looked at me, not saying anything but giving me a look that encouraged me to continue. This is one of the reasons I like Deborah so much; she never pushed where she didn't think she had the right. She would take the information you gave her and run with it, but she never forced anything out of you or made you talk about things you weren't ready to talk about.

I took a deep breath and continued, "I'm still sleeping in the guest room, but can at least go into our—my—bedroom now. I spend time in there daily, to get ready, change, and shower, but I'm not sleeping in there yet. It's just too much." My voice came out small and I stared at my hands, keeping my eyes low.

"What's too much?" Deborah probed.

"The memories! The emptiness! How quiet it is *all the time.* Connor worked from home and while he wasn't loud, I could still hear him in his office typing away on his laptop. I knew he was there. I could feel he was there and now...now there's nothing there. It feels like my house is trying to suffocate me all the time." My voice trailed off at the end, getting hitched by the lump that was forming in my throat.

Deborah reached over and put her hand on my knee,

looking at me directly. "Haley, what you're feeling isn't your home, it's grief. Remember how we have been talking about that? How it's not certain people or things trying to bring you pain or hurt you, it's grief?" I nodded silently. "Good. And you've worked really hard the last several months to learn strategies and skills that help you when your grief gets too heavy. Are you using them?"

"Yeah. Sometimes it's all just too much. It feels like I just lost him yesterday. It feels so fresh...like the wound is still wide open and throbbing." Tears started to form in my eyes as I admitted this to Deborah and she handed me a tissue.

"I know, sweetie. I know how real it all feels and how heavy it can be. And while I didn't know Connor personally, based on what you've shared with me about him, I don't think he would've wanted you to live this way. Do you?" I'm sure therapists aren't supposed to call their patients 'sweetie,' but the name made me smile and feel cared for.

I sniffed back some tears and wiped my nose with the tissue again. "No, I don't think he would have."

"Then let's keep working so you don't have to, okay?"

I smiled at Deborah and loved her even more for caring so much about me.

While I appreciated what she was hoping for, I wasn't so sure how much I believed it was possible.

———

THE NEXT DAY, Piper and I were sitting at my dining room table discussing the She Who Thrives Live! conference and everything that needed to get done between now and April. Because of the time I took off after losing Connor, we were woefully behind on planning and scheduling. Piper had asked if I wanted to cancel it this year, but I told her that would be a disaster and I would be fine. While that still wasn't necessarily true with only four months left before the conference, I was doing better than I had been six months ago.

"Okay, so we have the catering, serving materials, and waitstaff all through the convention center. Hosting it there also means we have lighting, audio, and video taken care of too." Piper was writing things down on a notepad, as she always insisted on doing, which sat on top of the MacBook Pro I bought for her last year. I stopped trying to understand why she had a thing for writing things down when she could just type them up.

"How are we doing on ticket sales?" I asked as I opened up a new window on my laptop.

"Uhhh…" I didn't look up from my screen but could hear the papers that were strewn on top of the table being shuffled around and knew she was looking for the piece of paper she'd written the number down on.

"Pipe—"

"Here it is!" she cut me off and gave me a sly grin before I could get on her about using her goddamn laptop. "I checked before our meeting and we are at 325 total ticket sales, which is great seeing as how we have four months left to get butts into those last 75 seats." She looked up at me and smiled, her grin telling me to leave her alone about her papers.

"Amazing, and we haven't even announced the full panel of speakers yet which will bring in those people. I'm glad we bumped the numbers up this year like we discussed." My eyes were back on my laptop, typing something into the search bar.

"Yeah, for sure. I think if we hit 400 this year, we can

waitlist the rest of the people who want tickets and then give them early access to next year's event to encourage them to try and purchase again." Piper continued talking but my mind had drifted to focus on the results of my Google search.

Beach homes for rent near me.

After meeting with Deborah yesterday, I couldn't get her suggestion out of my head. *You should work on getting out more,* she had offered, or some variation of that. *It's not your house that's suffocating you, it's grief.*

It sure as shit felt like it was my house, and coming home from our session yesterday had felt no different. Even now, sitting here with Piper, I could sense what felt like two hands around my throat, threatening to squeeze a little too hard. I hadn't considered leaving until Deborah suggested it, but now that the idea was there, I didn't hate it.

Actually, I really kind of loved it.

"With 400 chairs, we could arrange the room in a sort of—"

"We should go on a trip," I interrupted Piper, still not looking up from my computer.

"We should take a trip?" Her voice came out slowly, obviously confused as to where this idea came from.

"Yeah, you and me. We should take a trip." I looked up at Piper finally to find she was looking back at me with furrowed brows.

Piper set her pen down on top of her notepad, laced her fingers together, and looked at me. "Okay...where would you like to go?"

"We could go to the beach."

"The beach? YOU wanna go to the beach?" She raised her eyebrows at me.

"Yeah, that's what I just said. The beach."

Piper exhaled deeply and unlaced her fingers, placing them flat on top of her notepad.

"Haley, you *hate* the beach. You always have, which is why you live in the city and not on the water. Not that I don't love the fact that you want to get out, because I think a trip would be really good for you...but where is this coming from?"

I took a deep breath, knowing I owed my best friend an explanation for my sudden need to get the hell out of my house.

"Deborah suggested that I get out of the house more often, and the more I think about it, the more I think it's a good idea." I shrugged and looked at my friend who was watching with a disconcerting look.

"Since we're so close to the conference, we could use it as a business trip. We could rent a house for a few months, use it to plan and get new ideas for the event, and then come home and host it. Think of it like an extended work trip."

"This would be a *work trip*? Nothing else...?" She dropped her chin and pushed her eyebrows together as she looked at me from across the table. If she had glasses on, she would be looking at me over them like the cranky old lady does in the movies.

"I mean..." I paused and considered telling her the whole truth. I thought back to something Deborah had said before in a session about not having to carry the weight of my grief alone. Piper is my best friend, more like my sister, so I decided I could give her the whole truth.

I took another breath. "I also just need to get out of this house. I know I should be over it by now, but it's still so hard being here alone all the time. I don't know if you know this, but I still can't sleep in our—my—bed. I sometimes feel like I'm suffocating just being here." Too embarrassed to look

Piper in the eye, I settled on staring at the pen she had been using to write notes.

"Oh, sweetie, I'm so sorry." She reached over and took both my hands in hers, "I didn't know you were feeling like that. I knew you were still struggling, which anyone who went through what you did would be, but I didn't realize how hard it was to be here. But, just for the sake of being honest, I did know about the sleeping thing. Martha told me about what happened after the funeral and asked that I check to see if it looked like you were still sleeping in the guest room."

I scoffed and rolled my eyes. I should have known that my mom would have a spy on me. She always did, telling me when I was growing up that she had eyes everywhere and would know if I ever misbehaved when she wasn't around. I knew that this time though, her spy was only looking out for me, and I had a deeper love and appreciation for both her and my best friend.

"If you want to go on a trip, I will gladly go with you." Piper gave me a determined smile, pumping our hands up and down once on top of the table. "Which beach are you thinkin'?"

I turned my laptop to show her some of the houses I had pulled up and she gasped at the photos, instantly getting excited. We paused our conference planning and turned to planning our spontaneous trip to the beach.

After two hours and another coffee, we found a three-bedroom bungalow on the water that had an amazing kitchen and private office space we could use to work out of. We booked it through the end of March, giving us almost three full months there. After clicking 'Book' I was filled with a sense of relief I hadn't felt in a long time. I could almost feel the invisible hands around my neck start to loosen their grip.

It's time you get out and rejoin society, Deborah told me yesterday.

Well, Deborah, I'm getting out.

Question is, will I ever be able to fully come back?

14

CAM | NOW

I pulled into the parking lot of my hotel in downtown Wilmington just after lunch. After leaving the training center with my stuff, I headed home, grabbed my computer, and booked myself a room in the nicest place I could find.

I didn't have a plan beyond trying to run into Haley somewhere around the city just to be able to see her cinnamon-colored hair and freckled face in person one more time.

My brain went from *I have a few months of down time* to *that's a long fucking time to sit in my loft alone* to *I know someone else who is probably lonely right now* to *you're a fucking dick for thinking that* to *I can't stop thinking about her, I at least have to try.*

By the end of my spiral, I had a hotel room in Wilmington waiting for me. I quickly grabbed a suitcase, threw a bunch of clothes and other shit into it, and left the next day.

Being here now, I realized how much of a plan I was lacking. What are the chances I just run into her again like we had in Charlotte? I hadn't expected that to happen either, but it did. Surely fate was on my side, and it would happen again. Right?

Part of me regrets not asking for her phone number since I knew the one she had growing up was no longer hers. I remember one drunken night after I graduated college I had tried calling her only to get a very large-sounding man named Barry.

After checking in at the front desk, I went up to my room and dropped my bags on the floor. I had reserved the room for a week, figuring that I could just extend my stay if I needed more time. I didn't have to be back in Charlotte until late in the spring, so I was in no rush.

I've waited fourteen years to see her again–what's another couple of months?

Looking around, I was a little surprised by how nice the room was. When I booked it, I hardly looked at the pictures before typing in my credit card number. Apparently, I booked myself a suite, so there was a separate living room from the bedroom and it also had a small kitchen. The room was painted a deep navy blue and the bedding and furniture were all white. It felt clean yet welcoming.

I wonder if Haley would like it? I started thinking to myself. I thought about what I might do if I were to get Haley Jones alone with me in a hotel room. After so many years of disconnection, what would it be like to sit with her again? Would it be like old times? Would it be like it was before that night in her dorm room where I royally fucked it all up? I sat down on the edge of the king-size bed, my body bouncing a little as it gave way to my weight, and let my mind wander with my thoughts and memories.

That night in Haley's dorm room was one of the best nights of my life. Shit, that entire day with her on campus was the most fun I had had since leaving for school. It had been a few weeks since I had seen her, and even though we talked and texted a bunch, I missed her. I missed seeing her every day in the hallways at school and even missed seeing her around town. Our hometown was small. Small enough to not even be considered a city, so running into people you knew happened a lot. And thankfully for me, I ran into Haley or hung out with her almost daily.

Every time I got to spend time with her, my life just felt better. It felt brighter. By the end of our final summer together, the feelings I'd had for her for so long had only grown deeper. I was hoping they would go away once we both went our separate ways, but they didn't. They only grew stronger and started to consume me entirely. It was as if my body was going through withdrawal from being away from her, which is why I went to visit her. My body needed to be close to her.

And then I went and screwed it up.

Again.

I'd only gone to see her so I could be close to her again. Not to *be* with her. That's what happened though—almost, at least. We never actually had sex. But we did things, we both said things, and I promised her things I had never promised anyone else before.

I will never forget how she laid there next to me in the dark, one of her hands holding mine, our fingers intertwined. We talked about how we could spend winter break together and kiss on New Year's Eve when the clock struck midnight. Her voice bubbled with so much excitement I could hear the smile on her face. Her body felt warm next to mine and I loved how she fit in so perfectly next to me, her arm draped across my chest as she fell asleep. The sound of her breathing next to me brought me the purest form of contentment I'd ever felt.

I just remember thinking how crazy I felt for believing I was in love at eighteen. There was no denying it though, because when I was with Haley, everything just felt right.

The last time I went into something without a plan, I thought to myself, bringing myself out of my thoughts. *I royally fucked it up.*

This time though, this time I would do things right.

———

THE NEXT MORNING, I got up early even though I hadn't set an alarm and cursed my body for always getting me up before the sun. Didn't it know that the season was over and I could sleep in now?

I stretched my arms above my head as I put my feet on the floor, then stood up and looked out the window. It was still dark outside but I could see cars scurrying down the road, carrying people I assumed were headed off to work before traffic hit. After walking around my room and flipping through the TV guide for fifteen minutes, I was bored and decided to go for a run.

After getting dressed for a cold, mid-January morning run, I used my phone to look up some of the coffee shops that were within running distance of where I was staying. Haley always had a fixation for coffee, especially for the kind you could get from a cute, local coffee shop. I found three on the same block of my hotel and decided that I would go for a run and then stop at each one on my way back just in case I would find her inside.

But after a forty-five-minute run and looking like a borderline creep at each of the different shops, slowly walking by each of their front windows multiple times and looking in to see if I could spot a certain freckled-faced girl, I gave up and headed back to my hotel.

As I showered and waited for my room service breakfast to be delivered, I decided that my plan to go without a plan was dumb as fuck and I needed to come up with a better plan.

If only I could text her, I thought. Even if I could text her and ask where she was, she would want to know why I was asking. And if I told her, she would probably tell me to go fuck myself, which would be deserved. I hurt Haley all those years ago and while I wish she could forgive me, I also understood why she cut me out of her life and never looked back.

Suddenly, it hit me.

How I could see where I might run into her without actually needing to ask her myself.

Happy that I brought my laptop with me, I grabbed it from my backpack and set it down on my lap as I took a seat on the plush, navy suede couch that sat in the center of my "living room". I pulled the top open, swiped my fingers on the trackpad to wake it up, and connected to the Wi-Fi as quickly as I could. For such a nice hotel, the Wi-Fi sucked, and loading anything took forever.

The last time I did what I was doing now, I discovered the details of my childhood best friend's dead husband and went to his funeral the next day. This time, I was hoping I would find something a little less depressing but just as helpful.

As I hit enter on my laptop, her Facebook page loaded, slowly, and at the very top was a picture she was tagged in. It was of her and her friend Piper, standing on the deck of what looked like a small house on a beach. I squinted at the screen, looking for a date or location.

[Posted: 2 days ago]

Ready for some sea breeze and fresh ideas. Can't wait to plan an epic She Who Thrives Live! event for all the amazing babes coming out this April! See you in Wilmington!

At the bottom of the post was a link which I ignored, completely enamored by her face in the photo.

Her cinnamon-colored hair fell in loose waves around her shoulders. She was smiling but I could see sadness in her eyes. Her round, hazel eyes that would intoxicate you if you stared into them for too long now had a tinge of sadness in them. It had been six months since her husband died, but anyone who knew Haley would know she was still hurting. I felt the sudden urge and need to go to her, wrap her in my arms, and tell her she wasn't alone. That she would be okay. I was there to protect her, just like I did when we were younger.

Blinking away the thought, I scanned the post for a location, realizing that Haley wasn't in the city like I thought she was.

Where are you and why are you at the beach? You hate the beach, I thought to myself.

I reread the post several times before I realized Piper had been the one to tag Haley in the post, and Piper had tagged their location on her own Facebook page.

Bingo.

I called down to the front desk, letting them know I needed to cancel the rest of my reservation.

I was heading to the beach.

15

HALEY | NOW

I stepped out onto the porch, closed my eyes, and inhaled the salty sea air into the deepest parts of my lungs.

For the first time in six months, I felt like I could breathe again. Like a huge weight had been lifted off my chest. Exhaling, I opened my eyes again and blinked a few times as they adjusted to the morning sun.

Piper and I arrived at our beach house, which was more of a bungalow, a few days ago. Ever since we got here, I'd had this sense of calm and peace I hadn't felt since Connor's passing. I watched as the waves rocked in and out on the shore, nothing able to stop their movement, and was in awe of their ability to hold that kind of control over themselves.

Control.

That was something I felt like I had lost the second I got the call about Connor and I hadn't been able to get back since.

I was up before Piper which I didn't mind. It gave me time to sit by myself and let my mind just be. Plus, Piper was cranky in the morning if she was forced to greet the day before she was ready.

I took a seat on the porch swing and tucked my feet under myself. I started to take slow breaths in and out of my nose; something Deborah taught me to do when I was starting to feel overwhelmed by my emotions.

As I looked out towards the horizon, I thought about how anxiety and fear started to creep in after losing Connor. There was a feeling I couldn't shake that I would lose another person in my life suddenly, just like I lost him. Panic attacks and crippling anxiety overcame me and most days, I struggled to get out of bed. During our sessions together, Deborah taught me that I didn't need to let my emotions, or the feeling of being overwhelmed by them, control my life if I didn't want to. Then, she taught me how to breathe like I was now.

Deep inhale in. Hold. Deep exhale out.

At first, I thought it was dumb as hell.

But now I see its merit.

I couldn't seem to pinpoint exactly what had me feeling overwhelmed, but I knew the feeling was there. It's like the feeling you get when you're at a campsite in the dark and you can hear something moving around in the shadows, but you can't see what it is. You feel a sense of danger lurking around you, but you aren't sure if you will need to run like hell or stay and fight.

Maybe it was the fact that, since getting here, I'd felt this underlying sense of freedom that I hadn't felt in a long time. Maybe freedom wasn't the right word, maybe it's...*relief*?

Relief that I'm out of the house that's a constant reminder of something I've lost and will never get back. Relief that I'm no longer walking around in a town where everyone knows I'm a widow. Relief that I'm away from all the pain and grief I'd been carrying around with me for the last six months, even if it was just in a physical sense.

But feeling this freedom, this relief, it also made me feel a severe sense of guilt. As if my love for Connor wasn't deep enough for me to still feel the true weight of his loss anymore, even though I did. There's just something about being in a new place, away from all the darkness, that made me feel...a little lighter.

Maybe it's also the fact that you still can't stop thinking about the flowers a certain someone sent you after the funeral—ever think about that? I crushed my eyes shut, trying to silence the snide voice that spoke in my head.

I took another deep inhale, held my breath for a second, and thought, *or maybe it's that you have all these things swirling around in your brain but no one to really share them with.*

Sure, I had Deborah and Piper, and even my mom that I could talk to, but I couldn't talk to them like I needed to. I needed someone who would just listen, let me get all my words out without questions or interruptions, and then give me their honest opinion no matter what. Someone who wouldn't sugarcoat it or tell me what they thought I wanted to hear because they felt sorry for me.

Someone like Cam, the voice in my head said again. I swallowed hard at the thought of his name.

He showed up unexpectedly that weekend last August, not once but twice. First at the coffee shop, which was a total fluke, but then he came to the funeral the next day all on his own. I had to admit that I was touched by his attendance, even if it pissed me off at the same time. I hadn't seen him since we were eighteen and then he just showed up to my husband's funeral with no warning?

It's not the first time he'd shown up unannounced, I don't know why I was surprised.

The flowers, though, had surprised me. '*Thinking of you*' was all the card said and it was signed with his name. My heart swelled knowing he had taken the time to send them, and I felt a deep pang in my belly when I realized they were a bouquet of dahlias. Not only had Cam sent me flowers, but he'd sent me my *favorite* flowers.

I still felt guilty for how I blushed as I brought them inside.

Pulling myself out of my mind, I went to take another sip of my coffee only to realize I'd finished my mug. I looked down at my empty cup and frowned, sad that the coffee was gone too soon. My eyes moved back to the beach and spotted an elderly couple walking hand in hand along the seam where the waves were hitting the sand.

I will never have that, I thought to myself, and I felt the tears hit my eyelids within seconds. I wiped them away with the sleeve of my sweater.

Since it was mid-January, it was still chilly in the mornings as the sun started to rise. I took another deep breath and stood from the swing before slipping my feet back into my slippers.

I walked through the backdoor which led to the kitchen and living room of our small coastal bungalow. The house we had rented had just enough space for Piper and me to have our own rooms, and the third room had been converted into an office. I picked it out because I loved the light blue color it was painted and the fact that it had a wrap-around porch and a view of the ocean off the back. While I didn't love being *on* the beach—I hated how the sand felt on my skin—I loved how being *at* the beach made me feel. Something about the waves and the salt air made me feel alive and the cozy bungalow made me feel safe.

As I set my empty coffee mug in the sink, I craned my neck to look down the hallway. From where I stood, I could tell that Piper's bedroom door was closed which meant she was still asleep. While I was in no rush to get to work, I was starting to get hungry. We hadn't made it to the grocery store yet which was something I was starting to regret because I was suddenly starving. I decided to head into town and get myself some breakfast at the coffee shop we passed when we drove in. Since I was already going to be there, it only made sense to me to get another coffee. Not just to get through the day, but also to fight off the cranky morning Piper I would have to wake up if she still wasn't up by the time I got back.

I made a mental note to bring her home a pastry as an incentive for getting out of bed as I swapped my slippers for my Birkenstocks and headed out the door.

———

A LITTLE BELL chimed as I pushed open the door and I followed the sound with my eyes, discovering the bell just above the white, paint-chipped door that led into a small but quintessentially coastal coffee shop. Coastal Brews was just a few blocks away from the bungalow so I walked here instead of driving. As I made my way through town, some of the locals waved and said hello as they sat on their porches, enjoying the morning air. I smiled and waved back, feeling instantly more at home here than I had felt in Wilmington the last six months.

I don't know what it is about small local coffee shops, they just do it for me. The smells, the sounds, the people. They all just make me happy. Growing up, people would always go to the Starbucks in the center of town, but I always dragged anyone who would let me to the small shops instead. That person was almost always Cam, but he rarely complained about it.

Looking around, I could see that this was the place to be in the mornings. There weren't many tables inside the shop, but the ones that were there were almost half full already, and it wasn't even nine in the morning yet. Coastal Brews had so many of my favorite things small-town coffee shops had: old, refinished floors with scuffs and stains, hand-written chalkboard menus that changed with the seasons, and baristas with tattoos wearing knit caps even if it wasn't cold outside. I looked at the menu and tried to decide what I wanted before it was my turn to order. I hated when people stood in line and got to the front without knowing what they wanted.

When I stepped up to the register, I ordered my break-fast and a large, iced caramel macchiato with almond milk. I took the small number sign the barista handed me and moved to snag the last open table. As I set my coffee down, I reminded myself to grab Piper a pastry before heading home. While I waited for my food, I decided I would check the She Who Thrives Instagram and read some work emails on my phone.

I'd been scrolling for a few minutes and looking down at my phone when I saw a pair of shoes step up to my table out of the corner of my eye. Thinking it was a server bringing me my food, I looked up with a smile on my face, ready to thank them, and finally feed my stomach which at this point was now trying to eat itself.

But standing in front of me wasn't a server or even the barista who took my order.

The person in front of me was tall and built like a god.

The only thing I could focus on was the pair of dark emerald eyes looking back at me and the scent of pine and AstroTurf that was starting to fill the air around me.

Standing in front of me for the third time in less than a year was Camden Johnson.

16

CAM | NOW

After leaving Wilmington, I drove directly to the beach town Piper had tagged in the photo of her and Haley. Thankfully the coast isn't too far from the city, so it didn't take me long to get there. I hadn't even made a reservation before pulling up to the only hotel in the town. I prayed under my breath as I approached the front desk that they had a room so I wouldn't need to sleep in my car. Thankfully, the woman behind the desk thought I was cute, and when I told her I had no place else to go, she took pity on me and gave me their last available room, which happened to be a suite. I hung out for the rest of the day to give myself time to come up with a new plan.

My new suite was nice, not as nice as the last one, but still nice. It had more small-town charm to it than the last place, but I almost preferred that more. It had a king bed, a full dresser, and a full-sized bathroom on one side and on the other, a small living room space with a TV and a couch. Once I entered the room, I tossed my bag down on the bed, slipped off my shoes, and grabbed my laptop before sitting down on the couch.

My first search was 'local coffee shops near me,' knowing that without a doubt Haley would be all over them. I knew how much she loved going to any and all local coffee shops from all the times she would drag me to the ones back home growing up. Most kids just took the easy route and went to the Starbucks in town, not Haley though. She was never one to take the easy way out, not on anything.

My search proved helpful because this town was small enough to where there was only one coffee shop in town. *Coastal Brews* I read on my laptop screen. My hands came together in a prayer position and I brought them to my lips.

"Thank you, coffee gods, for making this easy." Looking at the hours of the coffee shop, I realized they were closed, and I would have to wait to go by until they were opened again tomorrow to see if I could find Haley.

Tomorrow, I thought. *You will go and maybe, just maybe, you'll get lucky again and see her. And if not tomorrow, the next day.*

I wouldn't miss the opportunity to try again with her.

Not this time.

Not again.

———

MY EYES SHOT open before my alarm went off at 6:30. Not that they had been closed much at all last night. The anticipation of even just *maybe* seeing Haley kept me up most of the night. I knew the coffee shop opened at seven and something in my gut told me I needed to go today. Unfortunately, it didn't tell me *when* I needed to go, so I just decided to get up, get dressed, and go for a run.

But after running for almost an hour, I still hadn't spotted her. And I was starting to smell. Unable to take my stench any longer, I retreated to my hotel room to shower, change, and head back out as fast as I could. By the time I was ready again, it was almost nine and I was starving. Before leaving my hotel room, I checked myself in the mirror. It was the middle of January and with the way the ocean air cooled off the temperature outside, I decided to put on my favorite pair of jeans and a long-sleeved gray tee shirt. I also grabbed a jacket in case I needed it.

This town was so fucking small that after my run this morning, I pretty much had the entire thing committed to memory. It wasn't a bustling downtown scene like Charlotte, so it wasn't hard to figure out. As I walked down the street, I took in my surroundings.

It was a brisk morning, and the sun was starting to reach its peak in the sky so that it warmed your skin when you stood in it. There was a park in the middle of the town square and on the other side was Coastal Brews. I'd just made my way up to the steps that led inside the coffee shop and was reaching for the door when someone in the window caught my eye and stole my breath all in one moment.

There she was, sitting toward the back of the coffee shop by herself. I watched her for a moment, scrolling her phone and tucking a piece of hair that had fallen from behind her ear. I didn't even realize how long I had been staring until someone behind me mumbled "Excuse me." I cleared my throat and held the door open awkwardly so they could go in ahead of me. Following behind them, I grabbed my spot in line and moved my body so that I was facing away from her. I hadn't thought about what I would do when I finally found her.

This is what you get for not coming up with a real plan, you moron, the voice inside my head said flatly.

My fingers started to methodically tap the side of my leg, which was only something I did when I was nervous. I could order, sit down, and be like, "Oh my gosh! Haley? I had no idea you were here!" and pretend like I hadn't borderline hunted her down. But she's smart and would see right through that. I could just walk up to her and say, "Hey." But was that too lame? I didn't want to come off as lame just as much as I didn't want to come off as a stalker.

All I knew was that I wanted to talk to her. That was the whole reason for coming to this town in the first place.

Before I realized it, it was my turn to order, and I had no idea what I wanted. I *hate* when people get to the front of the line and don't know what they want. That's literally the whole point of standing in line. To avoid slowing down the line too much, I ordered my usual coffee order, a plain black coffee, and the first food item I saw on the menu. I didn't even read what it was, it was just the first thing I saw so I told the barista behind that counter it was what I wanted. I nodded to the guy and took the number sign he handed me before moving out of line. Before really processing what was happening, my feet were taking me toward her. It was as if my body could sense she was near and it needed to be close to her. She never looked up from her phone until she noticed my feet on the floor in front of her.

Her eyes lifted toward mine and she had a smile on her face until she realized who I was. Her face transformed from warm and welcoming to pale white and confused. I could see the color disappear from her face when it hit her that *I* was the one standing in front of her.

"Jones." My lips turned up as I said her name. *So much better than "Hey."*

"What the *fuck*?" Her face froze. She'd spoken a little louder than I think she meant to, and some of the locals turned to look at us. She cleared her throat, trying to recover from dropping an F-bomb so loudly, and spoke again. This time through pursed lips and clenched teeth.

"Johnson."

"May I sit here? All the other tables are full." I motioned toward the empty chair at her table fit for two. Before she could respond, I pulled it out and took a seat, placing the number sign next to hers.

My eyes were fixed on her face and I could see her brain working out what was happening. That was something I had always loved about Haley: if you looked closely enough, you could see her thinking. A few seconds passed and before she said anything, she took a deep breath in through her nose and exhaled it out softly through her mouth.

That's new, I thought.

"What the hell are you doing here?" Her eyes pierced through me, and I could feel the heat of anger and confusion in her voice. I also sensed something else in her words, something I couldn't quite pinpoint.

"I believe that's what you said to me the last time we saw each other." I smirked.

She looked down and thought about it. I knew immediately when she put it together because a small grin flashed across her face before she looked at me again.

"That's what I said to you when you came to the funeral."

"It is. I feel like you've said those words to me before on *multiple* occasions."

"Maybe you should stop showing up to places unannounced and uninvited." She cocked her head, challenging me.

"Maybe you should start announcing where you'll be and invite me," I threw back.

She paused, putting our verbal sparring on hold. As I sat across from her, I tried to take in every fine detail of her face. From the freckles that scattered across her nose to the way the laugh lines spread away from her pink, plump lips. From where I sat, I could see the small flecks of gold that mixed with the hazel color of her eyes.

She took in another deep breath. "Cam, what are you doing here? *Really?*"

For a split second, I thought about lying. I thought about making up a story about how I was on a break between football seasons and I decided to hit the coast and it just so happened that she and I ended up in the same place at the same time.

But then another part of me decided she deserved the truth. So that's what I gave her.

"I haven't been able to stop thinking about you since we ran into each other six months ago and I wanted to see you again. Since the season is over and I had a few months of downtime, I decided to try and track you down."

Her eyes grew as I spoke but I didn't give her any space to cut in.

"First, I went to Wilmington and was hoping I'd just run into you somewhere but then quickly realized that was a stupid fucking idea, so I looked you up online. That's when I saw that you were here, in this town, so I drove down yesterday. I figured I would find you at a local coffee shop because you were a freak about them growing up, always dragging me to any new one you could find. Thankfully for me, there's only one coffee shop in town, so I committed myself to coming here until I saw you. I appreciate you being here so early, you saved me a lot of wait time." My lips were turned up and I gave her my best cocky grin.

Her face was frozen in an expression that you normally

only saw in TV shows or movies. Her brows were furrowed together, her jaw slack and hanging open, and her chin had dropped just enough to where she was looking at me through her lashes. Something about her stunned expression made me puff out my chest. I felt a deep sense of pride knowing I had made Haley Jones speechless.

A few moments had passed between us and Haley still hadn't said anything. I started thinking that I had scared her or worse, caused her to have a stroke.

"Jones...?" I leaned closer to her as I said her name.

She blinked a few times and shook her head, slowly coming back from wherever she had gotten lost in her mind. Her hands then rubbed her face and she tucked both sides of her hair behind her ears, exposing more freckles that were sprinkled down her neck. Noticing them made my core a little warmer.

"Cam..." She sighed, crossing her arms in front of her and leaning back in her chair. Her expression told me she was upset and I braced myself to hear her say that I was an idiot and needed to go home. "Did you call me a *freak*?"

My head fell backwards and I brought my hand to my chest as I laughed loudly in the crowded coffee shop. Out of all the things I just said to her, *that* was what she was focused on? I couldn't fucking believe this woman.

"Yes, I did call you a freak, because you are a freak," I started, still laughing. "I didn't even need to *try* to be able to know where to find you, Jones. You went exactly where I expected you to go because you're a *freak* for these kinds of places."

"Hey, I take offense to being called a freak," she started in on me and I was happy to let her. At the same moment though, a server came by with our meals and Haley bit back whatever jab she was about to throw at me.

We ate our breakfast in silence, both too focused on our food to say anything. As I ate, I tried to sneak a peek at her, but every time I tried, she was already looking at me. It surprised me how easy this felt. We hadn't seen each other in six months, and before that, over ten years. Being with her like this felt like putting on an old jersey that you hadn't worn in a few seasons. Worn in, comfortable, and kind of like home.

I cleaned my plate and sat back in my chair to look at her. I marveled at how beautiful she still was after all this time and begged the universe to let me live like this forever. Just watching her be her.

She finished her meal not long after I did and pushed her plate away from her. "So, how long are you here for?" I asked. She chewed on the inside of her lip before speaking, considering whether I was worth an honest answer.

"Through the end of March. Piper and I rented a place on the water to use as a planning hub for a conference I'm hosting for my business in April." She wiped her pale pink lips with her napkin and finished her coffee. I waited for her to continue, but she didn't.

I guess that's all I'm getting.

"That's awesome," I started. "Aren't you going to miss home though? That's a long time to not sleep in your own bed." I knew that Haley ran her own company, but beyond that, I didn't know what it was or what she did. I wasn't surprised to hear she was doing something big like a conference, she never shied away from a challenge, which is something I always admired about her.

She shifted uncomfortably in her seat and looked down at her hands, an expression of sadness on her face. I don't know what I said, but it had upset her.

When Haley spoke again, she said something that took

me back to a time we shared before. Another time in our relationship where I thought I had totally fucked things up for good between us. But again, Haley looked past it like she always did for me.

"You wanna go for a walk?"

17

HALEY | NOW

I couldn't believe what was happening right now. If you told me when I woke up this morning that *this* is what was going to happen, I wouldn't have believed you.

When I looked up to see Cam's deep emerald eyes looking back at me in the coffee shop, I didn't know if I was supposed to yell at him or throw up. A small part of me wanted to throw my arms around his neck and hug him. To allow the sense of safety and peace he always brought me growing up to fill my insides once again. Cam always made me feel safe growing up and it was one of the many reasons why I fell for him. He was a protector and you felt that when you were around him. At least I always did.

Now I was here, walking down the street with the man who used to be the boy I'd been in love with growing up. The boy I'd loved until the day I realized he couldn't love me back and I knew I needed to move on for the sake of my own heart. Years went by. Life happened. And I moved on, falling in love with a different man who could love me in the way I needed to be loved. But that man is gone now and a small piece of me was gone with him.

As Cam and I walked through town, passing the elemen-tary school and the park, my brain swirled with emotions. My thoughts were running around in my head and my heart felt tight in my chest. I needed another cup of coffee. Some people drank alcohol or smoked while they were stressed. I just drank copious amounts of coffee.

"So..." Cam started, pulling me out of my thoughts, "How are you?" He turned his head to look at me as we walked down the cracked sidewalk that was more sand than cement. The sunlight hit his face in such a way that I swear to God, made his deep emerald eyes sparkle.

"I'm okay." I started to give him the same spiel I gave everyone when they asked the sad mourning widow how she was doing but then decided that this was Cam, and I could be honest with him.

"Actually...I'm really fucking sad all the time. Sometimes I feel like I'm drowning in my grief. I started therapy months ago because things were so bad I couldn't get out of bed or leave my house. That's why Piper and I are here. I felt the walls caving in on me at home and I couldn't take it anymore." I took a breath and felt a wave of relief wash over me. It felt good to finally get the words off my chest.

He kept walking, matching my pace and watching his feet as we went. I watched him out of the corner of my eye and tried to guess how he would respond. I fully expected him to say he was sorry. Everyone always said they were sorry and it always pissed me off. I've never understood why people apologized for things they had no impact on creating or causing.

When we made it to the end of the block, I turned the corner that led us down the street the bungalow sat on. It was at the end of a dead-end road that, if you kept driving, would lead you straight to the ocean.

He still hadn't said anything after a minute and I started to worry that I had dumped too much on him. I was about to apologize when he finally broke the silence. *Here comes the apology.*

"That really fucking sucks," he said, keeping his eyes on his shoes and his thumbs tucked into his pockets.

"What?" I stopped walking and looked at him, surprised by his response.

"I said that really fucking sucks," he repeated.

"You aren't going to apologize?"

"Do you want me to?" He stopped and turned to look at me. I thought about it for a moment, trying to ignore the tingling in my belly as Cam and I held each other's gaze and realized that no, I didn't want another apology. They didn't change anything anyway and they didn't bring Connor back, so what was the point?

"No, I guess not."

"I bet people have been saying that a lot to you recently." Cam's head dropped slightly to one side with pity in his voice.

"Yeah, they have and it's really starting to annoy me," I hissed under my breath, starting to walk toward home again. He laughed through his nose and smiled just enough for me to notice. *God, he has a good smile.*

"Well, I won't add to the annoyance then. What you're going through sucks and you don't deserve to have to go through it." My lips pressed together into a tight smile, feeling a strange sense of comfort in Cam's willingness to acknowledge my feelings instead of trying to apologize them away.

"Thanks," was all I could muster up.

"So you said you're here planning something?"

I silently thanked him for changing the subject and took

the question as an invitation to explain She Who Thrives and what the live conference was all about. As I talked, he listened intently and nodded his head. He only interrupted when he had a question and when he did, I answered them eagerly. He was genuinely curious and interested in what I had built for myself and my heart swelled at how much he seemed to care. So many people in my life saw my business as a "cute little thing," but not Cam. He seemed genuinely interested in what I had created over the years.

"I'm not surprised." He gave me an admiring look as I finished explaining how we had almost sold out 400 seats to the live conference this spring.

"You're not surprised about what?"

"I'm not surprised that you built something from nothing and now have almost 400 women coming to sit in a room with you for three days. You always had this energy about you that drew people in. I know I've been drawn to it since we were in high school."

I felt my cheeks flush and dropped my head so my hair covered my face. I could only hope Cam hadn't seen how much his words impacted me.

When I looked up, he had his signature sly grin on his face and was looking at me out of the corner of his eye. We were walking side by side down the sidewalk, getting closer to the bungalow with every step. I was so surprised by what he had said that my mind couldn't come up with anything to say next. What was it about this man that caused my brain to go blank and my core to get so warm with just one look?

We continued our walk back to the bungalow without talking, letting the sounds of the small coastal town take over. While it was still too early for tourist season, there were still people here who, I assumed, were traveling here to escape some bitter winter back home.

We walked in silence, Cam with his hands tucked into his front pockets and watching his feet, his hair falling into his eyes. It reminded me of the walk we took in the park all those years ago when he tried to kiss me but I didn't let him.

I wonder where we would be now if I *had* let him kiss me. Would I have started She Who Thrives? Would we live in Charlotte? Would we have kids? So many what-ifs ran through my head that I didn't even realize we had made it back to the bungalow until we had almost passed it.

I looked toward the house, standing in front of the little white gate that led into the front yard.

"Well...this is me." I exhaled deeply and looked at Cam who was standing behind me on the main sidewalk.

"Nice place." His eyes traveled past the yard and onto the bungalow, taking in its wrap-around porch.

"Thanks, it's perfect for what we need it for," I said, swallowing hard. Why did I suddenly want to invite him in?

"I hope it brings you what you need, Haley." He nodded gently, his deep voice spoke with such comfort and knowing that I thought I might start crying.

I guess that's what happens when you've known someone for your entire life. They know what you need to hear even if you don't ask them to say it. They just know.

Cam was starting to walk away when I realized I hadn't asked him how long he would be in town.

"Cam!" I called out for him and he turned at the sound of my voice. My insides melted when I saw his smile and green emerald eyes looking back at me. "How long are you here for?"

After a beat, his lips curled up into a hopeful smile.

"As long as it takes."

18

HALEY | NOW

As long as it takes? As long as what takes? What the hell is that supposed to mean? I clung to his words as I stood on the front pathway, watching him walk down the sidewalk until he disappeared around the corner.

"As long as it takes to do what?" I whispered to myself before moving from the spot where my feet had been frozen and walking towards the front door. As my hand reached for the doorknob it hit me that I had forgotten to bring Piper anything home from the coffee shop like I told myself I would. Before I could decide if I should walk back and grab something or just get in the car and drive, the door swung open to reveal a very excited looking Piper.

"Is that who I think it was?" She had obviously seen who walked me home just a moment before and was gearing up to give me the third degree.

"I was going to bring you a pastry back after I got myself a coffee, but I forgot. Sorry about that!" I pushed past her, forcing my way into the front hallway, ignoring her question.

"Oh no. You are *not* going to get away from this one."

Piper grabbed my arm and spun me around, putting a stop to my plan of getting as much space between us as possible. "I saw who you just came home with! Where did you find him? Did you tell him you were here?"

"No, actually, *you* did!" I leaned into my words, emphasizing the fact that it was entirely Piper's fault that Cam was here in the first place.

"I did?!" Her face scrunched up in disbelief.

"Yes! You did when you tagged me in that post and *added the location to it!*" I pushed past her again, trying to make my way to the kitchen so I could make myself another cup of coffee.

"You need to remove that by the way, it's not safe to tag your location online when you're still there. Some creep might try to come and kill you." I lectured her using my best mom voice, trying to skirt past what Piper really wanted to talk about.

"So what, Camden saw the post and then came here? To see you? To be with you? What the hell is going on, Haley?" Piper spoke so quickly that anyone who hadn't been her friend for years wouldn't have been able to keep up. I suddenly felt very defensive.

"I don't know what's going on! Okay? I'm just as confused as you are!" I waved my arms over my head and nearly shouted at her. I'm sure anyone watching this conversation would think I'd lost my goddamn mind.

Maybe I had.

I did just walk through a small town I'd never been to with a man I had been in love with since I was fifteen.

Tears sprung in my eyes and my heart started to race from the overwhelming feelings swirling around in my body. I closed my eyes and tried to breathe deeply, focusing my mind on what Deborah had told me about how I control my emotions. They don't control me. I clasped my fingers together and put them on top of my head, keeping my eyes closed as I started to pace in small circles where I stood, trying to self-soothe before I had a complete and total meltdown.

Sensing my overwhelm, Piper moved across the hall and sat down on the couch in the living room. She waited in silence, watching me, until I finally calmed down enough to drop my hands and open my eyes. Moving toward her and taking a place next to her on the couch, I took another deep breath before speaking.

"I don't know what he's doing here," I offered as calmly as I could. "He literally showed up while I was waiting for breakfast and sat down. We talked; it was nice. I asked him to go for a walk with me and he did. Then we came back here and he left. That's it. That's all I know."

Piper didn't speak right away and studied me closely. I knew she wanted to ask me more questions, but she decided against it.

"So you forgot to bring me a pastry, huh?" Smiling at my friend, I laughed at her willingness to give me what I needed, which was time to think and process what had happened this morning.

Piper knew my history with Cam and she also knew how much I was hurting with the loss of Connor, even now, six months later. I was grateful she was giving me the space I needed to process what had happened this morning.

"Yeah, and I *really* am sorry about that. You wanna run back and get something before we start work for the day?"

"I will never say no to a coffee run with my best friend." She smiled back at me, threw her arms around my neck, and pulled me in for a hug.

After she pulled away, she walked toward her room

before grabbing the keys to my car so we could drive back to Coastal Brews. On our way up the road, my mind had already moved on to the coffee I was going to be getting tomorrow.

And the person I was hoping I'd run into again when I did.

19

CAM | NOW

The next morning, I woke up before my alarm again. This time, because I couldn't stop thinking about what happened yesterday.

I saw her. Fuck, I *hung out* with her and she didn't freak out or call me a creep when I told her how I found her. I would have understood if she did freak out—I did kind of hunt her down like a stalker. Not because I was trying to be weird, I just wanted to see how she was doing. I needed to know how she was. I needed to know that she was okay.

I could see the sadness on her face in the photo online, but seeing it in real life almost broke me.

Growing up, I'd always taken it as my responsibility to make sure Haley was safe and happy. But it was clear to me that right now, she wasn't. No matter how brave of a face she tried to put on, I could see right through it. She couldn't hide anything from me, and I didn't want her to.

Thinking back to our conversation, I was happy she had been honest with me about how she was doing. It would've been easier for her to keep her true feelings and struggles to herself, but she didn't. That was something we'd never done with one another, keep the hard stuff hidden. Not growing up, and clearly, not now either. I smiled to myself as I thought about it. It felt good knowing that Haley felt like she could still let me carry some of her baggage for her. We had grown distant after that night in her dorm room and fully grew apart once she got together with Connor. But based on our interactions yesterday, it was like we were never apart at all.

Still thinking about my morning with her, I rolled off the king-size, overstuffed hotel mattress and hopped in the shower. It was still early enough to where the sun wasn't up yet, but that didn't stop me from wanting to start the day anyway.

I showered, more quickly than normal because I didn't want to give myself enough time to get off on the images I held in my head of Haley. Just thinking about her freckled face and warm smile was enough to make me hard. It had been a minute since I had been with anyone, so it didn't take much. After stepping out of the shower, I pulled on a pair of running shorts and a long-sleeved shirt. Then, I pulled a hat onto my head and grabbed my headphones, popping them into my ears as I walked out the door.

Normally I would lose myself in my music. But as I ran today, I got lost in my thoughts about Haley and our time spent together from the day before.

She looked as beautiful as she did when I saw her in that coffee shop back in Charlotte. Her hair was longer than normal and I ventured to guess she hadn't had it cut since losing Connor. It still took my breath away. I wanted to run my fingers through it, pushing it out of her face to reveal the freckles on her cheeks and her round, hazel eyes. While she looked similar to the girl I grew up with, she also looked different. More mature, more grown up, and somehow, even more intoxicating than I'd remembered her.

My dick reacted to the thought of her and I had to awkwardly adjust myself as I ran past an older woman watering her garden, giving her an uncomfortable wave as I passed.

For fuck's sake, man, control yourself. You're going to make the little old ladies keel over with your indecency so early in the morning.

I continued running, wavering back and forth between thinking of how happy I'd been to have found her so quickly and of the things I wanted to do with her. The logically centered voice in my head reminded me that she was recently widowed and most definitely not looking for anything so soon. The other voice in my head, the one that I'm pretty sure speaks from my dick, was telling me that I could give her a hundred and one reasons not to be sad anymore.

You sick bastard.

While this finally felt like my chance to be with her, to be the man she always wanted me to be, I also didn't want to rush anything. She was hurting, she told me as such yesterday, and I didn't want to be another thing that brought her pain. It didn't matter that I wanted to invite her back to my hotel room and do things to her I'd only ever been able to dream of. I wasn't going to be that guy. She needed time to grieve and I wasn't going to rob her of that time.

As I turned another corner, I remembered the part of our conversation where she told me she was in therapy. It surprised me when she admitted this, because growing up, Haley was never one to accept help, even when she could've used some. I smiled as I jogged down a sandy path and was proud of her for getting help when she needed it.

After forty-five minutes, the sun was starting to come up for the day and I was starting to get hungry. I jogged back through town to head back to my hotel. Once in my room, I took another shower, changed into fresh clothes, then set out again for the second time. I walked toward the coffee shop to get something to eat and was silently hoping I would see Haley sitting at a table, just like I had found her yesterday.

I opened the door to Coastal Brews eagerly and couldn't deny the sense of disappointment I felt when I didn't see her anywhere inside. It wasn't as late in the morning as it had been yesterday when I found her, so maybe that's why she wasn't here.

Once it was my turn to order, I got myself a breakfast burrito and a plain black coffee. There was only one table open so I sat down and watched the windows, hoping to see a flash of cinnamon-colored hair through them. It wasn't long before a server brought me my food and I ate it without rushing, hoping that if I took my time, Haley might show up.

I sat at the table for well over an hour, holding my breath every time the door opened. When the person blatantly waiting for my table sighed loudly from the corner for the third time, staring at me while they did, I decided to call it quits.

I rose from my seat and motioned to the person that they could finally have my table. I started walking toward the entrance of the small coffee shop and reached my hand towards the door to pull it open. I wasn't paying attention as I walked through the door because I was too wrapped up in thinking about Haley when I slammed into someone who was walking into the door at the same time I was trying to exit.

"Oof! Oh my god, watch where you're—Cam?"

Looking down, I saw the cinnamon-colored hair I had been hoping to see all morning and my insides started to warm as I heard her say my name. I took a step back, my arms on hers to help steady her, and smirked.

"Hey there, Jones."

"You know it's polite to let people walk through the door when you open it for them, Johnson. It prevents situations like this from happening." Her voice was short but playful.

This girl was trying to fuck with me.

"How do you know that wasn't some secret ploy to get you in my arms?" I gave her a cocky smile and leaned close to her face as I spoke. *So much for taking it slow, you asshole.*

Her cheeks flushed and her lashes fluttered to the floor, a piece of her hair falling around her face. Someone behind her cleared their throat.

"While this is a nice little thing happening, we're all standing in the way of the door," her friend Piper spoke, moving her hand in a circle in front of her.

Realizing we were, in fact, standing in the way of other people trying to come in, the three of us stepped outside and out of the way. I remembered seeing Piper at the funeral, but we hadn't talked. The last time we had spoken to each other was that weekend back when I crashed her dorm room unannounced and then left without saying goodbye.

Fuck.

"Piper," I started, trying to give her my most charming look. Piper was small but she still scared the fuck out of me. The harmless looking ones are always the ones who get away with murder.

"Hello, Camden." Her voice was even but the smirk on her face made me nervous. She knew what I did to Haley all those years ago—she had to—and I knew she wasn't going to forgive me for hurting her friend. Part of me was deeply aware of how easily Piper could make me disappear without a trace, never to be found again. The other part of me was grateful Haley had found a friend who loved her as Piper did.

"How've you been?" I asked, trying to be the most charming guy she's ever met.

"I'd rather know what the hell you're doing in this tiny town of ours. Can't be a coincidence that you just *happened* to show up at the same time we did. What's that about, *Camden*?" She dragged my name out as if she wanted to drag me out to the back lot and beat the shit out of me. Piper is as smart as a whip and her straightforwardness could cut your carotid before you even felt it happen.

"Piper!" Haley's face whipped toward her friend.

"No, Haley, it's okay. She has every right to ask. I'm thankful she cares enough about you to call me out on my shit." Haley's cheeks were still flushed as I spoke to her.

I turned and looked at Piper again, her long blonde hair was pin-straight like needles. "I saw your post about being here and came to see how Haley was doing. After the funeral, I got busy with football and didn't have a chance to check in like I wanted to. Now that it's the off-season, I wanted to come and see Haley in person, to see how she's doing, and to make sure she's okay."

Piper never looked away from me, her eyes locked on mine like daggers. One of her eyebrows twitched just the smallest amount as I spoke. The movement was so small that if you blinked, you would've missed it. Piper had wanted to be a lawyer, I remembered, and her current behavior proves just how good of one she could have been. I stood my ground and never broke eye contact. After a few long moments, she finally blinked and exhaled deeply, as if to tame a fire that was raging inside of her.

"I just want you to know—" she took a step toward me and pressed a finger into my chest— "I studied law and finished one semester of school. And while that doesn't sound like much, it was enough to teach me how to cover up a crime and get away with it."

"I don't doubt it for a second." I pressed my lips together and tried to not let on about just how much I feared Haley's five-foot-two, blonde bodyguard.

"Well...this has been fun." Haley clapped her hands together in front of her chest and laughed awkwardly. Then, throwing her thumb over her shoulder she said, "We should probably get going now." She grabbed Piper by the arm and swung her around, pushing her down the wheelchair ramp that led into the coffee shop.

"Wait, we didn't get any—"

"It's time to go, Piper."

They walked down the sidewalk Haley and I had walked down together just the day before. As they moved away from Coastal Brews, their arms looped together, Piper looked over her shoulder to me a few times to check if I was still watching them. I wondered about what they were saying and hoped that they weren't talking too much shit about me.

Eventually, they turned the corner and were gone, headed down the street where their little bungalow sat, all the way at the end of the road.

I started to walk back toward my hotel, replaying how it felt to hold Haley in my arms. She was so close that I could smell her perfume and was instantly intoxicated by the scent. If I could bathe myself in it daily, I would.

The biggest thing I couldn't get over though, was how

cute she looked when she blushed. Her flushed face reminded me of a small girl who you just told looked like a princess. That she was the most beautiful girl you'd ever seen.

To me, Haley was the most beautiful girl I'd ever seen.

I just hoped that one day she'd let me say those words to her directly.

20

HALEY | NOW

"Well...that was interesting." Piper closed the front door behind her and followed me as I walked into the kitchen where my laptop was sitting. I opened it up and clicked on my email, fully ready to skate past this conversation as fast as I possibly could.

"Like I told you yesterday, I don't know why he's here." I didn't even try to meet her gaze, which I could feel was more of a glare. I just continued to type away on my laptop.

"You don't know *why he's here*? Are you serious?" She sounded incredulous. "Hays, that man is in love with you. It's written all over his stupid fuckin' face." I loved Piper, but sometimes she was so far out in left field with her accusations.

Cam was *not* in love with me. I hadn't seen him in over ten years. Not including the funeral, at least. There was no way he was *in love with me.*

I took a deep Deborah inhale and exhaled before speaking, "Piper, he's not in love with me. He just...he's just..."

"...in love with you." She looked at me, her eyes wide and her lips pursed together like a fish. I hate when she made this face at me, it made me feel like a child.

I rolled my eyes at her and picked up my laptop, walking away towards the office but she continued to follow me.

"We need to get to work. It's already almost eleven and we still need to go grocery shopping for food so we don't spend all our money on takeout." I took a seat at the long, white-washed desk and opened our conference planning spreadsheet on my computer. Piper planted her hand in front of my laptop, cutting me off from doing any work. I looked up at her where she stood next to my chair, her other hand on her hip.

"Hays, don't you think we need to talk about this? Camden, CAM, the boy who you were supposedly in love with all throughout high school and our freshman year in college is *here*. To check on you. To make sure you're okay. Don't you think that's something worth talking about?"

She started pacing around the room in circles as she spoke. "I mean, did you *see* his muscles, oh my god! He's a giant tool for treating you how he did, but holy shit, would I let him catch me if I fell out of a window. How are you not the least bit interested in exploring this?" Her words came out excited and I could tell she was getting riled up.

It was all too much for me though, and I snapped.

"I don't wanna talk about it, Piper. Just drop it, okay?!" Her face fell at my words, and I watched as her shoulders shrank.

Sucking on her bottom lip, she walked out of the room for a moment and returned quickly with a fresh notepad, a pen, and her laptop at the bottom of a stack of papers. She pulled up a chair across from me, opened her laptop, and started to write things down on the notepad. I could tell her feelings were hurt and I felt bad for shutting her down. She was only trying to be excited for me.

It was just too much to handle right now with losing Connor and now suddenly Cam returning to my life. I shouldn't have snapped at Piper though; she was only trying to be my friend. I reached across the desk and gave her right index finger a squeeze, our silent signal to say that we were sorry.

"It's just too much to talk about right now," I said quietly, chewing on my bottom lip.

She nodded her head, not needing to say anything else. She understood. Best friends like Piper always understood.

"Wanna talk about the seating arrangements?" she asked, pulling out a piece of paper with a million little squares and circles on it.

I smiled and for once, found comfort in her incessant need to have everything written down on paper. The predictability of the habit was comforting.

Piper and I worked on conference plans for a few hours before deciding to take a break to make a grocery list for the food we desperately needed. Thankfully for me, Piper loved to cook, so she handled all the meal planning for the week while I made sure we had enough easy foods on the list to grab and go.

Connor always made sure I was fed because I despised cooking. If it wasn't something I could make in a toaster or a microwave, I wasn't making it. He loved cooking though and would always bring me lunch when he worked from home. A wave of grief hit me as I thought about our lunchtime routines, and I had to blink away the tears that pricked my eyelids. Piper caught on to my energy shift and knew something was up, so she offered to go do the shopping for us so I could stay home.

Once she left, I made myself some coffee with what had been left behind by previous renters and took my mug out to the back porch. I've grown to love coming out here to sit on the porch swing that faced the water. I curled my feet under myself and held the mug in my hands as if it were a lifeline. That if I let it go, I would completely drift off into a sea of nothingness.

Looking out at the ocean, I started to think about my life and how I had ended up where I am today.

Up until six months ago, I'd had it all.

A business that I loved and built on my own, a house that felt like home, and a happy marriage to a man I was obsessed with.

Now?

Well now, I had lost one of those things and none of the other stuff seemed to matter that much. Now, I was sitting on the back porch of a beach house I rented because my therapist told me I needed to get out more and because my house was making me feel like it was slowly trying to suffo-cate me.

And then there was the Cam thing.

The 'Cam thing' being the fully grown Camden Johnson tracking me down and following me to a known-by-no-one beach town just to see if I was okay. Okay? Am I okay? My gut reaction told me no, but when Cam was around, I almost felt human again. It almost felt as if the giant hole inside me was starting to be filled in again, but with soil instead of cement, allowing for new and beautiful things to grow from it.

I shifted where I sat because of the nagging sense of

guilt and shame that was growing inside of me. I *shouldn't* feel this way so quickly after losing Connor—it's not right. If I did, it would mean that I didn't love him enough while he was around, when I did. I loved him with my whole self.

Thinking back to Cam, and how he came here to check on me, caused other feelings to stir inside of me.

The more I thought about him, the more an internal heat I hadn't felt in months started to grow. Suddenly, the feeling of Cam's strong arms around me was front and center in my mind from when I ran into him today at Coastal Brews. I hadn't meant to slam into him like I did, but when it happened and my hands touched his torso to catch myself, I felt every single one of his abs through his shirt.

And his muscles—*oh my god, his muscles.* I would never tell Piper this, but she was right when she said it would be okay if he caught you when you fell.

The thing that got me the most though were his eyes; his deep, emerald green eyes that I could see even with my eyes closed. The eyes that I would look for in the hallways, in the cafeteria, and that one sacred night where everything finally fell into place until Cam shattered it to pieces. I was almost mad thinking about that night until the image of Cam's cocky smile flashed in my mind.

Then I was just warm all over and I suddenly needed to put my mug down.

———

I SAT OUTSIDE on the porch, sipping my coffee and letting my mind bounce from one thought to another like a super bouncy ball until I heard the front door open and Piper call out to me from the entryway. We tag-teamed carrying in the groceries and were starting to find a home for everything when Piper locked her eyes on me. She watched as I put the milk away in the fridge and started to pull the salad from the grocery bag.

"So I was thinking about you while I was gone, and I feel as if it's my duty as your best friend to ask the question."

I sighed, unsure of what the question would be, but was ready for anything. I've known Piper for years and had learned to brace myself for whatever question she might throw at me. I looked at her and waited, my eyebrows raised, and gave her a small smile as an open invitation to ask whatever it was that she wanted to ask.

She paused for a single beat. "How are you?"

I looked at my friend and could see the concern in her eyes. She knew how much I had grown to hate this question because it was the only thing people seemed to ask me these days, so her asking it now was a big deal. I chewed on my bottom lip for a second, truly considering how I was before answering.

"I'm confused." Piper tilted her head to the other side and furrowed her eyebrows together at my response.

"Is it okay that I ask you why you're confused?"

Exhaling deeply, I moved around the counter and took a seat on one of the barstools before placing my chin in the palm of my hand like people do when they're thinking. "I guess I'm just confused about all the feelings I'm having right now."

"And what feelings are those? If you wanna talk about it!" she quickly added, remembering my outburst from earlier. I smiled at her and reached for her hand.

"I do want to talk about it," I started. "I guess I'm just confused about my feelings toward Cam, and how I feel like I shouldn't have any feelings for him at all. I haven't seen him in over ten years and he just comes waltzing in and my heart is all, 'Okay, time to turn to mush now!' It just feels wrong, like it's too soon. It hasn't even been a year since losing Connor. I'm a horrible person for feeling like this. I feel so guilty, so ashamed. It makes me feel like I didn't love Connor enough when he was still with us." A single tear slipped down my cheek as I finished speaking.

"Hays...hey...sweetie, look at me." Piper was sitting next to me and dropped her head so I could see her.

"There's nothing wrong with how you feel and you shouldn't feel guilty for having those feelings. Everyone grieves differently and everyone goes through this process in their own way. You are not a bad person for feeling something for Cam, he was a really big part of your life, right?"

I nodded in her direction while trying to swallow the giant mass that had formed in my throat as I fought back more tears.

She continued, "I know how hard it's been for you since losing Connor, and I know how fucked up things were left with Cam. None of this is easy but you're here, dealing with it the best you can. You are so strong, Haley, stronger than I would be."

"I don't feel strong at all. I feel like a horrible wife! I shouldn't be so quick to have feelings for anyone right now! And I don't even know what these feelings are." I brought my hands to my face, trying to cover the shame and guilt I felt. "Connor was the best husband and man to me. How could I betray him like this?!"

"You aren't betraying anyone, Hays. You aren't. I know it's hard to hear, but Connor is gone. You're still here. I know it hasn't been long, and I know you're still grieving and healing from the loss of him. But I think Connor would want you to be happy if you had the chance to be, don't you think?" Piper's hands were on my wrist and she spoke to me in a soft, comforting voice.

I thought about her words and a lost memory came to the front of my mind. It was one I shared with Connor, a conversation we once had. We had been talking about work and life and being together. One of us asked if we would want the other person to move on if something ever happened to us. We both agreed that we would want the other person to be happy, even if that meant moving on. I sniffed back some tears and my lips pulled back into a sad smile as I thought about it.

"Yeah, I think he would. I just don't know if I'm ready to move on yet."

"No one is saying that you have to, Hays. Just because you have feelings for Cam, whatever they may be, doesn't mean you need to act on them if you aren't ready. It's okay to have feelings and let them be just that—feelings."

I wiped my eyes with the back of my hand and Piper handed me a tissue so I could wipe the snot running from my nose. I flung my arms around her shoulders and pulled her into a hug, feeling even more grateful that she was my friend and she was here, standing next to me as I worked through my grief. There would never be enough words to express how much Piper meant to me.

"You're right, feelings can be just feelings. I don't have to act on them if I'm not ready."

Piper squeezed my right index finger, got up from her seat, and walked down the hallway to leave me with my thoughts.

Feelings were just feelings. I could agree with that.

But when would I get to the point of being ready to turn those feelings into something more?

———

SEVERAL HOURS PASSED as Piper and I worked to make progress on planning the She Who Thrives! Live conference. We didn't even realize how late it was until Piper's stomach growled so loudly that it broke both of us out of our focus. We laughed hysterically at just how loud it was.

"I guess it's time to eat," she laughed again before closing her computer and standing from the desk. She started toward the door and turned to look at me when I didn't get up right away.

"Are you coming? I got stuff to make salmon for us tonight."

"Uh, yeah, I am. I just want to finish this one thing first," I spoke slowly, trying to finish what was on my screen.

"Okay, I'll be in the kitchen when you're done."

I was in the flow of creating some social media content for the event that I wanted to finish before I walked away for the day. If I didn't, the creative juices would be gone for good and I would have to start over tomorrow. Sitting at the large conference-style table in the office, I continued to work until I heard the doorbell ring.

That's weird, I thought. *Who the heck is at the door?* From down the hall, I could hear Piper answer the door and start to speak.

"Oh...what are you doing here? Oh, my..." I heard her footsteps padding down the hallway, getting closer as she moved toward where I still sat.

Before I knew it, she was back in the door frame with a devious look on her face. I looked up at her with confusion.

Why is she looking at me like that?

"Special delivery," is all she said before I saw him.

I felt my jaw drop and my whole body started to tingle.

There was Cam, leaning over from behind her, two giant take-out bags full of what I assumed was food, hanging from his hands and a big goofy smile on his face.

As I locked eyes with him, I couldn't ignore the heat that I instantly felt in my cheeks.

21

CAM | NOW

Oh my god, she's so beautiful it hurts.

Earlier in the day, I'd decided to make what could have arguably been a horrible mistake of surprising her and Piper with dinner. After seeing her though, sitting in a chair and looking back at me with a small smile on her lips, I knew I'd made the right choice.

She was sitting at the end of a long table that had a lot of chairs around it as if it were meant for meetings. While she sat there on her own, she would have held the attention of anyone who filled the seats.

Her hair was tied up on top of her head, a few loose pieces falling into her face, framing it perfectly. She was wearing a light cream sweater and had the sleeves rolled up to her elbows, which were on the table. She had a pen in her mouth, which was something I remember she would do when she was deep in thought. *The flow,* as she called it. I wanted to pull it from her mouth and replace it with my lips. To feel her lips on mine again after all this time. I was awestruck by her, unable to form full sentences or create coherent thoughts.

"So beautiful..." I thought to myself again.

"Excuse me, *what*?" Piper whipped her head around quickly and looked directly at me.

Oh shit, did I say that out loud?! I cleared my throat and stood up straight as I was leaning around Piper to look toward Haley.

"So busy, I said 'So busy!' It looks like you're so busy." *And you look like a complete dumbass.* Haley let out an airy laugh and covered her smile with the back of her hand, her freckled cheeks now a faint shade of pink.

"Nice catch." Piper rolled her eyes at me and yanked the bags from my hands before she turned to head toward the kitchen with the food I'd just brought. I straightened my shirt and took a step forward, now leaning on the doorframe and looking at Haley again.

"Hey, Jones."

"Hey, Johnson." The way she bought into our old ways so fast made my heart skip a beat. Damn did this woman have me wrapped around her finger.

"I wasn't lying; you do look busy." I pointed toward her computer which sat open in front of her and the collection of papers that were strewn all over the top of the table.

"Yeah, well..." She took a deep breath and stood from her seat. "When you're planning a conference for 400 people, there's a lot that goes into that." She was standing near the edge of the table and it took everything in me not to close the gap between us, grab her face, and kiss her right where she stood.

"I see you still do that thing with your pen when you're deep in thought. Your 'flow' I think you called it."

Her face shifted into disbelief at my comment, "You still remember that?"

"I remember everything, Jones."

Haley's face fell and she took a step closer to me, my heart was beating fast and hard inside my chest. I don't know what possessed me to say that to her, but it was the truth. I remembered everything about her as if it were tattooed into my brain. Her laugh, her weird quirks that I thought were cute, even her favorite takeout order—which was Thai food, always. While she hadn't been part of my life in a long time, being with her now made it feel like no time had passed. It was as if she never truly left me at all.

We were standing in the office, within arm's reach of one another but not saying anything, allowing the silence between us to speak all the words we wanted to say but weren't sure if we should. The sound of Piper shouting from the kitchen broke the spell and made Haley nearly jump out of her skin.

"Let's go you two, time for dinner!"

I moved first, turning my body outward toward the hallway and motioning for Haley to go ahead of me. I was following closely behind her until Haley stopped in the hallway. I watched as she turned around to look at me, pausing for a moment where she stood.

She opened her mouth as if she was going to say something, then smiled and shook her head. Then, without saying anything at all, she turned on her heels and walked toward the kitchen where Piper and the takeout I had delivered were waiting for us.

———

DINNER WENT BETTER than I expected it to even though I came here with no expectations at all. Haley and Piper offered me a beer and poured themselves some wine as we ate around the kitchen table together and talked. It felt as if we'd all been friends for years.

I had picked up takeout from an Italian place down the street because I remembered how much Haley loved pasta and garlic bread when we were growing up. When she saw all the food, she gasped and her hands flew to her face in excitement. I almost melted into a puddle right there in the middle of the kitchen. I loved seeing Haley happy, but I loved it even more when I was the one to make her that way.

We all sat at the table that was next to a giant window overlooking the ocean, the sliding glass doors were opened to let in the late ocean air. I was sitting across from Haley at the table and every time there was a breeze, I would get a whiff of her perfume. I had to slyly adjust myself in my seat a few times because of the small bulge that was threatening to give me away.

Piper, Haley, and I talked about their work with She Who Thrives and I told them about Harvey and Coach Mike. Haley didn't act the least bit surprised about me being in Charlotte, and it made me wonder if she had kept up with my career after we had separated.

Piper was funny and quick-witted, and I was starting to like her even more as Haley's best friend. I could tell how close they were, almost like sisters, and knew that she was a big reason why Haley was doing as well as she was.

The three of us talked and ate for over an hour. When we were done, I offered to clear the plates and bag up the food while the girls finished their wine. I was returning to the table, a fresh beer in hand, when Piper looked toward Haley and then to me, and let out a huge, overly dramatized yawn.

"Ahhhhh...wow. I am beat. This wine just took it RIGHT

out of me. I think I'm going to turn in for the night and head to bed. You two enjoy your drinks now." A devilish smile was on her lips as she stood from the table and sauntered away, leaving Haley and me alone at the table. Haley looked dumbstruck by Piper and turned to me with an awkward smile on her face.

"Ha...uhh...okay then. It's just you and me then I guess." She drummed her fingers on the sides of her wine glass and looked around the room anxiously. I smiled to myself because we were alone, but also because I thought Haley's discomfort of us being alone was cute.

Stop it, you dickwad. She's a widow, remember?! Her husband just died! You shouldn't want to be alone with her. Stop. Thinking. With. Your. Dick.

"It's just you and me I guess." My words came out low and sultry. *You should be ashamed of yourself.*

"You want any coffee?" Haley offered, finishing her wine in two big gulps and standing from her seat with urgency.

I tilted my almost full beer toward her. "I'm fine."

"Oh...right. I'm just going to make some for myself then. You wanna go out on the porch? We can talk out there and not have to worry about keeping Piper up."

"Sure, I'll meet you out there." I headed out onto the back porch and leaned against the porch railing, taking a sip of my beer as I listened to the waves move in and out along the shore. I looked out into the distance, trying to figure out how far my eyes could see in the darkness.

The night air was crisp, not cold but not warm either, and I could hear people out on the beach enjoying the mild evening. As I was taking another swig of my beer, I heard footsteps behind me and the sound of the sliding door being shut. I turned to see Haley, freshly changed into new clothes, and holding a cup of coffee and a blanket. She smiled at me when our eyes met and moved toward the swinging bench that sat to the side of the porch.

"Wanna sit?" she offered as she sat down and tucked her legs under herself. She tossed the blanket over her lap and held it out for me, giving me the option to sneak in under it with her.

I took it.

We sat on the swing together, my feet gently swaying us back and forth for a few minutes, before either of us spoke. It reminded me of all those nights we would hang out after my football games on Friday night. Haley would come over to my house and we would sit on my back porch, just like this, and just be. I didn't realize how much I missed that until now.

"Can I ask you a question?" Haley broke the silence but didn't look at me. Her eyes were fixed straight out toward the water.

"Sure." I kept the swing moving with my foot and watched her out of the corner of my eye.

"How's life been?" She turned to look at me and I could see in her eyes that she was thinking about all the time that's passed between us. After I left her dorm room that night, we never saw each other again. I was an idiot, and leaving her like that was the biggest regret of my life.

I sighed and looked back toward the sand. "Well, I'm thirty-two, playing professional football making millions of dollars a year, and the only major commitment I have is my job."

Haley nodded her head and chewed on her bottom lip. "Millions of dollars a year, huh? Just to throw a ball around?"

I chuckled and took a sip of my beer which was starting to get warm in my hand.

"Yep...just to throw a ball around." I looked at Haley who was smiling into her coffee cup.

"Ever think about adding any other commitments to your list?" She didn't say what she wanted to ask, but I knew what she was getting at.

"All the time. My friend Harvey has three extra commitments, a wife and two kids, whom he goes home to daily. I've always wanted that in my life." My words came out earnestly because it was true. I had always wanted a family.

"What's stopped you from having it?"

"I guess I've just been waiting on the right woman to come along and be worth the commitment." My eyes were on her and when I spoke, she looked up at me and met my gaze. We were sitting close enough together that if I made one swift move, my lips would be on hers.

Haley swallowed hard and spoke again, "Are...are you happy at least?"

My words came out more as a whisper, our faces slowly moving closer together. "I am right now..."

Our breath was starting to share the same space and I could feel my dick starting to get hard, the image of Haley from my dreams coming to my mind as the Haley in real life looked like she was thinking about kissing me.

Then, somewhere out on the beach, a dog started to bark, startling us both and causing Haley and I to pull away from one another and look toward the sound.

That's it, I'm never getting a dog.

Haley untucked her legs from under her and dropped them so her toes were now helping me rock the swing. I cleared my throat, finished my beer, and set it down on the old, worn wooden deck. Even though her face was looking away from me and the sun had officially gone down for the day, I could hear Haley taking long, drawn-out breaths. I had noticed her do this when I found her sitting in Coastal Brews and was curious.

"Can I ask you a question?" I asked, dropping my head toward her.

One more deep breath. "Sure."

"What is that? The breathing thing you do? That was never one of your weird quirks growing up."

"Listen here, Johnson, I'm getting really tired of you calling me names. Don't think I forgot about how you called me a freak yesterday." She bumped our shoulders together playfully.

I knew she was kidding, but I wasn't. I wanted to know why she did it.

"I'm serious, Jones..."

Her face turned toward me again and she was chewing on her bottom lip, contemplating her answer. She let out a sharp breath from her nose before speaking.

"It's something Deborah taught me, she's my therapist. When Connor died suddenly, I was crippled by the fear that I would lose more people in my life unexpectedly like I had lost him—to the point where I couldn't even leave my house. Which didn't help either because being in my house is like being trapped in a time capsule of a relationship I no longer have because the man I loved for more than ten years is dead now. But that's a whole separate issue I'm working on." She paused, dropping her eyes to look toward her hands which were holding a now empty coffee mug.

"Anyway, Deborah taught me to do this when I was feeling overwhelmed by my emotions, to remind myself that I'm in control, even if my feelings are making me feel like I'm not. So...that's what it is. A way for me to handle everything going on inside my head because recently, there's a lot of shit in there."

I looked at Haley, the light from inside shining behind her, her face starting to become illuminated by the moon. Even in the near darkness, I could see her entirely for who she was. Kind, forgiving, fiercely independent, and just the littlest bit broken by what life had put her through. She was beautiful though, even her broken pieces.

"I'm really proud of you Haley," I remarked, giving her a lazy smile.

She scrunched up her face and looked out toward the water. "Proud of me? Proud of me for what?"

"For never being anything but you. For asking for help when you needed it. For being the strongest person I've ever met." I took her hand in mine and she looked at them as they intertwined, acting as if she thought they would catch fire at any moment. When she didn't pull her hand away, I continued, "You've always been the strongest person I know, even when we were growing up. I've always admired that about you."

"Thank you..." she whispered.

Haley's eyes hadn't moved from our hands which were still intertwined between us. This was the closest physical contact we've had since I ran into her at the coffee shop in Charlotte and wrapped my arm around her as she started to cry. Just like then, there was a growing heat in my core...and my pants.

When she sensed that I was looking at her, Haley brought her eyes to meet mine and we sat on the swing, eyes locked, for some of the longest seconds of my life. Our faces were only a few inches apart and her eyes were flashing between my eyes and my lips. Suddenly, Haley cleared her throat and was standing straight up as if she had been stung by something.

"It's uh...it's getting late. You should probably go." She

grabbed the blanket from the swing and walked inside, leaving me alone with a growing hard-on and an empty beer.

I followed her inside, placing my empty bottle in the trash can as I passed it, and met her at the front door where she was waiting for me. When I got to where she stood, she looked me up and down once more with her eyes, chewed on her bottom lip, then swiftly opened the door and made a motion with her hand that told me I was free to go.

Ask me to stay, ask me to stay, ask me to stay.

"Well, I guess I'll be going now..." I said, slipping my shoes on and slowly stepping outside.

Ask me to stay, ask me to stay, ask me to stay.

"Thanks so much for dinner, it was really nice of you. I'm sure Piper says thanks too." Her words came out short and quick. Why was she suddenly pushing me out the door? I swore we had just had a moment on the swing, but maybe I read it wrong.

"You're welcome," I spoke slowly, trying to delay my departure even more, "I'm happy to bring food or whatever you might need whenever you need it. I'm here for you, Haley."

"Oh, don't worry about us—"

I interrupted her and grabbed her free hand that wasn't holding the door open. "I didn't mean 'you' like you and Piper, Jones. I meant you and you alone. Whatever you need, whenever you need it. I'm here for *you*, Haley."

Her face was only illuminated by the single porch light on the side of the house, but I could tell her cheeks were a new shade of pink I hadn't seen before. Why do my knees suddenly feel like they're going to give out whenever this girl blushes? God damn. I squeezed her hand before dropping it, finally stepping out of the doorway and onto the front walkway.

"I'll see ya around, Jones." I turned to face her one more time and winked at her.

She blinked a few times, looking back at me. "Y–yeah, I'll see you around, Johnson." She slowly closed the door and once I heard it click shut, I stuck my hands in my front pockets and started walking back toward my hotel.

She didn't ask me to stay, I thought to myself, but she didn't pull her hand away either.

I couldn't believe how well this evening had gone. Way better than I expected it to when I picked up dinner a few hours ago. She let me stay and we sat under a blanket together for over an hour talking just like old times. She blushed. Every time she blushed, I wanted to drop to my knees in front of her.

My insides were buzzing like early spring cicadas and I was wired even though it was almost eleven o'clock by the time I got back to my room. I started to pace, trying to unpack everything that had happened when I decided to make a phone call.

"Hello....?" The voice on the other side of the line was groggy and disoriented.

"Harvey! Hey, man! What are you doing?" I spoke with energy and excitement.

"I'm sleeping, or at least I'm trying to. Go the hell away and call me in the morning."

"I can't do that, I need to talk to you," I added quickly before he could hang up.

"We can talk in the morning." Harvey's voice was drifting and I could tell he was starting to fall asleep again. Damn my friend and his inability to stay awake past eleven o'clock anymore. I guess that's what kids do to you.

"Harvey, I need to talk to you about Haley." My words tumbled out of my mouth and I braced myself for his reaction. Harvey had told me to stay away from Haley, to let her grieve in peace. I knew mentioning her now wouldn't make him very happy.

There was a pause on the other line. "What the fuck do you mean you need to talk to me about Haley?" There it was —his disappointed dad voice. I tried to tell him he had one after practice one day and the look he gave me almost killed me. I never brought it up again.

He had one though, and I was hearing it now.

"I, uh...I'm kind of not in Charlotte right now. I might have...maybe...looked her up and figured out where she was, and now I'm staying in a hotel room in this tiny town on the coast. I just got back from her place."

Harvey let out a deep exhale and I could just picture him massaging the space between his eyebrows with his fingers. "You just got back from her place?"

"...Yes?"

Another big exhale. "You're such a fucking idiot and I hate you. You know that?"

"Yes, I know, I kind of hate myself too, so we can hate me together, okay? I need to talk to you though."

He didn't speak right away, taking time to come up with his response. "Hold on a second...I also hate you for waking me up, you're such a dick." I heard rustling on the other end of the phone and Harvey mumbled something to someone —Monica, I assume—before he came back on the line. "Alright, you fuckwad, I'm in the living room and alone. What the hell do you need to talk about?"

I filled Harvey in on the last few days and my failed attempt to find Haley in Wilmington which then led me to the town I was in now. He called me a stalker and told me

I should go to prison, and for the sake of keeping the conversation going, I agreed. I then told him about running into Haley at the coffee shop yesterday, our walk, how we ran into each other again this morning at the same coffee shop, and then how I brought her and Piper dinner.

"I don't know this Piper girl, but I like her. She's right to give you shit," Harvey grunted through the phone, interrupting my story. He wasn't wrong.

I then finished by telling him about our time on the porch and how I thought Haley wanted me to kiss her, but we got interrupted by a barking dog. By the time I was done telling my story and dealing with Harvey's interruptions and disappointed dad sighs, it was past eleven thirty.

"So I just need to know..." I started, letting out a deep breath.

"You need to know what?"

"I need to know if it would be a bad idea to try and do something with her."

"*Do something with her?*" I didn't even need his answer, I knew Harvey was against this idea. "I don't know Camden, you tell me. Do YOU think it would be a good idea to do something with a recently widowed woman? I mean, for Christ's sake, she just lost her husband! She doesn't need some dumb fuck like you, *especially you,* coming into her life and making things more complicated for her!"

"But Harvey you weren't—"

"Camden, stop. Don't do this. You two have history—bad history, where you're the villain. She doesn't need this from you again. She doesn't need you rolling up like a knight in shining armor who's trying to rescue her. She needs a friend, Camden, you hear me? A friend. The kind of friend who doesn't try to kiss her, or bring her surprise dinners, or hold her hand, or tell her that you want her in your arms. Stop thinking with your dick and go home."

Maybe Harvey was right. Maybe I was trying to be a knight in shining armor. That's not what it felt like though. I held my phone to my face and played with a loose thread that was hanging off the pillow that sat on my bed. I could be just her friend, right? We felt like friends at dinner and when we sat across from one another yesterday at Coastal Brews.

I could be her friend.

"Yeah...yeah, you're right man. I'm being stupid. Sorry for calling you and waking you up. You can go back to sleep now."

"I'm serious, Camden. You need to leave her alone. She needs time to heal and get past this before she can really be with anyone and honestly, she might not ever be ready to be with another person. I don't want to see you get hurt if she isn't ready and you are." Harvey had just given me a verbal spanking but was still my friend enough to care about how I would fare in all of this.

"Thanks, Harvey, I appreciate that."

"You're welcome...and Camden?" Harvey said.

"Yeah, Harv?"

"I fucking hate you." The phone went dead.

I laughed as I looked at my phone before plugging it in. I started to pull off my shoes and my shorts and fully undressed by taking off my shirt. As I pulled it up and over my head, I hesitated and gave it a sniff. It smelled like her. I don't know how, but the scent of Haley lingered on my shirt so I pulled it back down over my head and left it on as I got into bed.

Maybe Harvey was right, maybe I needed to focus on being her friend. I could be her friend, hell, we were friends for eighteen years before I went and fucked it up. I could do it right this time.

I would do it right this time.

As I drifted to sleep, I tucked my nose into my shirt and breathed deeply, inhaling Haley with each breath.

I can be her friend, I thought as I dozed off. I could be her friend...and then maybe someday, I could have her as more than just my friend too.

22

HALEY | NOW

It had been a few days since the night on the front porch with Cam. I hadn't seen him once since he flashed me a grin that made my insides melt. I could still feel his strong hand squeezing mine even though it had been days since he touched it. Once he'd gone, I went inside and internally panicked about the entire exchange.

What he'd said, how I thought he was going to kiss me, how I kind of wanted him to kiss me, all of it. I paced the living room for almost an hour after he'd left, battling the voices screaming in my head. Ones telling me I should have let him kiss me and ones on the opposing side telling me I was a terrible wife and horrible human for how I was treating Connor. I couldn't shake the feeling that I was doing something wrong, being unfaithful in some way, for how I felt about Cam. I tried to explain my feelings to Piper in the morning and she told me I should set up a time with Deborah.

She probably wasn't wrong.

I half expected to see him the next morning when I went down to Coastal Brews for my morning coffee, but I didn't.

Nor did I see him the day after that when I decided I needed to take a break from conference planning and go for a walk. By the end of the third day of not seeing him, I was starting to think he had left town without telling me.

I wasn't surprised by the thought, but it still stung. That was Cam's M.O....get me on the hook, make me think he's changed, and then leave without notice. The man literally shows up unannounced and leaves just the same.

My alarm had gone off this morning promptly at 6:45 but I was already awake and staring at the clock, waiting for the alarm to sound. When it did, I slammed my hand down to turn it off, taking some of my pent-up aggression out on the unsuspecting clock.

Flinging off the comforter, I stood up from the king-size bed in my room and walked to the bathroom, passing a window as I went. It looked bright outside already, the sun starting to rise and peek out from behind the morning clouds. If it were any later in the year, the sun would be halfway in the sky by now but it was still only the middle of January.

I headed into the bathroom, feeling grumpy and annoyed, to take a long, hot shower. The water burned my skin and it was still a bright shade of pink by the time I got dressed and headed toward the coffee pot in the kitchen. How could Cam just leave? *Again?!* We weren't fucking kids anymore, the least he could've done was say goodbye.

I don't know how you expect him to do that though, the voice inside my head said. *You changed your number after college and never gave him your new one.*

I walked down the hallway that connected the bedrooms to the main part of the house and noticed Piper's bedroom door was still closed which meant she was still sleeping.

One major difference between Piper and me was that

she's a night owl and I'm an early bird. When we roomed together freshman year, there were countless nights when she would be going to bed as I was waking up for the day.

If I were in a better mood, I would walk down to Coastal Brews and grab us both a coffee and a pastry for Piper.

I sulked through the house and passed the front door, well on my way to make myself my morning coffee, when something through the pane of glass in the door caught my eye. Halting on my heels, I leaned back and turned my head to look through the glass a little more closely. The crystallized window of the old beach bungalow made it hard to see whatever was sitting on my porch, so I opened the door and looked down at the front stoop.

Sitting there with a note stapled to it was a large brown paper bag and a carrier tray with two coffees tucked inside. I looked up and down the street, which was empty, before picking up the bag and tearing the note off to read it.

Went for my morning run today and thought I would bring this by for you (and Piper). Iced caramel macchiato with almond milk. I know it's your favorite.
- Johnson

At the bottom of the note was a number that I assumed was his. I carried the bag of food and coffee into the house, closing the door with a giant stupid smile on my face. My insides started to thaw after waking up feeling as if they had iced over. He hadn't left and he remembered my order.

Setting the bag down on the kitchen counter, I reached for my phone and opened a new text message, typing in the number that was left on the bottom of the note. I reread my message three times to make sure it sounded okay and hit 'send' as I chewed on my bottom lip.

Nice touch this morning Johnson.

I was trying to be witty and smart, but also thankful for the food. I set my phone down and was starting to walk away when I saw the three dots pop up on my screen and scrambled to pick it back up.

Thanks Jones. I'm just trying to get back into Piper's good graces.

Just her good graces? What about mine?

I love ya Jones, but Piper could and would commit murder if she wanted to and I'm first on her hit list. You would never.

Did he just say he loves me? I'm just going to slide past that one for now.

I can't believe you remembered my order.

Holding the iced macchiato in my hand, I could feel my heart beat a little faster knowing that Cam hadn't forgotten that it was my favorite.

Like I told you before Jones, I remember everything about you.

About us.

I took a big inhale and released it slowly through my nose. I know he was being sweet, but I remembered every-thing about us too. Specifically, his propensity to leave without warning. Thinking about it now made me remember how I woke up in a foul mood but now the feelings had seemed to pass.

> You know I was starting to think you had left town and gone back to Charlotte. Haven't seen you in a few days…

The three dots were back on my screen, then they were gone. I stared at my phone with so much intensity, practically willing those stupid three dots to pop back up on my screen again. When they did, I exhaled sharply. I hadn't even realized I was holding my breath.

> I just didn't want to bother you is all. I wouldn't leave without saying goodbye.

That's a first, I thought, trying not to roll my eyes. He texted me back before I could type a reply.

> What are you doing today?

Thankful that Cam moved past the topic of abandoned goodbyes, I thought about the day ahead and what Piper and I had planned. We had already set the floor plan, speakers, venue, and timeline for the conference in April. Yesterday was spent dealing with caterers who didn't know their heads from their asses, which meant we were going to have to figure out the pop-up vendors we wanted to invite today. We were feeling good after checking ticket sales yesterday, noticing we only needed to sell fifty more over the next twelve weeks.

> Piper and I are going to be organizing vendors for the conference in April. It doesn't sound like a big task but we still need to source everyone, invite them, and then organize their setups.

Sounds like a big day. Another busy one I would guess.

> Yeah, we should be working most of the day.

Anyway you could cut out early and play hooky?

Texting Cam like this made me think of high school. We would text all day, even when we weren't supposed to, and never ran out of things to talk about. The big stupid smile was back on my face as I thought about it.

> I mean, I'm the boss so I do make the decisions.

Jones, you can be the boss of me any day.

My eyes got round and I reread his message twice to make sure he had sent what I thought he sent.

Was he trying to be sexy?

Why was my face suddenly warm?

> You're such a jerk.

Did I make you blush?

> I hate you.

I totally did ;) For real though, play hooky today and meet me. 3 o'clock work?

Screw Cam and his ability to know exactly what I was doing or thinking or feeling.

Fine. I'll meet you at Coastal Brews. Now leave me alone, I have a business to run.

Alrighty *boss*. I'll see ya later.

I set my phone down and tried to catch my breath. I read our conversation from top to bottom, still unable to believe what he had said.

You can be the boss of me any day? Was he for real?

The heat was still in my cheeks when I heard footsteps down the hall and looked up to see Piper standing in the hallway, looking at me with a confused expression on her face.

"Hays...you okay?" She was pulling her hair out of the bun she had slept in, her pin-straight hair falling down her back.

I stood up straight and flipped my phone face down. "Yeah, I'm totally fine. Why do you ask?"

She came closer, squinting her eyes at me. "Because you look like you just swallowed a bee. Did you go to Coastal Brews and get all of this?"

"No, Cam did," I said innocently. "He dropped it off sometime this morning before I came out. It was sitting on the porch."

I started to unbag the food that I had neglected while texting Cam and set it out on the counter. Piper dropped into one of the bar stools, crossed her arms, and placed her elbows on the counter. When I glanced at her, I could see the sly smile spreading across her face as she studied me.

"Oh, he did, did he?" One of her eyebrows raised.

"Stop."

"Stop what?! All I was going to say is that his gesture is *very kind*. That's all, I promise." She was using her innocent voice which she only used when she was acting not so innocent.

"Piper, he's just a friend. I didn't ask him to do this. He did it on his own accord. Don't read anything into it that it's not."

She looked at all the food Cam had brought for us and then at the coffees that were sitting on the counter. Her eyes shot back toward me again.

"Suuure, because 'just friends' bring you enough food to feed an army unannounced AND hand deliver your go-to coffee order to boot? And...wait a second, what is that?!"

She had spotted the note with Cam's number on the bottom and held it up to her face, reading what he had written. *Please let me be swallowed by a sinkhole right now, I cannot deal with this, just please take me now.*

"IS THIS HIS NUMBER?!" She wasn't even three feet away from me but Piper was nearly shouting as she shoved the note in my face, waving it around as if it were a golden ticket to see Willy Wonka's chocolate factory.

"Isn't that what it looks like?" I replied curtly.

"Well did you text him?" *Here we go, here come the questions.*

"Of course I did, I wanted to say thank you. I didn't wanna be rude."

"And what did you say?" Piper looked at me like she was a starving animal and I was offering her the first meal she'd had in weeks.

I weighed my options on whether I should tell her and decided that she wouldn't be able to let it go if I didn't. I grabbed my phone, unlocked it, and handed it to her.

I watched as her fingers scrolled to the top of the thread and her eyes took off reading, eating up every word like it was free candy. She made a few noises and then squealed.

"*YOU CAN BE THE BOSS OF ME ANY DAY?!*" Her eyes rolled to the back of her head as she clung my phone to her chest, her mouth wide open and gawking.

"I TOLD you he was in love with you! Holy shit, not only does he love you but I'm pretty sure he wants to fuck you," she said matter-of-factly. I watched her scroll to the top of the messages again.

"Piper!" I cocked my head to the side and looked at her. "I cannot believe you just said that! He does not wanna fuck me, oh my god."

"Hays...Haaaaaays!" Her eyes narrowed and she made a face at me. "He *totally* wants to fuck you. He pretty much told you he wanted you to *be the boss of him*. Hello?! That screams 'Please come fuck me.'"

I dropped my head and blew out a breath.

"Piper, I can't believe that. Not now, not so soon after losing Connor. I...I can't even think about being with another man like that so soon. It would feel like a betrayal."

Without warning and out of nowhere, tears were pricking my eyes, threatening to roll down my face like giant boulders down a hill. The energy in the room shifted instantaneously and the air was filled with sadness and grief.

"Sweetie...oh, Haley, I'm sorry." Piper reached across the counter and grabbed both of my hands. "I shouldn't have said that, I'm sorry. I didn't mean to make you feel like I was pushing you to move on from Connor. I would never do that."

Sniffing back my tears and wiping my eyes with the sleeve of my sweatshirt, I looked back at my friend. "I know you didn't, I'm sorry. Sometimes it just comes out of nowhere and it's too much to handle all at once. You're fine, it's okay." It was too late though and an onslaught of tears ran down my face uncontrollably.

Piper looked at me with sadness filling her eyes. She let me have my moment without saying anything but continued to hold my hands as tears fell down my face. It had been the first time in a few weeks that I had cried like this. The memory of Connor and being with him so intimately brought up a fresh wave of guilt and grief. Guilt that I was still alive and he wasn't, and grief because he was gone in the first place.

My shoulders were hunched over the counter, and I pulled my hands from Piper's to brace myself as I just let the tears come. Crying like this always left me feeling physically exhausted but emotionally lighter. As if releasing all the tears from inside of me was a way of releasing the sadness and grief I had stored up. Piper sat on the barstool across the counter until I was able to calm down again and collect myself.

"Feel better?" she asked. I nodded, unable to talk through the giant lump that was in my throat, which was now raw from my sobs. "Come here." She patted the seat of the stool next to her and I moved around the counter and took a seat. She placed her hands on my knees and looked at me with a soft smile.

"I'm going to say something that I don't know if you're ready to hear, but I feel as if it's my duty as your best friend to say things that are hard to hear sometimes. Hays, look at me." Following her direction, I moved my eyes from the floor to meet hers.

"I don't know what Camden wants or why he's here. I don't even know if you know. But what I do know is that you're allowed to be happy and you deserve to be happy *now* if that's an opportunity life is presenting you with. You love Connor, I love Connor, but you being happy with someone else isn't a betrayal to him. Ah—I'm not done." She held her hand up to stop me from interrupting her.

"I don't care if it's only been seven months. There is no timeline for things like this. Life gives us things on its own time, not ours, and it's up to us to either work with it or fight against it. You're allowed to work with it and take the happiness that life is handing you right now, even if it's in the form of a new person who very clearly loves you."

I swallowed hard, taking in her words. She was right, they weren't easy to hear. Part of me knew she had a point, that it was okay to want to let someone in so they could help me fill in the massive hole that's recently formed in my heart. But part of me knew Cam, and how he was, and feared that he wouldn't want to fill the hole for long. He'd left holes in me in the past, so how could I trust him to not do it again? I leaned across the two stools, and wrapped my arms around Piper's neck, pulling her into a hug.

"Thank you for being the best friend a girl could ask for. I seriously wouldn't be able to do any of this without you," I spoke into her hair.

"Damn right you wouldn't." She winked at me and smiled. "Now, why don't we take all this food and our coffees and get to work? Someone is playing hooky today and we have a shit ton of stuff to get done before that happens." I rolled my eyes at her and shook my head, getting up from the stool and collecting all of our things to head into the office.

Maybe Piper was right. Maybe this was life handing me

happiness and I needed to either fight it or figure out how to work with it. I wasn't sure how I would learn to work with it, but I decided to give it my best shot.

I've never been one to turn down a challenge before anyway.

23

HALEY | NOW

It had been several hours since my meltdown earlier this morning and every time a new hour passed, I got more and more restless.

I tried my best to focus on what Piper and I were working on, but it never lasted more than a few minutes. Piper tried multiple times to get me to refocus on what we were doing, but it never really worked. After too many redirects, she was over me.

"Oh my god, GO. I cannot deal with you anymore," she huffed, shuffling the stack of papers in front of her into a neat pile.

"What are you talking about?" I returned my glance to Piper, breaking my eyes out of a distant stare.

"Haley, you've been distracted all day. We have talked about the same vendor for the last thirty minutes and you still haven't answered my question."

"What was the question?" Honestly, I had no idea what she had been saying to me, my mind was focused on Cam and our...whatever was happening this afternoon.

"Exactly. I'm calling this workday closed. You can go

now." Piper dismissed me as if she was the boss and I worked for her.

I let out a sigh and stood from the conference table. I looked at the clock and it read 2:10. Under an hour until I was supposed to meet Cam at Coastal Brews.

I walked toward my bedroom and once inside, opened up the closet, looking at all of my options. I decided to throw on a sundress and a sweater in case it was colder outside than I expected. Looking at myself in the mirror, I brushed out my slightly longer than shoulder-length hair and pinned the strands around my face back so they stayed out of my eyes. I always liked it when I pulled my hair back like this because then the freckles on my face were on full display. My mom always called my freckles "angel kisses" which made me love them even more. Before leaving my room, I slipped on a pair of sandals and grabbed my purse.

Out in the kitchen, Piper sat on one of the barstools writing something down in her notebook. When she heard me approach, she turned, looked at me, and gave me a sly smirk.

"Well, well, look at you all gussied up," she teased playfully. Part of me felt like I was making a bigger deal out of this...whatever it was...than it needed to be, and I considered retreating to my room to change.

"Don't. Don't even think about it, I see it in your eyes. I'm just teasing you, you look beautiful, Hays."

"Thank you. I don't really know what we're doing today, so I hope what I'm wearing is okay." I nervously wiped my hands down the front of my dress to smooth it out.

"You're meeting at Coastal Brews?"

"Yep. Other than that, I don't know what we're doing."

"Is there something you *want* to do with Camden?" Piper

wiggled her eyebrows at me and my cheeks suddenly felt very hot.

"Goodbye, Piper." I rolled my eyes at her and walked toward the door. As it was closing behind me I heard her say, "Bye, have fun! Don't do anything I wouldn't do! Or do!"

The walk to Coastal Brews was short, just two turns down from where the bungalow sat, but today it felt like miles. My stomach was rolling with every new step I took. I was excited to spend time with Cam and had decided to just let life give me this potential happiness, but I was also still trying to resist the feeling that I was betraying Connor.

Grief is such a bitch.

As I got close enough to see Coastal Brews in the distance, I started to take in the image of Cam, leaning against the old, cracked, white picket fence that dotted the perimeter of the coffee shop. His muscular body was leaning up against a post, his hands tucked behind him.

He was wearing loose-fitted dark jeans and a gray t-shirt that hugged his well-formed arms. On his head was a baseball hat turned backward, covering up his dark brown hair. The afternoon sunlight highlighted the deep shade of emerald in his eyes and I could feel my insides turning into pudding.

I approached him and stopped just a few feet away, trying to catch my breath and fix my face before Cam noticed how my jaw was hanging open slightly more than it should be.

"Jones." He spoke first, my name sliding off his tongue like honey.

"Johnson." Our standard back-and-forth greeting came easily, and I was glad for it. I don't think I would be able to produce normal words otherwise.

"Your boss have any issues with you leaving work early

today?" His lips were pulled back into a smirk, and I could feel a smile starting to form of my own.

"I told you earlier, Cam, I am the boss."

"Yes, you are," he said it slowly, his voice gritty and low. I let out a breathy laugh through my nose and chewed on the inside of my lip. The thought of bossing Cam around like he was insinuating sent a shiver down my spine.

"So," he continued. "I thought we could go for a walk if you were up for it. It seems to be our thing. Plus, it's a nice enough day. What do you think?"

"A walk sounds nice." I nodded.

We walked down the sidewalk together and I followed Cam's lead. Piper and I had been here nearly a week but we hadn't had the chance to explore the tiny beach town beyond coming down to Coastal Brews. As we walked, Cam led us through what I'm sure was considered downtown. We passed several storefronts including a flower shop, a small library, a grocery store, and an Italian restaurant.

"That's where I got dinner from for you the other day," Cam said, pointing toward the restaurant window.

"The food was amazing. I could eat there every day if I knew I wouldn't put on four hundred pounds by doing so."

"You'd still be just as stunning if you did."

I tried to hide my smile and the fact that he had made me blush, *again*, and continued to follow him down the street. We weren't talking, just enjoying the time and space between us. Eventually, we hit the end of a boardwalk that connected the main road to the beach. Cam started down it but stopped when he realized I wasn't following him anymore.

"Jones...you coming?" His body was turned to face me and he gave me a confused expression.

"I don't like the sand," I stated apprehensively. For as

long as I could remember, the feeling of sand on my feet—or anywhere else for that matter—made me uncomfortable. This was a huge reason why whenever my mom and I took a trip, we didn't go to the beach.

"Oh come on, Haley, you can't come to the beach and not see the water. Come on, once we get to the end, I'll carry you so you don't have to touch the sand if you don't want to."

I looked at Cam to gauge how serious he was, and by the look on his face, he'd meant what he'd said. Curious to see if he would follow through on his offer, I followed him down the boardwalk until we hit the sand. When we did, Cam kicked off his shoes and turned so his back was facing me and tapped his shoulder with his hand.

"You want to give me a piggyback ride?" I asked incredulously. "Are you serious?" I hadn't been given a piggyback ride since I was probably ten years old.

"Why are you acting surprised? I told you I would carry you once we got to the end of the boardwalk."

"Cam, I cannot get on your back, I'm way too heavy. I'll hurt you and your body is worth, like, millions of dollars a year."

He turned and gave me a grin.

"While I'm flattered you just told me I have a million-dollar body; you are not too heavy for me to carry you. You're perfect, and so is your body. Stop arguing and hop on." He turned and tapped his shoulders again with his hands, waiting for me to follow his directions.

Chewing on the inside of my lip, I placed both hands on his shoulders and jumped up to wrap my legs around his middle. He wrapped his arms under my legs and shimmied me up a little higher on his back before starting towards the water. He carried me with such ease it was almost like he wasn't carrying me at all.

I slowly started to move my hands from his shoulders to be loosely wrapped around his neck and set my chin on his shoulder. He smelled like he always did, a mix of pine, earth, and AstroTurf. I was confused about how he still smelled like turf since he probably hadn't been on a field in weeks, but I breathed him in and let the smell comfort me anyway.

When we made it down to the shore, Cam stood with his feet in the water for a minute and I could feel him leaning into me. We stood just like this, Cam continuing to hold me, for a few moments before either of us spoke.

"Cam...are you going to put me down?"

"What if I say no?" He turned his head slightly toward mine, which still rested on his shoulder and our lips became dangerously close. "What if I don't want to?"

I laughed in his ear, butterflies taking flight in my stomach. "Cam, please, you can put me down now. I'm pretty sure I'm flashing everyone who is walking behind us."

He set me down and turned to look at me, a small smile on his face. "Well, we wouldn't want that. No one should get a free show that I can't also attend."

I smacked his arm and he flinched, trying to defend himself from my attack. When I went to playfully hit him again, he caught my arm and pulled me close to his face. My breath caught in my throat as I watched his eyes flicker down to my lips. Not letting him hold me in place long, I pulled my arm away without warning and took off down the beach, running as fast as I could.

"Are you really trying to outrun an NFL player, Jones?!" He laughed and shouted down the beach at me.

"I'm not trying, I'm succeeding! First one to the trash can down the beach wins!" I didn't slow down as I shouted back and tried to pick up my speed.

"Oh, you're so on!" I heard him say, and within seconds I could hear the water behind me splashing as we ran down the beach through the water.

I pumped my arms hard and tried to remember to breathe as I got closer and closer to our finish line. As I was about to cross the invisible line, Cam blew past me, laughing and whooting as he did.

I crossed the finish line as he turned on his heels and started to charge directly at me. I screamed as I saw him, and turned as fast as I could, running away as if I was being chased by an apex predator. But I was tired and my legs couldn't move as fast as they needed to escape him. When he caught up to me, Cam swung me around to face him and threw me over his shoulder. I hardly caught the edge of my dress and pulled it back down over my butt before it fell over my head, which would have fully exposed my ass to everyone on the beach.

"Cam! Cam put me down!" I was laughing harder than I had in months, tears coming to my eyes as he pranced around the beach with me still thrown over his shoulder. He was swinging me around like I was a trophy he had just won.

"I won! I won and you are my prize, Jones!" He laughed and spun around in a circle, holding onto me tightly to ensure he didn't drop me or I didn't fall. Feeling his strong arms wrapped around me like this made my insides grow hot.

"Cam! Please, Cam, you're going to make me sick!" Still laughing, I begged for him to put me down, hitting his back with my hand like a wrestler did as they tapped out of a fight.

Finally, he gave in to my plea and gently set me down. I placed my hands on his chest to steady myself, still dizzy from being spun around. When I brought my eyes up from the ground and realized where my hands were, I pulled them away quickly and took a few steps back.

Cam was trying to catch his breath and smiling at me. I don't know if it was his smile or the way his eyes shined when they looked at me, but my lungs suddenly struggled to produce air. I looked around the beach, taking in the ocean and the waves, trying to catch my breath. Being with Cam like this felt so easy, so light. Like nothing bad had ever happened to me or to us. When I was with him I started to feel whole again. My breath was starting to return to normal and I went to fix my hair as the pins that pulled it back had come loose.

Cam turned away from me and shoved his hands in his pockets. His eyes were fixed on the edge of the horizon and I could feel a shift between us. I stepped up beside him and followed the direction of his eyes. He shifted uncomfortably next to me and I looked up at him, confused by his sudden change in demeanor.

"What happened? What's wrong?" I could sense that something in him changed and I needed to know what it was.

"Nothing's wrong, not really. I just—I'm just trying to be respectful and not cross any lines with you." He swallowed hard and didn't look at me when he said it, his eyes still locked on the edge of the horizon.

"What do you mean, *not cross any lines with me?*" My voice came out small but I continued to look at him.

"Haley," Cam started. "Being with you like this—it makes me so happy. It also makes me wanna kiss you. Shit, it makes me wanna do *more* than just kiss you." He finally broke his stare and turned to me, his eyelids hanging low and his hands still in his pockets. "But I also know that you're still hurting, still healing, from losing Connor. I don't want to push you into doing anything you're not ready to do. I'm trying to be your friend, no matter how much I don't want to be *just* your friend."

I looked at Cam as his words began to sink deep beneath my skin, right down to my bones. *I don't want to be* just *your friend.* He was trying to be considerate and respectful of my feelings. This was not the Cam I grew up with. This Cam was more mature and thoughtful. He didn't want to hurt me like he had in the past, but part of me still felt the need to guard my heart no matter how much it wanted to break out of the Cam-proof box I'd put it in so many years ago.

I broke my eyes away from his, for fear that if I looked into them for too long, I would fall right into them. With my eyes back on the waves, I took a deep breath like Deborah had taught me to do when my emotions were becoming too much to handle. Out of the corner of my eye, I could see Cam studying me as I did, unsure of how I was feeling after hearing his confession.

"Being with you like this makes me happy too, Cam," I started, tentatively. "I haven't felt this light in a long time. Hell, I haven't *laughed* like this in months. It feels easy being with you. I would be lying if I said I didn't have feelings for you, but I think I always have. Those feelings don't ever go away, even if you move on and find someone new like I did." I chewed on the inside of my lip for a moment, feeling uncomfortable with the subject of Connor coming up.

"But I lost that person and I loved that person with everything I am. I don't know if I'm ready to move on from that yet. I'm sorry..." My eyes cast down to the hem of my sweater which I was now playing with.

"Don't apologize, Haley. You shouldn't apologize for needing more time. I just wanted you to know where I stood." Cam grabbed my hands and pulled them so that I was looking at him. "I want you to know that I'm willing to wait until you're ready. I'm not going anywhere, Jones. I promise."

I wanted to remind him of a promise he had made before, of all the promises he had made before. Of all the promises he had broken, leaving me a little broken each time he did.

I pulled my hands from his and crossed my arms across my chest, trying to keep my defenses up against Cam while also trying to stay warm as a chill ran across my shoulders. Without even realizing it, the sun was starting to set and the beach was starting to get dark. My eyes darted around and noticed that the only people left on the beach were Cam and me.

"We should probably get you home," he said, extending a hand out for me to take. I stared at it before taking it but decided that it might be nice to feel the touch of someone's hand in mine for once. Placing my hand in his, we walked back toward the boardwalk. As we reached the edge of the beach, where the wooden planks meet the sand, a sudden wave of bravery took over me and I turned to look at Cam under the single light that illuminated the boardwalk.

"I want you to know that I want to kiss you too." My words stumbled out of my lips as I forced my eyes to meet Cam's. "I just think my heart needs a little more time before I'm ready for that."

Cam's eyes met mine and he brought his free hand to my cheek. When he swiped his thumb back and forth across it, I held my breath and waited to see what he would do next. He had a small, reassuring smile on his face, and I could see his thoughts swirling behind his deep emerald eyes.

Without saying anything, he dropped his hand from my

cheek and started down the boardwalk again, leading me back to the sidewalk with one hand. He never dropped my hand the entire way back to the bungalow.

When we reached the front door, the lights were on inside and the windows were open, allowing me to hear Piper singing along to the music she was playing loudly from inside. It was right around dinner time and the smell of food wafting out from the windows made my stomach growl loudly, causing both Cam and I to start laughing. The sound of Cam's laugh brought me a sense of warmth I thought I would never feel again after losing Connor. I was still holding his hand as we stood on the front step, not wanting to let it go. My stomach growled again, begging for me to go inside and give it something to eat.

Grinning ear to ear, Cam looked down at our inter-twined hands. "You should probably go in and eat before your stomach stages a full-on coup."

I let go of his hand and placed it on my growling stom-ach, trying to get it to calm down. "I probably should..."

"Will you go out with me again? On Saturday? Let me take you to dinner." Cam's words came out quickly as if he hadn't planned on saying them. "I'm sorry...I shouldn't have asked that. You literally just told me you weren't ready to start anything. I'm such an ass." He looked down at his feet and rubbed the back of his head.

"No, it's okay. Wait...are you blushing?" My eyebrows shot up because even in the dimly lit front porch light, I could tell his cheeks had turned three shades darker. I couldn't help but smile and laugh under my breath. Camden Johnson was blushing, and it was the cutest thing I think I'd ever seen. I leaned my head down, bending just a little so that I could catch his glance. When I did, I smiled, reminding him that I was still there.

Deciding I should give the guy a little reprieve, I continued, "Cam, I would love to go to dinner with you on Saturday."

His head perked up at my acceptance and his eyes were back on mine. A warm tingly feeling was starting to grow in my core as we stood there, illuminated by the porch light, not saying anything but instead just sharing the same airspace. Cam grabbed both my hands, and then, just for a moment, I thought he was going to kiss me.

Instead of kissing me, I watched as he leaned in, closed his eyes, and pressed his perfectly plump lips to my forehead. It wasn't hard for him to do because of how much he towered over me. My whole body reacted to the feeling of his lips on my skin. I closed my eyes and leaned into them, breathing in his familiar scent.

I never wanted it to end.

When it did, Cam squeezed my hands gently before releasing them and started down the front walkway. I watched him leave and the tingly feeling inside me continued to grow as I stepped inside the doorway.

I was going on a date with Camden Johnson.

24

CAM | NOW

I let the door of my hotel room shut behind me and leaned against it, still smiling from the time I'd spent with Haley. God, did being with her feel so *easy*. It was like no time at all had passed between us and we were right back to how we were before we went off to college. I thought quietly keeping up with her social pages was enough, but being with her unlocked a raw type of desire and fulfillment I hadn't felt in a long time.

I kicked off my shoes and looked around my room. My eyes caught the clock and it told me that it was right around six. As I stood alone in my room, my stomach started to tell me how long it had been since I had eaten, so I called down to room service and ordered myself dinner.

I grabbed my phone and sent Haley a quick text, letting her know I had made it back to my hotel.

As I waited for her reply and my food, I decided to take a shower as the sweat and the salt from the day was starting to settle on my skin. I stripped off my shirt and shorts and tossed them on the bathroom floor. Slipping into the shower, I turned the water on and let the temperature rise as images of Haley started to flood my brain. The way her eyes crinkled in the corner when she laughed and how the freckles on her face seemed to dance. I remember how her hair bounced behind her as she ran from me down the beach, looking like pieces of silk blowing in the wind. The sound of her laugh was singing in my ears, making my entire body warm.

The more I thought about her, the harder I started to get and I could no longer ignore the urge to help myself along. I closed my eyes, letting the hot water hit the back of my neck, and took my dick in my hand. As I stroked myself back and forth, I let the images of Haley continue to play out in my mind. How she felt as I tossed her over my shoulder. The way I could feel her breath on my neck as I carried her on my back through the sand so she didn't have to touch it. How her soft hand slipped into mine like a missing puzzle piece, finally found.

Then, I recalled the dream I had of her so many months ago. How sexy she looked in only a lace set and how much I longed to see her like that in real life. My breath was starting to quicken as did my hand and I could feel myself starting to get close to the edge. I imagined what it would be like to touch the soft skin of her inner thigh and kiss the spot behind her ear. What it would feel like to wrap my hands through her copper-colored hair and pull her into me, tasting her lips for the first time in years. I created a scene in my mind where she was here, in my hotel room, naked and calling out my name as I took her to places she'd never been before.

The thought of her screaming my name pushed me over the edge and I finished in my hand. After a beat, I opened my eyes and took a few breaths. The thought of Haley on top of me, my name on her lips, wasn't helping my heart race slow its pace at all.

I finished my shower and grabbed a fresh pair of shorts, pulling them up and over my waist.

As I did, there was a knock on the door and I opened it to see someone from the hotel bringing in my dinner. I tipped the server and thanked him for the food before closing the door again. Setting the food down on the coffee table, I turned on the TV and flipped through the channels until I found ESPN. Some football game replay was on as I sat down to eat. I was halfway done with my meal when my phone lit up, notifying me of a new message. I snatched the phone off the table and hastily swiped my thumb across the screen to read the message from Haley.

> I'm glad a big strong man like you was able to make it home okay.

I smiled at her sarcasm and texted her back.

> Listen Jones, you can never be too sure. There could be some really dangerous people in this tiny town. The old lady in the house across the street from you is pretty fuckin scary if you ask me.

> Oh my god, you're ridiculous.

> Do you need someone to walk you home and keep you safe?

> You have no idea how hot the idea of you keeping me safe is Jones.

I replied quickly. Once I hit 'send' though, I second-guessed myself and wondered if I had crossed a line.

She just told you she wasn't ready for anything more, you asshole.

I saw the three dots pop up on my screen.

Cam please, we both know that between the two of us, YOU would be the one doing the protecting.

I like the thought of that...

And I will gladly protect you any day, from anything, as long as it's within my power to do so Haley. I would do anything for you.

My thumb tapped 'send' on the message and I waited for her to answer me. When she didn't for a moment, I started to picture what she might look like as she read my message. I could see her perfectly in my mind.

Her face was probably flush and her lips were probably pressed together, suppressing a smile. I wondered if Piper was reading her messages over her shoulder.

After a few moments, she didn't answer me, so I sent another text.

Did I make you blush Jones?

Shut up.

I totally did.

Damn I'm good.

While she couldn't see it, a cocky smile spread across my face.

I hate you.

Awww, love you too Jones.

If only she knew how much I meant that.

You're ridiculous and I have to go. Piper and I are going to watch a movie. I'll see ya later.

I didn't want to stop talking to her but I also didn't want to seem desperate.

I'll see ya around Jones.

I sat on the couch smiling and looked down at my phone. Scrolling through our messages, I reread them all from top to bottom, still unable to believe that the person I was talking to was Haley.

For so long after I'd screwed things up with her, I had let go of the hope that we would have any kind of relationship again. But here we were, so many years later, acting as if we had never lost touch.

My mind wandered to what our lives could have been like if I hadn't run away the morning after that night in her dorm room. The sportscaster on the TV droned on in the background as I finished my dinner and let my mind continue to create stories and images of the two of us and what we could have been.

Maybe we would've gotten married and she would have moved with me as I signed my first NFL contract. I imagined us having kids and loving her even more with a large, rounded belly. Thinking about the two of us being parents made me wonder why she and Connor never had kids of their own.

The sun started to set outside the hotel's windows and

the longer I sat on the couch, the more my eyes started to droop.

After falling asleep on the couch—twice—I finally crawled into bed with the idea of Haley as my wife still lingering in my brain. My heart ached as I thought about waking up next to her every day, bringing her coffee as she worked, and getting to watch her from across the table as we ate dinner together night after night.

The thought of getting to make love to her formed in my mind and just the thought of it made my heart start to race. Getting to be with her in that way, the two of us becoming one and feeling everything with her all at once, was enough to knock the breath straight out of me.

It was also enough for my hard-on to come back, and for the second time that night, I got myself off at the thought of a naked Haley crying out my name.

25

HALEY | NOW

"Haley, it's so nice to see you! How's beach life treating you, dear?" The southern drawl of Deborah's voice filled my ears and the warmth of it washed over me.

Piper's words about talking to Deborah about Cam have been running around in my head for days. After spending time with Cam on the beach, the feelings I had locked up in a box for so many years were starting to slip out. There were a few times I found myself unable to focus on anything other than Cam and what he'd said to me and I knew I needed to book a session with Deborah to talk about it. She and I hadn't met since I sat in her office, and she told me I needed to get out more. It wasn't until her face came up on my screen that I realized just how much I missed her.

"I'm good, Deborah. Thanks for meeting with me this way, I know it's not what you usually do, so I really appreciate it."

"Oh dear, I'd do anything for my favorite patients. But you didn't hear that from me." She gave me a wink and moved a notepad across the screen, ready to take notes as we talked.

Piper had been kind enough to give me the house while I met with Deborah and was out at the grocery store for some much needed restocks.

"I was so happy when I got your message yesterday asking for a meeting. I wasn't sure if I should expect to hear from you while you were away. I need you to know how proud I am of you for taking my suggestion to get out more. But I will say, I was a little surprised by how much you took the suggestion to heart!" She looked at me, inviting me to elaborate on why I decided to go all in on the 'get out of your house more' idea.

"Well, when you first suggested it, I was against it. The thought of leaving my house felt overwhelming. But the more I thought about it, and the more I thought about *staying* in my house, the more overwhelmed I got. Our home —my home—was starting to feel like it was collapsing around me, like the walls were caving in. So I left and came here." I brought my hands up to the camera to encapsulate the house in one fell swoop.

"And how does it feel to be there? In a fresh spot and somewhere where there aren't any reminders of Connor?" Hearing his name caught me off guard because I hadn't thought about Connor since the night on the beach with Cam a few days ago. It's not that I was forgetting Connor, more so that the thoughts of him were no longer strangling my mind like they had been since I lost him.

"It feels...freeing." I exhaled as I made the connection, realizing how right that word felt. It did feel freeing to be in a place, in a house, where there weren't any painful reminders of what I had lost. Every corner of my home back in Wilmington was like a sharp piece of glass waiting to cut me if I wasn't careful. Even being in town was painful because the people there knew I had lost my husband. But being here, where no one knew me, felt like a breath of fresh air that I had been struggling to take in.

Deborah looked at me through the screen and I could tell she was waiting for me to continue. "Back home, I felt like there were invisible hands around my throat, slowly squeezing until I wouldn't be able to breathe anymore. But here, I feel like I can finally fill my lungs for the first time. There's no pain here, no harmful memories of what I've lost, no dark cloud hanging over me. I'm finally starting to feel like myself again."

Deborah's eyes were squished together at the corners, a large smile growing on her face as she made notes on what I'd shared. "I'm so glad to hear it's been such a healing experience. I know how hard leaving must have been for you, but it sounds like you're starting to make progress toward getting back to your old self again. What else is going on? How's the conference planning going?"

Touched that Deborah had remembered the She Who Thrives conference, I filled her in on all the progress Piper and I were making. We had set the goal to have all the seats filled and a sold-out event by the end of February, which was four weeks from now. Deborah nodded her head as I spoke excitedly about the vendors we had booked, the catering we had scheduled, and the speakers we had invited to attend.

Pride rose in my chest as I thought about the conference and everything Piper and I had achieved, even through the darkest season of my life. Without Piper, and even without Deborah, I don't think I would have been able to accomplish everything we have.

"It sounds like things are going well! There is a vibrancy

in your voice I haven't heard before, Haley, and it makes me so happy to hear it," Deborah told me, tears pricking my eyes. Deborah reminded me so much of my mom, and hearing her say she was happy for me made me feel an overwhelming sense of gratitude.

"Thank you, Deborah. I've been trying to practice what you've taught me during our sessions and I feel like I am starting to feel good again. There are times though, that I feel unsure of if I'm making the wrong choices...like the choices I'm making are a betrayal to Connor and his memory."

"And what choices are you talking about, dear?" I hadn't told Deborah about Cam yet. I hadn't even told her about how Cam and I reconnected that day before Connor's funeral at the coffee shop. I quickly filled her in on *everything* that had ever happened between Cam and me, from the very beginning of our friendship and that night in my dorm room, all the way up to the moments we shared on the beach two days ago and how he told me he wanted to do more than just kiss me. I even told her how Piper swore he wanted to fuck me, but I didn't use that word when I shared that part.

Deborah listened intently, never interrupting me but laughing just a little when I shared Piper's comment. By the time I got to the end of my story, our session time was nearly up.

"I know that there's a chance Cam could run out on me again, he's done it before, even when I was honest about my feelings for him. But something in me is pulling me toward him. At the same time though, I feel like I'm betraying Connor's love and his memory by wanting to be with Cam in the way I want to be with him."

"Are you worried you're moving on from Connor too soon?" Deborah asked, her voice soft and open.

"That's the thing, it doesn't really feel like moving on with Cam. It feels like going home."

Deborah nodded, her lips pressed together, and her hand moving quickly as she wrote down more of what I was saying. I hadn't thought about how it felt to be with Cam, but once the words left my lips, I knew it was true. It felt like I was going back to something I'd always known, like an old, perfectly worn-in sweatshirt or the home you grew up in. It felt warm and safe to be with him, even if pain and heartache littered our past.

"Haley, I know how much you loved Connor and how much you still love him. I also know how confusing it must be to have someone as important as Cam come back into your life when he did. You're dealing with a lot of emotions right now, and I want you to know you are handling them in the best way you can. We are complex beings, us humans, and the work of the heart can make things even messier. Only we can decide when it's the right time for us to open up our hearts again when they've been bruised or broken. Do you understand what I'm saying?" Deborah's eyebrows were raised and her chin dipped, still looking at me through the screen.

While I understood what she was getting at, I didn't like her answer. I let out a huff and nearly whined, "So you can't just tell me whether or not it would be a huge mistake if I slept with Cam?"

Deborah laughed a deep belly laugh at my question. "You know I'm not supposed to laugh at my patients, dear, it's unprofessional." I sent her a smile. "But no, I can't tell you that. You must decide that on your own and trust that your heart will tell you when the time is right. As long as you listen to it, it'll tell you."

I pressed my lips together tightly, annoyed that Deborah wasn't going to give me a straight answer. I wanted to be with Cam because being with him made me feel like my old self. The woman I was before I lost Connor. I missed that woman. But the thought of being with Cam also brought me a deep sense of betrayal and guilt because it meant that I was moving on from Connor, and part of my heart was telling me it was too soon.

I repeated Deborah's words in my mind over and over until they were practically burned into my frontal lobe. *Only we can decide when it's the right time for us to open up our hearts again when they've been bruised or broken.* My heart had been both bruised and broken, but I could feel a small part of it, deep down inside me, starting to heal.

And that small part of my heart was telling me it was time to go back to what felt like home.

26

HALEY | NOW

The rest of the week went by in a blur and before I knew it, it was Saturday.

The same Saturday that I had a date with Cam.

Well, he called it dinner, but I was pretty sure it was a date. I woke up early that morning and did my morning ritual of coffee and quiet time out on the deck until Piper woke up and came to sit next to me on the swing. I had a blanket over my lap that she lifted so she could squeeze in next to me, our legs touching as she got comfortable.

It was the first weekend of February and the air was still brisk as it blew in from the shore. Piper's leg hung off the side and her foot kept the bench swaying slowly, forward and back. The two of us sat quietly next to each other on the swing, lost in our thoughts but enjoying one another's company.

"Whatcha thinkin' about?" she finally asked, breaking the morning silence, but keeping her eyes fixed on the water.

"About the conference," I lied. Truthfully, I was thinking

about how if my stomach didn't stop flipping over every time I thought about my date, I was going to hurl. "What are you thinkin' about?" I asked her back.

"I'm taking bets with myself on whether or not you're going to let Camden get you naked tonight." My eyes shot to look at her and my mouth fell open.

"Piper!"

"What? You know you've been thinking about it too, don't fucking lie. I saw the look on your face the other night when he left after kissing you on the forehead. I thought I was going to have to grab a bowl for you to melt into when you came inside." She laughed as she recalled my stunned expression and light-headedness when I came inside that night.

She wasn't wrong. I had felt like I was going to melt into a giant puddle right there in the entryway of the bungalow. I breathed deeply, unsure of how to feel about what Piper was predicting. She looked at me finally and chewed on her bottom lip for a moment before speaking again.

"Are you thinking about it?" Her voice sounded apprehensive as she spoke.

"Thinking about what?"

"Thinking about sleeping with him." Her eyes looked away and back toward me, unsure of if she was crossing a line. The last time we had spoken like this I had burst into uncontrollable sobs, so her apprehension was understandable.

"In the way you mean? Not really. I've thought about sleeping with him, sure, but I haven't really made up my mind on if I'm ready to do that yet. It just feels too soon, you know?"

Piper nodded and her lips pushed away from her face

like a duck. "Did you talk to Deborah about it?" she asked, turning her head back to me.

"Not about sleeping with him, no, but about being with him."

"And what did she say? If you're okay with sharing…"

I bumped my shoulder into Piper's and smiled at her. I loved how much she wanted to respect my conversations with Deborah and the privacy of them. But she was my best friend and I wanted to share this with her.

"She told me that we all have to decide for ourselves when it's time to open up our hearts again after they've been bruised or broken." I shrugged.

"I think that's pretty sound advice," Piper responded, her head bobbing up and down. She then scooted closer to me on the bench, roped her arms through one of mine, and laid her head on my shoulder.

"Hays, I feel as if it's my duty as your best friend to say this. Whatever you decide to do, I'm in your corner. Sleep with him or don't. I know that you'll do what's right for you. But if you do or if you want to, I want you to know that it's not a betrayal to Connor. He would want you to be happy, sweetie, even if that happiness is coming from someone else."

We both looked out toward the horizon, the sun finally starting to peek out above the shoreline.

Piper's words both stung and gave me relief at the same time. It was as if she'd ripped off a Band-Aid that had been stuck to my skin for too long. It felt like she handed a permission slip to be happy and to chase happiness again. That I didn't need to be weighed down by the feeling of loss or grief any longer if I didn't want to be.

Her words also touched the small part of my heart that I

felt healing deep inside of me and I was even more grateful to call Piper my friend.

———

CAM TEXTED me around four o'clock to let me know he would be picking me up at six for our date.

He even called it a date in his text and reading the word made me smile. I decided to wear the nicest dress I packed, which was only a simple sundress that dipped down low in the back.

When I packed for this trip, I wasn't expecting to go on any dates, so I hadn't brought anything overly sexy or alluring. This was going to have to do. I decided to curl my hair and pin half of it back, exposing part of my neck, and putting my freckles on full display.

When I walked out of my room, Piper gasped as if I was wearing a ball gown and diamonds.

"Oh my god, you look *so hot!*" she squealed and covered her mouth as she gaped at me. "Hays, you're stunning, seriously. You haven't looked this bright since before—" She stopped her words mid-sentence, not wanting to finish it. I knew what she was about to say, *since before Connor's accident.*

I grabbed her hand and squeezed her index finger.

"Thank you, Piper. And thank you for being so supportive. Part of me still feels like it's way too soon to be going on a date and the same part of me is also worried because of who I'm going on the date with. But you said it yourself, maybe this is life handing me happiness and I would be stupid if I didn't at least try to chase it."

I pulled out my phone to check the time and saw that Cam should be here in just under ten minutes. I was about to sit at the bar with Piper when the doorbell rang. We both looked at each other, surprised that Cam was early. Piper waved her hands at me and pushed me toward the door. When I opened it, a small gasp slipped from my lips.

Cam was standing on the cracked front step of the bungalow, wearing dark jeans and a white button-down shirt that he had cuffed at his elbows. The top few buttons of his shirt were undone, exposing his tanned and toned chest. His dark brown hair was tousled and slightly damp as if he had just taken a shower.

When I looked at his hands, I could see he was holding a bouquet of flowers, their bright pink and orange hues jumping out in contrast against his crisp white shirt. As I looked at the flowers further, I smiled as I discovered they were my favorite kind—dahlias.

"These are for you," Cam said, holding out the flowers for me to take. "If I remember correctly, they're your favorite." A flirtatious grin was on his face as he said it, knowing good and well that he was right.

"You remembered correctly. Thank you, Cam, they're beautiful." I took the bouquet in my arms and stood in the doorway, committing the image of a freshly shaven Cam bringing me flowers to memory. I must have been staring too long because I heard Piper clear her throat behind me.

"Here, Hays, why don't you leave those with me and I'll put them in a vase so they stay fresh and don't wilt." She took the bouquet from me and winked.

"Do you have everything?" Cam asked, my eyes turned back toward where he stood on the front porch. A nervous flutter swept through my insides. *Was I really about to go on a date with Camden Johnson?*

"Yep! I'm all set." I turned inside to pull the front door closed and caught Piper just inside the door flashing me a big smile and a thumbs up. I blew her a kiss from the doorway and pulled the door shut behind me.

Surprisingly enough, Cam drove his car to pick me up which I thought was odd because the town we were staying in was so small everything was walkable. He stood on the passenger side, waiting for me to approach, and opened my door for me. I could feel my cheeks burn slightly as I slipped in and took my seat. As I pulled the buckle across my lap, Cam slipped into the driver's seat next to me.

"You ready?" His eyes lit up as he looked at me and I could almost count each of his individual teeth, his smile was so wide. I let out a breathy laugh and nodded as he started up the car.

We drove through town, letting the sound of the music playing on the radio hold the conversation for us. The energy in the car was vibrant and nervous. I wondered if it was my nerves or Cam's that I felt buzzing between us. When we pulled up to the restaurant, Cam hopped out of the car and opened my door before I could even unbuckle my seatbelt. He offered me his hand which I took and helped me out of the car.

The restaurant he took me to was dark and intimate. Looking around, it seemed like it could only fit about ten tables inside the small, cramped space. The hostess showed us to our table immediately and Cam and I took our seats across from each other. After a few minutes of sitting at the table and getting used to the environment, my nerves started to disappear and I started to relax. As if picking up on my energy, Cam also seemed to relax after a few minutes. When the server came to our table, we both ordered a drink and our food before turning to one another once again.

We started to talk about old times and growing up in Pennsylvania. Cam told me about playing college football and how excited he was when he got drafted to play in the NFL. He asked me about my mom and She Who Thrives and the entire conversation felt easy and light. We only paused our conversation when the food came but picked up again once we had both cleaned our plates.

He told me about his friend Harvey and his wife and kids. As Cam spoke, I sensed a longing in him to have what Harvey had: a family of his own. Cam and I spoke for over two hours until the server came to ask us if we were ready for the bill or if we wanted another drink. I was perfectly content to sit at the table and talk until the staff threw us out, but I looked to Cam to see what his response was.

He looked at the server for a moment and then to me.

"There's a bar back at my hotel if you want to go get a drink there?" His voice teemed with apprehension, unsure of how I would take the suggestion. *This was it,* I thought to myself. *This was the moment where I either needed to work with what life was handing me or fight against it.* It took me less than a few seconds to decide I was tired of fighting.

"We'll take the check," I told the waiter with a smile.

As he walked away, I looked toward Cam who had a surprised expression on his face. The server brought the check back quickly and Cam handed him his card. Once we paid for dinner, Cam stood and pushed his seat back. I turned to grab my purse which I'd slung across the back of my chair and when I turned around again, Cam's hand was waiting for me to take, which I did.

We walked out of the restaurant together, holding hands, and sped off toward Cam's hotel once we were back in his car.

27

CAM | NOW

Holy shit. Holy shit. Holy shit.

I swiped the key card over the scanner and pushed open the door. Haley Johnson was in my hotel room, after going on a date with me, that I asked her on. When I picked her up from her house and she turned to hand Piper the flowers I bought for her, I had to quickly pick my jaw up off the ground after seeing her entirely exposed back. Ever since that moment, my pants have been tugging a little tighter across the front.

I held the door open for Haley to let her go in before me. Both to be a gentleman and so I could consume the exposed flesh of her back with my eyes once more. The tenderness of it made it look soft and it took everything in me not to place one of my hands on it. It was also sprinkled with freckles, just like her face, and I wanted to draw an invisible line between them with my finger. She set her bag down on the couch and turned in slow circles, taking in the room for the first time.

"Wow, Cam. This is nice." She raised her eyebrows at me

as she turned. My ego grew knowing that I had impressed her.

"You want a drink?" I held up the small room service menu for Haley to see.

"Absolutely, I do." Haley snatched the menu out of my hand and opened it, chewing her bottom lip as she studied her options, "What are you going to get?"

I'd been so fixated on how she was chewing on her lip, wishing I was the one doing the chewing, that I almost missed the question. Snapping my head back into the present moment I responded, "Uh...probably just a beer."

Between the exposed back and the mere fact that Haley was in my hotel room, I didn't have the brain capacity to come up with a better order.

"Then I'll get a glass of wine." She snapped the menu closed and took a seat on the couch while I called down to order our drinks. When I hung up the phone and turned, I found Haley with her legs crossed in front of her, continuing to study the room we both occupied. I'd known Haley for a long time, so I knew that she was deep in thought about something.

I could see it in her eyes.

"What are ya thinking about there, Jones?" She watched me take off my shoes and slip down on the cushion next to her. I pulled one knee up beside me so I could face her and rested an arm across the back of the couch. She looked away from me, brushed a piece of hair out of her face, and took a breath.

"It's just that..." Her hands were in her lap and she was spinning the ring she wore on her index finger. "We're here. I'm here. If seven months ago you told me that I would be here, sitting on this couch, in a room with *you*, I wouldn't believe it." She let out a small laugh and shook her head. I analyzed my next move for a moment and then started to graze my fingers across her shoulder.

Her skin came alive with goosebumps at the touch and I could see familiar shades of pink on her cheeks.

"I'm really glad you're here with me. If someone told me seven months ago this would be happening now, I wouldn't believe it either. But I'm happy it is, Jones." My voice came out deep and husky. My fingers continued to brush back and forth on her shoulder and my eyes traced the line between my fingers and her eyes.

She shifted in her seat until her legs were touching mine and brought her hand to my arm that was draped along the back of the couch. Her hand moved slowly up my arm and her fingers dragged on the edge of my sleeve. It felt like tiny bolts of lightning were shooting out of them.

When her hand met my cheek, I swore my whole face had caught on fire.

"I'm really glad I'm here too, Cam..." she whispered between almost-closed lips. Our heads were starting to come together and our eyes were darting between meeting each other's glances and looking at the other person's mouth.

Holy shit. Holy shit. Holy shit.

The sudden knock on the door made us both freeze as if we were sixteen again and being caught making out on the couch by one of our parents. We laughed when we heard, *"Room service!"* on the other side of the door. Our foreheads touched together and we both laughed again before I got up to answer the door.

After handing the server a five-dollar bill and taking our drinks, I slyly hung the "Do Not Disturb" sign on the handle of the door. I will not be interrupted again in my pursuit of kissing Haley.

Not by a dog and not by room service.

I carried my beer and Haley's glass of wine back to the couch and as I did, I noticed she'd kicked off her shoes and had her feet tucked under herself. She took the wine glass from me and smiled before taking a sip of her drink. A smile formed on my lips when I watched her start to play with her hair—something she did growing up when she was nervous. I sat back down on the couch next to her and bowed my head to whisper to her.

"Are you nervous?" I flashed her a grin and pulled the strand of hair she was twirling into my fingers so she knew what I was talking about.

When it registered what she was doing, she dropped her hair and punched me playfully in the arm.

"I hate you."

"You know...you've been saying that a lot recently."

"Yeah, well, if you weren't so dumb, I wouldn't have to say it."

For some people, this back and forth would get old. Not for me though. I could live like this, going back and forth with her like this, every day for the rest of my life if she'd let me.

"Yeah well if you weren't so god damn cute then I wouldn't be so dumb, now would I?" I retorted, mimicking the delivery of her words. Our eyes were locked together in an instant and I could see her chest start to rise and fall heavily.

Suddenly, everything started to move in slow motion.

Very carefully, she stood up and set her drink down on the coffee table in front of us. Bending at her waist, she turned around and brought her face eye-level with mine, placing both of her soft hands on my cheeks. She looked at me for a fraction of a second before pressing her lips to mine. Unable to control my hands any longer, I wrapped them around her head and through her hair. My hands gripped the back of her head as I pulled her closer to me, not wanting to be any further apart than required.

I heard her release a small noise from the back of her throat. The vibration shot through my body and straight to my dick. I remembered her exposed back and suddenly needed to get my hands on it immediately. I needed to remember just how soft her skin felt with my own two hands. Moving my hands down her back, I paused when they met her hips and I gently pulled her closer to me. Haley followed my lead and lowered herself down onto my lap.

Our lips never broke contact as my hands explored her back and hers continued to stay roped through my hair. She pulled at it which turned me on even more, making me kiss her even deeper and harder than before. Our tongues clashed and our breath felt like it was becoming one. We dug, clung, and pulled at each other until we were both out of breath, but neither of us seemed to want our contact to end.

Our kisses felt new and familiar all at the same time. Being with Haley like this—tasting her and touching her— was something I never thought I'd get the chance to do again. *God really does love me, I guess.* My fingers longed to feel more of her and were starting to stray to her front half. When my fingers made contact with the curve of her nipple, Haley took a sharp inhale at the touch and I suddenly worried I had gone too far.

"Sorry," I panted between breaths. "Too far?" I looked at her quickly, and her eyes flashed between mine and my lips. My hands shot away and were back to caressing her spine like I had been before, where I knew it was safe.

"No." She kissed me a few times, still breathing heavily, her hips grinding down on my lap. "Not far enough."

Her eyes lit up from within and I could see the fire behind them, begging me for more. Without wasting another second, I stood from the couch, grabbing under her ass as she wrapped her legs around my torso. She looped her arms around my neck as I walked us both from the couch into the bedroom and leaned over the bed to set her down gently. She didn't let go of me when her back touched the top of the mattress, so I held her where she was, bent over at my waist, and waited for her to release me.

"You know, Jones"—my words were coming out between heavy breaths—"we can't go any further if you don't let me go."

"What if I never wanna let you go?" Her voice was low and heavy with desire.

Using one of my hands, I grabbed her face and forced it to the side to expose her neck. I pressed my lips to it gently at first, then started to bite and suck the soft skin. She groaned in my ear and I could feel her grip starting to loosen. "I promise, Haley, you'll never have to let me go if you don't want to. I'm not going anywhere."

She blinked a few times and looked at me, taking a break from trying to force her tongue down my throat for the first time. Her arms were still around my neck and her legs were still wrapped around my torso. I had both of my hands pressed into the bed to prevent myself from falling on top of her completely.

"You promise?" Her question hung in the air between us. I knew she was recalling a time when we had been in a similar position that we are right now, and I made her a promise I didn't end up keeping. This time though, I was going to do anything I could to prove to her that I meant it.

I took her face into my hands, cradling it as if it were a precious piece of art because, to me, it was.

She was something so precious and I knew that if I dropped her, she would finally break for good. I closed my eyes and pressed my lips into hers, hard and with a purpose. We kissed deeply, both equally pushing into one another. I pulled away and in one breath muttered two words that I vowed to myself and Haley that I would never turn back on.

"I promise."

28

HALEY | NOW

I promise.

Two words I heard him say and as he did, a warm feeling in my core seemed to explode. It was a promise I'd heard before that had been broken, but something about this time felt different. Even if there was a nagging voice in the back of my head screaming, '*Stop! You're going to get hurt! You've been here before and he let you down. Don't you remember?! Hello?!*' There was a louder one telling me that I could trust him.

As soon as the words left his lips, I let him put me down on the bed completely and frantically grabbed at the buttons on his shirt. One by one, I unbuttoned them quickly and tore his shirt off. His chest was exposed to me for the first time since we were eighteen and I discovered he now had a full shoulder tattoo that covered the arch of his right shoulder and peck. I traced the outline of it with my finger and had to reel my tongue back into my head, practically drooling at the site of it. The tattoo was stunning. A mix of fine lines and abstract shapes that sucked you in and made your brain run a million miles a second.

"This is new..." My fingers ran across the front of Cam's peck, my eyes unable to look away from the tattoo and Cam's muscular chest. He was still holding himself up with his arms and leaning over the bed, looking down at me as I discovered new parts of the tattoo every second.

"I got it after I was drafted to play in the NFL and got my first paycheck. I'd always wanted one but never had the money, so once I did, I booked the appointment and had it done."

"I–I like it," I panted. My brain was starting to get fuzzy from how turned on I was by Cam, his tattoo, and his body.

He smiled down at me before whispering, "I like you."

His lips were on mine again, his tongue pushing its way into my mouth. He tasted as good as he smelled. I was still lying on the edge of the bed and as Cam finally lowered himself down on top of me, I couldn't ignore the strong force that was pressing itself into my pelvis. His hands explored every inch of flesh they could find as I continued to rope my fingers through his hair. My whole body shuttered when his hand met my breast again, playing with my nipple which was hard and showing through my dress.

He chuckled into my mouth, clearly proud of how my body reacted to his touch.

"Now, Jones," he started, pulling up the hem of my dress so that it was just above my hips. I was suddenly very happy I had decided to wear the lacey pair of underwear to dinner. "It can't possibly be fair that I'm down one article of clothing, and you aren't." A mischievous smirk started to spread across his face, like how I imagined the Big Bad Wolf looked at Little Red before he ate her.

"I didn't realize there was a level of fairness at play here." I was still grabbing at his hair and trying to avoid breaking contact with his lips.

"Haley, please, I'm a professional athlete and as a professional athlete, I only play when things are fair and even." His hand pressed down on my chest, pinning me down to the edge of the bed, then leaned over and whispered into my ear, his lips brushing against it as he spoke. "And when you play with me like this, everything is a one-for-one."

Then, in one fell swoop he wrapped his arms around my legs, yanked me closer to the edge of the bed, and ripped off my lace panties. Before I could even process what was happening, he spread my legs wide and reached one hand up to play with one of my breasts while the other found itself deep between my legs. My head slammed against the mattress, my senses completely overwhelmed by what he was doing to my body. It wasn't enough for him to play with my nipples on the outside of my dress, so Cam slipped his hand under it to find my exposed skin.

"You aren't wearing a bra?" he groaned, using his fingers to flick and rub my nipple.

"Backless dress, remember?" I responded between breaths.

"Holy shit, that is so fucking hot. Come here." He pulled me up from the bed and forced my dress up and over my head. I watched as he threw it to the other side of the room.

He took in the full image of me, naked and exposed, for what felt like a hundred hours. It turned me on even more when he licked his lips and slowly dragged his eyes from my face all the way down the full length of my body. Then, after taking every piece of me in with his eyes, he commanded, "Lay down."

I did as I was told, turned on by Cam's forcefulness, and pulled my hair out from under my shoulders so it could spread out on the mattress behind me. Cam was on his knees leaning against the edge of the bed on the floor, one hand tag-teaming my breasts and the other one teasing my center. My head was spinning and I was trying to remember to breathe when he pressed his thumb against my clit and started to move it back and forth. Arching my back, I thought I was going to lose it all right there when his thumb stopped and I heard him speak again in a low vibration.

"No, no…not yet, you don't. Not until I get a taste of you." I looked down at him and saw a flash of greed and anticipation on his face as he moved his head between my legs. Then, without another moment lost, I felt the warmth of his tongue at my center. As he moved his tongue back and forth on my clit, both his hands reached up and started to play with my nipples. Shockwaves rippled throughout my entire body and I could feel myself starting to climb.

"Cam…oh my god…*yes, yes…*" I clasped my hand over my mouth for fear we would be heard from the hallway, but Cam reached up and pulled it away.

"I wanna hear you scream my name. Let me hear you scream, Jones," he practically begged for it before burying his face between my legs again.

I moaned. "Cam, yes, oh my god. Don't stop, oh my god, you're going to make me finish…" I warned, but he only nodded. He kept his head where it was between my thighs, pressing his tongue to my clit and using his fingers to drive my nipples crazy. A few times, I would look down toward him only to find his eyes were watching me. The look in Cam's emerald green eyes watching me as he ate me out only made the entire experience hotter.

I felt the mind-numbing sensation start to grow in my toes and travel up through my center, behind my belly button, and up into my chest. Once it got to the top of my head, I couldn't hold on any longer and I let it take full control of me. My hips bucked and my head thrashed back and forth as I experienced one of the best orgasms of my entire life. I pushed Cam's head away from between my legs and lay there with my eyes shut, totally taken over by the feeling he just created in me.

I felt the bed give to his weight and sensed his body hovering over me, but my eyes remained closed. He nuzzled my face to one side and kissed my neck as I started to come down. Cam moved from kissing my neck to my cheek, then to my lips which had gone completely numb.

Cam started to push away from me but I grabbed him quickly, sinking my fingernails into his back. "Where do you think you're going?"

I could hear the smile on his face as he spoke. "Nowhere, I was just going to make things even between us again and lose the pants." My eyes flicked down and I remembered how I was completely naked and he was not. I pushed him back and sat up on the bed, reaching for his belt and working to unbutton his jeans as quickly as I unbuttoned his shirt.

"Jesus, Jones, if I didn't know any better I would think that you were trying to get me naked." he laughed.

I looked up at his face and gave him a devilish grin as I freed him from his jeans.

He stood in front of me, fully exposed. My eyes traveled up from his feet, pausing for a few moments on his cock which was standing at attention, before taking in the rest of him.

Looking at his body, it was no secret that Cam was a professional athlete. Every muscle on his body was taut and pronounced. While he didn't have a six-pack, his core was strong and he had those V-lines that pointed south which every woman got turned on by. My eyes worked their way up to the rest of his body, taking in his biceps and pecs, and his tattooed shoulder. The thing that took my breath away the most though, was his eyes. They pierced right through me like ice but were also warm and made me feel safe. When I made eye contact with him, Cam took a step closer to me and I moved back on the bed so he had space. Lowering himself down on top of me, I felt his muscles pulse, his dick on my core.

We started to kiss again, this time slower, more intentional, less feral. His hands swept up my sides as mine dug into his back, pulling him closer to me as if it were physically possible. I felt desire in my middle, begging to know what it was like to have him inside of me, and my hips started to grind against his as an invite.

"Cam..." I breathed into his ear.

"Haley..."

"Please...please let me have you."

"*Fucking finally*," he growled before pushing himself inside of me. We both let out sighs of relief as if being together like this had freed us from being trapped underwater.

He framed his hands on the bed beside my head and kissed me while he thrust his hips in and out. *So this is what it feels like to be with Camden Johnson*, I thought to myself. Hard, yet soft. Passionate, yet caring. This was an experience I'd thought about so many times before, but experiencing it in real life felt almost surreal.

I started to moan as Cam rocked back and forth on top of me. My hands needed to touch him and I clawed at his bare chest, trying to take any part of him I could get. Still on top of me, my breast fully on display, Cam leaned over and started to kiss and flick my nipples with his tongue, like he had been doing to my clit not even five minutes earlier.

Unable to control myself, I pulled him in and bit at his ear which caused him to flinch in pleasure.

"You are so fucking sexy, Haley Jones. This is so much better than my dreams." *His dreams?*

He continued to play with my breast and I continued to bite and grab at any open skin I could find. Cam was starting to thrust harder and deeper than before and the deeper he went, the more my body started to ignite. A few times he went so deep it almost hurt, but even then, my body begged for him to give me more. I could feel myself starting to ascend again, and I pulled Cam closer into my body.

"I'm going to finish and I want you to finish with me," Cam growled in my ear. He pushed me further back onto the bed and pushed up onto his knees before shoving one of his hands down toward my center. As he rode me hard, he had one hand playing with my clit and the other hand playing with my nipple. It took everything in me not to finish right then and there because I wanted us to finish together as he asked. My head pressed firmly into the mattress and my back started to arch again as Cam took me closer and closer to the edge.

"That's it Jones, you're mine. You've always been mine and I will have you as mine now. Say my name, Haley, scream it."

I let myself go at the sound of his words and did exactly as he asked, screaming his name as we finished simultaneously. Who cares if anyone in the hallway can hear us?

Cam nearly collapsed on top of me. After a minute to catch his breath, he pulled out from inside of me. Feeling him slide out of me brought me another wave of ecstasy I wasn't expecting. Rolling off of me and lying next to me, Cam gently kissed my shoulder and ran his fingers up and down my arm. I was lying there, looking at the ceiling when his eyes burst open and panic flooded his face.

"Holy shit, we didn't use protection. Oh my god, Haley, I'm so sorry, I should have said something, I—"

I cut him off mid-panic by rolling over on top of him and pressing my lips to his.

"It's fine, Cam, we're okay. I have an IUD, it's not a big deal." Remembering my choice of birth control now reminded me of the reason why I had it placed several years earlier. Connor hadn't wanted kids and we wanted to be extra sure about preventing them, so I got the copper IUD because it had the highest rate of protection. Thinking of Connor now, as I lay naked next to Cam, I couldn't fight the overwhelming sense of betrayal rippling through my body. I rolled over onto my back again and locked my eyes on the ceiling, trying to contain the tears that I felt welling up in them.

"But still, I'm so, so sorry. That was so selfish of me not to ask or offer, I just got caught up in the moment. I swear, I..." Cam looked toward me and noticed the wetness in my eyes.

"Haley...are you okay? Did I hurt you? Oh my god, if I hurt you..."

I rolled over to face him again and put my hand on his cheek, trying to dispel his concern. "No, Cam, you didn't hurt me, I promise." I sniffed hard, trying to collect myself before completely losing it.

"Then what's wrong, why are you upset?" His deep emerald eyes swelled with concern. This man, just looking at him now, I could tell how much he cared about me. I looked down at my hands before speaking because the thought of saying this to Cam's face was almost too much.

"It's just...this is my first time since losing Connor. And while it was amazing and it was something I wanted, I did...

it's just also something I didn't see myself doing so soon after losing him. I feel like I'm betraying him or like I don't love him enough to not be with someone else like this again. I miss him so much. And I'm embarrassed I'm having this conversation with you now, after what just happened." Tears streamed down my face and I brought my hands to cover my eyes, the embarrassment taking over. I can't believe I'm talking about this with Cam after he made me orgasm.

Twice.

I felt his arm reach across me and then he pulled the sheet over both of us so we were covered. A tender act of respect and care that made me cry even harder.

"Come here, Jones." His arm looped under my head and pulled me onto my side so my face was facing his chest. He shimmied closer to me and turned onto his side so we were now chest to chest. Wrapping his other arm over my waist, he pulled me close as I continued to sob. "Shhh...it's okay." He stroked my hair and kissed the top of my head.

"Can I say something?" I nodded my head under his arms which were still wrapped around me. "I can't pretend like I know what you're going through, but I want you to know that you shouldn't feel embarrassed. You lost someone really important to you and healing from that is hard. But I'm here for you in whatever way you need from me to work through this."

"Are you only saying that because we just had sex?" I squeaked through more tears.

Cam laughed and I moved at the weight of it.

"No, Jones. I'm not just saying that because we just had sex. I'm saying that because I care about you. And I want you to know that I didn't track you down to this small town just so I could get in your pants." He kissed my head again and I felt my heart swell in my chest.

"I don't know much about Connor, but I know how much he meant to you"—his voice trailed off—"and if you wanted to tell me more about him, you can."

The tears were starting to let up and I used my hands as best as I could to wipe my eyes. I squirmed in Cam's arms as he was still wrapped around me like a safety blanket.

"That means a lot, Cam, thank you. For now, I just want you to hold me." I nuzzled my face back into his chest and closed my eyes. Cam kissed my forehead and then I felt his chin on top of my head.

"I can do that, Jones," he whispered. "Anything for you. Forever and always."

29

CAM | NOW

I woke up with the feeling of something wrapped around my body.

Looking through partially closed eyes, I realized it was Haley's arm, looping itself around my torso from behind. I shifted slightly, feeling her head tucked against my back, and flipped myself around so I could see her. She was breathing heavily, still sleeping, and I noticed the sheet had slipped low, exposing her breast just enough to see her nipples.

Ignoring the erection I suddenly had, I pulled the sheet back up so she was covered, and ran my fingers along her arm. After she cried last night, I held her close until she told me she was okay. I then helped her get cleaned up with a warm washcloth before we got settled in bed. Then, she nuzzled herself back into my chest and fell asleep as I held her.

The image of her lying next to me now took my breath away.

Her cinnamon-colored hair radiated out behind her like ribbons blowing in the wind. Her freckles ran across her face like stars across the night sky, and I wanted to kiss each and every one of them.

My eyes peered down her arm and I gently pressed my finger into the moles that popped up on her skin every few inches. A piece of hair had fallen on her face as she slept, so I pushed it back behind her ear. I didn't want anything to block the image of Haley from my sight. As I pushed the hair behind her ear, she stirred next to me.

"Hi." Her groggy voice came out dry and raspy, her throat still dry from her sobs last night.

"Hey, beautiful," I hummed before leaning in and pressing my lips to her forehead. She replied with an audible, happy "*hmph*" and hearing the sound made my heart beat faster.

"How'd you sleep?" I asked her, running my fingers through her soft hair. She shifted and pulled the sheet a little closer to her chin. It made me feel better that I had covered her before she had fully woken up.

"I slept good. You kept me very warm." A smile formed on her mouth and she wiggled her body even closer to mine.

"I'm glad." I couldn't hide the pride in my voice. I lifted my chin to rest it on the top of her head. I like how she felt like this, tucked away and safe next to me.

"How...how are you?" I wasn't sure if now was the best time to bring up what happened last night, but I decided to do it anyway. I didn't want things to be weird between us and I also wanted to make sure she was okay.

"I'm okay. I'm mortified. But I'm okay." She moved out from under me and started to roll so she was facing away from me.

"Hey, don't do that. Don't turn away, you don't need to be embarrassed." I pulled her back toward me and slung my arm over her so she couldn't move. Her hands were on my chest and she avoided my glance by playing with the small hairs on my chest.

"Cam..." Her voice came out small, almost childlike. "We *finally* get together, like we did, and my reaction was to *cry*. And not just cry, but sob. I practically had snot running down my nose! That's enough to be mortified by if you ask me."

I looked down at her, begging her to meet my glance but she didn't, her eyes and fingers still fixed to my chest. I needed her to know it was okay, and that she didn't need to be embarrassed or ashamed for getting upset.

"Haley...Haley, look at me." Her soft hazel eyes fluttered to meet mine. I placed one of my hands on her cheek and she pressed her face into it lightly. "You lost someone who you loved and who mattered so much to you. It's okay to miss him and it's okay to be sad about him being gone. It's also okay to feel confused and unsure about...this. But I want you to know that I meant what I said last night. I would do anything for you and I will do anything for you. I'm not going anywhere."

Her cheeks flushed and she turned her face to kiss the inside of my palm. Her smile was back and I knew we were okay.

"I'll be right back," Haley noted, slipping out from under my grasp and taking the sheet on the bed with her. As she walked toward the bathroom wrapped up in the sheet, I saw her eyes flash to where I lay, naked and exposed, and chewed her bottom lip with desire. As the bathroom door closed behind her, I couldn't get over how cute she looked as she took in my body, shy yet full of lust.

I got up from the bed, pulled on some joggers that were balled up in the corner and laid back down in bed. After a few minutes, Haley opened the bathroom door wearing an oversized shirt and nothing underneath, her ass cheeks hanging out just below the hem of the shirt. Her hair was somehow toppled on top of her head in a way that was both messy and incredibly sexy. I wanted to pull her on top of me so I could watch her hair fall free again.

"Is that my shirt?" Noticing it now, I knew that it was. She didn't have any clothes here except for her dress which was still haphazardly thrown on the floor where I tossed it last night.

She stopped and looked down, her bare feet once padding across the floor now halted. She looked up at me through her lashes and almost looked nervous. "Yeah, I found it on the floor in the bathroom. Is that okay?"

I looked at her and took in the image that stood in front of me: Haley Jones, the girl I grew up with, who wore a denim skirt to school one day that turned my bones into pudding, was now standing in front of me more than ten years later wearing nothing but my shirt. *Yes, it's okay,* the growing erection under my joggers said.

"Yes, beautiful, it's more than okay." My arm reached for her and she moved to meet it, letting me pull her back into the bed we had made ours. She laughed as I pulled her down into bed and rolled her over so that she was on her side and facing me. I rolled over to meet her and propped my head up with my hand. Haley smiled back at me, her cheeks meeting her eyes, and I thought that if time froze like this forever I would be perfectly okay with it.

"Cam," she whispered after a moment of quiet.

"Yes, beautiful?" The name got me a scrunchy grin

"Cam..." Haley started to wiggle closer to me.

"Yes, beautiful?"

"Caaaam." She started to crawl on top of me. Swinging

one leg across my torso, she put her hands on either side of my head and sat on my lap leaning over me. Her hair fell from the top of her head and landed around our faces, closing us off from the world. Haley had a smile on her face as she sat her hips back, knowingly pressing down on my cock which was now noticeably hard.

She started to kiss me on different parts of my face that no other woman had ever kissed before. My nose, my eyelids, the right corner of my mouth, the spot where my jaw meets my neck. Everywhere but my lips. Over and over, Haley kissed me as my hands explored her body under the shirt she was wearing. She used her hand to pull her hair out of her way as her kisses got closer and closer to my ear. *Please bite it*, I begged to myself.

She didn't bite it, she whispered into it.

"I'm hungry."

My chest erupted with laughter and she giggled as I wrapped my arms around her to hold her in place so she didn't bounce off of me. This woman had crawled her way on top of me and started to seduce me, all so she could tell me she was hungry?

Un-fuckin-believable.

"Mmmm...I'm hungry, too." My hunger was not the same as hers though. I was hungry for her. I grabbed the back of her head and pulled her in close for a kiss. As I slipped my tongue into the inside of her cheek, she made a noise in the back of her throat that made me even more desperate to have her. Haley sat on top of me and pressed her hips into mine until I couldn't wait to have her any longer. I braced my hands on her back and flipped her over in one swift motion.

"Cam!" Haley gasped, unprepared for her sudden repositioning.

I dug my face into her neck, inhaling her scent and trying to commit it to memory. Sucking the small spot behind her ear got Haley to moan and the sound of it made me turn almost animalistic. My hands had a mind of their own and were inching closer to the hem of my shirt, begging to get under it. When they found what they were looking for, they pushed their way up and under the oversized shirt. My thumb brushed the tip of one of Haley's hard peaks and she shuttered at the touch.

"Caaam..." she moaned in my ear as I grinned to myself. I took way too much pride in knowing I could make Haley come undone like this. I kept playing with her as I dropped my lips next to her ear.

"Now, Jones, last night was beyond anything I could have ever imagined and beyond anything I have ever experienced. So much so that I'm hungry for more and need you now." Between what my fingers were doing to her breasts and the words that were coming out of my mouth, Haley's breath was starting to become labored. "But, I don't have any kind of protection right now and like I said last night, I'm always about playing fair. Do you know what I mean?"

She nodded her head.

"I'm starving for you already and I need to have you right here, right now." Without wasting another moment, I pulled the shirt off her body and threw it on the ground where her other clothes still sat. I crushed my hands into her breast, kneading them and swiping my thumbs over her hard nipples. Haley gasped and rolled her body in reply. I started to kiss from her neck down to the place right before her middle, only stopping at her breasts to suck on her nipples because I loved how it drove her crazy.

Haley hadn't put her panties back on and I was glad for it. It made getting to taste her again on my tongue that much easier. I made my way down her body and pushed her legs apart. She was already spread open, inviting me in, but I needed more. I wanted to be able to have every bit of her that I could. As I kissed her inner thigh, I felt a tremble of anticipation run up her body.

I continued to kiss her inner thighs and looked up at her as I sank one, then two fingers inside of her. She was propped up on her elbows and watched me as I played with her. When I pressed my fingers inside of her, her head fell backward onto the mattress, fully overtaken by the sensations.

"You...are the sexiest woman I've ever gotten to watch like this," I growled. My cock was hard and throbbing under my joggers. Haley let out another moan as I continued to play with her with my fingers, her pussy getting tighter and tighter. "Watching you like this makes me want you even more than I have you now. Do you want that, Jones? Do you want me to give you more?"

"*Yes,*" she hardly whispered.

"Good, because I can't wait any longer to have you." I pulled my fingers back and finally pressed my mouth to her, feeling a wash of relief and desire rush over me. My now free hands reached toward my joggers and pulled them down so I could release my dick from inside of them. As I tasted Haley again for the second time in twelve hours, I pumped my cock back and forth, giving it what it was begging for. It didn't take long before Haley was starting to pulsate under my tongue and as she did, I could feel myself coming hard and fast right along with her.

"Oh my god, Cam," her shaky voice begged, "please... please don't stop." I shook my head from between her legs and kept circling her clit with my tongue. My cock was right there with her, getting harder and ready to finish as soon as she did. I could tell she was close, so I used my free hand to slip two fingers inside of her as I continued to use my tongue on her.

"Oh...my...yes!" Haley shouted and convulsed as I brought her over the edge and when she did, I finished myself off in my hand. As she lay there, breathing heavily and coming back down, I could hear the seagulls outside starting to wake up for the day. Haley must have heard them too because she laughed and looked toward the window. Still on my knees, I watched her take in the morning until she turned her head again toward me.

"You know...I'm still hungry." Her fingers teased through my hair and I leaned into her hand as they did. Climbing back up on top of her, I nuzzled my face into her neck and kissed it lightly while smiling.

"Then let's go get you food." As I went to move off her, Haley quickly wrapped her arms around my neck and her legs around my waist, just like she had last night. I froze and looked down at her. She looked at me with deep longing and intention, and I could see what seemed like a hundred thoughts running around behind her eyes.

"You okay, Jones?"

"Yeah...I just want to be here, with you, like this, for another minute." She took a deep breath like she does frequently now and chewed on her bottom lip. "We can go."

Before moving, I leaned down over her one last time and planted a firm kiss on her forehead and I felt her relax. It felt like she had more she wanted to say, but she had kept it to herself. I won't push her, I thought to myself. She had the right to keep things to herself and I was going to be there for her whenever she was ready to share them.

I made her a promise last night and I was determined to keep it.

30

HALEY | NOW

Cam and I took some time to get cleaned up before getting dressed and heading down to the lobby to walk to Coastal Brews. Cam asked if I wanted to shower before he did, but I told him I was okay and cleaned up quickly before slipping my dress back on.

Part of me wanted to climb into the steaming shower with him, but my stomach was eating itself and a caffeine headache was starting to set in, so I opted against it. When he came out of the bathroom wearing only a towel wrapped around his toned waist, I regretted my decision. Once he was dressed, wearing dark gray joggers, a tee shirt, a backward baseball hat, and a sweatshirt on top, we headed toward food.

Thank god.

As we walked down the street, our hands brushed against one another's and I could tell that Cam wanted to hold my hand.

He's trying to be respectful, I thought to myself.

Then what the fuck was last night? Another voice in my head said. And this morning?

Me being me, I decided to make him squirm.

"Cam?"

"Yeah?

"You can hold my hand, ya know."

"I wasn't sure..."

I looked at him with a smirk and he rubbed the back of his neck. He was so cute when he was unsure. But I wasn't done making him uncomfortable yet.

"Cam, you saw me naked last night and had your head between my legs not even an hour ago. The *least* you can do is hold my hand."

"Oh my god, Jones. FINE." Cam swung his arm and took my hand into his.

"There, was that so hard?"

"*You are impossible, woman...*" he grumbled, looking away from me, still holding my hand.

"What was that?" I couldn't hide my smile and I looped both of my hands around his arm that was closest to me and pulled him in. He turned and looked down at me, exasperated.

"I *said*, you're impossible, woman!" He planted a kiss on my forehead before smirking.

"I'm not impossible, I'm just hungry. Now hurry up." He rolled his eyes at me as I picked up my pace, nearly pulling him down the street toward Coastal Brews.

When we walked in, the place was packed. Cam asked me what I wanted to order and told me to grab any table I could find, breakfast was on him.

Feeling butterflies in my stomach, I gave him my order and made sure he knew it was a caramel, iced macchiato with almond milk. I even had him repeat the order back to me to be sure he got it right. He gave me a knowing look but played along. He already knew my order because it hadn't changed since we were in high school.

Out the window, I could see an open table under an umbrella and quickly moved through the crowded coffee shop to snag it. While it was still technically winter, it was nice enough to sit outside, even if I was a little chilly in just my dress. As I waited for Cam to come out, the people of town started to fill the streets. Parents with their kids, people walking their dogs, and elderly couples walking hand in hand toward the boardwalk.

As I watched one elderly couple, the older man bumped hips with his wife and then pulled her in for a kiss. A pang of sadness stabbed at my heart as I thought about Connor and how that would never be us. As I was sinking into my grief, a voice came from behind me that warmed me instantly.

"Mhmph, that's nice." I turned up to see Cam watching the same couple I was, a look of longingness on his face. My mind wondered if he was hoping to have that someday just like I was.

"Yeah...it is nice." He took a seat across from me and set my coffee down in front of me. I took a long, drawn-out sip from it and felt the relief of morning coffee slowly bringing me to life. Piper always gave me a hard time about my incessant need for coffee, and Deborah always suggested that it was probably making my anxiety worse, but I happily ignored them both. Nothing would stand in the way of me and coffee.

Nothing.

"So, what are you up to today?" Cam asked, holding his black coffee with both hands.

"I don't know how you drink that." I scrunched my nose as I looked at his cup.

"That wasn't an answer to my question at all, but okay," he quipped.

"No, it wasn't, but still...I don't know how you drink your coffee like that!" I laughed.

"Why are you judging my coffee preferences?! What did black coffee ever do to you?" Cam made a face at me.

"Nothing...it did nothing to me. It's gross though, I just need you to know that."

"Some could say the same about the sugary milk you're drinking, Jones." His finger pointed to my cup with his eyebrows raised. I rolled my eyes at him and thought about the day.

"Well, it's Sunday, and Piper and I have virtually no food at the house so we will need to go grocery shopping at some point. I *really* need to shower and then, I don't know what else. I try not to work on the weekends even though with the conference so close, I might crack open my computer later and do a little work." As I talked about the conference, a million things that still needed to be done came to my mind. Roughly seven weeks stood between now and the first week of April, which was when the conference was being held back in Wilmington. While Piper and I had gotten a lot of the planning done, there was always more to do.

"Hmm...so you probably *can't* come back to my room tonight and let me taste you one more time? I would love to sink myself deep inside of you again if you'd let me." Cam leaned in as he said it, a coy smile on his lips.

"Cam!" I gasped and looked around the packed picnic area we were sharing with the locals and felt my face flush. "You cannot say those things here!"

"Come on, Jones. Come back to my room tonight. Let me have my way with you." He kept his eyes on me, the desire in them clear as day. I groaned, knowing that I couldn't do what he asked or what my body was now longing for too.

"I want to, Cam, but I can't. Piper and I heavy load our Mondays with things like meetings and calls. We try to get an early start to the day so we don't work too late. I would hate to have to get you up early if you don't have to. Plus, I already know Piper is going to be on me for last night anyway. I don't think I could take back-to-back interrogations from her."

"What is she going to be on you about? It's not like you did anything wrong. We're two consenting adults enjoying one another's company. That's all." As he finished talking, a server brought us our breakfast. I took a big bite of my breakfast sandwich before speaking again.

"Yes, but Piper knows you and our history and will just want to make sure I'm okay. Plus, she's going to want a play-by-play because she's living vicariously through all of this right now," I spoke with my mouth full.

Cam was watching me eat and smiling.

"*Are* you okay?" His voice was filled with genuine concern. I knew why he was asking the question. We hadn't spoken to one another since the morning after the dorm room incident when he left without saying goodbye. That was, not until I ran into him almost seven months ago at that coffee shop in Charlotte. Now we had slept together and were sharing a table at breakfast.

Was I okay or was I losing my mind?

"Can I be honest with you?" I asked, setting down my sandwich and looking at Cam.

"Of course you can, Haley. I always want you to be honest with me." My heart fluttered at the sound of his voice saying my name. It wasn't often that he said it, so when he did, my heart couldn't take it.

I took a deep breath and reminded myself that I could tell Cam anything. I did when we were growing up, and I wanted to believe I could now, too. His arms were crossed in front of his chest and he was leaning on his elbows on top of the table. A late winter breeze blew through the courtyard we were sitting in and I shivered as it ran across my back. The backless dress was a good idea yesterday when the sun was fully up and it was warm, but right now I was having second thoughts about it.

"Oh, here take this!" Realizing I was cold, Cam tore off his sweatshirt and stood up to hand it to me. Gingerly taking it from his hand, I held it over my lap for a second as if I had just been given a million-dollar check. Then, I pulled it over my head and I could still feel Cam's body heat inside of it. And it smelled like him.

Note to self: never wash this. Ever.

After pulling it down over my torso and pulling my hair through so it was behind my shoulders, I brought my eyes back to Cam who was looking at me with a grin.

"What are you looking at?" I questioned, tilting my head to one side.

"Just you, beautiful." I could feel the heat in my cheeks again and took a quick bite of my sandwich.

"You were saying something before..." Cam probed, trying to bring us back to what we were talking about.

"Yeah, right. You asked if I was okay and honestly, I am... but I'm also apprehensive."

He leaned back in his chair and his eyes glanced down toward the ground.

"I just, we have so much between us, Cam. And I wanted this—us to be together—for a *long time* when we were younger. And you knew it. Fuck, our *moms* knew it. But there was always something that had you running away. And after that night in my dorm room, I just couldn't continue being the one you didn't choose." My voice trailed off at the end and I braced myself for Cam to get up and leave, just like he had done in the past. I had my eyes on my plate as if my food was going to get up and run off when Cam finally spoke.

"Haley..." His voice was soft and my eyes flicked up to see he was back leaning on the table, his arm was reaching toward me, palm side up, asking me to take it. I paused and chewed my lip for a moment, considering, and then placed my hand in his. "I'm sorry for how I treated you then. It was wrong and stupid. I was stupid. But I made you a promise last night and I told you before, I'm not going anywhere. I will be here to prove that to you, for as long as it takes." Cam's green eyes swirled with what looked like hope and conviction.

I wanted to believe him. My heart wanted to believe him. But I'm a girl who has never ended up with a man who loved her enough to stick around for good. Even when I thought I'd found my forever, he left me too. Even if it wasn't his fault or something he could control.

Looking at Cam now, his eyes told me I could trust him. But something in my core told me I needed to play it safe and not let him in too quickly.

Because the last time I had, he was gone the next day without even saying goodbye.

31

HALEY | THEN

The sound of a slamming door in the hallway woke me up and I reached across my bed where I expected to find Cam sleeping next to me.

My brain was still fuzzy from the booze I'd had at the party, but I *knew* that what we had done and what he had promised me in the darkness wasn't just a drunken dream. As my arm searched for him, it only found a large empty hole where I remembered he had been last night when I fell asleep. My eyes burst open and I sat up quickly in my twin-size bed, searching the room for him. Looking to my left, the bed was, empty and void of any piece of him.

I glanced around the room, spotting Piper still asleep in her bed with the sheets pulled up and all the lights still off. I squinted in the darkness to see if I could find Cam's jacket, shoes, or backpack. I rubbed my head because the hangover was already starting to make my brain spin. As I looked around the room, it was as if he was never here. His shoes were gone from their spot at the end of the bed where he'd kicked them off last night and his jacket and backpack were missing too.

My toes hit the cold tile floor of my room and I reached for my desk, which sat next to my bed, to balance myself. My insides churned uneasily, both due to the alcohol sloshing in my stomach and because the small fears I felt last night were coming true. When my hand hit the edge of my desk, a piece of paper crinkled under it.

My eyebrows furrowed together as I pulled the small paper to my face so I could read it. I had to hold it unusually close because I was blind as a bat without my contacts, and my brain wasn't functioning enough to tell me to find my glasses. It was a post-it note from my desk, I discovered as I held it at the tip of my nose, and it had two words scribbled on it.

I'm sorry.

Recognizing Cam's handwriting, my heart sank into my chest as it pictured him climbing over me quietly, reaching into my desk to find something to write on, and then sneaking out without even saying goodbye.

I'm sorry?!

I couldn't believe it.

I didn't want to believe it.

My hands scrambled through my bed searching for my phone when I remembered I'd left it in my purse after coming home with Cam. Frantically, I grabbed it off the back of my chair and dumped the contents of it onto my bed, snatching my phone up as it tumbled out. I pressed the lock button a few times, trying to get it to light up and turn on, but it didn't.

Cursing under my breath, I reached for my phone charger that hung from the side of my desk and cradled my phone in my hands. My head was swirling with a million thoughts and I tried to take a few deep breaths.

Maybe he didn't leave. Maybe he went to go get coffee. Maybe he meant what he said last night and just had to get back to campus or something. We would still be able to spend winter break together and New Year's Eve like he promised. He didn't run out on me, he couldn't have. He made me a promise that we would be together.

He promised.

My phone finally illuminated in the dark room, the battery level showing me a measly 2% charge. I swiped my thumb across the screen and punched in my passcode, failing twice because I was going too quickly. My heart was racing and my brain was trying to keep up with the mixture of fear, abandonment, and anger that were rising inside my belly along with a heavy side of nausea.

I clicked on the messages app to see if he had sent me anything, but he hadn't. I also didn't have any missed calls or voicemails from him either. My hand came to my mouth to muffle the sounds of the panicked breath that was escaping me. I went to my address book, typed in his name, and called him.

No answer.

I called him again.

No answer.

I glanced at the clock and did the math. There was a four-hour drive between Cam's school and mine, and it was a little after eight. He would have had to have left before 4 AM to be back home now, which I couldn't believe he would do. Cam was an early riser, but not that early.

I decided to call him for a third time and got his voice-mail yet again. I left him a voicemail and calmly asked him to call me back as soon as he could. I also sent him a text message.

> Cam, where did you go? Why did you leave? You promised…

I considered what I was about to type and hit the backspace before sending my final text.

> Cam, where did you go? Why did you leave? Please call me when you get the chance.

————

> Cam, it's me. Please. You haven't texted or called me back and it's been like six hours. I just want to make sure you're okay and not dead alongside the road somewhere lol

> Please just call or text me when you can.

————

> Clearly you're back on campus, I saw you on Harvey's Snapchat. The least you could do is tell me that you made it back but whatever. I'm glad you're okay.

————

> Hello? Earth to Cam? It's been days and I'm starting to think I have the plague or something that you're trying to avoid lol

> Text me back, I wanna talk.

————

Cam what the fuck?! It's been a week and I have been trying to call you or at least get you to text me back but I don't wanna be a psycho either. PLEASE, can we talk? I'm not mad, just confused. Please.

————

Congrats on the big game win! I saw you catch the winning pass! I hope you go and have fun tonight but don't have too much fun.

I'm really proud of you Johnson.

————

Hey Johnson. I just got out of my public speaking class and it made me think of that presentation we had to do back in sophomore year for our final and you got so nervous you almost barfed in front of the whole class! HAHAHAHAH It made me smile thinking about it.

Anyway, I hope you're good and school is good.

————

Cam.

It's been over a month since you came to visit me and you still haven't texted or called me back. Don't worry, I've gotten the message. But I want you to get the message too.

I can't do this anymore. I can't be the girl who is always waiting for you on the sidelines just hoping you will choose her. I can't continue to be your second choice. I've done it for literally *years* and I can't do it anymore. I've sat back, watched you date other girls, kiss other girls, and even help you get other girls' numbers, all while pretending it didn't bother me.

But it did. It always did.

Because I wanted it to be me and not them.

Then you showed up at my door, unannounced, and I just let you take my heart right out of my chest. You protected me that night from that lame ass at the party. You held me that night in my bed as I fell asleep. We…did things together that I had only ever dreamed I'd get to do with you. That meant something to me, Cam. It means so much to me. And I thought it meant something to you too but clearly not.

I want you…no, I need you to leave me alone. I'm done. Please don't text me anymore or call me, but that shouldn't be too hard seeing as how you've been avoiding me for weeks now. I need to move on and stop holding onto something that is clearly never going to happen.

Goodbye Cam.

Oh, and one more thing.

> Don't think for a second that I was asleep when you said what you said. I might have had my eyes closed, but I heard you say that you loved me that night.

> And I think that's what hurts the most.

> Because I love you too, Cam.

———

> Haley, wait…

I DIDN'T READ the rest of the message before deleting it.

Camden Johnson wouldn't have the last word and I wouldn't cry over him anymore.

Not until after tonight at least.

32

HALEY | NOW

Once Cam and I had finished eating, he walked me back to the bungalow, holding my hand as we went. I chewed my lip as we walked, thinking about what he had said last night and again at the table this morning.

That he wasn't going anywhere and that I could trust him.

I wanted to trust him. But I had trusted him so many times before and then he would break that trust. We would get close, talk about being together, and then suddenly he would ice me out and bolt in the opposite direction.

The last time he and I were as close as we were last night was our freshman year in college. But after the heartbreak he put me through, I swore I would never go down this road again.

Yet here I was, on the same road.

Again.

You're going to get hurt, you stupid girl, the voice inside my head said. *You're a horrible wife to Connor, how dare you betray him like that? You never deserved him in the first place. No one will love you enough to stay, not even Cam. You can't trust him, remember?*

I pushed the voice out of my head and tried to focus on how good Cam's hand felt in mine. It was strong and callused from throwing a football a hundred times a day. The way it caged itself around mine made me feel safe. I couldn't help but feel like it fit perfectly into mine.

When we reached the old oak door of the bungalow, Cam squeezed my hand and kissed me on the cheek.

"Just the cheek?" I raised my eyebrows at him, surprised by the move. He rolled his eyes at me and leaned in, stopping just before his lips reached mine.

"Jones, if I do anything more than just kiss you on the cheek, I won't be able to stop. And I don't think your old lady friend across the street would like to watch me take you right here on the front porch."

My face burned and I bit my lower lip as he kissed my cheek again.

"I'll see ya around, Jones. Thanks for the best date ever." He winked at me before heading down the front walkway. He turned once he hit the gate and turned to wave before walking back down the street. I stood on the front steps for a moment, watching him go until I couldn't see him any longer. My head was spinning and I could feel the stupid grin on my face as my fingers laced in front of me.

That's when I felt the sleeves of Cam's sweatshirt between my hands and I looked down to realize I hadn't given it back to him. I almost ran down the street after him, but after sinking my nose into the collar and taking in his scent, I decided against it.

Realizing I'd been standing on the porch for an unreasonably long time now, I turned and pushed the front door open, still smelling the collar of my new sweatshirt.

As soon as I stepped inside I could feel her eyes on me from the kitchen. My eyes slowly moved from the floor up toward the bar to find Piper sitting on a barstool, one leg crossed over the other, with her hands crossed on her knee.

She had a welcoming smile on her face and anyone who didn't know this smile would think they were safe. In reality, this was Piper's way of luring you into a false sense of security. Making you think you were safe before she tore you open with a million questions.

"Hi, Piper..." My voice came out slow and I braced myself for her attack.

"Sup, slut." Her nice smile slowly turned into a shit-eating grin as my mouth fell open.

"How do you know we even did anything?!" I shouted at her, kicking off my shoes and walking toward the coffee pot. I was going to need another cup of coffee to get through her cross-examination.

"Well, let's look at the facts." *Oh boy, here we go, she has facts.* "One, you're coming home *the next morning* after going on a date with him. Two, you're wearing his sweatshirt and are practically chewing on it like a starving animal. And three, your dress is on inside out." My eyes flashed down toward the hem of my dress and sure enough, there was the tag on the outside, all the inner seams exposed to the world.

"Shit, that means it was like that at breakfast this morning." My hand palmed my face and I was suddenly hoping no one at Coastal Brews noticed. Piper burst into a fit of laughter and I thought for a second she might fall off the barstool.

"You went to breakfast looking like that?! Do you want the entire town to know you and Camden fucked last night?!"

"It's not like we know these people! They're total

strangers to us!" I was mostly trying to convince myself that I would be fine if the old ladies around town started to whisper about me.

"Oh, Hays, you crack me up. So, how was it?" Piper swung herself back around on her stool and straightened herself again, facing me. Resting both elbows on the counter, she looked at me with anticipation, like a small child waiting for someone to tell them a story.

"The date was nice. Food was good. Service was good. We should go sometime." I set the coffee mug down in front of me and stirred in some creamer, completely avoiding Piper's gaze and the real question she was asking me.

"That's nice, sweetie, I'm so glad you had a nice date. Now tell me what I really want to know."

"What do you really wanna know?"

"His *dick*, Haley. Tell me about his dick. Was it good? Bad? Too big? Give me all the gory details and *don't* leave anything out." She wiggled her eyebrows at me and grinned ear to ear.

My lips pursed at her bluntness but I couldn't really be mad. This exact personality trait is part of the reason I loved Piper so much. She never beat around the bush and she always kept things straight with you.

I shooed my hand at her and took a sip of my coffee, reliving last night and this morning in my head. I sucked my lips under my teeth and squeezed my eyes shut, then started to smile and laugh. When I opened my eyes again, I finally met Piper's gaze.

"Oh my god! IT WAS GOOD! AHHHH!" She started to squeal and clap her hands. We sat there squealing and jumping around together, laughing as we did. It was totally ridiculous to be acting like this at thirty-two, but I was living for it.

"Okay, okay. For real"—Piper took a deep breath and held both hands out in front of her, palms down, trying to get serious again—"I need more than just giggles and stupid smiles. *Tell me everything.*"

I took a seat next to her at the counter and gave her every juicy detail from dinner to our after dinner dessert. She nearly fell out of her stool again when I told her about how Cam wanted 'to keep things fair' and squealed again when I gave her the play-by-play of Cam's pre-breakfast feast.

By the time I was done, her eyes were wide and her mouth hung open.

"Holy fucking shit, so it was like, *really* good," she gushed.

"Holy fucking shit, it was like, *really* good," I repeated back, looking into my coffee mug with a smug smile.

She was nodding her head at me when she spoke again. "And he didn't get upset that you brought up Connor? Not even when he just had his dick inside of you?"

"Could you not say it like that please?" I rolled my eyes at her. I loved Piper but sometimes her frankness was just a little bit too much. "No, he wasn't. He was actually really sweet about it and told me that if I ever wanted to talk to him about Connor, I could. I don't think I will but still, it's nice to know that the door is open."

"Yeah that is really sweet of him," she paused for a moment, "So, now what?"

I inhaled, bringing my shoulders to my ears, and on the exhale dropped them heavily down my back.

"I don't know. We didn't talk about dating or being together or anything. Shit, I don't think I'm ready to be in another relationship officially yet. Part of me is still trying to even believe it's okay to be with Cam like this so close to losing Connor. And..." I trailed off, not sure if I wanted to vocalize the last bit of my thought out loud.

"And you're worried you can't fully trust him after everything you guys have been through before," Piper finished, knowing full well about the crap Cam and I have been through.

"Yeah..." I worried my bottom lip, thinking about all the times Cam had let me down in the past.

Like in middle school, when I told him I had a crush on him and he laughed and told me to stop being stupid. Then, during our sophomore year, I swear he looked at me differently, like more than a guy looks at his friend who is a girl, just to show up a few weeks later dating an older girl. Even senior year, after the last home game of the season, Cam had won the game for our school and he ran into the stands and kissed me on the cheek in front of the entire student section.

Then there was that night in my dorm room. The one where he promised to be there for me and whispered in my ear that he loved me, just to vanish the next day and not text me back for over a month. After I deleted his text message, I never heard from him again and I never reached out to him either. I had clicked send on my texts and made a vow to myself to move on.

The next year I met Connor, and the rest is history.

"Do you want my opinion on the situation?" Piper's voice broke me out of my memories and brought me back to the present.

"Isn't it your duty as my best friend to give me your opinion whether I want to hear it or not?"

"Oh my god, I'm so glad you agree!" She rolled her eyes and flicked her hand at me. "Here's what I think. I think you need to give him a chance. You've been hurting for so long and I haven't seen you as happy as you were when you walked through that front door an hour ago in months. You don't need to be official to have fun with the man, so just have fun. Keep your heart protected but try to believe that what he is saying is true. He's given you reason not to trust him in the past, but men are idiots, especially when they're only boys. But if we always closed them out, we would never have any orgasms or things to gossip about, now would we?"

I laughed at Piper because I knew she was right. Cam had told me, multiple times now, that he was here to stay and that he wasn't going anywhere. Maybe this was our chance to start over, start fresh, and let this new beginning be the start of us. I didn't have to date him in order to just have fun with him, right? That's what this could be, just some fun while Piper and I are here planning the conference.

As my mind started to replay last night and this morning, the space between my legs started to tingle.

I guess I was already ready for some more fun.

33

CAM | NOW

When I dropped Haley off at home on Sunday morning, I didn't realize it would be several days before I saw her again. I also didn't think that I would miss her this much so quickly. We'd been apart for over ten years, and I never really missed her then.

Okay I did, but not like I do now.

Now, I crave her like a starving man craves a Big Mac. My body ached for her touch every hour I didn't get to be with her. And my dick? Well, it was aching no matter how many times I got myself off in my hotel room replaying our time together last weekend.

She'd texted me a few times each day, telling me how busy she was with work and she would try to sneak away, but something always prevented her from coming over. She apologized over text multiple times and I told her I understood and not to worry. She was busy, I could respect that.

The sensible side of me could at least. The caveman side of me who wanted nothing more than to throw her over my shoulder and drag her back to my hotel bed could not.

By the time Wednesday rolled around, I was going crazy

having not seen her, so I decided to surprise her in the morning with coffee from Coastal Brews.

I got up early, showered, and started toward Coastal Brews so I could get it to her before I knew she would be making some at home. It was early February, and the sun was starting to come up a little earlier each morning. While it wasn't warm by any means, it was nice to see the sun before noon and feel it on your skin. The people who lived in town were also starting to come out earlier, and many of them waved to me as I walked by their front porches and picket fences.

Knowing I was going to be staying here longer than just a few weeks, I made a deal with the hotel that they could charge me weekly for my room until I told them otherwise. The other thing I did this week while trying to distract myself from missing Haley—and being horny as fuck—was get a gym membership. The gym here was nothing like the training center, but it would do for the time being. Plus, it was helping me work off some excess energy that was building up.

When I got to Coastal Brews, I waited until it was my turn to order and got myself a black coffee, Haley an iced caramel macchiato with almond milk, and Piper a vanilla latte. I also grabbed a few pastries from the case just in case the girls needed breakfast.

I had to finagle a carrying system for everything I had ordered but managed to make it to the bungalow without any issues. Standing at the door, I grabbed the bag of pastries with my teeth, held the drink carrier in one hand, and pressed the doorbell with the other. I waited for a moment before I heard footsteps on the other side of the door. It swung open quickly and on the other side of it stood a very surprised looking

Haley. *How does she look this pretty so early in the morning?*

"Cam? What are you doing—oh my god, let me help you with that!" She grabbed the paper bag out of my mouth and waved me inside. The back side of the bungalow faced the water and the entire wall was made of oversized windows. The view of the ocean was so amazing it almost took my breath away.

"Cam, what are you doing here? I was on the back porch sitting on the swing when I heard the doorbell and was so confused. It's not even 8 AM!"

I placed the coffee on the counter and walked toward Haley, who was standing on the inside of it, closer to the kitchen. I couldn't help myself and looped my arm around her waist, pulling her closer to me. She was wearing tiny pajama shorts that showed the bottom of her ass and my sweatshirt from our date last weekend. The sight of her made my knees weak.

I would get on my knees for this woman if she asked me to.

Putting my nose close to hers I whispered, "I missed you, Jones. I thought a coffee bribe would finally get you to say yes to seeing me again." A small smile crept across her lips and she didn't pull away from me.

"You know I'm a sucker for iced coffee," she whispered back.

The sound of her morning voice is what broke my self-control completely and suddenly I was pressing my lips to hers right there in the kitchen. She wrapped her arms around my neck and looped her fingers through my hair. With my hands on her waist, I pressed her against the countertop and dug my hips into hers. She reacted to the feeling of my hard-on with a low groan in the back of her throat.

Clearly, she missed me too.

As we stood at the counter consuming one another, I heard the faint sound of a door opening down the hall and feet padding across the floor.

"Holy shit, do I smell coffee?" Piper came walking out of her bedroom, rubbing her eyes, still in her pajamas. When we heard her voice, Haley and I jumped apart from one another and I turned away, pushing my erection down as if that would do anything to get it to go away.

"Oh! Well hello there, Camden. Are you here to get in our Haley's pants so early in the morning?" A devilish look was on Piper's face as she said it.

"Piper, knock it off. He brought us coffee." Exasperated, Haley held up their coffee cups and shook them.

"And was your payment for said coffee shoving your tongue down his throat? And why does Camden look like a fifteen-year-old boy trying to cover up his dick? Camden"— she turned, talking to me now—"I agree with you that Haley is smokin' hot, but I've seen a man with an erection before. You don't need to be embarrassed."

"Oh my god, shut up and drink your coffee or I'm dumping it down the drain!" Haley shoved the latte into Piper's hand. With my erection finally under control, I turned around and started unpacking the pastry bag.

"Ohh, not only does he bring coffee, he brings food too. Whatta guy," Piper swooned, taking a seat at the bar.

"Only for you, Piper." I winked at her, playing into her game.

"You're both annoying and I hate you." Haley looked between us and took a swig of her coffee. I moved from standing beside her to behind her and looped my arms around her waist again.

Bringing my lips down and speaking softly into her ear I

hummed, "Don't worry, Jones, there are things that I will save to do *just* for you."

Her eyes got wide and her cheeks flushed instantly. Piper stared at us uncomfortably for a beat before making a gagging sound and pretended to throw up on the floor.

"And that's my cue to leave." With one finger in the air and holding her latte, Piper bolted out of the kitchen and went back to her room, closing the door loudly behind her.

Haley started laughing and feeling her happiness under me made my insides flip. She felt so good standing in front of me like this. My eyes flickered down the back of her neck and I couldn't stop myself from nuzzling my nose into it, taking in her intoxicating scent.

Welcoming me in, Haley took a deep breath and pressed herself against me. We stayed like this, me standing behind her with my arms wrapped around her waist and her pressing back into me, stroking my arms, for what felt like a lifetime.

"This was really nice of you. Thank you for bringing us coffee. It was also nice of you to bring Piper something too, even though her behavior this morning did not earn her such a treat."

"Jones, she's your best friend. I need to get in her good graces and if coffee is the price of admission, I'm more than happy to pay it. Plus, part of me truly believes she could kill me and get away with it, so I'm just trying to keep her happy."

Haley spun around in my arms and was now leaning against the counter, palms propping her up, my arms still caged around her.

"The person you should really be afraid of is *me*." She was cute when she was trying to be intimidating.

"You? You think I need to be afraid of you? You really

think you're so scary, Jones?" I teased. "Here's what I think about how scary you are!" Without warning, I pulled her in by her hips and dug my teeth playfully into her neck, pretending to be a monster who was eating her, sound effects included all while tickling her sides. She burst into a fit of giggles and squeals, trying to push herself away from me, but I was too strong and held her close.

"Cam! Cam! Okay, okay!" She laughed. "I'm not scary! You win! Stop!" More laughter. Hearing her beg for mercy brought my dick back to life. "Cam, please! I beg you! Stop!"

"You have three seconds to get away from me, pretty girl, and then you're mine!" I said in my most menacing voice. She squealed again and took off as I let her go and I counted, "One! Two! Three!" at lightning speed.

From across the living room, she yelled, "Hey, no fair! That wasn't a full three seconds!" But I was already closing the distance between us again.

Haley tried to leap up and over the couch, but I reached for her in time with my arm and pulled her down with one hand. Turns out my football skills had a use off the field too. Both laughing hysterically, we collapsed together on the couch and I pulled Haley onto my lap. I touched my forehead to hers and soaked in everything that she was.

Funny, smart, and everything I have ever wanted in a woman.

And I'm totally in love with her.

"Ohmygosh", she said in one breath. "I haven't laughed that hard in SO long." Her head fell backward as she tried to catch her breath.

"I'm glad I can be the one to make you laugh."

"I'm glad you are too. I'm glad you came over this morning. I missed you." Her hazel eyes were on mine as her breath started to slow. She had her arms wrapped around my neck and her legs draped over my lap.

"I missed you too." I leaned in and kissed her on the forehead and then on the lips once more. We were starting to lean into each other more when Haley pressed her hands against my chest and broke away.

"Cam, it's not that I don't want to do this, I do. But Piper and I are super packed this week planning for the conference, and I already know the first few hours will be spent having Piper grill me for your surprise appearance this morning."

"What's wrong with me coming here? Am I not allowed to?" Part of me started to worry I had crossed a line I didn't know about.

"No, you are! It's just that with you, Piper wants to ask me a bazillion questions and interrogate me on what's going on when I don't really know what's going on. I'm just having fun and letting things go how they go."

"Mmm, I can show you fun." I went to kiss her again but she pulled away before I could reach her.

"Cam, for real." Her eyes locked on mine and turned serious, "What is going on with us? What are we?"

I knew what she was asking, but I didn't know what answer she wanted. Did she want me to call myself her boyfriend? Are we just friends with benefits? I know that I want the former, but maybe she wants the latter?

"What's going on..." I started, pulling her up and onto my lap entirely now, helping her move so her legs were straddling my lap. She rested her hands on my chest as I looked up from here where I sat. "Is that I would like to take you on another date on Friday. And again on Saturday, if you'll let me. How does that sound?"

"That sounds nice."

"Good, then it's a date. It's two dates." I kissed her and pushed a loose piece of hair back where it belonged behind her ear. She then stood up from my lap and held out a hand, helping me stand up too.

We walked back toward the front door after stopping by the kitchen to get my coffee and phone from the counter. She opened the front door and we lingered there, looking at each other.

"You're sure I have to go?" I begged, giving her my best, charming smile.

She groaned and dropped her head back slightly.

"I don't want you to, but you're too much of a distraction and we have less than seven weeks before the conference. I need to be focused and I really need Piper to be focused. She's only as good as her environment, and if you're here, nothing will get done. I'll text you tonight, I promise."

Without meaning to, I reached for her face and took it in the palm of my hand. Almost instinctively, she rubbed her cheek against it and smiled up at me.

"I get it, you're the big boss doing big boss things. Honestly, it's a huge fucking turn-on."

"Ohh, you like it when I'm the boss, huh?" she teased, a coy grin on her face.

"*Yes.* Very much so."

She took a step closer to me, closing the space between us until her tits grazed my chest.

"I'll remember that for this weekend then." Her voice came out low and gravely. My erection was back in an instant.

"Geezus fuck, Jones." I exhaled at her tone, instantly turned on and warm all over. "I'm gonna go before I take you right here in the front door. I don't think Piper would appreciate us doing it out in the open like that."

Haley was laughing again. "No, I don't think she would. Goodbye, Cam." She playfully pushed me out of the house but before she closed the door, I stole one more kiss from her.

"Goodbye, beautiful."

I WAS LYING in bed when my phone buzzed from my nightstand. I paused the game I was watching to pick it up.

I couldn't help but smile reading her name.

Hey Johnson, you still up?

I glanced at the clock and noticed it was eleven.

Are you just getting done with work?

No! God no, Piper and I got done a few hours ago. I'm just having a hard time falling asleep.

Is something wrong? Do I need to come over?

My severe need to protect her kicked in without warning.

No..that's nice of you to offer though :)

I'm just…restless I guess. I had therapy today and I guess it's just sitting weird in my head…

I was proud of Haley for going to therapy, but every time she brought it up, I wasn't sure how to talk about it. I wanted her to know I supported her in going, but didn't want to push her to talk if she didn't want to.

Do you wanna talk about it? Or talk about something else?

Mmm..I wanna talk about something else.

Okay..what do you want to talk about then?

How about what I'm hoping we do after our date on Friday?

Well, I wasn't hard before but now…

I will happily talk to you about that. What are you hoping for?

I could name a few things…

She was playing coy.
If she was going to be like this, I would too.
I texted her back.

Why don't you then?

I imagined her curled up in bed, under the covers, hopefully wearing nothing, while picturing all the things I did to her last weekend.

What she didn't know was that I was ready to give her all of that and more this weekend when I finally had her alone again.

My phone buzzed in my hand and I quickly swiped my thumb across the screen to unlock it.

> Well first I want to go out somewhere with really good food and a good wine menu. I plan on wearing an evil dress that turns you on just at the sight of me.

> Then after we eat, I want to go back to your hotel room and I want you to have me for dessert. Ever since last weekend, my body has been craving to have you on it again. To feel your fingers on my skin…to have you between my legs.

> God I'm soaked just thinking about it.

Without even realizing it, my hand had slid under my shorts and I was jerking myself off as I read her text.

> But you know what I *really* wanna do this weekend Johnson? I wanna get on my knees for you and take you in my mouth. I wanna see how hard I can get you, how close I can take you to the edge. I want to hear you scream my name for once.

Before taking myself too far, I texted her back quickly.

> Holy fuck Jones, you have me there already.

> Show me.

She sent back quickly and my eyes went wide at her text.

Was Haley Jones asking me for a dick pic? I didn't think women liked those.

Not wanting to deny her request, I leaned over and flipped on the bedside lamp and without showing too much, I snapped a picture of my hand down my shorts and sent it back.

> If I wasn't turned on before I am now...

She texted back after a moment.

> Show me.

I sent, throwing her demand back at her.

Within a moment, I got a very similar text back, but instead of a photo, it was a video. It was dark, but you could see what was happening.

Haley, stripped down with nothing but a pair of red lace panties with her hand slipped under them, playing with herself. You couldn't see her face; all you could see was her waist down.

That's all I needed to see to fully lose control.

> Holy shit Haley, that is so hot.

> Just thinking about you gets me hot.

> Are you still thinking about what you want me to do to you this weekend?

I watched the three bubbles on my screen dance as she typed back while I continued to stroke myself long and hard. My dick getting harder with each pump.

Yes..and I'm getting really close to coming.

Thinking about her getting herself off, fucking herself, and burying her fingers deep inside her pussy drove me fucking crazy.

Do it. Play with yourself and make yourself come. I want you to think about how I will be the one to make you come over and over this weekend. You better be ready Jones because once I take you out and show you off on my arm, you're mine. And I will show you how much you are all night long.

My breathing was starting to become labored and my chest was rising and falling heavily as I typed.

I can't wait until I can slip my fingers inside your tight pussy and play with your perfect tits. I'm starving without getting to taste you, wet and delicious on my mouth. The neighbors will know exactly what's going on too because I'm going to make you scream my name over and over until you have no voice left. Then I'm going to do it all over again the next morning.

When she didn't text me back right away, I figured it was because she was doing what I was doing, which was coming completely undone.

I played the short clip Haley sent me over and over again. She hadn't muted the sound before sending it and when I turned the volume all the way up on my phone, I could hear her breathing heavily in the background. A small, audible groan at the very end. It drove me crazy, that sound. I wanted to listen to it over and over again on a loop.

I could feel the tension in my body growing and it didn't

take me very long to reach my peak, a warm sensation washing over me and my stomach when I did.

I lay there, stunned at how good the orgasm was that I just had without Haley even being here. I'd never sexted before but holy shit, I would do it every night if Haley asked.

After catching my breath, I got up and walked to the bathroom to clean up quickly before coming back to check my phone. I'll shower once I know she's asleep, I told myself.

Sure enough, when I reached my bed again, there was another message on my phone.

> Cam...

> Yes, beautiful?

> That was amazing.

> I couldn't agree more beautiful.

> You can't see me right now but every time you call me that I can't help but smile.

I couldn't see her, but I could picture her, and what I pictured was beautiful.

> I'll call you that every chance I get then if it means I get to see your smile. Because just like you, it's beautiful. And I lov--

I thought about what I was about to text and hesitated. Quickly backspacing, I reread my text and hit send.

> I'll call you that every chance I get then if it means I get to see your smile. Because just like you, it's beautiful.

> You're too sweet Cam.

> I'm not. I actually don't think I'm sweet enough. You deserve all the sweetness, and kindness, and happiness someone can offer you. I hope you'll let me be that person.

I watched the three bubbles dance again on the screen, then disappear. They reappeared after a moment but were gone again. I got the sense that Haley had something she wanted to say but wasn't sure if she should.

Maybe I had gone too far? Finally, a new message popped up at the bottom of our NSFW thread.

> I'm getting there...

While it wasn't a, "I would love for you too, Cam! I love you, please never leave me!" like I had hoped, it wasn't a no either.

I could work with 'getting there.

> I'm here for as long as it takes. I'm not going anywhere Jones, I promised you that and I mean it.

She didn't text me back for a long time and I was starting to think she had fallen asleep when my phone buzzed once more.

> It's getting late and I'm kinda falling asleep. I'll talk to you tomorrow Cam. Thanks for helping me wear myself out a little tonight.

> I'm always here to please ;) I'll talk to you tomorrow beautiful.

When the three dancing dots didn't pop up on my screen, I knew she'd put her phone down for good. Feeling suddenly energized and wide awake, I decided to hop in the shower and clean myself up.

As I stood in the shower, the warm water running down my chest, my mind wandered to Haley and everything she and I had been through.

We'd been friends since the first day of kindergarten when Haley stomped on my foot for calling her small. Smiling at the memory, it dawned on me that I'd never called her small again. Ever. She and I were somehow always in the same classes, shared similar interests, and our mothers had even grown close.

When she came to school that day in ninth grade, wearing that short denim skirt that hugged her hips in all the right places, I was never the same.

I was whipped, intoxicated, and so totally in love with her. But something, *something* inside of me made me question if it was right. To love her like I did. That's why I always did stupid ass things like date other girls and leave without saying goodbye.

Something about loving her felt wrong. Like I was putting her happiness in jeopardy.

What if I loved her and I fucked it up? What if I loved her and it wasn't enough? What if I wasn't enough?

But keeping her at a distance never worked either. All it ever seemed to do was hurt her more.

I knew how much it hurt her when I left that morning after sleeping next to her all night, yet I did it anyway. And when she continued to try to get me to talk to her, I ignored her completely. I thought that if I just kept her as my friend, and kept her at a distance, everything would be fine. She and I could just be friends and be happy with being friends.

But when she texted me all those years ago saying she couldn't do it anymore, I knew I had fucked up. And I knew

I had blown up any kind of relationship we had into a million little pieces when she never texted me back. I couldn't even be mad that she hadn't, because I had just done the very same thing to her. When I saw her update her profile to 'Dating' a year later, I vowed to leave her alone for good. She was happy, finally, and I needed to let her be happy.

What we have now, though—it feels like a second chance. It feels as if the universe is bringing us together again for a reason, and I wasn't going to fuck it up.

I love Haley.

I've loved Haley for almost twenty years and this was my chance to try again. To make it right. And no matter how much time she needed or how much space she asked for, I would give it to her. I will fight for her and show her that I can be the man she needs me to be for her.

That I'm a man of my word and I will do whatever it takes to make her happy.

Because I will.

Forever and always.

34

CAM | THEN

Haley, wait.

Please give me another chance. I'm so sorry for leaving and for not texting you back. I was an idiot and I was scared, but I'm not now…and I want to be with you.

I came to visit you a few weeks ago because I felt this hole in my gut that wouldn't go away. I felt this emptiness in me that I never felt when we were back home and for a while, I thought it was because I was homesick. But after my parents came to visit and I even took a quick trip home, it was still there. That's when I knew it wasn't home I was missing, it was you.

It was your laugh and how your smile shows all your teeth. It was how you punch me in the arm when I'm being stupid and when you do, my whole body starts to tingle. I was missing your freckles and how they splash across your cheeks like stars in the night sky. And your hair, your soft hair that I wish I could run my fingers through right now.

And after that night in your room, I miss your lips and how they feel on mine. I miss feeling your skin brush against me, so soft and warm. I miss how good you smell and how it feels to bury my nose into your neck just so I can inhale every ounce of you. I miss every part of you.

Part of me feels like I'm starving without you.

The last few weeks have sucked because I've wanted to text you, but I couldn't bring myself to do it. I wanted to say all of this to you that night and every day since, but I didn't because I was scared. I've only ever wanted to make you happy, Jones. But part of me worries I won't always be able to make you happy enough and that kills me on the inside. Maybe I was wrong though, maybe I could. I would really like to try if you'll let me?

I love you Haley Jones. I've loved you since we were in the ninth grade and I think I'll love you forever. You've ruined me and made me better all at the same time.

I'm so sorry I hurt you. Please, give me another chance.

I love you. Forever and always.

35

HALEY | NOW

The week went by quickly enough and before I knew it, it was Friday.

As promised, Cam picked me up for our date promptly at 6:30. He had texted me earlier that afternoon and told me to bring a sweater and something I could wear while sitting on the ground. When I tried to ask him why, he told me that questions weren't allowed and that I needed to be patient. I was both annoyed and curious but made sure to follow the directions given to me.

After standing in front of my closet and wishing I'd brought more clothes with me on this trip, I settled on a long, floral maxi skirt with a long-sleeved shirt underneath and a cream, cable-knit sweater to throw on top if I needed to. It was the first half of February and when the sun went down, it got chilly outside. I hoped that by doubling up on my layers, I would be okay if we were sitting outside for an extended period of time.

When Cam rang the doorbell, I could feel a rush of butterflies in my belly. I don't know why I was so nervous. Cam and I had been a part of one another's lives since we were six. Things were different now though, and it felt exciting to feel this way towards another person again.

Towards Cam again.

Piper got to the door before me because I was still slipping on my shoes when he got to the house. I could hear her from down the hall.

"Well, well, well, Haley's suitor is back again. Don't you look handsome?" She spoke with her fakest nice voice. Even though I couldn't see her, I could picture the shit-eating grin I knew she was sporting. I hurried to grab my bag so I could go and rescue Cam.

"Hello to you too, Piper." Cam stepped inside the doorway and sure enough, he did look handsome.

He had shaved recently; I wasn't sure when because I hadn't seen him since he came to the house earlier in the week. With the cleaner cut, his jaw was more defined and somehow he looked even hotter than before. I felt good about my outfit choices since he was wearing dark, loose-fitting jeans, a white long-sleeved shirt, and a pullover that accentuated his strong arms. Not super fancy, but still dressed up enough for a date.

When he saw me walking down the hall, a smile grew on his face and his cheeks touched his eyes. A warm feeling grew in my belly as I got closer to him. Between his smile and his dark emerald eyes, all he had to do was look at me the right way and I was ready to take all my clothes off.

"There she is", Cam said, extending his arm for me to take his hand, which I did. "You look beautiful. You ready to go?"

"I'm ready." I nodded at him, still holding his hand, and started to follow him out the front door. "Bye Piper." I turned and waved to her with my free hand.

"Bye, sweetie, be good tonight...or don't!" She winked at

me as she closed the door. I made a mental note to yell at her for the comment later.

"I'm sorry for her. She has no self-control, I swear."

"Jones, you do not need to apologize for anything. Piper is your best friend, I would expect nothing less from her." He leaned in and kissed me on the side of my head, making my heart do a flip. "Plus, I think she's funny."

"Oh god, *please* don't tell her that. She'll never stop if you do."

When we reached the passenger side door of his car, he wrapped his arms around my waist and pulled me close. The space on my cheek burned with electricity when he leaned down and kissed it. I couldn't help but smile at him.

I loved it when Cam showed me how he felt about me with these small gestures. Physical touch is one of my top love languages, so moves like this caused my heart to swell. Part of me hoped that I would get to have him like this forever.

As soon as I had the thought, though, a small voice in the back of my head said, *"Remember when you wished it was Connor who would be your forever? You're horrible for replacing him so soon. You're a despicable, terrible wife. You don't deserve this kind of love from anyone. You should be ashamed of yourself."*

I shook my head, trying to silence the voice.

Cam looked at me funny. "I'm sorry, do you not want me to do that? I won't if you—"

"No," I cut him off. "I do. I do want you to do it, it's just... it's nothing. I'm sorry." Pushing myself onto my tip toes so I could reach him, I gave him a quick kiss on the cheek before lowering myself into his car. Cam closed the door once I was in and took his place next to me in the driver's seat. He reached across and set his hand on my thigh, and I slipped my fingers under his. It felt nice to have his hand in mine.

"So where are we going?" I asked, still in the dark about our destination.

"You'll see soon." He looked mischievous and almost giddy as he pulled out of the driveway. I didn't know where he was taking me, but knowing Cam, it was somewhere I wouldn't expect.

———

I GASPED as we walked up and I saw where we would be having dinner.

As it turned out, Cam had spent the afternoon setting up a beachside picnic for us at the end of the boardwalk we'd walked down the last time we came to the beach. Knowing how much I hate the sand, Cam offered to walk me to our spot via piggyback, which I gladly accepted. When we reached it, I couldn't believe what I was seeing.

A massive rug had been placed in the sand with small lanterns that were illuminated at each corner of the rug. In the center sat a low-sitting table just big enough for two. Around it were pillows and cushions to sit on and somehow there was music playing even though I couldn't find a speaker. Waiting for us was our food which was still steaming hot and ready to be eaten. A bottle of wine sat chilling in a cooler and two glasses were on the table waiting to be filled. The whole scene, mixed with the ocean in the background, took my breath away.

"Oh my god, Cam." My eyes moved to take in the whole setup as we approached. I turned my head to look at him, but he was already looking back at me.

"You like it?"

"I love it. Thank you!"

He kissed me on the forehead and motioned for me to sit. Lowering myself down, I slipped my feet under the table and set my sweater down beside me. I was glad I brought it out here with me because it was already starting to cool off. I sat with my hands on my cheeks, taking it all in before I started to eat when I heard Cam chuckle.

My eyes went to him. "What are you laughing at?" I asked defensively.

"Nothing, I just think you're cute." I felt my face blush. "Let's eat before it gets cold."

We both started to eat and Cam poured us a glass of wine. As I watched him pour mine, I couldn't believe that this was happening. And what I really couldn't believe was that it was happening with *Cam.* Instead of questioning it too much like I would normally do, I decided to try and live in the moment and enjoy it. The last thing I wanted to do right now was get lost in my thoughts and let it ruin the evening.

As we ate, Cam asked me how things were going with the conference—good, but we still had a lot to do—and I asked him how he felt about the next season—good, but he was hoping for a better final record than last year. I also learned that in the last week, he'd joined a gym and that during the day while I worked, he was either running, working out, or watching old football game replays back in his hotel room.

"I've made great friends with the support staff at the hotel. I know most of their names and they are always happy to bring me whatever I need when I call down," he shared, taking a big bite of his dinner.

"Yes, well, when you tip them twenty bucks every time they come, I'm sure they are *happy* to do whatever you ask."

He shrugged and wiped his mouth with a napkin. "My family didn't have a lot growing up and I don't think these people have a lot either. I have more than enough to go around, so if I can give back to the people who are helping me out, I will."

My heart swelled, knowing that Cam was truly doing what he was doing because he wanted to, not for recognition or validation. He cared for the people in his life, and he always did what he could to show them that.

It wasn't long before the sun had started to go down and the temperature started to drop. I pulled on my sweater and pulled my legs under my skirt to use it as a blanket. We had both finished eating when Cam noticed me shiver.

"Are you cold?"

"No," I lied.

He cocked his head at me.

"Yeah, you are, Jones. Let's go. Let's get you somewhere warm." He stood up, walked around the table, and gave me his hand to help me stand.

"And where might that be?" I smirked at him as I stood. Cam pulled me in and wrapped both his arms around me, trapping me against him.

"Beautiful"—his voice was deep and low—"I think you know *exactly* where that might be."

My breath caught in my throat for a moment and I licked my lips in anticipation. But then I remembered our dinner setup and worried. "Don't we need to clean this up first?"

"No, someone will be by to do that for us. Can we go now? I really wanna get you warm." The grin on his face and the way his hands slid down my back to land right on the spot where my back meets my ass told me he wanted to do more than just that. Suddenly though, I was ready to get warm too. *Very* warm.

"Yes, please. Let's go get me warm." I nearly begged him.

Cam turned and I jumped on his back again to avoid walking on the sand and once I was on, he nearly ran back to his car.

We were both ready to be very, very warm.

36

HALEY | NOW

We couldn't get into his room fast enough, pushing and pulling at each other like animals.

My hands reached under his pull-over and made contact with his abs, sending a shiver of pleasure down my spine. His hands reached under my sweater and worked to pull it up and over my head. We moved as one across his room and toward the bed. Since Cam was in a suite, we had to maneuver around the couch and other furniture in the living room. After bumping into an end table, Cam lifted me easily and carried me the rest of the way. I wrapped my legs around his waist and giggled as he laid me down on the bed.

"What are you laughing at, Jones?" he growled in my ear, making quick work at getting my skirt off.

"I'm just laughing at us. At this. It almost feels unreal...it almost feels like a dream."

"This is my dream, Jones. I've had this dream before." Cam kissed my neck and was starting to play with my breasts, my bra pushed up so they were exposed. My eyes rolled to the back of my head, almost getting lost in his touch when his words hit me.

"Wait"—I pressed my hands against his chest, stopping him—"you've dreamed about this before?"

"I dream about you all the time, beautiful."

My eyes were locked on his but before I could respond, his lips crashed into mine, filling my entire body with the taste of him. With his hands still on my chest, I arched my back as his fingers started to pinch and flick my nipples. When he brought his mouth to them, my breath got caught in my throat.

"Take this off now," he demanded, pulling me up onto my elbows and unclasping my bra behind my back in one try. His hands then moved to remove my panties.

"Damn, Cam, you're really good at that. Have a lot of practice?" I teased.

"I'm good at a lot of things, Jones. Let me show you what else I'm good at." He reached behind my back and set me upright and had me watch as he quickly undressed in front of me. The tingling in my body grew as his jeans fell to the floor and exposed his very hard cock.

"Now come here," he demanded.

"You're kind of bossy," I said playfully.

"You make me like this. One day I'll let *you* boss me around, but not tonight. Now come here, *please*."

He didn't wait for me to follow his commands before he pulled me up from the bed, picked me up again as if I weighed nothing, and then stepped up onto the bed still holding me. Carefully, he lowered us both down until we were sitting on the bed with me in his lap. His back was against the headboard when he grabbed both my legs and pulled me even closer to him. His hard cock under my lap caused even more wetness to pool between my legs.

Facing one another, Cam and I pressed our lips together hard and deep, as if this was the first kiss we'd ever shared. I laced my hands through his hair, pulling him closer to me. One of his hands played with my nipple while the other slowly slid down my stomach. My back arched instinctually and I took a deep inhale as his strong fingers found my center and started to rub back and forth slowly.

Between Cam's hands playing with the two most sensitive spots on my body and his lips gently biting my neck, I almost came sitting on his lap. I tried to breathe through the pleasure and bring him with me. I reached between us and started to play with him. The more I played with him, the harder he got in my hand. Stroking him up and down only made him work harder on me and suddenly we were both starting to pant.

"*Fuck, Haley*," he growled in my ear. He pulled both of his hands away from my body and gently pushed me back. I caught myself with my hands, relinquishing his cock in the process.

"You are so fucking good at that but I'm not ready to be done yet. I need more of you tonight before I let you finish me completely."

I expected him to move me off of him and push himself inside of me. Instead, he kept one hand on my hips, keeping me where I was on his lap. My hands were braced behind me and I was leaning away from him with my legs still wrapped around him. He leaned over and brought his mouth to one of my breasts, flicking my nipple with his tongue. His other hand found my clit and started to play with it. When he pressed his thumb hard against my clit, I could feel myself starting to climb, the pleasure Cam was bringing me consuming my entire body.

"Cam..." I moaned. "You're going to make me finish if you don't stop."

"I'll be mad if you don't. Come for me beautiful. I want to feel you come on my fingers." Hearing his words turned me on even more and when he slipped two fingers inside of me, I completely unraveled. My whole body tensed up and stars filled my eyes. All of the things Cam was doing to me became too much and I experienced one of the best orgasms of my entire life.

"That's my girl." I was still coming down as he said it and I punched him in the arm with as much force as I could muster.

"'*That's my girl*'? Are you for real?"

Cam laughed under his breath and pulled me back up to meet his eyes again. He pressed his mouth to mine again before slowly rolling me off of him and lying down next to me.

"Admit it," he hummed in my ear, biting it just enough to send another shiver down my spine. "It turns you on when I call you that."

"Mmm...it kinda does." I turned my head and grabbed his chin with my hand and pulled him in for another kiss. "You wanna know what else turns me on?" I asked, pulling him on top of me now, his hips now squarely on top of mine.

"What's that?"

"Watching you fuck me."

Cam's face dropped for half a second before he caught it, then a sly grin spread across his face. "Does it now?"

"Yes, it does. Now come here," I repeated his words back to him.

"You're kinda bossy," he snapped back. *He was paying attention.*

"Cam, you don't know how bossy I can be. Now, do what I say, and fuck me. I'll even say please if you want."

"No need, beautiful, I'm happy to give you exactly what you want." Leaning over, he opened up the bedside table, pulled out a condom, and slipped it on quickly. He then pushed himself inside of me and the stars were back behind my eyes.

Being with Cam like this was better than I ever imagined it could be.

He was strong, and big, and knew exactly how to move, where to press, and how to go just a little deeper. Maybe it was because I wanted this for so long, but something about being with Cam *like this* took the entire experience to the next level.

As he pushed himself further inside of me, I arched my back inviting him to go even further. His hands were on top of the headboard, giving him all the leverage he needed to go even harder and deeper inside of me. With every thrust, a small cry escaped my lips.

We looked into one another's eyes as he moved back and forth, hitting my clit with his pelvis every time he drove deeper inside of me. My eyes flicked down and watched as his hips moved in rhythm, in and out of my pussy. I'd never been one to watch before, but watching Cam do what he was doing turned me on like crazy.

Cam's eyes were locked on mine, a small smile brimming with pleasure on his face. The way he was looking back at me made me feel free and sexy. Letting the feeling fill me up, I reached my arms above my head and grabbed onto the headboard.

"I want you to suck my nipples." He did without hesitation. "Now play with me while you fuck me." Again, he gave me what I wanted.

With Cam deep inside of me, his tongue going back and forth between my breasts, and his finger playing with my clit, I started to climb again. I wanted him to finish with me this time, so I kept talking.

"You're so good at this. You're making me want to finish already," I groaned into his ear.

"Then why don't you?" He asked before bringing his lips to my neck.

"Because I want you to come with me, Cam. I want you to finish when I do."

He moaned and nipped at my ear as he continued to push in and out of me. He started to quicken his pace, so I know my words were bringing him closer to the edge.

"You...can fuck me...any day of the week. As long as you do it like this," I moaned. He bit my neck and I yelped out. "Your cock is so hard, every time you go deeper inside of me another part of me comes alive. Please, Camden, fuck me deeper. Fuck me harder."

"Jesus Christ, Haley, you're going to make me finish if you keep talking like that," he growled and tried to pull away, but I wrapped my legs around him and dug my fingers into his back, not letting him move. He moaned deeply as my fingers sunk deeper into his skin. Cam's back flexed under my fingers and his arms started to shake as he continued to sink his hips deeper inside of me.

"*Please*. Please come. Please fuck me. I need you too, I've been waiting all week for you to do this to me. *Please, Camden.*"

As soon as the word left my lips, both Cam and I crashed into one another, falling over the edge at the same time. Dropping down to his elbows, Cam was breathing heavily into my neck as the pleasure continued to rip through my body. With my legs still wrapped around him, I pushed my hips up into his, sinking him a little deeper inside of me causing him to suck in a breath.

"That is not fair," he groaned, pushing my head to one side with his nose and lightly sinking his teeth into the sensitive spot behind my ear. It sent a shiver through me and I pushed my hips up into his again.

"Lucky for me, I'm not a professional athlete so I don't have to play fair." I bucked my hips up one last time and took pleasure in the feeling of all the muscles in his body contracting at once.

"You are evil." His voice was raspy as he was still catching his breath, but a smile was on his face and his deep emerald eyes were locked on mine.

"And you love me."

"Yeah, I really do."

I froze under him and the words we had both said hung in the air. My words had tumbled out before I even realized what I'd said, but Cam had agreed without hesitation. Looking at him now, I couldn't read his expression. He looked as if he wasn't sure if he had said something wrong. My eyes searched his as my brain tried to come up with the right words to say next.

But it came up empty.

Sensing the awkwardness, Cam leaned down and kissed me on the forehead, dispelling some of the tension that had filled the air.

"I'm going to go get cleaned up." He slowly pulled out of me and stood up. He moved to the bathroom and closed the door behind him. For a second, I thought that was going to be the end of the exchange, but after a moment, the door to the bathroom slid open again and his head popped out from the other side. "You wanna join me?"

———

AFTER CLIMBING out of the shower, I pulled on the tee shirt that Cam had left for me on the bathroom counter, smiling as I did because it smelled like him. *I will be adding this one to my collection.*

When Cam asked me to join him in the shower, I almost wasn't sure if I should say yes. He had kind of told me he loved me—maybe? I'm still trying to figure that out—and I wasn't sure if the awkwardness from bed would follow us into the shower.

Thankfully it hadn't and taking a shower with Cam was oddly sweet. He checked to make sure it wasn't too hot and he gave me plenty of space even though he was huge and took up most of the shower. He also offered to wash my hair, which no one had ever offered to do before. It was sweet and tender, and extremely hot without anything we were doing being outright sexy.

Things like this just felt different with Cam.

A good kind of different.

As I walked out of the bathroom, I found my underwear on the floor and pulled them on. Cam was spread out in bed wearing a pair of joggers and nothing else. He smiled up at me as I got closer and reached for my hand as I made it to the side of the bed I slept on the last time I stayed.

"Feel better?" he asked as I sat down next to him on the bed.

"I do. I feel very clean. Thanks for the shirt." My hand touched the sleeve of the shirt and I posed for him.

"You're welcome. You look good in my stuff; you should wear it more often." His voice came out deeper and he pulled me into him. My hands braced themselves on his chest as our lips met again. I could feel him smiling as our lips touched. We kissed like this for a few minutes, pressing into one another hard and deep.

"Scooch over," I told him, pulling the blankets back and wiggling myself down under them. I nestled myself at his side, his toned arm wrapped under me like a pillow. He was warm and I loved how his warmth made me feel safe. Like nothing bad could happen to me. To us.

"There you go again, being bossy," he joked.

"Hey, if I remember correctly, you once told me that me being the boss turned you on." I slapped him playfully as I pressed my body against his. He caught my hand as it made contact with his chest.

"It does." He kissed me again. "You can boss me around whenever you want, Jones, and I will *happily* comply with your demands."

"Be careful what you wish for, Johnson," I teased. Suddenly very sleepy, I leaned over Cam to look at what time it was. "Holy shit, it's almost one in the morning!"

"Time flies when you're getting what you ask for," he joked. He brushed his nose against my neck and kissed it softly. He sounded tired too. I looked back toward his face and sure enough, his eyes were closed and heavy.

"Cam..." I whispered. "Are you tired?"

"No..." he whispered back. His body was starting to get heavy next to me and I could tell he was falling asleep. I pulled his arm around me tighter, breathing in his familiar scent. Pine, earth, and AstroTurf.

"Cam..." I whispered again. "Did...did you mean what you said earlier? About loving me..."

His eyes didn't open and his body didn't move. Breathing heavily next to me, I thought he had fallen asleep. My heart sank as disappointment started to creep in. I needed to know if Cam had meant it when he said he loved me. Did he mean it, or did it just slip out? I didn't mean to say what I had said, but did he? I also didn't regret saying what I'd said, but maybe he did. I needed to know or else I was going to go crazy.

He started to shift beside me, turning over so he was on his side and facing me. Without opening his eyes, he draped his arm over my waist and pulled the covers up closer so we were both under them. Then, he leaned in and kissed my forehead with his eyes still closed. Our faces were close and I could feel his breath on my lips as he whispered one single word that made me realize that this wasn't just a fun fling anymore.

That this could be real.

That the feelings I'd had for Cam so long ago never truly left my heart. It was as if they were a book I started to read but never finished, waiting on a shelf for years until I was ready to pick it back up again.

One single word that told me exactly how he felt for me, and exactly how I felt for him.

"Yes."

37

HALEY | NOW

I'm starting to believe that time moves faster when you're happy.

When I lost Connor, the days felt as if they were five hundred hours. Now they felt like they were five seconds.

Without realizing it, two more weeks had passed and it was the end of February. The She Who Thrives! conference was six weeks away, which meant Piper and I only had four weeks before we would be leaving the bungalow and heading home.

Thinking about leaving made my stomach sink because I had started to feel so at home here. Both in the bungalow and out of it. The people around town waved at Piper and me when we went to grab coffee at Coastal Brews and we were even on a first-name basis with the elderly couple across the street. Dianne and Dale were sweet, and one morning, Dianne brought over fresh cookies for Piper and me, which we ate for lunch because we hadn't made it to the grocery store. Again.

The biggest thing that made me anxious about leaving the bungalow though, was Cam.

Ever since that night in his hotel room, after our date on the beach, things were different between us. *Good* different.

I replayed that moment in my head at least once a day when he told me he meant it when he said he loved me. How he looked. How he smelled. How safe I felt lying in his arms, feeling his breath rise and fall in his chest as he fell asleep next to me. How I wanted to say it back, but I didn't. Not because I didn't think I loved him, but because we had been in this place before and it nearly broke me.

He'd told me he loved me before but by the next morning, he was gone. I wanted to believe him when he said he wasn't going anywhere, but something in my heart had me guarded and unsure if I could trust him.

Instead of telling him I loved him, I kissed him on the cheek and rubbed it in with my thumb as he fell asleep. The next morning, we went for round two before walking to Coastal Brews to get coffee.

During the day, Cam was sweet and kind. He held my hand, told me I was beautiful, and offered to bring me coffee or Piper and me food whenever we wanted it.

Once the sun went down though, he became a completely different person.

He was hungry, ravenous even, and wanted me to sneak away to his hotel room every night as if we were in high school and breaking some kind of rule. As much as I wanted to, sometimes I just couldn't. Piper and I still had so much to do before the conference and running off to play sex kitten with Cam every night of the week did not help me get my work done.

The past two weekends I have spent both Friday and Saturday night in Cam's bed, staying up till the wee hours of the morning with him between my legs. Or on top of me. Or under me. Anyway we could have one another, we would.

When we were alone, things were hot and heavy and we were doing things I'd *never* done before. Role play, dirty talk, and one night, Cam tied my arms behind my back and didn't untie me until I came. *Twice.* And that was before he even got inside of me. I didn't even know it was possible to have three orgasms in one night, but Cam proved that it was.

Things were *good* with us, really good.

But still, a part of me worried that the end of our trip would also be the end of what we were growing here. Could we make it work once we were home? He was a professional NFL player for god's sake, he probably didn't have time for a relationship. Did we feel this way because of where we were? It's not like the bungalow or this tiny town was anything crazy romantic, but being in a new place can stir up new emotions.

Could Cam love me longer than just this trip? A voice inside my head was trying to convince me that he couldn't. Or that he wouldn't.

I was sitting at the office table with my laptop opened in front of me, chin in my hand, when I heard Piper say something.

"Hello? Earth to Haley? Helloooo, you in there?" She started to wave her hand in front of my face. Shaking my head and snapping out of my thoughts, I looked at her.

"Oh, yeah. I'm here, sorry. What were you saying?"

Piper sighed deeply and pushed the pile of papers away from her and set her pen down on top of them.

"Hays. What's going on with you? You've been distracted *all week*. Caught in a sexy daydream?" She wiggled her eyebrows at me. Piper had demanded I tell her *everything* every time I came home from being with Cam. I didn't tell her *everything*, but I did tell her a lot. She would know what would be included in my sexy daydream if I had been having one.

"*No.*" I sighed. "I was just thinking about how soon the conference is and how soon we'll be heading back to Wilmington. It's crazy, we've been here for over a month now..."

"A lot has happened in a month..." Piper mirrored my apprehensive tone. "How are you feeling?"

I took a deep inhale and let it out slowly. Deborah would be proud. "I feel...unsure. But good. I don't know, it's hard to explain. I'm so happy, and things with Cam are so good. But the voices in my head keep telling me I'm a horrible wife for moving on so quickly after losing Connor and that once the trip is over, everything with Cam is going to blow up in my face." I dropped my head into my hands and slumped over the table.

"Okay, well, for starters...we've talked about the feelings connected to Connor and I know you've talked to Deborah about them too. Yes?" Piper was speaking in her lawyer voice and suddenly I was annoyed. I wish she would just wallow with me for once.

"Yes," I started. "You and I have talked about them before and I've talked with Deborah about them too."

"Okay, and what does Deborah say about it?"

"She says that we all move on in our own time and if I feel like it's my time to move on, then it's okay to move on. She keeps reminding me that Connor wouldn't want me to be lonely forever and that I'm not being unfaithful by being with Cam."

After the night Cam told me he loved me, I booked a last-minute appointment with Deborah the following day. We spoke for over an hour—and she charged me as such—because there weren't enough deep breaths I could take that would help me calm down. By the end of our session, Deborah had made me feel better even though she hadn't told me what I was supposed to do next. When I asked her if I should tell Cam I loved him, she told me she couldn't give me that answer and then laughed when I whined about how annoying it was that no one would just tell me what to do.

"I couldn't agree with her more. Now, onto item number two. Cam hasn't given you any reason to believe that once it's time to leave this place"—she swung her arms, making a motion that referenced the bungalow—"things are going to fall apart."

"*This time*," I interrupted her. "This time he hasn't given me any reason to think that, but in the past, he has. Remember freshman year? He told me he loved me then ran away the next morning without even saying goodbye."

It was her turn to interrupt me.

"Oh my god, Hays, I love you, but you have got to let. That. *Go*. It was years ago and we were young and stupid. He was young and a boy, which means he was extra stupid. You can't seriously be letting the decision of an eighteen-year-old boy be the reason you won't let something amazing happen with a thirty-two-year-old man, will you?" I sat up again and blinked at Piper, stunned by her words.

"Piper, you were there. You saw what he put me through!"

"Yes, sweetie, I was there and I remember all of it. But that was a long time ago and I think you need to let it go if you don't want to be the one who burns it all to the ground this time. History doesn't repeat itself if we don't let it."

History doesn't repeat itself if we don't let it. Her words sunk deep into my brain and I started to chew on the inside of my lip. My brain was starting to get tangled in my thoughts when I felt Piper squeeze my right index finger. Looking toward her, I saw a small smile on her face, which I returned.

"You know I love you, Hays. I just want you to be happy."

"I know, Piper. Thank you." I squeezed her right index finger back. "I don't know about you, but I'm kinda done for the day. Wanna go for a walk or something?"

"I would love that. Why don't you invite Cam over and we can all cook dinner?"

My smile grew at the thought of Piper, Cam, and I cooking together. It would be nice to have my two favorite people together for once. Normally, I went to Cam's because we didn't want Piper to feel uncomfortable, so it was nice that she was the one who invited him over.

"Yeah, I like that idea. I'll text him. But first, let's go for that walk."

Rising from the table, Piper and I cleaned up the papers and closed our laptops before getting ready for our walk. It's moments like this that I was grateful to have a friend like Piper. One who will listen to me talk, but also call me out when I needed it. She kept me honest and genuinely had my best interest at heart.

And I loved her for it.

ALWAYS RIGHT ON TIME, Cam arrived at the house at six just like I'd asked him to hours earlier. I opened the front door of the bungalow to find him carrying two bags of groceries and looking as sexy as ever. There's just something about a guy wearing a pullover and a backward hat that did it for me.

As he leaned in to kiss me, his scent swarmed around me and I happily breathed it in. There were certain things about Cam that I wanted to remember forever. His deep emerald eyes, his strong arms, and jawline, and how he smelled.

"Hey, beautiful," Cam said as he stepped inside after we kissed on the front steps.

"Hi." I smiled back at him and suddenly felt seventeen again. I don't know what it was about him, but Cam made me feel as if I had never been loved before and this was my first time.

He set the bags down on the floor and looked around to see if Piper was within eyesight. When he saw that she wasn't, he wrapped his arms around my waist and pushed me against the back of the front door. I giggled as he pressed his lips to my neck and buried his face behind my ear. Tingles filled my body as he kissed me and held me in place with his hands. My arms were pressed between us so I couldn't do anything but let him have me.

"I missed you today," he murmured, pressing more kisses into the side of my neck.

"I missed you too," I replied, turning my head to meet his.

He paused for a moment and gave me a cocky smirk. His eyes flashed from my eyes to my lips before he kissed me hard.

Finally releasing me, I was able to rope my arms around his neck and pull him close as he leaned into the kiss, pushing his tongue into my mouth. The taste of him made me feel like I was floating.

"Oh my god, *get a room!*" Piper shouted as she exited her room and saw us at the door.

We both laughed and moved away from each other. Cam picked the bags up off the floor and followed Piper and me into the kitchen.

"So, what are we eating tonight?" Piper asked, sitting at one of the barstools as Cam and I unloaded the groceries.

"I would like to point out that you guys invited *me* here for dinner, yet I was the one who had to go grocery shopping," Cam joked, pulling out a jar of pasta sauce from one of the bags and setting it on the counter.

"*Actually*, it was Piper's idea to have you over for dinner. All I did was send a text." I looked at him with a half-smirk.

"Oh, so what you're saying is you *don't* want me here then? Should I just leave the food and go?" Cam set the groceries down on the counter and started to walk back toward the front door.

"No! Don't go!" I started after him nearly begging. "If you leave, who will cook us dinner?"

He gave me an incredulous look when I grabbed his arm and pulled him to face me. When I started to laugh, he turned around quickly and started to tickle me. I tried to run, but he held me tight and was bear-hugging me before I could escape. He continued to tickle me and I squirmed under his grasp, laughing uncontrollably.

"Say it, Jones, say you want me to stay!" he growled as he continued to make me laugh deep in my belly.

"Stay! I want you to stay!" I could hardly get the words out because I was laughing so hard. "Please, Cam, I want you to stay! Stop tickling me, I'm about to pee myself and if I do, you'll be the one who has to mop the floors!"

He stopped, thankfully, and all three of us were laughing. Once he released me, I punched him playfully in his arm as we walked back toward the kitchen. He looked at me again, and I saw a look of admiration and affection in his eyes.

"You two are cute, but you're also making me sick.

Someone better feed me before I barf all over the floor because of how much you disgust me."

I rolled my eyes at Piper's joke and continued to help Cam unpack the groceries. As we did, I thought about how nice it felt to do this with him. Unpack groceries. It's such a mundane thing, but with Cam, it felt special.

Everything with Cam felt special. It felt comfortable.

It felt like home.

———

Two hours later and several glasses of wine down, Piper, Cam, and I cleaned up the kitchen and were sitting on the couch discussing the conference.

I loved how many questions Cam asked about it. He wanted to know everything about She Who Thrives and it made my heart swell seeing how much he was interested. I especially loved how much he supported Piper working for me. He talked to her like she was working any other kind of job, which I knew was important to her.

Piper didn't talk about it much, but I knew she felt a little weird about coming to work for me. She had big plans to become a lawyer, but when life didn't work out according to her plan, she came to work for me. I didn't think of her as any less for not making it as a lawyer, but I knew she did. It made me happy to see Cam be just as supportive of her as he was of me.

Just after eleven, Piper got up from her spot on one of the couches and announced she was going to bed, leaving just Cam and I in the living room. He was sitting across from me on the oversized couch that took up most of the room. His arm slung over the back of it and his hand propped up his head. He was looking at me with a small smile on his face, not saying anything.

"What?" I asked him as I pulled my feet under my butt.

"Am I not allowed to just look at you?"

"No, you are. I just wonder what you're thinking about when you do."

"I'm thinking about how beautiful you are."

I could feel my cheeks getting hot without even needing to touch them. He started to move closer to me, his body approaching my side of the couch slowly but intentionally.

"I'm also thinking about how lucky I am that I am here with you." A little closer.

"And I'm thinking about how much you mean to me." He was within kissing distance now.

Placing my hand on his cheek, I pulled him in for a soft, gentle kiss. His words filled me up with so much life that I could feel all the broken pieces inside of me starting to heal.

"I feel pretty lucky too," I confessed as Cam sat back in his own space. Without meaning to, I yawned and quickly covered my mouth with my hand.

Cam laughed and cocked his head at me. "Tired?"

"I guess so. I didn't realize I was until now."

"Do you want me to go?"

"No!" I was a little too eager and Cam laughed. "Why... why don't you stay?"

"Stay the night? Here?"

"Yeah. Piper knows we're sleeping together and I honestly don't think she'll care if you stay." *At least, I hope she won't care. We hadn't really talked about this.*

"Okay." Cam shrugged. "If you want me to stay, I'll stay. Anything for you, beautiful." He kissed me on the cheek and rubbed it in with his thumb before giving me a smile that made my insides melt. I suddenly had a strong desire to straddle him.

I got up from the couch and started toward my room.

When I realized Cam wasn't following me, I turned around to see him fluffing up a pillow on the couch and pulling the blanket off the back of it.

"Cam?" I asked as my eyebrows started to meet in the middle of my forehead, "What are you doing?"

"I'm getting ready to go to sleep?" He said it as if it was the most obvious thing in the world. I dropped my head to one side and looked at him.

How do boys make it anywhere in life?

"Cam, you can stay in my room with me." I chuckled. "You don't have to sleep on the couch."

"Oh!" He jumped up from the couch and closed the space between us quickly. "I wasn't sure if that's what you wanted."

"Of course it's what I want." My hands were on his chest and our faces were close enough that if I leaned in even a little, I would have been able to kiss him again. "There's a lot I want right now." My eyes fluttered to his lips as desire oozed off my words.

"Is that so?" A coy half smile was on Cam's face and he cocked his head slightly to one side.

"It is so." I held his hand and led him down the hallway toward my bedroom.

"Well, Jones," he said in a husky tone as we stepped inside my room, "I'm happy to give you whatever you want tonight."

"I'm glad you say so," I said slowly, closing my bedroom door behind us. "Because tonight, I'm the boss."

38

CAM | NOW

Haley was still holding my hand as she led me to her bed where she motioned for me to sit down. Once I took a seat, I took in her room for the first time.

While I knew it wasn't *really* her room, it felt like I was in a sacred space that I wasn't supposed to be in with the door closed. Maybe that's because whenever I was in Haley's room growing up, the door always had to be open.

"Stay there." Haley's voice was low and firm. "I'll be right back." She walked toward the bathroom that was connected to her room with a coy smile painted on her face. My cock was starting to get hard as I watched her go, her long, cinnamon-colored hair trailing behind her shoulders as she disappeared behind the bathroom door.

As I waited for her to return, I looked around the room. It matched the decor of the rest of the bungalow; nice yet cozy and not super modern. It felt homey and welcoming, like your grandma's house, but it didn't *smell* like your grandma's house. It smelled like Haley. Her perfume lingering in the air, slowly intoxicating me as I sat there waiting for her to come back. The bed was big, probably a king, and I started to imagine what it would feel like as I fucked her in it.

She's in charge tonight though, I remembered. Hearing her say she's the boss made my dick jump in my pants almost instantly. I loved when Haley took control and it turned me on to think about how she might boss me around tonight.

"Hey there, player." Her sultry voice pulled me from the dirty images running around in my head. When I looked toward the bathroom door where she stood, I couldn't stop my jaw from nearly hitting the floor.

There, in the doorway, was Haley Jones wearing my football jersey. Just my jersey. Well, it wasn't *my* jersey, but one I assumed she'd ordered online. The number 32 big and bold across her torso with my team name across the front.

She spun around, her hair floating like ribbon as she did, and stopped when she was showing me her back. She pulled her hair to the side to expose my name across her shoulders. With her chin turned into her shoulder, she looked at me over it and smirked.

"Whatta ya think?" *I think I just came a little in my pants.*

"I think..." She turned around and took a few steps toward me, just close enough so I could reach out and grab her by the waist. "You look hot as fuck in that."

My chin tipped up as she lowered her head down to meet mine, pressing a soft kiss to my lips. Her hair cascaded around us, closing us underneath it. I reached one hand behind her head, pulling her even closer. A low moan escaped from the back of her throat as I pushed my tongue into her mouth.

She took a few steps closer and spread her legs so that she was standing with them on either side of mine as I sat on the bed. Pulling away from her, I took in everything she was as she stood in front of me. Her legs with strong, muscular calves and thighs were on full display below my jersey. Her round ass teased me when she turned around to show off my name across her shoulders. Her waist curved in and felt like the greatest thing under my hands.

My eyes made their way up past her breast which filled out the top of my jersey like a dream and landed on her eyes, which were looking back at me, just like always. Those two hazel eyes that I would kill to be able to look into every single day for the rest of my life.

"Like what you see?" She bit her lip and ran her fingers through my hair which was getting long enough to need a haircut. I liked the way it felt and I pressed my head against her hand as she did it.

"I *love* what I see." My hands flipped the bottom of the jersey up just above her hips, exposing a pair of light blue, lacey panties that let her ass cheeks hang out just enough to drive me crazy. They matched the color of my jersey almost perfectly.

"Geezus, *fuck*," I growled, unable to hold back just how much they turned me on. If I wasn't hard before, I was now. I reached behind her and grabbed her ass with both hands, yanking her closer to me and pinching her playfully. She let out a small yelp and then giggled before slapping me playfully on the shoulder.

"Ouch, Camden!" She leaned down, swung her long hair over her shoulder, and bit me on my neck. I think it was supposed to hurt, but all it did was send a shockwave down my spine.

She must have noticed because for a moment she paused, smiled, and then bit me again. "Ohh, so you like it when I bite you?" Another shockwave ripped through me as her teeth nibbled on my neck. She continued kissing and biting my neck as I continued to grab her ass, kneading it with my fingers. I was tired of her not being on me, so I looped my hands under her legs and pulled her down onto my lap, my hard dick making contact through my pants with her center as she came down.

"Camden..." she whispered into my ear as her hips gyrated on my lap. *Holy shit, Haley Jones is giving you a lap dance right now while wearing your jersey.* I tried to take a deep breath and calm down because if I didn't, I was actually going to come in my pants.

"Haley..." I fought to keep my focus. "If you don't settle down, I *will* flip you over right here and fuck you from behind. You have me so hard right now."

"Mmm..." she groaned and ground her hips even harder on my lap, making my breath catch in my throat. "But I'm in charge, remember? So you have to be good and do what I tell you."

"Tell me what to do, Jones. Boss me around, I'm begging you." A devilish smile spread across her face as she stood up again, freeing my cock from her sensual hips.

"Take your pants off. Leave nothing behind," she commanded.

I'd never been a man to not follow directions, so I stood, undid the button on my jeans, and let everything fall to the floor without wasting another second. Haley licked her lips as she stared at my cock, which was standing at attention.

"Now sit."

Again, I followed her directions. Once I was perched on the edge of the bed, she put her hands on my shoulders, spread her legs, and took a step forward so the insides of her thighs were pressed against the outsides of my legs. She leaned down and her lips brushed against my ear.

Hardly above a whisper, she purred, "I am so wet right

now. Wanna see how wet you make me, Camden?" She moved one hand so it was hovering just above my cock and grazed it with her fingers.

"Yes." My arms were holding me up on the bed but I needed to see just how wet she was. When I reached for her center she took a small step back before I could touch her.

"I want you to beg for my pussy." Her words were so delicious and sounded like music to my ears.

"*Please*, Haley. Please let me touch you. I need to feel you on my fingers *now*," I begged. Fuck, I would grovel for this woman if she asked me to. I would get down on my knees right here at her feet and plead just to get a taste of her.

She looked like she was contemplating whether or not my request was good enough, and it drove me crazy.

She drove me crazy.

And I fucking loved it.

Finally, she took a step forward and let me have her.

As my fingers moved quickly over the top of the lace that was the only barrier between me and her center, I knew she was telling the truth. She wasn't just wet, she was *soaked.*

A moan escaped me as I started to rub the outside of her panties, realizing I was the one who made her like this. Pride swelled in my chest knowing that I made Haley this turned on.

"More. I need more, Camden. I know you want more too," Haley murmured, her fingers still grazing my cock as she stood over me. She was right, I did want more. Pushing the dainty fabric aside, I slipped my fingers between her pussy, moving them back and forth through her center. As I rubbed against her clit, she shivered and I felt her legs buckle just a little. I held her hip with one hand, steadying her where she stood, while the other hand continued to play with her pussy.

"You feel so good, Haley. Can I do this to you every day? Please, I will pay all my millions to be able to finger fuck you just like this if I have to."

She took in a sharp inhale as I flicked her clit with my finger. While she was starting to stroke my cock with one hand, her other hand was braced on my shoulder, helping her stay upright. Her head was resting on top of her hand and when I looked at her, I could see she was watching what I was doing to her.

This girl likes to watch and I find that so fucking hot.

"I want you to finger me." Her breath was starting to become labored. "But I want to be able to see you do it and this jersey is in the way."

Haley crossed her arms in front of her to strip off the jersey, and I helped her take it off as she pulled it over her head. As it landed on the floor next to our feet, I finally got to see what was *under* the jersey.

I'd never seen anything like it. She was wearing a bra the same color blue as her panties, but it hardly covered anything. It had straps that had small pieces of lace on them that asymmetrically crossed over her chest. Her nipples were fully exposed and hard, like two small peaks that my tongue was begging to touch. It didn't seem very practical, but it was the hottest thing I'd ever seen.

I closed my eyes for a moment and thanked whatever god might be out there for letting me be the man who got to see Haley Jones like this.

"What do you think?" she stood confidently in front of me, placing her hands on her hips, pulling her shoulders back, and pressing her breast out toward me just a little more.

"I think..." I grabbed her hips and yanked her back toward me, she let out a little giggle as she fell forward toward me again. "You're *mine*. And I'm ready to give you whatever you want tonight."

"I want you to fuck me with your fingers first." She paused just long enough to kiss and bite the side of my neck. "Then, I want you inside of me, fucking me until I come for a second time." I let out a low growl at her words.

"Then you better sit down so I can get to work on that delicious pussy of yours, beautiful. You're mine tonight and I'm yours. Let me give you what you asked for."

Her eyes lit up and her lips turned up.

She spread her legs to get closer to my hands, her breast just at eye level. She placed both hands on my shoulders this time and I leaned forward to take one of her nipples between my lips. As I sucked and flicked one nipple with my mouth, the other was being taken care of by one of my hands. Every pinch, flick, and lick caused Haley's breath to catch in her throat.

"More, Camden. I need more," she begged, and I didn't waste another second before giving her what she wanted.

I reached toward her hips and gently pulled the lace panties she was wearing down until they fell to the floor at her ankles. Returning one hand to her breast and playing with her nipple, I slowly dragged my other hand down the side of her leg. I moved impossibly slow, wanting to tease Haley as my hand made its way to the inside of her thighs.

"*Please. Inside of me. Now,*" she begged again, her head dropping to my shoulder like before. Her eyes were locked on my hand as it disappeared between her legs.

Ever so slowly, I rubbed one finger up and back through her pussy, feeling how wet she was. I could tell she was getting closer to the edge by the way her body started to shake. Playing with her like this made my cock throb.

Finally ready to give her what she wanted, I slipped one

finger inside her pussy and took pleasure in how tight she felt around my finger.

"*You are so tight*," I growled in her ear, and goosebumps sprang across her skin.

"Give me two."

I had to think for a moment about what she meant and then I realized she was asking for *two fingers*. I grinned and wanted to see how much I could unravel her. I wanted to watch her face as I gave her what she asked for. Using my free hand, I grabbed her chin and moved her face from my shoulder to force her to look at me.

"Look at me as I make you mine, Jones. Keep your eyes on me as I fuck you like this."

With our eyes connected, I slipped both my index and middle finger inside of her. Her eyes rolled to the back of her head and she moaned as I did it. With her legs spread and straddling me and her head being held in place in front of me, I took in the whole picture of what I was doing to Haley.

She was sexy and beautiful. Strong and begging for more. She was the girl from my dream and she was *mine*.

"Three. Give me three." Her voice came out more like a whimper than a command and I could tell she was getting close.

I pulled her face to mine, smashing my lips to hers as I slipped another finger inside her tight, wet pussy. With three fingers inside her, I could feel her muscles starting to contract as she edged closer and closer to the finish. Feeling her like this on my fingers made my cock throb so I released her chin and started to pump myself with my hand.

"Oh my god. I love watching you do that to yourself. Don't stop." Haley braced herself against my chest, her eyes locked on where my hands were. We made eye contact and she gave me a devilish smile that almost sent me over the edge. I continued to pump my fingers in and out of her, crooking my index in a way that touched her G-spot.

"Yes, yes...Camden, yes!" Her head dropped to my shoulder again. "I'm going to come, you're going to make me come."

"Do it, beautiful. I want you to. I want to feel you come all over my fingers."

Haley dropped lower onto my fingers and I felt every muscle of her pussy convulse as she reached her peak. Her hips bucked and she threw her head back, her chest pushing out toward me as she did. She moaned and her body jolted when I tried to bring one of her nipples to my mouth. Feeling Haley Jones completely fall apart on me like this was the greatest feeling in the world.

"That's my girl," I whispered, pulling my fingers out of her slowly and pulling her into my chest. She was breathing heavily, her eyes still closed, when I heard a small laugh escape from her mouth.

"You really like calling me that, don't you?" she murmured, her voice raspy as she was still coming down.

"I like calling you a lot of things. Beautiful, Jones, Haley, but my favorite thing to call you is *mine*."

She opened her eyes then and looked at me with an expression I hadn't seen on her face in a long time. She looked...free. Like she had just been brought to life and everything inside of her was illuminated.

She moved her hands so that they were on either side of my face and she pulled me in for a kiss. One that was deep and long. Our tongues clashed against one another and our breath became one. Haley's hands moved to the back of my head, her fingers roping themselves through my hair and she held me where I was.

It felt as if she thought that if she didn't hold me tight enough, I would disappear without notice.

Not this time, I thought. *Never again.*

"I need you inside of me." Her lips pulled away from mine as she begged. Reaching down, she took my cock in her hand and started to play with it. I needed to be inside of her too, but there was something I needed to do first.

I grabbed both of her hands and stood from the edge of the bed. She looked up at me and I swear, between her hazel eyes and freckles, she almost brought me to my knees.

"I need to be inside of you, beautiful, but first..." I spun her around and undid the clasp of her bra, releasing her from all the ties and straps it had. I then reached toward the floor and picked up my jersey. Looking at Haley, I smiled and said, "I want you to wear this while I fuck you tonight."

Her devilish grin was back and she raised her arms above her head, inviting me to slip it on. I watched as it fell, covering her torso, and she pulled her cinnamon-colored hair out from under the jersey. As it fell, I caught a whiff of her shampoo and I suddenly wanted to bury my face in her hair.

"Lay down," she commanded.

Back in charge, it seems. I pulled my shirt off finally and laid myself back on the bed, my head resting against the headboard. Haley licked her lips as she took in every part of my fully exposed body.

Watching her at the edge of the bed, I had a flashback to the dream I had months ago and almost laughed at the irony of it all. When I'd had that dream, I thought that would be all I would ever have with Haley. But now here I was, living the dream I once had. Haley stepped out of her panties that were still at her ankles and slowly started to crawl toward me from the bottom of the bed.

So much better than my dream.

"Now, Johnson," she purred as she crawled toward me. "I'm in charge tonight. You understand that, right?" She was just passing my shins, crawling on all fours. Watching her like this made my dick jump.

"Yes, Jones, I understand."

"Good." Her eyes crawled up to meet mine and she paused once her head was just above my hips. "Ready for your rules?"

"There are rules?"

"There are rules. Do you agree to follow my rules?"

I paused and looked at her. Her mouth was just inches from my dick and I thought for a second how badly I wish she would drop her chin just a little more.

"Sure, Jones, I agree to follow your rules."

The devilish smile was back.

"Rule number one..." Her head dropped and I watched as she opened her mouth and licked my dick from shaft to tip. I took in a sharp breath and my hand reached toward her, but she stopped me before I could touch her. "Is no touching unless I tell you to."

I groaned because all I wanted to do was touch her, to feel every part of her with my fingers. She licked my cock again, sending another shockwave through my body.

"Do you agree to rule number one?" she asked, clearly enjoying herself.

"Yes, yes, I agree with rule number one. What else, Jones?" My heart was starting to race and if I didn't get inside of her soon, I was going to completely lose it.

"Rule number two..." She waited for me to look at her and when I did, she grabbed me in one hand and placed her entire mouth around my cock. My hips raised to meet her and I groaned again as she pulled me out. "Is that you come inside of me."

"Holy fuck, are you serious?"

She was stroking and licking me but then gave me an almost annoyed look because I had questioned her.

"Yes, Camden." Now she was growling. "I'm 100% serious." She took my cock in her mouth again and bobbed her head up and down. I grabbed her hair with one hand and pulled her off of me, afraid that if I let her go too long I would finish before I could follow rule number two.

"Then you better stop doing that, beautiful, or I'm going to finish in that pretty little mouth of yours."

She smiled and looked dangerously pleased with herself.

"Do you agree with rule number two?" She started crawling up my body again, her chest finally square to mine, her hips hovering just above my hard, throbbing cock. She leaned over me, her hair cascading to one side and my jersey brushing against my stomach. Her lips were less than an inch from mine and it took everything in me not to pull her down on top of me.

That would be breaking rule number one though, so I resisted.

"Yes, Jones, I agree to rule number two."

"Good." She smiled and reached her hand down toward my cock. "Now, I'm going to ride you while wearing your jersey and you're going to watch. Remember rule number one, though. If you break it, I'll stop."

As she slid me inside of her, a visceral moan escaped my throat and I had to grip the sheets with both hands to abide by rule number one. It took every ounce of self-control and restraint to not put my hands somewhere on her body. I wanted to touch her, grab her, and play with her more than anything else at that moment.

But Haley was in charge and nothing turned me on more than watching her be in charge.

I watched as she pushed off her strong, lean legs, riding my cock as if it was the greatest thing in the world to her. When she dropped her head back and her hair fell down the back of my jersey, I almost lost it completely. I'd had women fuck me like this before, but nothing compared to having Haley on top of me. Especially while wearing my jersey.

"Holy shit, Haley...you are so sexy. Watching you like this, in my jersey, it's almost too much." My hands reached for her thighs as they moved up and down, pushing her on and off of my cock. Before they could make contact, she grabbed my wrists and held them down on the bed at my sides.

"Ah, ah, ah, Camden Johnson, remember rule number one. No touching unless I tell you you're allowed." She was breathing heavily, becoming breathless as she took me all on her own. The look on her face told me she was thoroughly enjoying herself as she tortured me in this way.

"I don't like rule number one anymore."

She laughed as she pulled as far away from me as she could without me fully leaving her body, and then slowly welcomed me back inside of her, taking me all the way to the hilt. A sharp breath caught in my throat as she did it again, taking me deeper and deeper inside of her with every thrust. Watching her take me like this was unreal.

She continued to ride me, alternating from sitting straight up on my lap and leaning over me. When she was close enough, she would bite at my neck and ear which brought me even closer to the edge. Never breaking rule number one, I moved my hips with hers, helping to hit her G-spot with every thrust, and making her come closer and closer to the edge.

"Cam..." she said breathlessly. "I want you to touch me now."

"You don't have to tell me twice, beautiful."

Without wasting another second, one hand went to her pussy and started to play with her clit. My other hand grabbed her hip and followed her rhythmic movements. *So much better than my dreams,* I thought to myself again. The more I watched her, the harder I got and the closer I got to my own finish.

"Haley...I'm getting close." My breath was getting short and I could feel myself grow inside of her.

"Mmm, I can tell." Her bottom lip was tucked under her front teeth and seeing it drove me wild. "But we aren't finishing like this."

She stopped moving just long enough to lean down and whisper into my ear, "I want you to take me from behind and I'm going to watch as you finish inside of me. Can you do that for me, Camden Johnson?" Her words were like honey, and I thought my heart might stop. Haley's eyes flicked toward a mirror that was leaning against the wall just to the right of the bed.

She wanted to watch.

Never in my life did I think I would find a woman's desire to watch me fuck her so hot.

"You better get off of me so I can make that happen then, beautiful."

She pulled herself off of me and moved to position herself on all fours, but this time in front of the mirror. I squared my hips with hers and locked eyes with her in the mirror, both of us fully visible in it. A sultry smile grew on

Haley's face as I lined myself up with her hips and slowly pushed inside of her again. She moaned deeply from the back of her throat as I buried myself deep inside of her.

"Holy shit, you feel so good there," she breathed.

"Jones?"

"Yes, Johnson?"

"Do I still have to follow rule number one?" I knew she had freed me from the rule, but I wanted to hear her ask for me to touch her in all the places my hands were dying to explore.

"No, Johnson, you don't have to follow rule number one. You can touch me, have me, and take me in any way you want." She was watching me thrust in and out of her through the mirror. I reveled in watching her eyes roll into the back of her head every time I pushed myself a little bit deeper.

"*Thank god.*" My hands, finally free to do what they had wanted to do, reached for her breasts under my jersey. I flicked, pinched, played, and squeezed as Haley's breath started to become short and heavy. My eyes danced back and forth from watching her from behind and catching her in the mirror. Every time my eyes hit the mirror, Haley was watching me fuck her from behind.

"Jones, I'm not going to last long like this. You are too fucking beautiful and too fucking sexy to hold out for too long." Watching her take me like this, on her hands and knees, was enough to drive any sane man over the edge.

"Then don't," she said between her moans and I knew she was getting close to the edge too. "Remember rule number two, Cam."

"Are you sure?"

"Camden, please, I want you to come inside of me. I want to feel your heat and your cock come inside of me. I—"

Her head dropped as I thrust deeply inside of her. "I want to feel you finish inside of me again. *Please.*"

The final 'please' is what sent me over the edge. I pushed myself in and out of her, going deeper with every thrust, and it didn't take long before I felt myself finish inside of her. My cock throbbed as the heat inside of me exploded. Haley buried her face into the sheets of her bed to muffle her cry as she came undone under me. Unable to hold myself up any longer, I fell down around her, bracing myself with my arms to avoid completely falling on top of her. She looked up again and our eyes met in the mirror.

Her lips spread slowly into a smile, a look of satisfaction and enjoyment on her face.

Then, like a small child who intentionally does something bad in front of a grownup, she pulled away and pushed her hips back into me, causing my whole body to convulse as her pussy slid off and on my cock. Doing this to a man after he's already finished is a mean trick. But I loved it.

"You are a very bad girl, Haley Jones," I gasped, looking back at her with my own devilish smile.

She did the thing with her hips again. "And what are you going to do about it?" She was challenging me. She enjoyed watching me suffer.

I grabbed her hair and pulled it gently, pulling her head back as I did. Not enough to hurt her, but enough to keep her in place and show her that I was in charge again. I brought my mouth to her shoulder and nipped it, causing her to yelp out as my teeth pinched her skin.

"I'm going to make you pay for your misbehavior, don't you worry, Jones. Next time, I'm in charge."

"I can't wait to see how you take control, Johnson. Now

pull out of me, but slowly, you feel so good and I want to enjoy it as long as I can."

I placed my hands on both of her hips and slowly pulled myself out of her. Before moving from behind her, I pushed the jersey she was still wearing up a little further, leaned over, and kissed her on the soft of her back. She peaked at me from over her shoulder and let out a small "hmph" when I did it again. I went to kiss her back a third time, but she wiggled underneath me and flipped over before I could.

Looking down at her, I took in every freckle on her face and made a mental note to try to count them one day. Hundreds of small dark spots sprinkled across her cheeks, nose, forehead, and chin, and I wanted nothing more than to be able to commit each and every one of them to memory.

Haley's hands reached up to cup my face and I gently brought myself down to lay on top of her. She was warm and her skin was soft. She wrapped her legs around me, locking her ankles behind my back, trapping me in this position.

"What are you thinkin' about?" she asked just above a whisper. Her thumbs rubbed back and forth across my cheeks. Her eyes were swimming with a mix of emotions. Contentment, maybe? I couldn't tell.

"I'm just thinking about how beautiful you are. And how much I love your freckles. And how sexy you are." She started to laugh, so I continued, "And how smart you are, and how happy you make me, and how much I love you."

I stopped on that last one and watched as her face went from being warm and happy, to falling and landing somewhere in the realm of disbelief. Her hands froze for a split second on my face before she started to trace my features with one index finger. She traced my mouth, then dragged her finger over my eyebrows, then moved it from the bridge of my nose to the tip. I watched her eyes and knew that behind them, her mind was running away with her thoughts.

After a moment of complete silence, I attempted to pull her back to me. "What are you thinkin' about?"

She looked at me, her eyes meeting mine, and dropped her hands. She chewed on the inside of her lip, giving herself away. She was nervous, anxious even, and I could see it all over her face.

"I'm thinking about whether or not I should believe you." Her eyes searched my face for a reaction. I understood her hesitation, but it still hurt hearing her say it.

"Haley..."

"It's just that you've said it before and then you were gone. You've made promises in the past just to bail on me without any notice. I've told you how I felt before and you played it off like it was a joke. I know that was a long time ago and I should let it go, but I'm finding it really hard to take your word and trust that you won't disappear again, Cam." She took a deep breath in and slowly released it.

Oh shit, not the breathing thing.

I brushed a piece of hair back from her face and leaned down to kiss her softly. She returned it, but I didn't miss the hesitation I felt in it.

"Haley"—I took a breath myself before continuing—"I know I fucked up when we were younger. I know how much I hurt you and I'm so sorry for being a dick. I've never regretted anything more than how I treated you back then. I wished and dreamed and hoped that one day, *one day,* I could maybe get the chance to fix things between us. I held onto that hope for ten fucking years."

She looked up at me and started chewing on her bottom lip again.

"When I saw you in Charlotte, in the coffee shop, I took it as a sign that this was my chance to make things right. Even if I could only be your friend again, I was okay with that, because it meant I could have you in my life again." I rubbed her cheek with my thumb before continuing.

"I promise, when I say this, I will do anything to keep you in my life. I will do anything to show you that I mean it when I say that I love you, because I do. I have ever since we were kids growing up in the middle of nowhere, Pennsylvania. I just wasn't brave enough to show you then." I kissed her again.

"But I am now, and I promise you, I will do anything to show you that I mean it. Whatever it takes, Haley, I will do it. Because I love you and I will show you that I love you every fucking day if you let me."

I watched her blink back tears and my insides grew warm as her lips started to lift into a small smile. She roped her arms around my neck and she hugged me tightly.

"You have no idea how long I've wanted you to say that to me," she whispered into my ear. I pressed my lips into her neck.

"Forever and always, Haley."

"Forever and always, Cam."

39

HALEY | NOW

The last few weeks went by in a blur and before I knew it, it was the middle of March, and Piper and I only had two weeks left at the bungalow. We'd booked it through the end of the month, and once we were home, we would have two weeks left to finalize everything for the conference. Thinking back to the beginning of January when I booked this place, it felt like a lifetime ago. I booked it to escape the pain I was trapped in. To escape my house that made me feel like I was being suffocated. To escape the constant memories of what I'd lost.

But now, almost three months later, I couldn't remember the last time I felt any of it. The pain. The grief. The crippling anxiety that left me unable to leave my home or sleep in my bed. The other missing thing in my life recently, I've realized, were my thoughts about Connor.

Connor used to consume every thought I had every minute of every day. I thought about him as I worked. I daydreamed about our future together while I was at the gym. I would send him steamy texts during my meetings with Piper whenever I worked outside of the house. So much of who I was as a person was wrapped up in Connor. When I lost him, I felt like I lost a part of myself.

But now, I'd started to remember who I was again.

When I realized it had been over a week since I had thought of Connor, I booked a session with Deborah to talk about it. Part of me felt bad for not thinking about Connor as much anymore. Another part of me felt excited about who I was becoming.

I was starting to feel lighter.

I was starting to laugh deeper.

I was starting to feel happy.

While I would love to give myself all the credit for putting myself back together, I couldn't. I couldn't because I knew deep in my core that if it weren't for Cam, I would still be a shell of my former self. Well, Cam and Piper.

But mostly Cam.

He came into my life again like a freight train, knocking every wall I had built up to protect my heart from him down in one fell swoop. It was like when you watched him on the field and he caught a forty-yard pass to run it into the end zone. He made it look so effortless. That's how things felt when we were together—effortless. And the more time we spent together, the more he carefully and thoughtfully put my broken pieces back together.

We had fallen into a routine over the last two weeks since Cam stayed over and slept in my bed with me. Both of us making a sacred promise that only we understood.

Forever and always.

It was something we'd said to one another growing up, but as adults, it meant so much more. It meant he wouldn't leave me—even though part of me held onto a fear that he would—and it meant that I would work to let him in—which I was trying to do. It also meant that we were an 'us.'

And being an 'us' with Camden Johnson lit my entire soul on fire. My mom nearly cried when I told her. She had always liked Connor, but she always loved Cam.

On the days I wasn't waking up with Cam next to me, I would have a 'Good morning, beautiful' text waiting for me on my phone. He would go for his run, stop at Coastal Brews, and bring Piper and me coffee before we got started on our workday. When he stopped by, he would pull me outside and kiss me against the front door, not caring if any of the neighbors saw. He would then offer to bring over lunch for Piper and me, and I would tell him no for the hundredth time. Then he would pull me in for another kiss and say, "I'm just trying to find an excuse to come by and see my girl."

If we worked late or I hadn't texted him by a certain time in the evening, he would show up with dinner from one of the beachside restaurants and feed us. Piper would never complain and I was always happy to see him.

Then there were the days that I did wake up with Cam next to me. The days when, even when Piper and I had worked past ten and I was so exhausted I could fall asleep on my laptop, I would sneak out of the house and jump into Cam's car to go back to his hotel room with him. We would talk, have incredible, mind-blowing sex, stay up until two or three in the morning, and then in the morning, Cam would walk me home and hold my hand the entire way there.

My favorite days were the ones where Piper and I would wrap up the workday early and Cam would come over and sit on the porch swing with me. Sometimes we would talk, but most times we just sat together, fitting into one another's sides like perfectly matched puzzle pieces, watching the waves go in and out.

These were the moments I wanted to commit to

memory. How Cam looked at me while I drank my coffee or read my email on my phone. The way he would press his nose into my neck and try to slyly sniff my perfume as if I didn't know what he was doing. Or how he would banter back and forth with Piper, my chosen sister, as if they had known each other forever. With every passing moment, I could feel myself coming alive again.

I knew I was falling in love with Cam. I knew from the moment I saw him almost ten months ago in that coffee shop in Charlotte that I had never really stopped loving him. It was as if I had put my feelings for him on a shelf, and when the time came, I pulled them back out and brushed off the dust that had settled on them. He made me feel safe and secure. He made me feel like I wasn't broken, even though I could still feel where I was in some places. He made me laugh and told me I was beautiful and brought me coffee without me even asking. And I loved him for it. Even if I hadn't said the words to him quite yet.

Things were good.

Really good.

And while I knew that things were good and wanted to believe that things would stay good, the voice in the back of my head was always there. Whispering to me as I tried to work or fall asleep or read.

He's going to leave you. You aren't worth sticking around for. Just wait, you'll see.

He'll leave you too.

Just like every other man in your life has.

40

HALEY | NOW

A smile spread across my face unwillingly as I read his message.

It was nearly three o'clock on Thursday and Piper and I had just wrapped up a video call with some of the speakers who were flying in to speak at the conference. She walked back into the room holding two fresh cups of coffee and looked at me.

"Tell Camden I say hello. And that we still have one more call for the day so he can't come and try to jump you before five." Her words came out pointed, but playful. She loved to mess with me when it came to Cam because she knew it always riled me up.

"Piper!"

"What? I'm not the one with a stupid smile on my face while reading a text message." She took a sip of her coffee, trying to hide her smirk. "What, did he send you a dick pic?"

"Oh my god, Piper." I rolled my eyes at her. "You need to grow up."

"You're going to sit there and try to tell me you *wouldn't* be open to receiving a dick pic from him? While I haven't *personally* seen it, based on the stories you've told me and the bulge I've seen in his pants while he looks at you, I'm sure it's not a bad one to look at."

"I'm telling him you said that," I threatened, hoping it would get a rise out of her.

"Good. I'm sure he'll be flattered we're talking about his dick," she said with an added wink. *Dammit.*

> It's good. We're talking about your dick.

> Oh? And why's that?

> Because Piper asked if you sent me a dick pic and that's why I was smiling at my phone. She then told me you probably had a nice looking dick and getting a picture of it from you wouldn't be such a bad thing.

> She's right, I do have a very nice dick. I think you would agree ;)

I rolled my eyes at his message.

> She said you would be flattered.

> I am flattered.

> I find it cute that you were smiling at your phone when I texted you. I'd love to see your smile right now if I could.

This had me smiling again, butterflies taking flight in my belly as I read his message again.

Sorry Johnson, Piper said you're not allowed to come over and try to jump me until after five. We have another call for the conference in half an hour and I need to be on my A-game for it.

I thought you were the boss?

I am. But right now, I am a very distracted boss thanks to you.

I could send you something that would be really distracting, but I won't.

Please do, it would be okay.

Instead, I will ask you to go on a walk with me tonight. Down on the water. What do you say?

Only if you promise to give me a piggyback ride until we hit the water. You know how I feel about sand.

Without even a second passing, he texted me again.

It's a date. I'll pick you up at 6 beautiful.

Go crush this call like the boss I know you are. I can't wait to hear all about it during our walk tonight.

———

As PROMISED AND NEVER LATE, Cam knocked on the front door of the bungalow right at six o'clock that same evening.

Since we were getting closer to spring, it was still warm outside even as the sun was starting to set. I decided to wear a dress I bought when Piper and I went shopping last weekend and carried a sweater I could pop on in case it got chilly. I loved this dress the instant I saw it. It was floral and longer, just hitting around my shins. It had a sweetheart neckline and little lace around the edges that made me feel pretty.

But seeing Cam's eyes on me as I wore it made me feel even prettier. When I came out of my bedroom and walked toward him in the entryway, a big grin spread across his face.

"You look beautiful." His hands wrapped around me and pulled me close, planting a sweet kiss on my cheek. I loved the feeling of his stubble rubbing against my skin. It looked like he hadn't shaved in a few days and the way his face looked with a five o'clock shadow did something to my insides. I squeezed my thighs together as I took him in.

"Thank you," I hummed as he pressed his lips to my cheek. "You don't look so bad yourself, handsome."

He blushed just enough for me to see.

"Have everything?"

"Yep! Let's go." I smiled at him and laced my fingers through his as he pulled me through the door.

"Bye, kids! Have a great time! Remember to practice safe sex, no one wants any accidental love children now!" Piper shouted from the kitchen. At this point I had a long list of comments like that to yell at her about.

We walked to the beach, hand in hand the whole way. When we reached the end of the boardwalk, Cam turned and patted his back which I took as my invitation to jump on so he could give me a piggyback ride down to the water. I placed both my hands on his shoulders and counted to three before jumping up and letting him catch me. I wrapped my legs around his waist and roped my arms around his neck. As he walked toward the water, I dropped my chin into his neck and started to kiss it.

"That's not fair, Jones," Cam groaned as I pressed my lips harder into his neck. When I bit him just a little, he growled.

"We've gone over this, Johnson. I'm not the professional athlete in this relationship, so I don't have to play fair," I mewed in his ear.

He squeezed my ass with his fingers and I yelped out in a mixture of pain and pleasure.

"If you don't stop, I'm going to carry you back to your room, bend you over, and show you just how unfair I can be, pretty girl." His head was facing toward mine as he made the threat.

As much as I wanted to let him do that, I was also looking forward to our walk. Walking had always been our thing.

"Okay, okay, I'll stop. You can put me down now."

We had made it to the edge of the shore where the sand meets the water. Cam set me down gently and spun me around to face him before I could walk any distance away from him. Now facing one another, he wrapped both his arms around my shoulders and kissed me hard. His tongue grazed my lips and I opened mine, letting him in.

Kissing Cam turned all my insides into pudding and this kiss was no different.

He pulled away from me and smiled, "I love your dress, Jones. You're the most beautiful woman I've ever seen. The girl of my dreams. Thank you for coming on this walk with me tonight."

If my insides weren't pudding from the kiss, they were now because of his words.

"You don't have to thank me, Cam. I was happy to come when you texted me earlier. I was starting to miss you." I took his hand in mine and started to lead him down the beach. We walked in silence, enjoying one another's company before he spoke.

"So...it's almost the end, huh?"

Panic struck my belly instantly. What was he talking about, the end? I looked at him with a confused expression.

"What's almost the end?" I asked, the voices in my mind were already starting to run away.

The end of us? The end of our time together? Was this his way of telling me he was leaving?

Was he seriously going to leave me, *again*?

"The end of the trip. You and Piper, you have to head home soon, right? She mentioned the end of March or something?"

Oh, he meant the end of the trip, one voice in my head said, relief started to settle over my already racing heart.

But then another voice spoke; a meaner, nastier one.

Yeah, and the end of you two. You don't even live in the same city. This is his chance to break things off with you. A clear ending point. An easy out. He never really loved you, he just wanted to sleep with you. And you were stupid enough to fall for his games, just like he knew you would be.

I took a deep breath and tried to settle the growing anxiety in my head and stomach before speaking.

"Ye–yeah. The end of March. We have the bungalow through the last weekend of the month and then we need to head back to Wilmington to finish planning the conference."

Our walking had slowed, but his hand was still in mine.

"That means I'll also be heading home soon too..." Cam's voice trailed off and he didn't look at me when he said it. He kept his eyes on the water as it came in and out. His body language was awkward, almost uncomfortable, and he continued to avoid my eyes.

I couldn't believe what I was hearing. Cam was leaving and by the way he was talking, he was going to be leaving me when he did.

My fears were coming true. He was going to leave me just like every other man in my life had. My father when I was just a girl, Cam when we were in college, and Connor who was supposed to be the love of my life. I can't believe how stupid I was to let Cam back into my life like I had. I should have told him to go home when he found me here two months ago. I should have told him to fuck off and leave me alone. I'd cut him out of my life entirely and I should have left him like that.

I couldn't believe he was going to leave me *again.*

"So I guess that means you're leaving me then too, right?" My stomach flipped as the words left my mouth and I ripped my hand from his.

He turned to look at me when I did.

"What?"

"You're leaving me, that's really what you mean. *'I'll be heading home soon,'*" I mocked, "What you really mean is that you'll be leaving *me.*"

"Jones, *what are you talking about*?" His face was screwed up into a confused expression but I knew it was just a cover. He was mad because I'd figured him out and was calling him out on it. I was getting to the punchline before he could this time.

"You, Cam! I'm talking about you, and how you're leaving me. Again! You're taking the easy way out with the end of the trip and are going to leave me just like you did before!"

I started to walk back toward the boardwalk, my hands crossed in front of my chest.

"Haley, come back here! Stop walking away. I don't understand what you're talking about!" I heard him calling out to me but I was moving quickly back toward the boardwalk and he had lost some distance on me. The sand on my feet made me cringe but I didn't care because the thought of standing there next to Cam any longer was worse than feeling it on my feet.

The tears burned in my eyes as I stomped off the beach and made my way toward the road. Feeling stupid and ashamed, I kept my eyes forward as I heard Cam trying to close the gap between us and catch up.

I wouldn't be the one left behind. Not this time.

This time, I would be the one who left.

41

CAM | NOW

I continued after her, watching her long, cinnamon-colored hair blow behind her back as she made her way toward the end of the boardwalk. She had stormed off so quickly that she'd gotten a good lead on me, but thanks to my training and my literal job being to run fast, I caught up to her before she hit the road.

She didn't stop to look at me until I was on her heels and was close enough to grab her. My arm reached for her and I spun her around to look at me. She tried to wrestle her arm out of my hand, but I held on just tight enough so she couldn't escape.

"Let go of me, Camden," she hissed, not looking me in the eye as she did. Tears were in her eyes and it nearly killed me to see her this upset.

"No, not until you explain to me what the fuck is going on." I moved so my face was in front of hers and she had to look at me.

"What's going on?! What's going on is that you're *leaving,* Cam. Just like before. Just like every other fucking man in my life has!" She whipped her arm free and started to walk quickly down the sidewalk. My head was spinning trying to follow her logic.

"Haley, I said I was leaving to go *home,* not that I was leaving *you.* I wouldn't do that, I promised you I wouldn't and I meant it." I was walking quickly, trying to keep up with her as she stormed down the road toward the bungalow.

"Oh yeah? Then what, Cam? We have a long-distance relationship?" she scoffed. "I don't see you being willing to do that. You might as well just leave now; it'll be easier that way."

"Hey, stop!" I grabbed her again and turned her around so she was facing me again. When her face met mine, I could see the tears starting to fall down her freckled cheeks. Her expression was a mix of anger and disappointment. "I'm not going anywhere, I made you that promise weeks ago and I intend on keeping it."

She tried to turn away from me but I grabbed her chin and held her face to mine.

"Do you remember what I said to you, all those years ago, do you remember what I said to you in your dorm room? I told you I loved you and I fucking meant it. I told you I loved you a few weeks ago, and I meant it then too. Dammit, Haley, I love you right now even though you are trying to push me away and I don't understand why." My eyes searched hers for any kind of answer, but I couldn't find one.

She stayed silent as a single tear slipped down her cheek. I wiped it away with my thumb and tried to pull her closer to me.

"I'm not leaving you, Haley. I will never leave you. I promise. Forever and always." I nearly whispered the words to her as I reminded her of my promises.

"I don't believe you," she said through gritted teeth. Her

words felt like a knife to the chest. Even after telling her over and over for weeks that I wouldn't leave her, she still didn't believe me.

She still didn't trust me.

"Haley, I will fight for you, but I will not fight you. If you don't want this, want us, you need to be the one who decides that instead of trying to push me away. I'm not leaving this time, I know I did before but I was an idiot, a stupid kid who was scared." I took a breath and watched as more tears streamed down her face. "But I'm not scared anymore, not to love you. Not to tell you you're beautiful every day. Not to tell other people how amazing I think you are or how much you consume me. I'm not afraid to be here, next to you, telling you that I love you, every day, forever and always."

She didn't speak for a long moment and I thought, just for a second, that she had come to her senses and realized that what I was telling her was the truth, because it was.

"Let me go, Cam, please. I want to go home now." Her words stunned me but I didn't want to force her to stay if she didn't want to.

So I let her go.

But I didn't *let her go*.

No. I promised her I wouldn't leave her and I intended on keeping that promise. Even if she was trying to push me away.

After I released her from my hold, she spun on her heel and stormed off down the street back toward the bungalow.

And I followed close behind her the entire way back.

42

HALEY | NOW

I knew he was following me as I hurried back toward the bungalow but I refused to turn around and tell him to stop. I couldn't even look at him for fear that I would fall apart completely. He wouldn't get that out of me and I wouldn't give him that kind of satisfaction.

But I knew he was there, following just close enough to keep me in eyeshot. Partially because I could hear his footsteps on the pavement and partially because my back tingled where his eyes burned into it.

I quickened my step as I got closer to the bungalow, pushing through the white picket fence gate and slamming it behind me to cut Cam off. I made it to the front door before he could reach me and slammed it shut behind me.

I heard him call my name from the other side of the door.

"Haley. Haley, please!" he shouted through the thick mahogany. "Jones, open the door. Please talk to me."

"Go away, Cam, there's nothing to talk about!" I shouted back at him.

Behind me, I heard Piper's footsteps coming from the

hallway. She leaned out of her bedroom and looked at me, concern filling her face.

"Hays, what's going on?"

"Please, Haley, just open the door. Please!" Cam shouted again.

"Cam, I don't want to talk to you! There's nothing to talk about, just leave!" Frustration and anxiety were building in my throat and tears were burning my eyes.

You're so fucking stupid, the voices inside my head said. *He never loved you and you're a fool for thinking he did.*

I could feel the panic building in my stomach, a large knot forming as Cam continued to beg for me to open the door.

"I'm not leaving you, Jones. I promised you I wouldn't and I meant it!"

"Haley..." Piper put her hand on my shoulder and I tried to ground myself in how it felt. I could feel the anxiety building and needed something to help ground myself in what was real.

What are five things you see? I thought to myself, running through a strategy Deborah taught me when I felt an anxiety attack coming on. I looked around the room and tried to name five things, but the tears in my eyes blurred my vision.

You were never meant to have him, the nasty voice inside my head said. *He saw that you were weak and alone. He just wanted to get you in bed, make you love him, and then leave. He would never stay for you; you aren't worth sticking around for.*

Why do you think your dad left? And Connor? They never loved you enough to stick around and neither does Cam.

You're worthless. Unlovable.

That's why every man leaves you.

"That's not true," I whispered to myself, trying to catch my breath.

Just wait, next it will be Piper. Then your mom and Deborah. You're broken and who wants to be with someone who's as broken as you are?

My hands were starting to clench at my sides and I dug my fingernails into my palms to try and hold back the tears. The feeling that I hadn't felt since coming to the bungalow was back. Like two hands were wrapped around my neck and were slowly starting to squeeze all the air out of me.

"Hays, are you okay?" Piper's voice felt so distant, even though I knew she was standing right next to me.

My heart raced and the feeling of being suffocated was growing. My eyes burned, my nose was running and my stomach was knotted like old ivy to a brick building. I couldn't breathe. I felt like I was underwater and drowning. Nothing felt real or safe or stable. Everything I worried about was coming true.

Cam didn't love me.

He just wanted to use me.

And I fucking let him.

Again.

"Haley, can you hear me? Breathe, sweetie, you're having a panic attack. You're safe. You're okay."

I fell to my knees, my hands on the floor in front of me, Piper knelt next to me, speaking slowly.

All of the voices in my head were screaming, and I tried to speak, but the lump in my throat had completely cut off my ability to form words. I worked to raise my eyes to look at her mouth as she spoke, trying to process what she was saying. Trying to escape my mind and the horrible place it had trapped me in.

"I'm okay..." I questioned through panicked breaths.

Tears fell from my face and landed on the backs of my hands.

"Yes, you're okay, sweetie. Breathe." She soothed and took some deep breaths, encouraging me to mimic her.

"Jones? Jones, are you okay?!" I could hear Cam's hurried and panicked voice through the front door but did nothing. I couldn't see him. I couldn't open the door and let him see what he had done to me.

"Camden, shut up!" Piper shouted back to him, "Just give us a minute!"

She looked back at me and held my cheeks in her hands, forcing me to look at her. So I had to focus on something real instead of the voices and fears that were spiraling inside my head.

"Sweetie? Are you in there? Can you hear me?" Piper had experienced my panic attacks in the past after I lost Connor and she always knew how to bring me back.

She spoke slowly, didn't force me to talk or do anything I wasn't ready to do, and never told me I was being crazy or overdramatic. She kept her cool, took things slow, and helped me come back to real life on my own time.

"Yeah...yeah I hear you, Piper," I said slowly. My breath was starting to slow and my eyes were starting to dry. I looked down at my hands which were flat against the floor and started to count each of my fingers. Something that always helped me when I was having an anxiety attack was rooting myself in things that I could see. Things that I could see were real.

"Okay, good. Now tell me five things you see around you."

I did what she asked and thought about how much I loved her. Piper was always in my corner and always tried to make me feel better. I couldn't have asked for a better friend.

"Are you ready to get up now?" she asked, sitting on her knees and offering me her hands.

"I'm tired," I whispered, trying to meet her gaze again. Something most people don't know about anxiety attacks is that they're physical and exhausting. They take everything out of you no matter how big or small they are. And this one was the biggest I'd had in months.

"I'm sure you are, sweetie. Can you stand? I'll take you to your room so you can sleep." She offered me her hands and we stood together.

We walked down the hallway, Piper's arm wrapped around my waist as she led me to my bedroom. Once inside, she helped me change out of my dress and into my pajamas. She pulled the covers back on my bed and pulled them up to my chin once I was safely tucked inside.

Piper was my best friend, but right now, she was acting like the sister I always wanted.

Before she left my room, she leaned down and kissed my forehead, a tight smile on her lips as she pulled away.

"You gonna be okay, Hays?" she whispered in the doorway before she left my room.

I didn't answer her and turned over so I was facing away from her. She took that as her answer and left my room, closing the door behind her. Once I heard the small click of the door shutting behind her, my eyes squeezed together as tears sprung in them once more.

I couldn't answer her question because giving her an answer felt too painful. It felt like if I vocalized it, I would break into a million little pieces all over again.

No, I'm not going to be okay, I thought to myself. *Because Cam doesn't love me and now he's leaving me again. This will be the thing that ruins me for good.*

I cried into my pillow as quietly as I could to avoid

having Piper come in and check on me. I wanted to be alone. I figured I should get used to the feeling since it was clear that I will be alone for the rest of my fucking life.

I don't even remember falling asleep, eyes still wet with tears, and my heart breaking into a million little pieces.

43

CAM | NOW

It'd been ten minutes since Piper yelled at me through the door and I was losing my fucking mind standing on the porch. I knew I could have just walked in, I didn't hear anyone lock the door, but I also wanted to respect Haley's space.

I wanted her to come back to me.

To choose me.

To let me in.

But she didn't, and when I heard her start to cry and Piper asked if she was okay, I panicked.

Was she hurt? Did she need help? Should I just say fuck it and go inside? I wanted to be next to her so badly but I also knew that I was part of the reason she was hurting.

I scanned my brain through our conversation over and over again, trying to pinpoint what I had said that upset her. I mentioned going home, but not leaving her. The whole point of asking her to go for a walk was to talk to her about me staying with her for a few more weeks in Wilmington until I had to report back for spring training. We didn't even get that far though before she ran off and got pissed at me.

As I was dissecting every syllable of our conversation and pacing on the front porch of the bungalow, the front door swung open. I turned quickly and my heart dropped when I saw that it was Piper, not Haley, standing in the doorway.

"Where is she?" I asked hastily.

"Come inside and be quiet." Piper's tone was short. I could tell she was pissed by the icy expression she was shooting me.

I did as I was told and slowly stepped inside the door, Piper closing it softly behind me. I slipped my shoes off and followed her as she waved her hand at me. We walked through the kitchen and out onto the back porch. Piper closed the sliding glass door behind us and sat down on the porch swing. The last time I was out here I was with Haley, her head in my lap as I stroked her hair and we watched the waves come in and out on the shoreline.

"Sit down." Piper's words were sharp and stung like venom. I felt like I was being scolded by my mother or my very scary fourth-grade teacher, Mrs. Brownstein.

I sat down next to her, not saying anything, my hands anxiously rubbing against my knees. Piper didn't look at me and sat sitting straight up on the swing, her eyes facing the water. Anger, fear, and a hint of sheer insanity sat on her face and I braced myself for the verbal lashing I knew she was about to give me. Piper was a great person until you threatened or harmed the people she loved. Then she was a lioness out for the kill. No mercy. No holds barred.

"What the fuck did you do?" She looked at me, her eyes cutting me to the core.

"Nothing, I swear!" I defended myself but a little too loudly and Piper was quick to shush me. I lowered my voice and spoke again, "Nothing. I swear, Piper."

"Then why the fuck did my best friend just have a complete and total meltdown? I haven't seen her have an anxiety attack this bad since the first week after she lost Connor. *Clearly*, you did something!"

"She had a panic attack? Is she okay? I need to go see her." I stood from the swing but Piper grabbed my wrist and yanked me back down.

"To hell you are. You aren't going to go in there just to set her off again. I will sooner kill you and throw your lifeless body into the ocean to become fish food before I let you go in there and see her."

"Piper, I swear to you, I didn't do anything. We were walking on the beach, having a good time. We were just talking, and then suddenly she was upset and stormed off!" I waved my hands in front of my face as I explained what happened.

"What were you talking about?" Her posture hadn't changed and I could tell she was on the offensive. Ready to gut me like a fish as soon as she figured out where I had slipped up and caused Haley so much pain.

"We were talking about the end of the trip and how you guys only had two more weeks here. She mentioned heading back to Wilmington and I mentioned going home too, back to Charlotte. I was about to ask her if I could stay with her in Wilmington for a few weeks when—"

"Wait, you mentioned going home?" Piper cut me off.

"Yeah, I said that I would be heading home too since you guys are leaving. I was only staying here as long as you guys were, but your trip is about to be over which means I'm going to head home too. When I said that, she totally freaked out."

Piper suddenly relaxed in her seat and pushed her hair out of her face with both hands. She looked up into the dark sky and let out a long, deep exhale. I wondered if she picked that up from Haley. She looked at me for the first time since letting me into the house.

"She thought you were leaving her, instead of just leaving *here*, didn't she?" Piper spoke so matter-of-factly.

"Yeah...how did you know that?"

"Because Camden," another deep breath, "I know my best friend. And for the last two months, all she's worried about is you leaving her. So, when you said you would be going home, I'm sure she took that to mean you were leaving *her*."

"But I've told her so many times that I *won't* leave her. I've done everything except tattoo it across my forehead. I don't understand why she doesn't believe me. I don't know what I need to do to get her to believe me." My words sounded exactly how I felt, exasperated and confused. "That also makes no sense. Why would me talking about going home mean that I was really talking about leaving her?"

"It doesn't need to make sense to you, Camden. It makes sense to her, to her anxiety. You said 'I'm going home,' and she heard 'I'm leaving you.' It doesn't need to make sense to you for it to feel very real to her."

What was she talking about? Haley doesn't have anxiety...

"What are you talking about? What anxiety...?"

Piper took a deep breath and stood up for a moment from the swing causing it to move slightly. She reached out to steady it before sitting back down, tucking one leg underneath her as she did. She was fully facing me now, her arm wrapped around her knee that was bent in front of her. She looked at me with understanding and sadness.

"Camden, Haley isn't the same girl you used to know growing up. Losing Connor...it changed her. It planted a seed of doubt and worry in her that wasn't there before the accident. That seed has now bloomed into anxiety. Full-fledged, hard-to-manage, deeply-rooted anxiety. She does a really good job at covering it up, but it's there. I see it every day, running around behind her eyes."

My mind started to race, suddenly picking up on cues that I'm sure were her anxiety peeking out when I thought they were just new, weird quirks she had picked up during our time apart. The breathing, the long pauses before saying anything, the chewing of her lip.

"That's part of the reason she's in therapy," Piper continued softly. "When she lost Connor, she didn't leave her house for almost a month. Shit, she didn't even shower for almost two weeks and she only did when her mom practically stripped her down and forced her to. Has she told you that she hasn't even slept in her bed since Connor passed?"

"No..." I had no idea Haley was hurting like this. She hadn't told me and I felt like a complete ass for not asking. For not noticing how much she was still struggling.

"So when you said you were going to be going home..."

"She thought she was going to lose me too," I finished Piper's thought. She nodded her head slowly and pursed her lips together. "*Shit.*"

"Yeah, shit." Piper looked at me for a long moment before moving her eyes to the water. The sun had set completely and it was well past nine. It was dark out near the water but you could still hear the waves crashing into the shore.

"So tonight," I started after a few silent moments. "She had a panic attack?" The thought of Haley being in this kind of pain made me want to hold her close and protect her at all costs. I was angry at myself now that I knew the pain I had caused her and sad that she was struggling in this way.

She didn't deserve to suffer like that, especially because of something I had said.

"Yeah, a big one too. She hasn't had one this big in months."

My heart dropped into my stomach.

"Does she have them a lot?"

"Not recently she hasn't. She hasn't since we've been here actually. She's almost seemed...like her old self again. The Haley we knew before losing Connor. But back home" —Piper took a breath and looked back out toward the water, her mind going somewhere else, to a memory—"back home, she was struggling. She had them a lot after losing Connor and they take everything out of her. She's exhausted once she comes out of them and usually sleeps the rest of the day."

"You've helped her through them?" I asked, my heart swelled with gratitude knowing that Piper had been there for Haley through all of it.

"Yep. Me and her mom. We've figured out how to help her through them and how to bring her back to us when she's having them. It's horrible, watching her struggle and feeling like you can't do anything to help. I would do anything to take that pain away from her." Tears were forming in Piper's eyes and her voice hitched in her throat.

I reached over and squeezed her hand, trying to console her.

"You're a good friend, Piper. You're the best kind of friend. I can't speak for Haley, she would kill me if I tried, but I want you to know how grateful I am that you're part of Haley's life. Thank you for helping her. Thank you for being there for her as she works through this."

Big, wet, heavy tears fell from Piper's eyes and she gave me a big smile.

"Thank you, Camden. I love Haley like my sister. I would do anything for her. Including killing you if you hurt her—don't forget that." She playfully punched me in the arm and we both laughed, Piper's coming out more like a cough. I didn't need her to remind me, I knew that she would.

The two of us sat on the porch swing and talked for almost an hour.

Piper filled me in on everything Haley had been struggling with before coming to the bungalow. She told me about how losing Connor changed Haley and how seeing Deborah had really helped her start to heal. Piper also taught me what to do when Haley was having a panic attack, which I was grateful for. While I hoped I'd never have to witness her in so much pain, I wanted to know how I could best support her if I did. I wanted to be able to support Haley through anything, including this if she needed me to.

Before going to bed, Piper told me I could stay and sleep on the couch if I wanted, which I did. I wanted to be here in the morning and show Haley that I meant it when I told her I wasn't leaving.

I wanted her to see that, even in her darkest, hardest moments, I loved her and would stand by her side no matter how hard she pushed me away. I wanted her to know, to see, to believe, that no matter what, I loved her. That I wasn't going anywhere. That I would be by her side, as long as she would let me.

Forever and always.

44

HALEY | NOW

My eyes were raw and red when I woke up the next morning. I didn't even remember falling asleep, but based on how puffy my eyes felt, I knew I fell asleep crying. I rubbed my eyes as I sat up in bed and slipped my toes onto the floor, finding comfort in feeling something real.

Last night was bad. Last night was the worst I had been in a long time.

When I first lost Connor, panic attacks like the one I had last night were a weekly occurrence. Sometimes even happening multiple times in a week.

But ever since coming here, to the bungalow, I hadn't felt anxious like that at all. Like my whole world was slipping out from under me and I was being swallowed up in quicksand. But hearing Cam's words completely set me off and turned my entire world upside down.

His name felt like poison in my mind. Just thinking about him made me sick to my stomach. I can't believe how stupid I was to fall for his games again. How naive I had been to believe that this time, he really loved me. And that I could be loved by him in the way I had wanted to be loved for so long. The thing that hurt the most was that I knew I loved him back.

You're such a fucking fool, I heard the voice inside my head spit. I shook my head, trying to ignore the ever-present voice that always made me feel like shit.

Pushing myself up from my bed, I headed toward my bathroom. When I saw myself in the mirror, I almost didn't recognize the girl looking back at me. My hair looked familiar, the same shade of red it had been since I was little. My freckles were all still where they had always been, scattered across my nose and cheeks like paint splatters on a canvas.

But my eyes...they looked different. They looked sad and hollow, like all the light in them had finally gone out.

"You fought a tough battle. But everyone hits their breaking point," I said to myself, splashing my face with water and pulling my tangled hair back into a messy bun. I didn't have the energy to brush it. It could become a tangled mess, just like my heart, for all I cared. Normally I would change into regular clothes before going out for breakfast since it was a work day, but I didn't have the energy for that either. I knew Piper would understand and not make me feel bad for wearing baggy sweats and an oversized tee shirt while we worked.

As I walked toward the door, my hand moved to grab the sweatshirt that was folded on the chair in the corner of my room but stopped before my fingers reached it. It was Cam's, the one he had given me after our first night together in his hotel room. I'd kept it, telling him he would never get it back. Now it sat there like a cruel reminder of the game I had lost.

Leaving the sweatshirt behind, I pulled the door open and headed toward coffee. My feet padded across the old hardwood floor as I passed the living room. I had almost made it to the kitchen when I saw a large, broad-shouldered, finely chiseled figure rise from the couch. Unsure of if my brain was playing a trick on me, I turned slowly to face it.

"What the hell are you doing here?" My voice was flat. Emotionless. Just like how I felt inside.

"Why are you always asking me that?" *Is he trying to be cute right now?*

"I told you to leave."

"And I told him to stay." My head whipped toward the hallway where Piper was exiting her room, already fully dressed for the day.

"What? Piper, what the hell?" I wasn't sure if I should be angry or annoyed with my best friend. I settled on both.

"I know you're pissed and you can yell at me about it later. But, sweetie—and I'm saying this because it's my duty as your best friend to do so—you two need to talk." She was now in front of me, placing one hand on my shoulder.

"I don't want to talk to him." My eyes were set on Piper, avoiding Cam at all costs.

"Well, I'm done talking to him and I think you're crazy if you don't. I'm heading out for a few hours, I'll be back later." She turned to face Cam. "I'll see you later, Camden. Good luck. And don't fuck this up because I will kill you if I have to. And I won't feel bad for doing it."

My eyes followed Piper as she walked toward the entryway and when I heard the door click behind her, I knew I was alone with Cam once more.

Without even thinking, my body rushed toward my room so I could close the door and lock it behind me. Cam anticipated the move though, *damn football player,* and cut me off in the hallway. Using one arm to block the hallway and one arm extended in front of him to stop me, I didn't have anywhere to go. For a split second, I thought about running out of the house behind Piper, but that would be totally immature and embarrassing.

Plus, I'm pretty sure Piper would haul my ass back here if I tried.

"Jones..." Cam started before I interrupted him.

"I don't want to talk to you." I turned away from him and walked back toward the kitchen. If I was going to make it through this, I was going to need some coffee. Cam's footsteps followed closely behind me to the kitchen.

My hands reached for the filters, coffee, and mug with very little thinking. Over the last eight weeks, this process has become part of my morning routine and I could find everything I needed for my morning fix with my eyes closed.

"Haley, please, can we just talk?" Cam pleaded.

"We don't need to talk. We talked enough last night. I'm done talking."

"Okay fine, I'll talk," he said, trying to get his body in front of me as I moved around the kitchen. "Haley, I'm so sorry for last night. I didn't mean to upset you and I—Haley, will you stop and look at me."

I continued to ignore him, thinking that if I did it well enough he would just disappear from my kitchen and be gone for good.

"Haley...Haley, look at me, *please.*" Cam's words came out as a plea and his hands laced around my waist, forcing me to spin and face him. Twenty-four hours ago, the move would've made my heart skip a beat. Now it just felt like being pricked by a thousand tiny needles.

"Haley, look at me." I may have been facing him but I

was staring at his chest. He was still wearing his clothes from last night, which meant he hadn't left.

"Please, beautiful. Please look at me."

I closed my eyes and took a deep breath. I held it in for a few seconds before slowly releasing it. I forced my eyes to look up into his and tried to keep myself from getting lost in the only pair of eyes that ever made my heart completely melt.

"There she is..." he whispered with a small smile on his face.

We were close, our bodies only a few inches apart, and I could smell him.

Pine, earth, and AstroTurf. Just like always.

"Why won't you just leave me alone?" I grumbled, trying to pull my eyes away from his but failing miserably.

"Because I love you, Haley Jones. And I made you a promise that I would never leave you. I intend on keeping that promise, no matter how hard you try to push me away." His words came out like honey, sweet and thick.

My heart started to beat faster and there was a growing heat in my core. *Stop it. Keep your walls up, woman. You will not fall for his games so easily.*

"What are you thinking about?" Cam's eyes were searching mine. I turned my face away from him, trying to conceal the thoughts that were running around in my head.

"Come on, Jones. I see it behind your eyes, you're thinking about something. Tell me, please."

"I'm thinking about what a fool I am. How stupid I was to believe you when you said you weren't leaving. How hilarious you must find this entire situation," I spat out at him and tried to push him away from me, but he held me in place effortlessly. "Oh, I got her again! Jones really thinks I love her, time to deliver the punchline!" I mocked.

Cam's face slowly morphed into one of sadness and disappointment, but he didn't pull away from me. We stood there in the kitchen, chest to chest, as the coffee maker spurted and bubbled on the countertop. Neither of us said anything for a few, long moments.

Then, as the coffee machine beeped to let me know my coffee was ready, Cam leaned down and pressed his lips to my forehead. It felt like my heart was healing and breaking into a million pieces all at once.

"Can you please tell that brain of yours to stop making shit up?" he whispered, pressing his forehead to mine. "And the voices, can you tell them to shut the fuck up too?"

I pulled my face away from him quickly and looked at him in shock. How did he know about the voices?

"Piper," he said, knowingly. *Of course, Piper told him.*

"Haley, I wish you'd told me sooner that you were struggling."

I chewed on my bottom lip, trying to stop the tears from coming to the edge of my eyes.

"Hey." He swiped his thumb over my lip. "You don't have to do that. You don't have to hold it back or pretend. You're safe with me. You don't have to hide."

Again, I tried to move away from him, to hide in my bedroom until he left, but he wouldn't let me go. He kissed my forehead again and my heart, the little traitor, flipped behind my sternum.

"I'm fine, Cam," I lied. Because I wasn't fine. I hadn't been fine in almost a year.

That's why I had Deborah. That's why I did the breathing exercises and chewed my lip until it bled. That's why I would consider and reconsider my words a hundred times before speaking them aloud. It's why I didn't leave my house or change my clothes or sleep in my own bed. It's why

I couldn't believe Cam when he told me he wasn't going to leave me. That he loved me. That he wanted to be with me.

Because I wasn't fine.

And Cam was seeing that now.

Just how unfine I actually was.

And I knew it would be another reason he would use to leave me for good.

"Jones, I've known you since we were six years old. I know when you aren't fine and you're not. I see it in your eyes." He tilted my chin up so I had to meet his gaze. "But I promise you, I love you anyway. Whether you're fine or not fine, *I love you.*"

I don't know if it was his eyes or how he smelled or the way he spoke, but a small flutter of hope started to swell in my chest.

"I get it now. Why it's so hard for you to believe me when I say that I love you or that I won't leave you." He paused. "Well, I don't totally understand it, but I hope you will talk to me about it more so I can start to understand."

A small laugh escaped me because I knew what he meant.

"And I hope"—he planted a soft kiss on one cheek—"that with time"—he kissed the other cheek—"and daily reminders"—he kissed my nose—"that you start to believe" —and then my neck—"that I love you and that I'm never leaving you. Ever."

He took my face in both hands, his strong fingers on both of my cheeks and sealed his promise with a kiss.

When his lips touched mine, I felt the words start to sink in. They didn't feel like words, they felt like something real. Like something I could hold in my hands or steady ground that I could stand on. It felt different this time, hearing him tell me he loved me. That he was never going to leave me.

Maybe it was the electricity that shot through my veins every time I felt his lips on my skin or maybe it was because when they did, all the voices in my head went silent. For once, there was silence.

No panic.

No worry.

Just silence and safety.

I couldn't hold back the tears anymore and started to cry as we stood in the kitchen, kissing one another softly.

When Cam felt the wetness on my cheeks, he pulled away and looked at me with concern.

"Haley, beautiful, what's wrong? What did I say? I'm sorry I didn't mean to—"

"Cam." I brought my hand up to his cheek and he leaned into it like he always did. "I love you."

His face fell and I knew I had stunned him with my words.

"You what?" Cam nearly stuttered and I had to bite back a laugh. He was so cute when he was thrown off guard.

"I said"—I mimicked his actions and kissed one of his cheeks—"I"—my lips moved to kiss the other cheek—"love" —then his nose—"you." And I sealed my promise with a kiss, just like he had.

A slow growing grin bloomed on his face before he laughed and wrapped his arms around my waist. He lifted me off my feet as I wrapped my arms around his neck and buried my nose into his neck. When my feet were back on the ground, he grabbed my face again and kissed me hard this time.

"I've been waiting almost twenty years to hear you say that, Haley Jones," he said breathlessly, breaking our lips apart.

"And I've been waiting since I was sixteen for you to be mine, Camden Johnson," I confessed.

"Beautiful, I'm all yours. Forever and always."

As he pulled me back into his lips, I knew he meant it.

45

HALEY | NOW

I was standing in the entryway, taking in the last few images of the bungalow.

Looking around, so many memories from the last ten weeks swarmed my mind. The late nights when Piper and I would drink wine on the couch. The time Cam showed up with bags of food and coffee one morning and left his number on the note. When Cam stayed in my bed for the first time after coming over for dinner. It had only been ten weeks, but to me, it felt like an entire lifetime.

When I booked the bungalow, I was trying to escape.

Escape my house that felt like it was suffocating me. Escape my mind that was holding me hostage. Escape a horrible nightmare that I could never wake up from. But now, as I was leaving it, I didn't feel like I had to escape anymore. I felt like I had finally been freed and I could breathe on my own again.

The final week and a half at the bungalow was a dream I will never forget.

Cam stayed with me every night and Piper and I finalized all the last-minute details for the conference. When we weren't working, the three of us cooked dinner together, sat on the back porch sipping wine and beer, and laughed until we were too exhausted to function anymore. Then, I would take Cam with me to bed and we would whisper under the covers as if we were in high school doing something we weren't allowed to do. He thought it was fun to try to get me to cry out while his head was between my legs or we were having mind-blowing sex with Piper asleep across the hall. We didn't *have* to be quiet, but we didn't want to be rude either.

A few days ago, Cam and I walked to Coastal Brews and sat at the same table I was sitting at when he walked up to me back in January. It was weird to think that it was only ten weeks ago, but sitting at the table filled me with a sense of nostalgia I wanted to hang on to forever. As we sat together, Cam eating a bear claw and me sipping on an iced macchiato, he asked me if he could stay with me in Wilmington until after the conference was over.

"I have spring training starting soon, but I want to stay with you until it starts," he'd said, "Would that be okay? I can rent something there if it's weird for me to be at your house."

My heart swelled at his offer. I had told Cam how I felt about being in the house Connor and I called home, and it meant so much to me that he didn't want to cross a line. He found a condo to rent for a month downtown that same morning as soon as we got back to the bungalow.

I wasn't sure how we would make things work between us once we got home, with him needing to be in Charlotte and me needing to be in Wilmington, but I knew we would. Cam reminded me of such every night before we fell asleep.

"Just so you know, I love you and I'm never leaving. It might not be perfect, but we'll make it work. I would do anything for you, beautiful," he would say before kissing my forehead. Every time he pressed his lips there, all the voices in my head would go quiet.

I knew it wouldn't be easy, but I also knew I could believe him.

"You ready, beautiful?" Cam's warm voice from behind me pulled me from my thoughts and back into the present day.

He had a bag slung over his shoulder and another in his hand and was standing in the front doorway of the bungalow. His teeth were showing through the smile he was giving me and his eyes caught the light in such a way that I swore, they sparkled. I took a deep breath and swept the inside of the bungalow one more time with my eyes before turning to him.

"Yep! Let's go."

We walked out of the bungalow together and I turned to lock the door behind me. Piper was standing next to my car, keys in hand, looking at Cam and me with a knowing look.

"You two lovesick kids ready or what?! I wanna get home and sleep in my bed and not have to listen to you two fucking across the hall for once!" She shouted across the driveway as she lowered herself into the car.

"Piper!"

"Oh stop, sweetie, I'm just teasing. I'm always glad to hear that Camden is making you happy." She winked at me and pulled the car door closed. I rolled my eyes at her as Cam opened my door for me.

"I'm so sorry for her," I said to him as I slipped into the car.

"I'm not. I'm glad she can tell how crazy I make you just by the sounds you make." A cocky smirk spread across his face. I shook my head at him.

"I hate you. Get in the car." He closed my door gently, checking to make sure I was in before he did.

Cam took his place next to me in the driver's seat and we waved at Piper as she pulled out before us. I looked to Cam, who gave me a warm smile before leaning over the dash to give me a quick kiss.

"I love you, Haley Jones. Forever and always."

"I love you too, Camden Johnson. Forever and always."

As we pulled out of the driveway, with Cam's hand on my thigh, I looked back to the little bungalow that had been nothing more than a picture on my laptop screen ten weeks ago. A place I didn't know, a place that was a stranger to me. Leaving it now though, it didn't feel strange at all.

As a matter of fact, coming to this little bungalow felt a lot like coming home.

46

CAM | NOW

If you had told me eight months ago that I would be driving back to Wilmington with Haley Jones in the passenger seat of my car, I wouldn't have believed you. If you had told me eight months ago that Haley Jones and I would be *dating,* I would've told you that you were hooked on some kind of drugs and needed to seek professional help.

But here we are.

And there she was, sitting next to me in the passenger seat, singing loudly to a Taylor Swift playlist.

She didn't even ask if we could listen to it but instead, just plugged in her phone and turned the volume all the way up. I didn't care though. I was happy to let her be happy like this. Shit, I would learn every word to every Taylor Swift song if she asked me to.

As we packed up and left the bungalow, I couldn't believe how far we'd come. When I ran into her last August in Charlotte, I never imagined this would be where we were eight months later.

Together and in love.

And watching her now out of the corner of my eye, I don't think I could've asked for anything better. Her cinnamon-colored hair was blowing in the wind because she insisted on having the windows down until we got out of town and her freckles shined off her skin. I always thought Haley was beautiful. Ever since that day in ninth grade when she was walking toward me in that denim skirt, I thought she was the most beautiful person in the world.

I looked at her again as she sang loudly and without shame and my heart skipped a beat. She must have felt my eyes on her because she turned and looked at me with an inquisitive look.

"What are you looking at?" She smiled and I could feel the blood rush to my face when she did. Before answering, I paused to really take in what I was looking at.

A woman who had fully consumed me and changed me forever. The girl I used to run around with on the playground and try to catch a glimpse of from across the cafeteria. My better half and the person I would move mountains for just to make her smile.

"I'm just looking at you, beautiful." I grabbed her hand and pressed it to my lips, kissing the back of it. "And I can't wait to look at you like this, forever and always."

EPILOGUE

HALEY | ONE YEAR LATER

Cam's hand was on my knee as we drove down the two-lane highway that took us to the place where we fell back together just a year ago.

The place where he borderline stalked me just to get the chance to see me one more time. The place where he bought me coffee, gave me piggyback rides, and told me he loved me. The place where we had fallen in love all over again.

This past year had been totally insane. The She Who Thrives Live! conference went off without a hitch and we'd already sold out this year's event which was in another month. I told Cam I was too busy to make the trip here but he insisted that we come at least for the weekend.

After the conference was over last year, Cam had to head back to Charlotte to start spring training and I went with him for the first few weeks. It was so fun to see where he lived, explore his city, and spruce up his loft—which was really an apartment, but he called it a loft. I was surprised to see how well it was decorated until he told me that he had paid someone to do the decorating for him.

Men.

Over the summer months, Cam and I traveled back and forth between Wilmington and Charlotte in order to spend as much time together as we could.

Being back home was nice until after a few weeks, the feeling of two invisible hands around my neck started to creep in and consume me. I listed the house Connor and I once shared by the end of that week and moved into a new, smaller, but still nice, condo by the end of the month.

Piper helped me move into my new place, which was in the same neighborhood as hers since Cam was tied up with training. We FaceTimed that night so I could show him my new place and then promptly had a round of long-distance phone sex.

Once the season started, I was in Charlotte for every home game. I would drive up a few days before the game, stay with Cam, and then watch his game with the other player's wives and girlfriends. I finally got to meet Harvey and loved sitting with his wife and kids during the games. Whenever Cam traveled, he offered to fly me out to wherever he was playing, which I did whenever I could.

It wasn't an easy situation and I missed him like crazy when we were apart, but we made it work. Every day we were together, Cam would pull me into his arms and tell me he loved me and that he was never leaving me. On the days we were apart, he would call me and tell me the same thing. I'd stopped needing the reminder to know it was true but I never told him to stop saying it.

Even with all the travel, game days, conference planning, and business running, I still made it a weekly priority to meet with Deborah. Not because my anxiety was bad or I was still in the darkness of grief, but because I knew it was good for me. Plus, I liked Deborah and didn't like the idea of not seeing her anymore. When I told her about Cam and me, she told me how proud she was of me, and I cried.

"We're here," Cam said, tapping my thigh with his hand, pulling me out of my thoughts.

As we pulled up to the bungalow, I couldn't help but smile. This little house on the coast changed so much of me when I was here last year, and being here now felt like being home. I looked at the chipped, white picket fence around the front and the big mahogany front door. Memories from last winter filled me up and made my insides swirl with joy.

Cam turned the car off and quickly came to my side of the car to open my door for me. Reaching out, he offered his hand to me and I took it, pulling myself out of the car with his help. We stood in front of the car and took in the bungalow together.

"Oh..." My heart dropped suddenly. "Someone bought the place."

My eyes looked at the big red and white "*SOLD!*" sign that was in the front yard as sadness filled my belly. While I knew people had stayed in the bungalow since we had left it a year ago, it made me sad to think we wouldn't be able to come back here to visit again. Cam weaved his fingers through mine and pulled me toward the front door, pushing through the little gate as we went.

"Cam, stop, we can't do this," I said as we walked up the front walkway. "Someone else owns this house. I don't think it's a rental anymore. We're trespassing." Fear and worry were starting to sink into my belly, and I looked around panicking that a cop would roll up any second.

"Jones." He kissed my forehead once we were standing on the front step of the bungalow. "Tell the voices in your head to be quiet. We're fine." He pressed another kiss to the spot on my forehead and I felt the voices in my head start to settle.

"But Cam, we can't—"

"We can, beautiful." That's when he pulled a single key out of his back pocket and dangled it in front of his face. My eyes went wide staring at it before they went back to Cam's.

"Cam...what did you do?"

"Are you happy?"

"Cam, what the hell did you do?"

"Why are you always asking me that?" The cocky grin I loved so much was on his face. I squealed and jumped into his arms and he picked me up and spun me around.

"Oh my god, I can't believe you did this! We can't live here though, you play back in Charlotte and I have the condo in Wilmington."

He was unlocking the front door as I spoke.

"I know we can't live here, not yet at least. But I'll be retiring in a few years and then I thought we could move in here together. Until then, we could use it as a place to escape when we want to be alone or just get away." His voice was behind me now as I walked into the front entryway. Looking around the bungalow, I had never felt more at home.

"Oh my god, Cam, I can't believe you—"

I turned to face him again and stopped when I found him down on one knee. My breath caught in my throat and my heart started to race.

"Cam..."

"Haley Jones"—he took one of my hands and kissed the back of it—"I have loved you since we were fifteen and trying to figure out life in a small town in Pennsylvania. I may not have been able to get my shit together right away, but I have now."

I laughed a little as tears started to prick my eyelids.

"When I saw you in that coffee shop in Charlotte, I knew I wasn't going to be able to let you get away again. I made a promise to myself that very day that I would do anything, *anything*, to have you in my life again. And now that I have you, I will do anything to keep you in it." He stood and I had to lift my chin to keep my eyes on him.

"Jones, I promise to tell you I love you every single day and to remind you that I will never, not ever, leave your side. As long as you will let me, I will be here for you. Keeping you safe and making you feel loved. You're mine, beautiful, and I never want to let you go. I love you, Haley, forever and always."

Tears streamed down my face and he moved his thumb to wipe them away.

"I love you too, Camden Johnson. Forever and always."

"Will you make me the luckiest man in the world and be my wife?"

When he opened the box he had been holding, I gasped.

The ring was modest in size but covered in diamonds. A center set stone with a halo and a diamond-studded band with rose gold metal. The exact ring I had wanted since I was a little girl. The one I would dream about casually with Cam when we were growing up.

He had remembered.

"Yes!" I squealed and jumped up to wrap my arms around his neck. Cam slipped the ring onto my finger and kissed me in the entryway of our new home.

"She said yes!" he called out and then my mom and Piper came racing out of one of the bedrooms down the hall. Both were crying and Piper was squealing right along with me as I showed her my ring.

I turned to Cam after gushing with Piper and my mom. He was standing behind me and watched me as I closed the space between us, a look of contentment and happiness on his face. I wrapped my arms around his neck and dug my nose into his neck, taking in his scent. Earth, pine, and AstroTurf. Just like always.

"Are you happy?" he whispered just loud enough for me to hear.

Piper and my mom had moved to the kitchen and were pouring champagne.

"I'm so happy. And you know what else?" I pulled back and looked into his deep emerald eyes.

"What's that, beautiful?"

"I'm hungry."

Cam let out a big belly laugh which caused my mom and Piper to look over at us. He dipped his head back toward mine.

"What would you like to eat, beautiful? I'll get you whatever you want."

I looked up at Cam and felt a deep sense of comfort and safety standing in his arms. As he looked at me, I knew that he would be my protector, my biggest cheerleader, and my safe haven. Forever and always.

Being with Cam didn't feel like moving on from Connor.

Being with Cam felt like coming home.

"Can we order Thai?"

THE END

ACKNOWLEDGMENTS

Writing this story was never something I saw myself doing, but damn am I happy that I did. It came to me one day as I was driving down the road, listening to Taylor Swift's Foolish One, and had a chokehold on me for weeks before I finally sat down, opened up a Google Doc, and started writing. From then to now, there are so many people who have celebrated me and supported Haley and Cam's story that I would like to celebrate now.

First and foremost, my beautiful alpha reader and dear friend, Jess, who was the first person I told I was writing this book. Sending you that message at 9:45 at night changed something in me and your unwavering support for this book will never be forgotten. Next, to the cute blonde boy who inspired so many of the best parts of Cam, thank you for always being in my corner. I know I come to you with a lot of wild ideas, but you didn't even flinch when I told you I wanted to publish a book. Thank you from the bottom of my heart for always being in my corner.

This book would not have been made possible without my incredible beta readers: Jenah, Conor, Chelsea, Ambrosia, Skye, Courtney, and Wren. The feedback you gave me to make this story great was invaluable and I will forever be thankful for your kindness as you read the earliest version of this book. I would like to give the award for best reaction to this book to my close friend Janice. Thank you for nearly falling out of your chair when I told you I had pulled this off in the wee hours of the night and thank you big time for always telling me I can do big things. To Elle, who always speaks positively about me in rooms I'm not in and for always talking about author life with me. You are the friend my heart has been longing for and I am so grateful you are part of my life. Finally, I would like to thank my mom whose reaction was, "What is this?" when I handed her the first version of my book and followed it up by asking me if I would be part of Reese's Book Club. Maybe one day Mom.

Finally, I would like to thank you, dear reader holding this book. I am so grateful you decided to give this book, and me, a chance. I know you could have chosen from thousands of other incredible authors and stories out there, but you chose this one, and I'm grateful for it. I can't wait to continue to bring you more swoon-worthy men and the women they're obsessed with in the years to come.

XO,
    Rebecca Wrights
    Forever and always.

ABOUT THE AUTHOR

Rebecca Wrights is a romance author writing stories about swoon-worthy men and the women they adore. She is all about creating stories and characters that her readers can connect and relate to, while also falling madly in love with them. Small-town romances and steamy love scenes can be expected in each of her stories.

Be sure to follow along with her writing journey on Instagram, @RebeccaWrightsAuthor. Want more books from her? Stay tuned for her next series, The Nat. 20 Series coming later this year!